**"Listen, Shane."**

Lexi jabbed at his chest. "Regardless of how or what I feel, you cannot kiss me while I'm at work, even if you do own the place! Who knows who saw that kiss? I have a reputation to maintain, so I suggest you get your butt on that plane and focus on your next ride."

"After you admit you still love me." Shane leisurely leaned against the stall door.

Lexi closed the distance between them and carefully kept her tone low so no one would overhear. "You arrogant, egotistical— How can you think for one minute— We just started—"

"Yep, I knew it." Shane slapped his thigh with his hat. "Some things never change, *mi ángel de fuego*."

Taken off guard, Lexi was surprised to hear Shane refer to her as his "angel of fire." The last time she'd heard the nickname was before they broke up. Struggling to compose herself, she stared at him, afraid to speak.

"Whenever you get riled up like this and can't finish a thought, I know I'm right, and it kills you," he said.

If he only knew how much it all really was killing her...

# A Ranch Called Home

**Patricia Thayer & Amanda Renee**

Previously published as *Her Rocky Mountain Protector*
and *Blame It on the Rodeo*

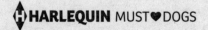

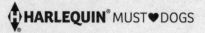 HARLEQUIN® MUST♥DOGS

Recycling programs
for this product may
not exist in your area.

ISBN-13: 978-1-335-50745-7

A Ranch Called Home

Copyright © 2021 by Harlequin Books S.A.

Her Rocky Mountain Protector
First published in 2013. This edition published in 2021.
Copyright © 2013 by Patricia Wright

Blame It on the Rodeo
First published in 2014. This edition published in 2021.
Copyright © 2014 by Amanda Renee

This edition published by arrangement with Harlequin Books S.A.

For questions and comments about the quality of this book,
please contact us at CustomerService@Harlequin.com.

Harlequin Enterprises ULC
22 Adelaide St. West, 40th Floor
Toronto, Ontario M5H 4E3, Canada
www.Harlequin.com

Printed in U.S.A.

# CONTENTS

**Patricia Thayer** was born and raised in Muncie, Indiana. She attended Ball State University before heading west, where she has called Southern California home for many years.

When not working on a story, she might be found traveling the United States and Europe, taking in the scenery and doing story research while enjoying time with her husband, Steve. Together, they have three grown sons and four grandsons and one granddaughter, whom Patricia calls her own true-life heroes.

### Books by Patricia Thayer

#### Harlequin Western Romance

*Count on a Cowboy*
*Second Chance Rancher*
*Her Colorado Sheriff*

#### Harlequin Romance

*Tall, Dark, Texas Ranger*
*Once a Cowboy...*
*The Cowboy Comes Home*
*Single Dad's Holiday Wedding*
*Her Rocky Mountain Protector*
*The Cowboy She Couldn't Forget*
*Proposal at the Lazy S Ranch*

Visit the Author Profile page
at Harlequin.com for more titles.

# HER ROCKY MOUNTAIN PROTECTOR

## Patricia Thayer

To the strongest and the most stubborn woman.
I'll miss you every day,
but I'm happy you're with Dad now.
Love you, Mom. Rest in peace.

# Chapter 1

Regina Williams rolled over and stared up at the peeling paint on the ceiling of her bedroom and smiled.

Two weeks. That was how long she and Zack had been living in the little bungalow on Cherry Street. Even with the endless projects to do, and the sparse furnishings, they'd found joy moving into their very first home.

Of course, there were thirty years of payments ahead, even with Lori's help as co-signer and a good interest rate. That was as far as Gina would let her wealthy big sister go. She had to do this on her own. She had to prove to herself and her son they could be independent.

She had a good start, with her staging business and thrift shop and new friends and now, a wonderful place to live. Destiny, Colorado, was a great small town to raise her seven-year-old son. Zack was thriving in school and he was making friends. He was finally coming out of his shell, and maybe putting their old life where it belonged. In the past.

She climbed out of bed, slipped on her robe as she walked into the hall. She hesitated at Zack's door, then decided to put on coffee first. In the kitchen, she drew back the curtains at the French doors that overlooked the backyard.

This was the view that had sold her on the house—also the acre of land out back. Springtime in Colorado was an array of color and she had already planned out her flower garden in her head.

Right now she'd better get her busy day started. Coffee made, she walked down the hall, knocked on her son's door and opened it. "Rise and shine, kiddo." No response. Zack had always been a slow starter. She went across the hall to the bathroom and turned on the light, then the shower.

"Come on, Zack," she called. "I need to get to work and you have school." She walked back to the bunk beds, to find the top bunk empty. So she glanced under to the lower bed, but no child.

"Zack," she called, and pushed around the blankets. "Honey, we don't have time to play around. So come out of hiding."

Fear began to build as she glanced around the room. That was when she saw the curtains blowing from the open window. She rushed over to find the screen missing.

"No, God. No!" Her heart stopped then started racing as she frantically checked the closet, then under the bed, calling her son.

"Zack. Oh, God. Where are you? Please come out." Even as she pleaded, something in the back of her mind told her that her worst nightmare had come true. She returned to the bed, jerked back the blankets and found the proof. A crumpled piece of paper.

A familiar feeling of helplessness hit her. Hard. Instinctively Gina knew it was a note from her ex-husband. A shiver ran through her as she picked it up and read, *"I found you, babe. Now I got what you want. You'll be hearing from me."*

Grady Fletcher parked his truck in front of Destiny's sheriff's office and glanced up and down First Street. Mid-morning and the main street was busy with people going about their business, paying no attention to him. Just how he liked it.

He pulled up the collar of his coat and climbed out. He checked the area once again. Although he knew he was safe, old habits died hard. "Stay," he said to his trusted companion.

The German shepherd, Scout, sat in his spot in the backseat. The retired military working dog's ears perked up, waiting for his command. Grady gave a hand signal and the animal lay down. "Be right back, boy."

Grady was adjusting to his new life, too. Suddenly becoming a civilian after twenty years in the army wasn't an easy transition, especially after his last tour of duty. So temporarily living at his grandfather's old cabin was a good thing. It gave him time to heal physically and think about the future. He'd loved the solitude he found in the San Juan Mountains until he found there was a trespasser on his land.

He was going to let the sheriff handle it.

Grady walked through the front door and the room was a buzz of activity. He removed his cowboy hat and looked around. He could sense something was wrong. That was when he caught sight of the small dark-haired woman seated next to the desk. Worry was evident on her face, along with her tears. He decided his business could wait and started to leave when Reed Larkin came out of his office.

The woman stood and hurried to the sheriff. "Please, Reed, we need to start looking for Zack right now."

"And we will, Gina. First, I had to issue an Amber Alert on the boy, and find a description of Eric's last-known vehicle." He glanced over the paper. "That was a 1998 primer-gray Ford truck, Colorado license." He read off the numbers. "I have all the state agencies involved in the search, Gina."

That description sparked Grady's interest. He walked up to the twosome. "Maybe I can help."

They both turned to him, but his attention went to the pretty brunette with the wide green eyes. Grady quickly turned to the sheriff, shielding his injured side.

"Hey, Grady, I haven't seen you in town for a while."

"There's been no need, until today. You're looking for a gray truck? I might know where you can find it."

Gina forced herself to draw in her next breath as she looked up at the giant of a man. He had a head full of sandy-brown hair that curled in thick waves. His dark eyes were deep-set and edged with tiny lines. His chiseled jaw was firm and clean-shaved. She caught a glimpse of an angry red scar on the side of his neck.

Gina gasped. "Where?"

Suddenly the man turned his intense gaze on her. Her first instinct was to back away from the intimidating man, but she forced herself to listen to what he had to say.

She forced herself to move closer. "Did you see a little boy, Mr...?"

"It's Fletcher, ma'am. Grady Fletcher. There's a truck with that description on my grandfather's property. But I haven't seen anyone."

The sheriff spoke up. "This is Gina Williams, Grady. Her seven-year-old son has been taken by his father. Eric Lowell was recently released from prison for drug possession and abuse. He kidnapped the boy from his home sometime during the night. We believe he's dangerous, so any help would be appreciated. Where did you see the vehicle?"

Grady nodded. "On the northeast section of my grandfather's property," he told them. "The truck is partly hidden off the road just below Rocky Top Ridge."

Reed Larkin frowned. "Where your granddad's old mines are?"

The man nodded. "As far as I can tell the truck has been there a few days. I came in to report it. I figured they were thinking the mine is abandoned, or they're trying to jump Fletch's old claim."

"Oh, God," Gina gasped and turned to the sheriff. "Eric's been in town that long, stalking us?"

"It's okay, Gina. We're going to get him." He looked

back at Grady. "When was the last time you saw the truck?"

"At dawn this morning," the man said.

Reed nodded. "Did he see you?"

"Not unless he was out walking around early. There wasn't anyone in the truck when I found it."

"Good, we have a possible location," the sheriff said. "My bet is he's holed up in one of the old mines. Can you take us there, Grady?"

He shrugged. "It's pretty rough terrain, but my dog might be able to pick up the trail. Are you and your men experienced hikers?"

Larkin nodded. "We've all had survival training. I hope the weather holds out today."

They started to walk away. Gina went after them. "Wait," she called. "Please, take me with you."

Reed went to her. "Gina, no. You can't handle the climb."

She blinked. "You have no idea what I can handle, Reed. My son is up there with a man who swore he'd get even with me. I'm not going to stand by and wait while he takes his revenge out on Zack."

The sheriff shook his head. "It's not safe."

"I can do this. And I know Eric. I know what pushes his buttons. Besides, he doesn't want Zack, or he'd be on the road heading for parts unknown."

She exchanged a glance with Grady Fletcher. "He wants me." She stood straight. "And as long as my son is safe, I'm willing to make a trade."

Minutes later, Grady stood out of the way as the sheriff made arrangements to leave. It hadn't taken long for Reed to give in to the mother's plea. Grady didn't like this plan, not one bit. Take this woman with them. No way.

He shook his head. He didn't need this problem. All he had to do was take them up to the mine, then leave the sheriff to handle the rest. Right. He wasn't made that way. In the army he'd become a take-charge-guy as a means of survival. But that was before the explosion, before he gave up his career. He shoved the memory aside and turned his thoughts to the problem at hand.

This Lowell must be a crazy bastard to come in and steal his own kid. It definitely could turn out badly.

Just then Gina Williams came out of Reed Larkin's office. She'd changed into hiking boots laced up at the bottom of her jeans. A sweatshirt under a quilted down vest would keep her warm against the cool day. She had her hair pulled back into a ponytail and a wide-brimmed hat to protect her from the elements. Springtime in Colorado was unpredictable. It could mean anything from rain to a full-blown snowstorm.

A blonde woman walked out behind the boy's mother. He recognized her as Lorelei Hutchinson Yeager. She'd pretty much owned this town since her father's death last year. Grady knew about the Hutchinsons only because of his grandfather's stories. Old Fletch had a strong dislike for any members of the town's founding family. It had something to do with disagreements over land rights.

Grady stood straighter when the two women walked his way. Ms. Williams had a stuffed toy in her hand.

"Mr. Fletcher, this is my sister, Lori Yeager. Lori, Grady Fletcher."

He nodded. "Mrs. Yeager."

She managed a smile. "It's Lori. And I can't tell you how much I appreciate your help finding my nephew. Zack means the world to us. If there's anything you need, let Reed know."

Gina looked at Grady. "The sheriff said you have a dog who can track."

He wasn't about to explain that he'd been through hell and back. "Scout was a military working dog. We're both retired now."

Gina held up a floppy-eared rabbit. "This belongs to Zack. Do you think he could pick up his scent?"

Since Scout's injury, he hadn't been put to the test. "It's worth a try."

She hugged her sister and they all walked outside. The sheriff and his two men had loaded up the white four-wheel drive SUV. After instruction to lead, Grady climbed in his own truck and Scout greeted him.

"Looks like we got some work to do. You up to it, fella?"

Surprisingly the animal let out a bark as the passenger-side door opened and the pretty Gina Williams peered in. "The other car is full. Would you mind if I rode with you?"

It seemed to take forever to get to their destination. The longest twenty minutes in Gina's life, but thanks to Grady Fletcher she now had hope of finding Zack.

She tried to calm herself as she stole a glance at the beautiful scenery along the gravel road leading to the dotting of tall pines in the distance. A stream ran alongside the winding path. She thought of Zack. Was he warm enough? Had Eric hurt him? She tensed. He'd better not have.

Suddenly she felt a nudge on her arm. She started to pull away, then discovered it was Mr. Fletcher's dog. "Hey, fella."

She looked at the man who filled up the truck cab, making Gina very aware of his presence. "Is it okay if I pet him?"

He gave her a curt nod. "It seems Scout wants the attention."

She ran her hand over the shepherd's soft, nearly black coat. "He's a beautiful dog. You said he's a military dog?"

"Yes. He served overseas until last year."

"Were you with him?"

Another curt nod.

Gina continued to rub the dog's fur. She found it gave her comfort, but nothing could stop the fear she felt for her son. She'd thought she'd been so careful. That Eric would never find them.

Out of the blue, Mr. Fletcher said, "Tell me about your…about Eric. How experienced is he with survival skills?"

"Really good. Every year, he'd go with his brothers during hunting season." She had been glad when he was away because it had meant she was safe from his abuse. "Don't put anything past him, Mr. Fletcher." She couldn't forget the times she had, and he had made her pay. *Oh, God, Zack,* she cried silently. "Eric wasn't supposed to find us here. Destiny was our safe place." She worked to hold it together, but wasn't doing well. "We didn't tell a soul that we'd moved here. We changed our names while he was in prison." She released a sigh. "Why can't he leave us alone?"

For a long time the man didn't say anything, then added, "The sheriff will get him and he'll go back to prison."

"I pray that happens. Right now, all I'm concerned about is my son's safety."

Grady went across the stream, then drove several yards off-road, coming to a stop under a tree, next to some large boulders at the base of hillside. Before he could shut off the engine, Gina jumped out of the truck and had started up the hillside when she felt his hand on her arm.

"Hey, you just can't go running off half-cocked. At least wait for the others."

Before she could argue, a rifle shot rang out, and something hit the tree above their heads.

With a curse, Grady pushed Gina to the ground and covered her body with his. He had to get her out of there. He grabbed her close, hearing her gasp, then rolled them over and over until they were behind the tree.

Gina landed on her back and was swiftly aware of this large man. He braced his arms on either side of her head so his full weight wasn't on her. Still, she was very mindful of the fact of his powerful size. Oddly, she didn't feel panicked or threatened. She had her son to worry about.

He raised his head and those dark brooding eyes locked on hers. "You okay?"

She managed a nod. Again she caught sight of the scarred skin covering the side of his neck.

Another series of shots rang out over their heads. He

moved her just as the sheriff's vehicle pulled up and parked in front of them as a shield.

Reed climbed out of the truck. His men scrambled to find cover behind large boulders. The sheriff reached them. "You two okay?"

Grady moved off the woman, trying to forget the awareness he felt. Their gaze connected for an instant before she sat up. This was trouble in more ways than he could count.

"I'm fine, but my son isn't. So I need to go up there."

She started to stand and Grady pulled her back down. "Lady, I know you aren't thinking clearly right now," he growled. "And running up there isn't going to get your son back. That maniac is holding a high-powered rife on us, and he wants you to pay."

Before Grady could stand, Gina Williams gripped his arm. "I don't care how you do it, Mr. Fletcher—just get my son out safely. Please." Tears filled those mesmerizing green eyes. "My life doesn't matter without Zack."

"We'll do whatever it takes to get the boy out of there." Grady moved away, praying he could keep his promise.

*I'm so scared. Mom, help me.*

Wiping away more tears, Zack sat up on the blanket and began pulling at the ropes that held his wrists and feet together. He had to get away before his dad got back. Struggling with the ropes again, he wished he were strong enough to break free. With only a little light from the lantern, he glanced around the dark cave, but couldn't see anything.

He was all alone.

He bit down on his lip, trying not to cry again. He had to get out and find his mom before Dad hurt her again.

"I got to get loose," he whispered and began to wiggle his hands back and forth feeling the burn, but continuing to fight to get out of the ropes. Using his teeth, he loosened the knot and finally his hands came out. Excited, he untied the ropes at his ankles. He stood, careful not to make any noise. He grabbed the lantern and headed toward the light in the opening. Outside he heard rifle shots so he turned and ran off in the other direction. Far away from danger.

# *Chapter 2*

Grady stood behind the large boulder as he scanned the rocky rim with binoculars. He followed the dark figure of a man as he moved cautiously among the trees and brush. He'd seen a picture of the suspect and recognized him.

He nudged the sheriff beside him. "Lowell's up there, but I can't see any sign of the boy. Can you?"

Reed looked through his glasses, then said, "No, no sign of Zack, but that's definitely Eric Lowell. We can't rush him. The boy could get hurt. If this guy came all this way to take his son away from his ex-wife, he isn't going to give up easily."

"He'll never give up."

Grady looked over his shoulder to see that Gina approached them.

"I thought you promised to stay in the vehicle. It's not safe here."

She shook her head. "He's got Zack. My child isn't safe with him."

The panicked look on her face tore at Grady. It sent him a painful reminder of what he'd lost. Only he never deserved to have a family in the first place.

"You've got to let me go up there, Reed. Make a trade. Eric wants me. He wants to punish me. Please, Reed," she pleaded. "Eric knows he's going back to prison. So he has nothing to lose." She wiped the tears that escaped her eyes. "I can't let him hurt Zack. I can't."

When she started to walk into the clearing, Grady grabbed her right arm as another rifle shot rang out. He pulled her back against the rock wall and shielded her. Grady had to work to get his breathing and heart rate under control. That was too close. This lunatic was playing for keeps. "Lady, you've got to stop with the crazy stunts," he growled.

She tossed him a stubborn look. "It doesn't matter. Nothing matters without my son."

"What do you think will happen to Zack if you get yourself killed? You need to let the sheriff handle this."

"Okay, but you don't understand. I can't leave my son up there." She nodded to the ridge. "I promised Zack. I promised him I wouldn't let his dad hurt us again. Please, you've got to help me."

He hated that this woman got to him. As much as Grady wanted to, it was impossible to walk away from this. He turned to Reed Larkin. "What's your next move, Sheriff?"

"I wish I had an answer. I can't take a chance that

he'll harm the boy." Larkin gave him a hard look. "You know the area, Fletcher. Is there a back way in?"

Grady nodded, remembering the summers he'd tracked after old Fletch. "You can come in along Miner's Ridge. It's pretty narrow, and it'll take about fifteen minutes, but if Lowell is focused on watching for his ex-wife, we might be able to catch him by surprise. Give me a little time to scope the area."

Grady started to walk back to his truck to arm himself when Larkin stopped him. "I can't ask you to do this."

"You didn't. I volunteered."

"Then I'll need to deputize you first. Do you have a problem with that? I can't let a civilian get involved."

Grady paused as he looked at this woman still gripping that floppy-eared rabbit. Suddenly memories of his past life flashed before him, the picture of the stuffed animals that lined the shelf in his infant son's room. Toys the baby never got the chance to see or play with. He quickly shook it away. "Do what you need to do."

After the sheriff had sworn him in, Grady hurried back to his vehicle and opened the door. Immediately the shepherd stood in the backseat. Scout hesitated. The dog hadn't worked since Afghanistan when he'd been injured. Yet since they'd returned home, Grady had adopted Scout, hoping to get involved in some search-and-rescue operations. It was a good time to test him.

"Come on, boy. We've got a kid to find." The shepherd jumped out of the backseat and waited for his next command.

Grady reached back inside the vehicle, took the Glock from under the driver's seat and tucked the gun in the waistband of his jeans against his back. He was going to be prepared for anything.

Reed appeared. "I see you don't need me to issue you a weapon." The sheriff looked concerned. "I'm going to send one of my men with you."

"No. Alone. I'll move faster and with less chance of being seen." He stared at the sheriff. "You have to trust me on this."

"Okay." Reed Larkin handed him a small radio. "Here, you'll need this to communicate with us."

Grady took it, then walked over to Gina Williams, seeing the fear on her face. "I'll do everything I can to bring the boy back. So don't try anything stupid, or the sheriff will send you back to town. Let us handle this."

She nodded. "Just hurry. Please!"

Grady settled her in the truck and then he went to the sheriff. Grady knew these mountains. His grandpa had taken him around every mine and cliff along this face of the mountain range. He glanced at his dog. "Come on, boy, let's find Zack." He prayed that his words would come true. Maybe this time he would be there when someone's child needed him.

Gina watched as Grady and Scout started up the back side of the mountain. She began to pray that they would be able to get to her son before any harm came to him. She closed her eyes and could feel her ex-husband's slap across her face just as if it were happening again.

But it never stopped at just a slap. There were also those closed fists that slammed into her body. A tear dropped to her cheek and she quickly wiped it away.

No! She wasn't going to let Eric win again. She was

going to make a life for her son here in Destiny. Zack was going to have a happy childhood. She wasn't going to let Eric hurt her little boy again. Even if she had to stop him herself.

"Gina."

She opened her eyes to see Reed standing next to the truck. "I wish I could tell you everything is going to be all right, but I can't. Only you know your ex. Has he ever hurt his son?"

"He hadn't until the last time. That's when Eric learned that he could inflict more pain on me by making Zack his target."

Reed's nostrils flared. "I swear, Gina, we'll do everything possible to get Zack away from him. Grady Fletcher is retired army. He's served overseas and is combat trained." The radio squawked. "That's Fletcher."

He pulled the radio out and spoke into it. "Larkin, here."

"I've reached the mine. He could be inside, or Zack could be there. Since I can't see Lowell, I don't know. You need to draw him out."

"Roger." The sheriff looked at Gina. "We need to draw Eric out in the open."

"Use me," she said, and started out of the truck. "I can distract him." She wanted Grady Fletcher to get a good shot at him.

"Give me a few minutes," the sheriff said, then signed off. "Gina, don't do anything foolish. Your ex isn't worried about leaving here. He wants revenge on you."

"I don't care. Zack is the only thing that matters."

"But he needs his mother, too."

"Just not a mother who's let him down so many times," she breathed. "But not this time, not any more."

Grady was pressed flat against the rock wall as he moved toward his target. He gave the hand signal for Scout to stay behind and continued around the boulder. There he heard the sheriff call to Lowell.

"Hey, Eric, your wife wants to talk to you."

Nothing. There was no movement, no sign of the guy. "Come on, you bastard," Grady breathed.

Then he heard Gina's voice. "Eric!" she called. "Eric, please talk to me. I know you don't want to hurt Zack. So I want to make a trade. Zack for me."

Lowell finally spoke. "I'm not falling for that," he told her.

Grady got a location. The kidnapper was just on the other side of the boulder. He looked down at Scout to see the animal's ears go up. He gave a hand signal to stay. The animal obeyed.

Again, Gina called out. "Please, Eric. I'll do whatever you want. Just don't hurt Zack. Please."

"I like to hear you beg, Gina," Lowell said. "Come on, convince me some more."

That was when Grady saw him. The man came out just enough to get into his line of sight. He looked to be around six feet tall. His body was lean and strong, probably from working out in prison. Grady wasn't impressed. Not by a man who used his strength to beat up on women. He just hoped the guy wasn't too smart.

Lowell called his ex-wife a few choice names. "Tell me what you want, wife. You always want something." The man moved toward the ledge. He knelt down for protection. "I'll need more than just you, if you want my son. That big sister of yours inherited a boatload of money. I want a cut."

"How much?" Gina asked without hesitation.

"A few million should get me where I want to go. I'll also need transportation."

There was a pause, then Gina said, "It's going to take some time."

"You got an hour," he told her.

Grady saw his chance and took it. He came out behind the guy, just as he turned around. Grady managed to knock Eric's rifle out of his hand, but that didn't stop him.

Lowell charged at him, landing several blows, then Grady got in a good one, knocking the man down. He called to Scout once he had subdued Eric on the ground in a choke hold.

"I got him," Grady yelled down to the sheriff, then to Lowell he said, "I wouldn't move if I were you." He nodded toward the growling dog. "Scout will catch you. And I haven't fed him today."

Eric cursed but didn't put up a fight as Larkin and his men showed up. One of the deputies took charge and cuffed Lowell. Larkin finished reading him his rights when Gina Williams showed up.

She ran to her ex. "Where is Zack?" she demanded.

"Go to hell," he said. His words were slurred, his eyes glassy. Drugs, in all likelihood.

Grady walked up. "Let's check the mine," he said, taking out his penlight and heading to the opening that had once been boarded up but now showed signs of some of the boards having been pulled away. He stepped through the slats, Larkin and Gina right behind him.

"Come, Scout," he called to his dog.

The shepherd immediately went into the darkness and Grady turned on the flashlight, and followed.

Gina cried out, "Zack! Mom's here and you're safe. Zack!" There wasn't a sound, then a bark from Scout. They walked carefully through the maze of rocks and mining equipment. Then they reached the wide opening. That was where they saw the light and sleeping bags and camp lanterns. There was a pile of ropes abandoned on the blanket.

Gina searched around. "Where's Zack?"

"Not sure," the sheriff said. "Maybe Eric moved him." He flashed the light around the cave and over the piles of blankets to the empty food containers. Then he picked up the knotted ropes. "Do you think Zack could have got away?" He glanced at Grady. "Is there another way out?"

Grady had to think a minute. Then he heard Scout's bark again. "This way." He started off and the others followed. They were led through a maze of rocks until they saw some light and were outside in the back of the cliff. There was no sign of the boy.

"Where is he?" Gina demanded.

Not waiting for an answer, she returned to the front of the cave. Marching over to her ex-husband, she began pounding him with her fists. "Where's Zack? Tell me. Damn you, tell me."

Lowell tried to move, but the deputies held him there. "Get her the hell away from me."

When Reed Larkin finally pulled Gina back, Grady

could see her tears on her face. He was about ready to give her something to beat the SOB with.

Gina couldn't hold back any more and sobbed. "Where's my son?"

An evil grin appeared on the jerk's face. "Hell, Gina, I hid him so deep, you'll never find him."

Suddenly Grady reached out and gripped Eric's shirt, getting the man's attention. "You'd better hope that's a lie, because if anything you said has one ounce of truth in it, I'll personally take care of you myself. So I suggest you don't push any more of my buttons, or I'll bury you so deep no one will find you," he said through clenched teeth, then he finally released Lowell, causing him to stumble backward.

"Hey, he threatened me," Eric cried.

"I didn't hear anything," the sheriff told him, and the deputies agreed. "Maybe you better talk, and fast."

"Who the hell are you?"

Fletcher moved closer. "Your worst nightmare. I've done two tours of duty in Afghanistan. I know a lot of ways to torture someone, and get rid of the body."

Lowell's eyes grew wide. "I swear, I left Zack back in the cave and he was tied up when I came out. I don't know where he is now."

Grady got in his face again. "I'd better not find out you're lyin'."

Eric cringed, looking like the coward he was. "Sheriff, get him away from me, I told you everything I know."

"Take him down to the truck," Reed said.

After the deputies took Lowell off to the vehicle,

Gina turned to the sheriff. "We've got to go look for Zack."

"We will, Gina," Reed promised, and turned to Grady. "Could Scout find the boy?"

"We can try." Grady looked around the dark area, but Scout wasn't there. He put two fingers in his mouth and whistled. "Scout. Come." There wasn't even the sound of a bark. Now it was time for Grady to panic.

"Please, don't hurt me," Zack cried as the big wolf came toward him. He raised his shaking hand and waved, hoping the animal would leave his hiding place. "Just go away. Please."

Zack took off running. He wasn't sure what he was more afraid of, the animal or his dad finding him. He climbed the rough hillside, and went through a group of trees, but every time he looked back the big wolf was still following him. He tripped on a rock and cried out as he fell. He rolled over and saw his bloody palms. It hurt so bad, but he wasn't going to cry. He just had to get away.

He got up and started to walk again, hoping he could find someone who would get him back to his mom. He looked up at the sky. It was getting late and it was going to be dark soon. That scared him. Nighttime was when bad things happened. He glanced over his shoulder to see the wolf was still following him. Zack climbed over the next rock and stopped. There was a coyote, then soon there were three of them.

Suddenly the wolf following him took off after the wild dogs. The animals fought, and soon the coyotes ran away, but not the wolf, who came back to him. Afraid,

Zack backed away, but the animal still came closer. Then he saw a collar and a tag hanging from his neck. "You're a dog?"

As if he understood, the animal barked at him.

All at once the wind began to blow and Zack hugged himself. It began to rain, and lightning and thunder weren't far behind.

The dog barked again and started off, but stopped and waited for him. Maybe the dog was taking him home. Zack went after him, but they came to another mine and the dog slipped inside, showing him the way.

Shivering, he went inside the dark old mine. He didn't know what else to do. Inside, he stayed close to the opening, and the fading light, but couldn't help but be curious by all the treasures. An old mining car sat on tracks. He wished there were some blankets to keep him warm. It began to pour rain outside and he stepped back. The dog came up beside him, and Zack stood very still, then he reached down and petted him. His fur was soft.

"Good dog," Zack managed to say.

The animal nudged him away from the entrance and Zack sat. The dog sat, too. "Can I see your collar?" Zack carefully reached for the silver tag and read the letters. "U.S. Army. Your name is Scout. Wow, you're an army dog. You can protect me."

Scout laid his head on Zack's leg, and he was beginning to feel a little better. Now, if only his mom would find him.

# Chapter 3

Three hours later, and exhausted from the search, everyone stood next to the sheriff's vehicles to figure out the next move. They'd had to wait out the heavy rain, then had gone back out and combed the area once it let up, but any trail of her son had been washed out.

"But we can't leave Zack out there," Gina cried.

A frustrated Reed Larkin said, "Of course not, Gina, but it's getting dark. I need to go back to town and get more volunteers and we'll start out again at first light. The men need to eat, and get some rest."

"It could be too late by then," Gina argued.

The sheriff turned to Grady Fletcher. "Is there a chance your dog might be with Zack?"

Gina was hopeful. "Is that true?"

Grady nodded. "Scout might have got the boy's scent

and gone after him. If the dog couldn't get the boy to follow him back to us, he'd stay."

She was hopeful. "So Zack's not alone out there?"

"It's a possibility," Grady told her. "I don't know for sure." He hesitated. "Scout had some injuries while in Afghanistan."

Gina frowned. "Injuries? So you don't know how he'll act? Could he harm Zack?"

Grady shook his head. "Scout wouldn't hurt anyone unless he's given provocation. If he found your son, he's been trained to stay with him. He'll protect him with his life."

The sheriff stepped in. "I know I can't get you to go back to town, Gina, but I can call Lori."

"No, I don't want her out in this weather. She's pregnant and Jace is out of town."

"So you're going to spend the night in a truck?" the sheriff argued. "And there's more rain expected."

"I'll be all right." She turned to Grady. "That is, if you'd be willing stay, too. Of course I'll pay you for your time."

The man straightened. "I don't want your money. I'll stay for the boy and for my dog. But a better plan might be to go to my grandfather's cabin up the road. At least dry off and get something to eat."

Reed Larkin stepped in. "That's a good idea, Gina. You can't just keep wandering around these mountains. You'll get lost. That isn't going to help Zack."

How could she leave her son? "How far away is the cabin?"

"About a half mile from here," he offered. "You'll at

least be close by, and if Scout leads the boy out, he'll bring him to the cabin."

She looked back at Reed. "Go, Gina," he told her. "You're chilled to the bone. I'll be back at first light."

It had been a long time since she'd trusted a man, outside of her new brother-in-law, Jace, and a few of the townspeople. It looked like she didn't have much of a choice.

"Thank you, Grady," Gina said. "I promise I won't be a problem."

Grady knew that wasn't true. Gina Williams had already caused him the kind of trouble he didn't need right now. "I know. And you'll at least dry off and get some food in you."

The sheriff stopped Grady. "I'll be back at dawn." He handed him his card. "If anything happens before then call my cell phone."

Then the men loaded into the vehicles and drove down the road.

"Come on, let's get you warmed up." Grady helped Gina into the truck, then turned on the heater, trying to stop her shivering. The temperature had already dropped with the fading daylight, and with the combination of the rain, it was damn cold. He, too, was worried about the boy, praying he had found cover.

He drove along the bumpy road that led to the old log cabin that he'd called home for the past three months. In the dim light, the place didn't look much better than when he'd officially moved in a few months ago, knowing his grandfather needed a lot of help for his recovery.

After parking the truck, he got out to help his guest, but she'd already jumped down by the time he reached her. He climbed the steps to the porch that sorely needed to be replaced. It was one of the many things on his list. He would get to that in time. But it meant he wasn't exactly ready to have guests.

He unlocked the door and swung it open and allowed Gina to step inside. He followed and quickly went to the back room and switched on the compressor, then returned and turned on the table lamp.

"Oh, my," she said. "It really is rustic."

He glanced at her. "There's a generator for the refrigerator and lights, but wait until you need to use the facilities. They're still out back."

She shrugged. "Then maybe I should head there now."

With a nod, he showed her the little house toward the back of the cabin. He waited on the porch as the last of day turned into night. It only took a few minutes before she came hurrying back to the cabin.

Inside again he watched her examine her surroundings in the main room. A huge stone fireplace and rough log walls were as far as the rustic charm went. It got worse with the old sofas and two chairs that were covered in a faded fabric. A big scarred table took up most of the kitchen area. He'd like to get rid of a lot of it.

Old Fletch had had the entire space crowded with furniture. His grandfather never threw out anything. Thank goodness he hadn't inherited that trait from the old man. Since he'd heard about his grandfather's accident, he'd been doing double duty. Once he'd arrived here from Texas, he'd been going to the nursing home to oversee Fletch's recovery from his broken hip. He'd also been trying to clean up this place by hauling things off to the dump.

He handed her a blanket and lit the logs in the fireplace. "It'll be warm soon."

"I'm fine, really," she said, unable to stop her shivering. "I can't tell you how much I appreciate you letting me stay here. I just need to be close by."

"I understand." He went into the kitchen area. "I'm going to reheat some stew I made last night."

"Please don't feel you have to wait on me." She stood by the fire. "I'll probably just sit right here."

"I'm going to eat, so you might as well."

She nodded. "Okay, what can I do to help?"

He nodded toward the cupboard as she came into the kitchen area. "The bowls and spoons are in there."

Gina did as he asked. She was surprised at the cabin, especially the array of furniture crammed inside. The cabinet that held the dishes was an antique. "You have a lot of…things."

"It all belongs to my grandfather. He's been in a nursing home. I've been trying to clear out most of this stuff since I came here a few months ago."

She looked at him. "Are you selling the furniture? I might know of someone who's interested."

"In this junk?"

She raised an eyebrow. "Your grandfather has some nice pieces. This cabinet is probably an antique. It's a Hoosier." She glanced over the scarred wood. "It might need work, but it's worth some money."

He turned up the flame on the camp stove and set the pan on top. "Really?"

Gina once again saw on his neck the long burn scar

that ran past his collar. She didn't want to stare, but it was hard not to. "You said Scout was injured by a bomb. Were you with him?"

He stopped, but didn't answer for a while. Then he looked at her with those dark brooding eyes. "Are you asking if that's where I got my scar?"

She nodded.

"Yeah. It's not pretty, but I was one of the lucky ones."

Grady tried not to think about that day, or the two men he'd lost.

"I'm sorry. It must have been horrible."

"Yeah, war usually is."

Grady thought back to the two young soldiers, Jimmy and Vince. After he'd been well enough to leave the hospital, Grady had made a trip to West Virginia to visit Jimmy Prescott's family, then he'd gone on to Georgia to see Vince Johnson's kin.

Gina drew his attention back to the present. "What about you?" she asked. "Do you have any family?"

He didn't like where this was headed. "You sure are full of questions."

She shrugged. "Seems you know everything about me and my sordid past."

He frowned. "It's not sordid. You did nothing wrong. The man beat you. There's nothing lower than that. You did the right thing by sending him to jail."

"Not as soon as I should have," she admitted. "I had the misconception that I could love Eric enough to make him stop." She raised her chin. "He just didn't love me enough to want to. Now, my son is paying for it."

He stopped himself from going to her. She didn't

need the kind of comfort he was willing to give. "Hey, we all have regrets," he told her. Hell, he had a boatload of them. "Sometimes love isn't enough." Removing the pan from the stove, he carried it to the table and emptied the stew into the bowls. "Sit down. You need to eat."

She did as he asked. "I'm really not hungry."

He sat across from her. "Eat anyway. You need strength to hike around the mountains. I don't need to have to carry you out of there tomorrow."

She took a small bite and chewed slowly. "You're good at giving orders."

He swallowed a spoonful of stew. "I've had a lot of years to practice."

Those deep green eyes widened and he felt a stirring of awareness. "How long were you in the army?"

He watched her take another bite. "I went in the day I turned eighteen, and got discharged last December. Twenty years." When had he suddenly become such an open book?

"You don't look old enough."

And she looked far too young for him to think about anything beyond helping to find her son. So he needed to stop the direction of his thoughts. "Spoken like a respectful youngster."

She raised an eyebrow. "I'm not so young."

"What, twenty-five?"

"Twenty-seven…my next birthday."

Still far too young for him. Think of her as a kid sister. That didn't work, either. He was drawn to her intriguing eyes once again, then his gaze lowered to her mouth and he felt the reaction like a slam in the gut. He glanced away. It had been nearly two years since he'd reacted so strongly to a woman. Not since his marriage had fallen apart. Definitely not since the accident. He stood. "Do you want any more?"

"No thank you. I'm finished."

"Okay, if you need to use the bathroom again, I suggest you go now." He looked out the window. "It's started to rain again."

She nodded. "I'm fine."

Well, he wasn't. So the sooner they found the boy the better. Then he could get back to his life.


*"You think you can get away from me? Think again, bitch."*

*Gina huddled in the corner, trying to protect her body from Eric's vicious blows. "Please stop!" she cried, praying he'd tire and let her alone.*

*"Never. I'll always find you. You'll never get away. Never." He stepped back, stumbling drunkenly.*

*Zack suddenly appeared. "Stop hurting my mom," he cried, and began hitting his dad. "Go away. Leave us alone."*

*Eric grabbed the boy, swung back his fist and she screamed. "No! Don't hit him! No!"*

"Gina! Wake up"

She felt someone shaking her. She finally opened her eyes and saw the large figure leaning over her. She gasped and pushed him away. "Please, don't," she cried and scurried to the end of the sofa.

Grady stepped back and raised his hands in surrender. "Hey, it's me, Grady. You had a bad dream. I woke you, that's all. I'm not going to hurt you, Gina. You're safe here."

Gina brushed her hair back, trying to slow her breathing. "Oh, God, Grady, I'm so sorry." She glanced up to see the man standing there in the dark shadows in a pair of Levi's and a T-shirt over a well-toned body. "Please tell me I didn't hit you. Are you all right?"

In the shadowed light, Grady stared back at her, knowing it best to keep his distance. He wished he could get his hands on Lowell again. "Question is, are you?"

She nodded, but avoided any eye contact. "The nightmare must have been triggered by Eric taking Zack."

At least she'd got a few hours of sleep. He'd covered her with a blanket before going into the one bedroom in the cabin.

She finally looked at him. "Is it light enough to start searching again?"

He nodded. "I expect by the time we have some coffee, it'll be daylight." He sure wasn't going to get any more sleep.

After Grady dressed in fresh jeans and a shirt, he made coffee and they pulled on their coats and headed to the truck. It only took a few minutes to get back to the original spot where Eric's truck had been parked the day before. Where Gina Williams's nightmare had started.

Grady ended the call to the sheriff and put his cell phone back into his pocket. "Larkin said they'll be here in ten minutes."

"I can't wait." Gina opened the truck door. "I'm going to head up." She was out of the cab.

Grady jumped out and went after her. He grabbed her by the arm, and she immediately jerked away. He raised his hands in surrender.

"Sorry. I just don't want you to run off. You don't

know the area and could get lost, too. Besides, I want to check out another mine, the Lucky Penny." He pointed to a different direction. "We didn't get to it last night."

"Why not?"

They started climbing the slope. "For one thing, it was too dark and it's a lot farther."

"Why do you think Zack could be there?"

"Scout knows the mines around here. I've been working with him there on some search-and-rescue training."

Gina was frustrated. Her son had been out in the elements all night and all she wanted was to find him. "Okay, let's go there."

He nodded and they started their hike to the Lucky Penny.

She managed to keep up with him. "Do you think Zack would follow your dog to safety?"

"Your son seems pretty resourceful. He was smart enough to get untied and run away from his dad, then he's smart enough to stay out of the weather."

"But he doesn't know that he's safe from his dad. He might still be hiding."

Zack was shivering when he woke up. He'd been cold all night, even with Scout sleeping beside him, keeping him warm. He was still next to him now. He wished it were his mom with him. He was so scared and his scraped hand hurt.

"What do we do, Scout? I don't want my dad to find me. He's mean, and he hurts Mom." He stroked the dog's fur. "He'll hurt me, too, because I ran away." He brushed away a tear, hating to cry.

The dog got up and gave a bark.

Maybe Scout could protect him. But his dad had a gun. He wiped away more tears. "Why can't my dad just leave us alone?" he said, making a fist. "I don't want to go away and have to hide again. I like living in Destiny with my mom, Aunt Lori and Uncle Jace and my cousin Cassie."

The dog cocked his head as if he were listening to every word.

"We have a new house and I'm gonna try out for baseball next month. I get to have a birthday party this year." He didn't care about that. He only wanted his mom.

The animal made a whining sound and looked toward the cave opening.

Zack was suddenly afraid again. What if his dad got his mom, and hurt her? He didn't know what to do.

Suddenly the animal jumped up and went to the opening, then he looked back and barked. He came back several times, and nudged at him before he ran outside.

"Wait, Scout," Zack cried and took off after him. Once he was outside, the sunlight nearly blinded him. The dog barked again, then he heard a voice calling his name.

He tried not to cry, but he couldn't help it. "Mom!" he yelled, and followed Scout. "Mom!"

Gina stopped when she heard the sound. She grabbed Grady's arm. "I hear something."

Grady paused and the next sound was that of a dog barking. He put two fingers in his mouth and let loose with a loud whistle. He was rewarded with another bark.

"This way," he said. "It's coming from the Lucky

Penny." He pointed toward their left, then took her hand and helped her climb up the slope. When they reached the cluster of boulders, a dog and child appeared.

Her heart was beating wildly. "Zack," she cried, and ran to her son.

"Mom," he cried, throwing himself into her arms.

"Oh, Zack." The tears poured out of her as she hugged him tight, breathing in his familiar smell. Even with the mixture of dirt and sweat, it was heavenly. "Oh, thank goodness you're safe." She pulled back and did a quick examination. "We were so worried. Where did you go?"

The child looked worried. "When I got untied, I was afraid Dad would come back to get me. So I ran away. Where is he?"

"Oh, honey." She smiled. "Don't worry. Sheriff Larkin has your dad in jail. Mr. Fletcher helped capture him." She hugged her son again. "He's never going to hurt us again. I promise, Zack. I promise. You must have been so scared."

Her son pulled away. "I was at first." He glanced down at the dog. "Scout came and stayed with me." His brown eyes widened. "Mom, he's a military dog."

She managed a nod. "I know. He's trained to find people and I'm so grateful that he found you."

"He kept me warm all night long." Zack looked at Grady. "Is he your dog?"

"Yes, he is." Grady stood next to the animal, who sat perfectly still. "We've been in a lot of tight situations together. Scout was trained to find bombs. I guess now he can add little boys to the list."

Gina had completely forgotten about the introductions. "Zack, this is Mr. Fletcher. He's helped me search for you."

"Thank you. I'm glad you had Scout." Zack went over to the animal. "Can I pet him?"

"I know Scout would like that."

Grady watched the affection between the two. This was a new experience for Scout. A child was hard to resist, could even be distracting. Grady glanced at Gina Williams. So was his mother.

"Maybe we should head back down," he said. "You need to get warm and checked out to make sure you're okay."

They started walking down the slope just as the sheriff's vehicle appeared next to his truck. The next ten minutes were chaotic as Grady stood back and let the paramedic look over the boy. Then they all piled into the vehicle.

"I can't thank you enough for all you did, Grady." She smiled for real this time and he found he liked it too much. "My son is everything to me," she managed to say.

"Then you'd better go tend to him." Scout sent a bark toward his new friend in the SUV. Grady watched Gina get into the vehicle and drive off. Suddenly he was alone once again, and realized it wasn't what he truly wanted at all.

*Be careful what you wish for.*

# Chapter 4

Four hours later Gina stood at her sister, Lori's, family room entrance and watched her son sleeping on the pull-out sofa bed. She still felt shaky, thinking about the thirty-six-hour ordeal. Worse, how things could have turned out.

A tear fell against her cheek. Zack was back safe with her. She had so many people to thank; one in particular, Grady Fletcher. The stranger who had put everything else aside and led the sheriff to Eric, then had stayed with her the entire time, keeping her sane until they found Zack. And Scout. What a special dog to protect her son.

"Is he asleep?" Lori whispered as she came up behind her.

Gina nodded, and followed her sister into the kitchen. "I promised I'd stay close by."

Lori motioned for her to take a seat at the large kitchen island. "I think we're close enough to hear him if he wakes."

Technically her half sister, Lorelei Hutchinson Yeager was a pretty blonde with big brown eyes and a generous heart. Last fall she'd come to Destiny when she inherited her estranged father's fortune. She'd fallen in love and married a building contractor, Jace Yeager, and moved into his house with his daughter, Cassie. Just recently they'd got a big surprise when Lori learned she was pregnant.

Gina glanced around the newly remodeled room. Jace had done a great job of refinishing the fixer-upper home, especially the kitchen. The large space had custom maple cabinets, granite counters and top-of-the-line stainless-steel appliances.

Gina was proud she'd helped Lori add some special touches with the burnt-orange paint and bright yellow accents.

Lori set a cup of hot tea in front of her. "Here, drink this."

"Thanks," Gina told her. "You should sit down, too. You have to be tired."

"I'm fine. Really."

When Gina was growing up, Lori had been more than a big sister. She had filled in where their mother couldn't or wouldn't. Still Gina had become a rebellious teenager when she'd met wild boy Eric Lowell. Lori had never deserted her though, especially when things had got rough and Eric had begun knocking her around.

Last fall when Lori had come to Destiny to claim her inheritance from her father, Lyle Hutchinson, she'd sent for Gina and Zack, hoping they all could start a new life here together. Then somehow Eric had found them.

Gina felt the emotions churning up again, but this time she couldn't push them away and she began to sob.

Lori shot around the island and pulled her sister into her arms. "Oh, honey. Let it out. You've been through hell the past two days."

Gina cried until her throat was raw and she finally wiped away the last of her tears. "I thought we were safe. How foolish could I be to think Eric would leave us alone?"

"Well, he's going to be staying away now. He'll be in jail. If the kidnapping charge doesn't stick, shooting at the sheriff and at you should carry some weight."

Heavens, she prayed that would work. "He's got off before."

"This is his third offence, Gina. That hateful man took my nephew and he isn't going to get away with that. Not this time."

Gina thought back to all the people who'd helped her in the past few days. The entire town had volunteered. They'd cooked meals, asked to be deputized and searched for Zack, or just prayed for his safe return. Once again she thought of the one man who had truly helped her find her son.

"Lori, what do you know about Grady Fletcher?"

Her sister blinked at her question, then smiled. "Not much, only that he's been in the bank a few times. I know more about his grandfather, Joe Fletcher. The old miner is recuperating from a broken hip at Shady Haven Nursing Home. Since Grady was listed as next of kin, he's been handling things until Fletch gets back on his feet. I'm not sure that's going to happen since his grandfather has to be in his eighties."

"So he doesn't live here?"

Lori shrugged. "It would be nice if he did. From what Reed told me about what happened on the mountain, I'd say Grady is a take-charge kind of guy. And for what he did for Zack, he's pretty high on my list of good people. Not bad-looking, either."

Gina wasn't surprised by her sister's assessment. She hadn't had much time to notice, but once the dust had settled, she had taken a look at the handsome man. "You'd better not let Jace hear you talk like that."

Lori smiled. "He has nothing to worry about. I only have eyes for my husband."

"That's good to know."

They turned around to see Jace Yeager standing in the doorway. The tall, dark and handsome man was smiling at his wife. "Because I'm kind of crazy about you, too."

Lori rushed across the room, wrapped her arms around him and rewarded him with a tender kiss. "I thought you weren't coming home until tomorrow," she said.

"My family needed me. So I made it happen." He walked over to Gina and pulled her into a big hug. "I'm so sorry I wasn't here for you and Zack."

She nodded. "It's okay, Jace. We got him back and that's all that matters."

That was when they heard a child's cry from the other room. Gina jumped up and hurried to the sofa bed.

"It's okay, honey." She sat on the edge of the bed and pulled her son into her arms.

There were tears in her son's eyes. "Mom, I dreamed Dad was coming after me."

"Never. He's never going to get near you ever again." She looked up at Lori and Jace. "Hey, Uncle Jace came home so he could be with you."

Jace walked to the sofa. "That's right, partner. I heard you had a rough few days."

The child nodded eagerly. "Yeah, I got tied up in a cave."

Gina saw her brother-in-law stiffen, working to control his anger. He kept his voice calm. "Man, that's bad. I'm proud of you for being smart enough to handle it." He messed the boy's hair. "So you spent the night in a cave."

The boy's eyes grew wide. "Yeah, but Scout was with me. He's a big German shepherd. I didn't get scared too much because he was there to protect me from other animals and bad people."

"Sounds like Scout is a pretty neat dog."

Again the child nodded. "He was in the military. He's a hero like Grady." Zack looked at his mom. "I wish I had a dog like Scout. I wouldn't be afraid then."

All eyes turned to Gina. "Yeah, Mom," Jace mimicked. "A dog would be good protection."

Gina had always planned to get her son a dog once they were settled. Her house had a fenced-in yard. "I guess a dog wouldn't be a bad idea."

Her son nearly jumped into her arms. "You're the best mom in the whole world."

Those words were enough to completely sell her on the idea, and to remind her how close she'd come to losing her son. "And you're the best son in the whole world."

* * *

The next morning was Saturday, and as Gina promised, she drove her son out to the cabin to thank Grady. Even for her small all-wheel-drive vehicle, it was slow going over the pitted dirt road. She wasn't sure that she was headed in the right direction until she came through a grove of trees and finally saw the cabin in the clearing.

"Oh, boy." It wasn't much of a clearing. More like a junkyard. Something she hadn't noticed when she was here before. Suddenly she was rethinking her decision to come, wondering if Grady Fletcher just wanted to be left alone.

"Grady might be busy, Zack. I'm not sure if we should just drop in on him."

"Come on, Mom. We don't have to stay long. I want to give Scout my present."

They'd spent all morning shopping for a reward for the dog. "Okay, but if he doesn't have the time, then we leave. Mr. Fletcher is a busy man."

Then the cabin door opened and the German shepherd came out and greeted them with a bark, but stayed on the porch. Gina's heart skipped a beat when the tall man stepped through the door. He was dressed in jeans and a dark thermal shirt, showing off his muscular build. Her body reacted, not in fear but in awareness. Well, darn.

"Scout!" her son called and jumped out of the car. Zack took off running to the dog before she could stop him.

Grady stood rooted on the porch, surprised to see Gina Williams again. Then she stepped out of her car and he found his heart suddenly beating faster. He wasn't happy about that, or about the lack of sleep he'd had since the night she'd invaded his cabin.

Dressed in jeans tucked into boots and a sweater and thermal vest, she reached into the backseat and took out a cellophane-wrapped basket.

She walked toward the steps. "I hope we're not disturbing you."

She didn't want to know the answer to that. "I can take a break." He looked down at Zack. He was glad that the boy looked to be doing well. "Hey, Zack. How are you feeling today?"

He stood on the bottom step, and Scout sat eagerly on the porch waiting for a command to go greet his new friend.

"I had a nightmare last night, but then I pretended that Scout was with me and felt better." The boy waited. "Mom said I need to ask you first if I can pet Scout 'cause he might be in training." Both kid and dog looked up at him waiting for an answer.

"When he's not working he can play. And he's not working now."

Zack grinned. "I got Scout a present. Mom got you something, too." He pulled a long tug rope with a handle on the end from the bag he was carrying. "Is this okay?"

It was okay for Scout, but he didn't want anyone bringing *him* presents. Especially a distracting woman with a little boy. "Yeah, it's okay, but Scout can pull pretty hard."

"I know he's really strong."

Grady pointed to a cleared spot. "Go over in the yard."

The bright sunlight seemed to highlight all the junk

that littered the area. Two rusted-out vehicles, a mess of mining equipment. "I've been trying to clear away most of this stuff, but couldn't do much until the snow melted."

Gina nodded. "I'm sure you can get a lot for the scrap metal."

"I might have hell to pay from my grandfather, but I've got someone coming here in a few days. I'm hoping it will all be cleared out." He sighed. "Then I plan to cart some stuff out of the inside so I have room to move around." He shook his head. "I don't know how the man didn't kill himself. What am I saying? He broke his hip."

The boy called Scout and they ran off to the yard. That meant he was left alone to deal with the mother.

Gina carried the basket up the steps. "I wanted to talk to you about that."

"About what?"

"Your furniture. Well, your grandfather's that is." She stepped onto the porch. "I have a thrift store in town called Second Best. If there are things you want to get rid of, I can sell them for you on consignment...."

That surprised the hell out of him. "That's what you do for a living?"

She nodded. "I kind of fell into it. I started by staging my sister's business complex, then she asked me to decorate some bank-owned properties. I got the idea for a store when I ended up with all this furniture people left behind." She nodded toward the cabin. "Seems like you have extra furniture, too. If you want to get rid of some things, I'd be happy to have a look."

"I'll check with Fletch when I visit him the next time."

"Good." She held out the package in her hands. "I also brought you a little something."

Though embarrassed by her gesture, Grady couldn't refuse her gift. "You didn't have to."

"It's not much. Really. Just some turkey and ham and cheeses from the sandwich shop in town. We wanted to thank you for everything you did. Especially having to put up with me."

Spending time with her hadn't been a burden. Finding her son had been the good part. "Hey, I was in the military for years, so I'm used to taking orders."

She made a face, but it didn't take away from her beauty. He doubted anything could. "Was I that bad?"

"You were just willing to do whatever it took to get your child back. I'm glad everything came out okay." He motioned her toward the door. "Please come in."

First, Gina glanced at Zack to see he was okay with Scout then turned and told Grady, "He makes a great babysitter."

"Scout hasn't been around kids much, but I can see that I don't have anything to worry about. And since I've adopted him and am training him for search and rescue, I was impressed with how well he did finding Zack."

"Will you be staying here after your grandfather comes home?"

"My plans are to go back to Texas, San Antonio, outside Lackland AFB. That's where I plan to do my training with my partner."

"I see." Gina wasn't sure of what else to say as she crossed the threshold so she concentrated on her surroundings. In the daylight, she was able to get a better look. There was some junk, but she'd been right the night she stayed here. There were several good pieces, too. "Do you know what you'd like to keep?"

When she heard his sigh, she realized how close he was standing to her. "About half this," he told her. "I can barely move around as it is. "I'm going to throw out two of the sofas."

She set the basket down on the table. "Which two?"

He pointed out the two worst of the three. "I'll take them," she told him.

"You're kidding?"

"No. They're older, but the frames look to be in great shape. I can reupholster them and sell them in the shop."

"They're yours," he assured her.

Gina examined all the different antique pieces that interested her. He told her no when she asked about the Hoosier cabinet. She'd expected that, but she got a nice sideboard and two end tables to sell on consignment. And he just gave her the old rocking chair.

"Is there more?"

He arched a brow, and she caught a gleam in those dark brown eyes. Then a smile tugged at the corner of his mouth and there was a strange feeling in her stomach.

"Show me?" Her voice was a little throaty.

He didn't say a word as he walked to the doorway leading to another room. She followed tentatively as he opened the door and she stepped through into the next room.

She immediately saw the huge bed that took up most of the limited space. She got closer to the metal frame to see that it was brass, heavily tarnished, but definitely brass. "Oh, my. This is quite something."

"Oh, yeah, it is," Grady agreed. "And my grandfather was very proud of this bed."

"I take it he had it for years."

He nodded. "Ever since I can remember. And I spent a lot of summers here as a kid. Fletch was so proud that he bought it with one of his first gold strikes."

Gina walked around to the other side. "Of course he wouldn't want to sell it?"

He shrugged. "It does take up a lot of room, but probably not."

She glanced around. Like the other space the room was crowded with furniture. "There would be more room to move around if you removed one of these armoires." She went to one cabinet and examined the hand-carved detail on the doors. "This is a lovely piece. I'm not an expert, but I could have an appraiser look at it."

He hesitated, so Gina moved on to the other cabinet. "This one is nice, too. Not as well made, but I could sell it for you if you want."

This was the last thing Grady thought he'd be doing today. When Gina Williams showed up on his doorstep, he didn't think they'd end up in his bedroom. *Whoa, don't go there.*

"Grady?"

He shook off the thoughts. "Sure, I'll check with my grandfather and get back to you. Just leave me the bed and something to put clothes in. Right now my focus is working on the outside."

"Well, I should let you get back to it. I'll go."

She turned to leave and Grady reached for her arm. Then hearing her gasp, realized his mistake. He also saw the panicked look in her eyes and released her. "Sorry. I didn't mean to startle you."

"It's okay. I'm still a little jumpy."

"No, I had no right to grab you like that. Look, you don't have to leave. It's just my frustration with all this stuff in the cabin. Hell, I don't know what to do with fifty years of junk around here. I wouldn't know an antique if it bit me."

"Are you trying to get ready to sell this place?"

He shook his head. "No, but my grandfather can't continue to live like this if he wants to come back here. I'm training dogs, and since I'm staying here longer than planned, I need to build temporary kennels.

"First, I need to clear an area outside. A guy is coming Monday to haul off all the things in the front yard. So the inside of the cabin isn't a top priority."

She smiled. "You're going to train more dogs for a living."

He wanted to make a living at something he enjoyed, and that was working with dogs. "Since I'm retired from the army, I need to do something. Of course, Grandpa Fletch could be a handful." He couldn't abandon the old man who had always been there for him.

"Sounds like a interesting man."

"He has his moments. I'll ask him about the furniture the next visit, because I can't concentrate on the cabin until then." This bedroom was getting smaller by the minute. Her scent drifted in his direction, reminding him of the things he'd lost, that he'd chosen to walk away from.

She followed him back into the main room. "Then we're out of your hair."

She headed for the door, then paused and turned back to him with those sparkling green eyes. "I have an idea. How about if when you get the okay from your grandfather, I'll handle organizing the inside of the cabin for you?" She walked back to him so he got the full effect of her beauty. Her flawless skin and perfect mouth. All that thick brown hair brushing her shoulders made his hands itch to touch it.

"There's no need for you to do that."

"I know, but you rescued my son. There's no way I can repay you for that. Please, let me help you."

He'd pretty much been a loner since his marriage had ended. His choice. And this woman wasn't helping his solitude. "Do you have someone to help you cart off this stuff?"

She nodded. "There's a man who works for my brother-in-law. He does pickups and deliveries for me, too."

He sighed. "Okay, let me check with Fletch and I'll get back to you."

Just then Zack came rushing inside. "Boy, Grady, your dog is really smart."

Grady wasn't used to having kids around. "He's been well trained."

"By you?"

"No, I'm not his first handler. A soldier named Vince Richards worked with him while in Afghanistan."

"Why do you have him?"

Grady shot a glance at Gina, then said, "Because

Scout is retired and I adopted him. I've also adopted two more military dogs. They should arrive next week."

The boy's eyes widened. "Wow. I wish I could have a dog like Scout. Mom said I could get a puppy."

Grady arched an eyebrow. "A dog is a lot of responsibility and work."

The boy nodded. "I know. Mom said I have to feed him and take him for walks."

And Gina added, "And make sure he doesn't have accidents in the house."

"And I want him to protect me, too." Zack turned to Grady. "Can you help me teach a dog to do that?"

Grady hesitated, knowing the boy was still traumatized over what had happened. "I'll see what I can do."

# Chapter 5

Grady drove his truck through the gates of Shady Haven Nursing Home. With the brick and red-cedar shingles, the two-story building looked like a mountain resort. That was only part of the facility, too. There was also a drug rehab center on the far side of the property. And they'd added a newer section, the senior assisted-living apartments.

He walked through the double doors and the inside was just about as impressive. A large reception area had a fireplace and gleaming hardwood floors. In an adjoining room, Grady could see several patients in wheelchairs. One of them was old Joe Fletcher.

He walked in past residents playing games at different tables. His grandfather was playing cards, no doubt taking their money, too.

"Hey, Fletch, what are you up to?"

The thin man with the leathered skin glanced in his direction. "Hey, Grady." He smiled. "Good to see you. Hey, everyone, this is my grandson. Master Sergeant Grady Fletcher."

He pulled up a chair, swung it around and straddled it. "Come on, Joe, I'm retired now. It's just Grady."

"But you're a hero." Those same dark eyes looked back at him. "I heard about the boy."

Grady was surprised. "That was an accident. I found someone trespassing on your land. I told the sheriff."

The old man gave him a toothy grin. "I'm proud, son. Now, can you break me out of here?"

"Whoa, you aren't even healed yet. You need physical therapy." He leaned forward. "And about coming home. It's a death trap there."

Those bony shoulders lifted in a shrug. "So I've collected a few things."

Grady arched an eyebrow. "A few! I'd say, in certain circles you could be known as a hoarder." He sobered. "I need to get rid of a few things so you can get a walker around the place."

The old man grumbled some, then said, "Whatever you think is best, son. Just leave my bed alone."

It was a few days before Gina heard from Grady when he gave her the okay to come out. It took another day before she could get Mac Burleson and his brother, Connor, to drive up to the Fletcher place. They both had other jobs, working for her brother-in-law at Yeager Construction. She couldn't pay them the same money as Jace and she didn't need them too often.

She was reluctant to come along, not knowing if Grady really wanted her there. She also wondered if it was his burn scars that kept him out of town and on the mountain. Somehow, she thought he might just be a solitary man by nature. No sign of a wedding band. Of course, that didn't mean there wasn't someone special. Maybe he was at a loose end since he retired from the army and had to stay here until his grandfather got better.

She shook away any personal thoughts of Mr. Fletcher. It was none of her business. She was interested only in his furniture, not him. She pulled her car up next to the familiar truck, leaving room for Mac's vehicle. She climbed out and that was when she noticed the changes.

The rusted old cars that littered the yard were gone, along with the mining equipment. The grass had even been mowed. Along with the Burlesons, she went up the walk and saw the new wooden steps to the porch. The door opened and Grady came out.

"Good morning," she greeted him, trying not to notice how the long-sleeved T-shirt hugged his wide shoulders and flat stomach. "Looks like you've been busy."

"There's a possibility of snow flurries tonight. I needed to get things done."

"Well, we're here to help. Grady, this is Mac and Connor Burleson."

The men shook hands and then quickly started with their tasks. The brothers loaded the two old sofas onto the truck bed, and went back for some smaller pieces that Grady had told her to take. In about thirty minutes the job was finished. Mac and Connor tied the furniture down, and then they were on their way back to town.

Back in the cabin, Gina began rearranging the furniture that was left behind. She placed the sofa toward the fireplace and tucked a large quilt over the back, then put a braided rug in front of it to cover the rough wooden floor. Since there was room now, she pulled the kitchen table away from the wall and placed a checkered tablecloth she found in the cupboard over the scarred surface.

She stood back and examined her work. "Not bad."

"It looks a helluva lot better than it did."

She turned to see Grady. "Sorry, I hope you don't mind that I moved some things around."

He shook his head. "No. You made it look so much better and I can get around the room now. More importantly, my grandfather will be able to."

She thought it looked cozy. "Well, I should probably get back."

Grady looked at her. "If you have a few minutes, I've got something to show you."

Gina was surprised and intrigued. "Sure." She followed him out the door to the side of the cabin. That was where she saw a high fence and the small building.

"You built a kennel."

"It's temporary."

She saw Scout. He barked and came to the fence to greet her. Soon another shepherd came into view. A lighter color, more golden. "That's Beau." Then two others appeared. "And that's Rowdy and Bandit."

"Oh, Grady. They're beautiful. Can I pet them?"

"I want to work with those two awhile first." He gave a hand signal and the dogs sat, and he managed to retrieve the smaller shepherd named Bandit. Once outside, the lovable animal was all over her. "Well, aren't you a lover."

"Hey, stay back," Grady ordered. It worked, but the little guy began to whine when she moved away.

"I thought you were only getting two dogs."

"When I picked these two up at the Durango airport, my partner, Josh, told me about Bandit. He didn't complete the program, but I didn't want him to go into a shelter." Grady turned that dark gaze on her. "If you're serious about getting a dog for Zack, this guy would be a good one for him."

Gina looked back at the dog. He had the gold and black markings of a shepherd, with two circles around his eyes. "Is he safe for kids?"

"These dogs are socialized before they even start with any other training. I'd never recommend him if he wasn't safe. Of course he needs a little discipline, but yes, he'd be a good companion dog for Zack. And a good watchdog for the house, too."

"Is Zack old enough to handle a big dog?"

"Owning any pet is work, Gina."

She was a little surprised when he said her name. He'd never been that personal before.

"If you have a yard, and can afford to feed him, Bandit will be a great dog for a child. But only if you feel you want a pet."

She refocused on the cute dog. "Okay. Okay, you sold me. What do I owe you for him?"

He shook his head. "Nothing, Josh and I are just glad that we could find him a home. I would like to hold on to Bandit for a few days, just to see what needs to be worked on. I'll bring him into town this weekend. Will you be home?"

"I work Saturday, so is Sunday okay?" At his nod, she went on to say, "Plan on staying for supper." She began to laugh like a silly girl. "Oh, Zack is going to be so excited, especially since you've picked him out. He hasn't stopped talking about Scout and you." She added silently that she'd done her fair share of thinking about this man, too.

Sunday afternoon Grady drove his truck off Main Street onto Cherry Street, a tree-lined street with well-kept family homes. The Williamses' house was a green clapboard bungalow with a large front yard and spring flowers that edged a big porch.

He pulled up to the curb and parked his truck and glanced around. This reminded him of another lifetime. He'd once had a home that looked a lot like this. It had taken them a while before he and Barbara had been able to get their first place, especially since the army had moved him around every few years.

Then he'd been stationed in Texas to stay for a two-year stint. But he hadn't stayed, he'd left to go back to fight a war. He closed his eyes, not wanting to remember the rest. Maybe because he wanted to forget the pain of a bad marriage, and the child he'd never know.

He leaned back against the headrest, recalling the whirlwind romance with the pretty blonde, Barbara Dixon. They'd met at a nightclub while he was on leave, he'd ended up going home with her, and had just stayed. They'd married within weeks, just days before he was deployed.

Nearly a year later he'd come home from overseas and found they were strangers. They were. In all fairness, he hadn't worked that hard at being as social as Barbara needed him to be. He'd tried over the next year to be as attentive as he could.

She struggled with him being gone so much, but he felt helpless to change it. Their marriage suffered for it. Then while deployed again in Afghanistan, Barbara shocked him with the news that he was going to be a father. Excited, he hoped to be home when his child arrived into the world. Then complications had set in and Barbara had gone into labor a month early. He'd got emergency leave, but by the time he arrived home, it was too late. He couldn't even share the loss with his wife. She wanted nothing to do with him. His son was gone. The marriage was over, maybe before it had even had a chance.

Grady shook away thoughts when he heard his name and looked to see Zack running toward the truck. Scout barked from the backseat, causing a chain reaction from Bandit.

"Okay, boys, I want you two on your best behavior." He climbed out of the truck. "Hey, Zack. How's it going?"

"Fine." He nodded toward the truck. "Who's with Scout?"

"What?" He turned and looked at the dogs. "Well, how did he get in my truck?" Grady opened the back door and signaled for Scout to come out. He was grateful that Bandit stayed, but obviously he wanted to get some attention, too.

"You call him out." Grady showed the boy a hand signal.

Zack motioned and Bandit jumped out of the truck. "I did it." He glanced over his shoulder. "Mom, did you see what I did?"

Gina walked up to them. "I saw. Boy, this sure is a pretty dog."

Grady could only stare at her. Gina Williams was the pretty one. She was dressed in jeans and a blue sweater, showing off her trim figure.

"What's his name?" Zack asked, drawing his attention back.

"This is Bandit."

"Wow! That's a cool name. Are you going to train him to rescue people, too?"

Grady shook his head. "No, I have Scout. And my two other dogs, Beau and Rowdy, are back at the cabin. This guy is pretty young and he needs a home."

"Really? Can anyone adopt him? I mean even a kid?"

Grady nodded again.

Zack looked at his mother. "Mom, can we adopt Bandit and have him live with us?"

She acted like she was thinking it over. "That depends. Are you sure this is the kind of dog you want?"

"Yes! He almost looks like Scout."

"A dog is a big responsibility."

Grady took over. "You'll need to feed him, Zack. Not just when you have time, but every morning and evening." He petted the shepherd. "He needs to be walked, and most importantly, clean up after him."

"Oh, I promise I will." He turned to his mother. "I really promise, Mom. Every day."

Something tightened in his chest. This boy had been through a lot in his short life. He had been braver than most adults. "Bandit will need his training reinforced."

Grady glanced at Gina. "He hasn't been worked with much. So he's not as good at taking orders as Scout."

The boy nodded. "I'll work with him, I promise."

Grady nodded. "Then I guess he's yours."

The boy threw his small arms around Grady. "Thank you, Grady. I promise I'll love him and take care of him."

"I know you will, son," he said, feeling a funny tightening in his chest.

Then Zack moved away and went to his mother and hugged her. "Oh, thank you, Mom."

Grady moved away from the touching scene and went to the truck bed and picked up a large bag of food and a dog bed.

There was the sound of a horn and he looked up to see an SUV pull up behind his truck. Gina's sister, Lori, got out, along with a man he recognized as Jace Yeager. A young girl climbed out of the backseat and went straight to Zack and Bandit.

So this was going to be a family dinner. Great.

The sisters hugged and Lori turned toward him. "It's good to see you again, Mr. Fletcher."

"It's Grady, ma'am," he said and saw the resemblance between the sisters. The hair and eye color might have been different, but the shape of the face, and the flawless skin was shared between the two sisters.

"I'm Lori, remember? This is my husband, Jace." The two men shook hands. "And that's our daughter,

Cassie." Lori glanced at her husband. "Brace yourself, she's gonna want a dog now."

"She's got a horse," Jace argued.

The attention turned back to Grady and Lori said, "I don't think I ever thanked you for finding Zack."

"No need. I've been thanked enough."

"Maybe so, but I have to say it again. Thank you, Grady Fletcher." She quickly changed the subject. "How is your grandfather doing?"

"He seems to be recovering nicely."

"Is he up for visitors?"

"Who wants to see him?"

"I wanted to stop by and speak with him about some land that there's a question about."

"If this has anything to do with Billy Hutchinson, I'm not sure I want you stirring up any trouble."

"No trouble, Grady. It's righting a wrong that my grandfather did years ago. Once I took over the bank, I discovered a title to a piece of land that I believe belongs to Joe Fletcher. Maybe when he's feeling better I can correct this…mistake."

Gina stood back and watched the change in Grady's demeanor. How different he'd been with just Zack and her. Now that the group was bigger, he seemed tense. He wasn't comfortable around people.

Grady didn't have time to reflect on Lori Hutchinson Yeager's confession as they herded both kids and dogs to the backyard. Grady followed Gina to put away the bag of dog food in the cupboard on the utility porch. The oversize dog bed was placed next to the clothes dryer.

"I doubt Bandit will be sleeping in here," she said. "I know Zack wants him to be in his bedroom."

Grady nodded. "This dog has been kenneled at night, but I'm sure there won't be a problem with Bandit sleeping in Zack's room. Just not in the bed."

"Okay, but you have to tell Zack, along with any other rules about caring for the dog."

"I will." He looked into her green eyes and started to get distracted. "How's Zack doing?"

"Better each day, but he still isn't sleeping in his own room. Jace is going to replace the windows and put in higher ones so Zack will feel safe again. Right now he's sleeping in another room that I've been using as my office." He saw her watery eyes. "And we have an appointment tomorrow to go and talk to a therapist about what happened."

Grady tensed. He'd love to get his hands on Lowell again. *Who does that to a child?* "He's gone through a lot. It'll take time."

He couldn't help but think about what Gina had gone through, too. The years of abuse from a man who claimed he loved her. "What about you? How are you handling this?"

She looked surprised at the question. "I'm okay, as long as Zack recovers from this."

The sounds of giggles coming from the backyard got Gina's attention. She smiled and his heart skipped a beat. "I guess having a dog is a start. Thank you."

"Not a problem," he told her, wondering why her praise meant so much to him.

"Come on, Grady, let's join the fun."

She started out the door, but he hesitated. It had been a long time since he'd done any family things. He'd never been very good at it. The army had been his family. And now he didn't even have that. He wasn't sure what he had.

An hour later Gina, Grady, Jace and Lori were sitting on the patio finishing their hamburgers while the kids played with the dogs.

Gina loved that her family was all together, at her house. She'd never expected to have someone like Grady Fletcher sit beside her, but he seemed on edge all during the meal. Finally he'd gotten up and taken Zack out to teach him how to work the dogs.

She glanced at her son, running around the yard with his dog. Zack was so happy.

Grady had given them some tricks to work on and that was all it took. The kids started burying things, and soon the dogs were retrieving toys and returning them. Bandit got distracted pretty easily, but some training would help that.

Gina's attention went to the ex-soldier standing alone. Did he have a problem being around a lot of people? She'd noticed how his demeanor had changed when her sister and her family had arrived.

Lori turned to her husband. "Mark my words, Cassie will ask for a puppy before we get back home."

"If you really want one, I bet Grady can find you one."

Jace groaned. "Don't give your niece any ideas." He hugged his wife. "We're hoping a new baby will distract her from wanting any more pets."

They all three laughed as the back gate opened and

Gina saw Claire and Tim Keenan walk in. Gina rushed over to greet them both with a hug.

"I hope we're not intruding," Claire said, holding out a covered dish.

Gina hugged the two. "Claire and Tim, of course you're not, you're always welcome. Please, join us."

"Oh, no, we just wanted to drop off this pie and tell you how happy we are that both you and Zack are back safe."

"I insist you stay. We're about to have some coffee and now some pie."

"I can go for that," Tim volunteered as they walked toward the others on the patio.

Gina introduced Grady, letting him know they owned the Keenan Inn, a historical bed-and-breakfast in town.

"Sheriff Larkin is married to their daughter, Paige, who is an attorney. Their oldest daughter, Morgan, is the mayor. Their youngest daughter, Leah, is a photo journalist. They all came back to Destiny to raise their families."

After they shook hands, Tim said, "Sounds like a Chamber of Commerce ad." The older man smiled. "I remember you, but it's been a while. You were just a kid. Old Fletch used to come into town and bring you along."

Gina watched as Grady nodded. "That wasn't very often," he admitted. "He didn't like people much."

So that was where he got it from. Was Grady a loner like his grandfather, or was it the scar?

Tim Keenan laughed. "No, he didn't. Most of the old miners kept to themselves. I think they were afraid someone would jump their claims if they left them for long."

Grady gave a rare smile. "Yeah, I used to hear a lot of those stories. I feel bad I wasn't around to help him more."

Claire added, "Rest assured, the Shady Haven Nursing Home is a wonderful facility. I volunteer there, so I see how happy their patients are." She smiled. "I hope you don't mind, but I stop in to see your grandfather from time to time."

"I appreciate it." Grady was ashamed that his own personal problems had interfered with spending more time with his grandfather. "I didn't get to see much of him the past few years."

Claire smiled. "Fletch understood, and let us know on more than one occasion that you were defending our freedom," she told him. "And we, too, thank you for your service."

He nodded. "I'm retired now."

Tim stepped in. "I hear you're already starting a new career, training dogs for search and rescue." He looked out toward the shepherds. "Are those two of them?"

"Just the one," Grady said as he pointed to the bigger dog. "That's Scout."

"He found Zack," Gina added. "The other younger one is Bandit, he's Zack's new dog."

Claire looked from Gina toward Grady. "That's really nice of you to get the boy such a special dog. Are you planning to move here permanently?"

"No. I'm going back to Texas once Fletch is settled and on his feet again."

"Oh, do you have family there?"

Grady knew where this was going. Mrs. Keenan was already putting Gina and him together as a couple. "No, it's just me." He glanced around. He needed to leave, and soon.

Suddenly as if Gina saw his distress, she interrupted. "Oh, we need some plates for our dessert," she said, then rushed into the house.

Grady knew that he couldn't get away as easily. What was he thinking, getting involved with them? He wanted to come here and sit on the mountain while his grandfather recuperated. Why couldn't he be left alone?

Over the past several nights his solitude had been invaded by a lost boy and a beautiful single mother. None of which he needed at this point in his life. Probably never. Gina Williams had her own issues. So did he. She needed a patient guy who wanted a family. Grady didn't do family. He'd tried and failed, never again. He'd stick with animals.

"They're beautiful dogs." Tim Keenan came up to him. "Were they overseas, too?"

"Scout was. He's completed his service so I was able to adopt him. Bandit didn't make the program, but he's still an excellent dog."

"Even better that Zack gets to have one, too." Tim shook his head. "That boy has been through hell, and he was just starting to open up when this all happened. I think Bandit will be a great therapy dog for him."

"I'm glad I could help. I need to get back before dark." He stood and whistled for Scout. The dog stopped then ran toward him and sat. Grady said goodbye to everyone as he started to leave.

"Don't be a stranger in town," Tim said as he walked

with him to the gate. "Get to know people here in Destiny. You'll find we're pretty easy to get along with."

Grady just wasn't sure he wanted to form any attachments. He'd be leaving soon. Definitely the best idea before he got distracted by one pretty brunette.

# Chapter 6

Three days later Gina stood at the front window of her shop on First Street. The Second Best Thrift Shop had an ideal location right off the town square.

She could see the large fountain and park, along with several other storefront shops. Destiny Community Bank was across the street, next door was Paige Keenan Larkin's law office and the Rocky Mountain Bridal Shop. The sheriff's office was on the next block along with the U.S. post office.

Gina had been lucky to get a space in a prime location. The front of the shop was her thrift store. The showroom was still a little sparse, but once she cleaned up the pieces she'd gotten from Grady Fletcher, it should add a lot to the window display.

Her thoughts turned to the man who had upset her

tranquillity. She still didn't know much about the ex-army master sergeant who lived on the mountain. Only that he'd seen war, and had to have suffered greatly with his obvious burns. She'd seen the pain in his eyes. Yet, from the way he stood back from people, she somehow doubted it was all physical.

Still he hadn't hesitated to help find Zack. That alone made Grady Fletcher pretty special. The part that bothered her was that she found she was drawn to him. She'd spent just over twenty-four hours with the man, and oddly, she felt safe around him. Given her past record with men, she hadn't found it easy to trust. And she might never find it easy.

She couldn't help but recall the width of Grady's shoulders and chest. Her breath caught in her throat as she remembered his gentle touch, with her, Zack and his dogs.

She shook away the direction of her thoughts. She was in no way ready to think about a man in her life. Besides, Grady Fletcher would be leaving for Texas soon. That right there should make her keep her distance. Not that he would ever want her, not with all her baggage. Not with her fears of intimacy. She could never measure up to what Eric wanted in a wife or a lover. He'd let her know time and again that she couldn't please him.

She shook away the memories. No, she didn't need a man. She was happy with her life as it was. She was independent and had her family.

Most importantly, Zack. This was his first day back to school since the ordeal. Even though she'd talked with her son about the situation, she knew it would be a long time before he got over the events of those harrowing twenty-four hours. Their new dog helped a lot.

She smiled, thinking about Bandit. He'd been the best medicine ever. Boy and dog had been inseparable the past two days. So there had been sad faces this morning when she'd taken Zack to school. Maybe she should go home at lunch to check on Bandit, just to make sure he was okay.

Gina checked her watch. Right, she needed to get to work herself, so she walked toward the back of her store. In the work area she saw the two sofas from Grady's cabin. Marie, her young helper, was already removing the dirty, worn fabric.

"How bad is it, Marie?" she asked the young mother of a twelve-month-old little girl, Sophie.

The tall, willowy blonde was about Gina's age. She had an easy smile and a real talent with a sewing machine.

"Not bad. The frame is solid and with new padding and fabric it will look great."

"That's what I was thinking when I saw it." Gina grinned. "And it was free." She eyed the other sofa. "How about you reupholster this one, and I'll do the camelback sofa? Since I can't pay you what you're really worth, how about you take sixty percent of the sale?"

"Oh, Gina, you don't have to do that."

"Yes, I do. I'm barely paying you now. And don't tell me you can't use the money."

Marie's husband was finishing college and could only work part time. "But how many bosses let an employee bring her kid to work?"

Not many that Gina knew of, remembering when she

herself had tried to find work with Zack in tow. "Hey, a business should supply a daycare, even if it is a small storage area in the back of the store."

"It's perfect. And thank you for that."

"Let's just get these sofas finished so we can sell 'em."

Marie looked toward the wide doorway that led out to the alley. "I think we have a visitor."

Gina turned around. She couldn't be more surprised to find Grady Fletcher. He looked big and intimidating. Did he do that on purpose?

She put on a smile and went to him. "Grady. It's nice to see you again."

He gave her a nod and stepped through the doorway as if he wouldn't be welcome. "Didn't mean to disturb you, but I thought I'd come around back to drop off some things I found in the shed."

"Oh, really?" Gina glanced over her shoulder. "Marie this is Grady Fletcher. Grady, Marie, my jack-of-all-trades."

"Nice to meet you, Grady."

Grady tipped his cowboy hat. "Ma'am."

He turned his attention back to Gina, causing her to feel nervous. "As you can see, we've started tearing apart the sofas you gave me."

He walked over. His gaze searched the furniture. She wondered if that was how he looked when he inspected the troops.

"Looks like a lot of work."

"It'll be worth it once they're finished. Right, Marie?"

"Right," the pretty blonde agreed. Gina planned to

put them in the front display window. She put on a big smile. "Of course, they won't be there long, once we work our magic."

"Well, good luck with that."

Gina pulled his attention back. "You said you have some more furniture?"

Grady nodded, wondering what he was doing here. One look at Gina Williams, and already he was distracted. She looked fresh, young and so pretty. Dressed in those nice-fitting jeans and a denim blouse, she could pass for a teenager. Too young for him. And it seemed every time he got near her, he couldn't seem to act normal.

"I was clearing out the shed when I found some things." He pointed over his shoulder. "They're in the truck."

She smiled and his heart began to pound hard. "May I see them?"

"Sure."

They walked out to his truck. Scout spotted her and barked in greeting from the backseat.

"Well, hello, fella." When the dog stuck his head out the open window, she went to him and began to pet him. "Oh, I know a little boy who misses you," she told the animal.

"How is Zack doing?"

She turned to him. "Good. He went back to school today, but as a mother, I worry. What if the kids start saying things? Teasing him?"

Grady leaned against the truck door, then realized he was close enough to inhale her soft scent. "I would think the kids would be more interested in Zack spending the night in a silver mine, more than his dad kidnapping him."

She looked up with those moss-green eyes. "Thank you for that, but I can't help but be overprotective."

"You have good reason to be. But now, you know you and your son are safe from your ex."

She sighed. "You can't imagine how good that feels. We can finally concentrate on making a life for ourselves."

He wondered if that included finding someone to share that life. It wouldn't take long for the men in this town to come sniffing around.

She smiled. "Like you are," she added.

He nodded, but he wasn't sure what his permanent plans were. "Thanks to my grandfather I have a place to live for now. On the downside, Old Fletch is a packrat—my immediate future is filled with a lot of work clearing out the place."

"Your grandfather is a man after my own heart." She rubbed her hands together excitedly. "So what did you bring me?"

He couldn't help but smile. "I don't know if this stuff is even worth bringing in." He walked to the truck bed and unfastened the tarp and pulled it back, then let down the gate.

"Oh, my," she said, and began to climb up on the bumper. Grady reached out, gripped her waist and boosted her up into the truck.

Gina froze momentarily, but then realized this was Grady touching her. She trusted him—as much as she would ever trust a man—not to hurt her. What truly scared her were the feelings that he did stir in her.

She quickly concentrated on the treasures he'd brought her. Another rocking chair, a cedar trunk, a Tiffany lamp. But it was a small pedestal table that got her attention. She pulled back the tarp further and was rewarded with a leather top in nearly perfect condition.

"Where did you find all this?"

"Buried in the shed out back." He climbed up and stood next to her. "Why?"

Gina examined it more closely, pulling out the single drawer to see the name stamped inside. "It a Mersman pedestal table with a leather top." She ran her fingers over the camel-colored softness. "How is it in such perfect condition?"

"Like I said, it was protected by a tarp and buried under a lot of stuff. I think it belonged to my grandmother. Maybe after she died, Fletch just put her things away."

She gave him a questioning look. "Are you sure your grandfather is okay about selling these things?"

"I saw him yesterday. He agreed that the cabin needs to be cleared out. He gave me first pick on these things. Except his bed. He wants me to keep my hands off that bed."

She smiled. "Your grandfather seems to be quite a character."

"Joe Fletcher was a miner, which wasn't an easy life. He once lived in Destiny, but after my grandmother passed away, he moved up to the cabin to work his claim. My father didn't like the life there so he didn't hang around after he turned eighteen. He didn't come back here much, either." Only to drop his kid off so he didn't have to deal with him, he added silently.

Gina studied him. "But you like it here."

"Old Fletch wasn't so bad." Their gazes locked, and he found himself saying more than he'd planned. "I was sent to spend my summers here after my parents divorced."

"It's nice you had him, but it must have been hard…" Her face brightened, and he could hardly draw a breath. "I bet those times were fun."

Yeah, he loved the old guy. "No one taught me more." He glanced around at the mountain range. "I hiked this area a lot of summers."

"Must be some nice memories," she said and sighed. "I want that for Zack. I want him to be able to erase all the bad that has happened to him."

Grady studied her pretty face. He found the need to reach out and touch her, but he fought the attraction. Making any kind of connection was a bad idea. "You have a good start here."

"I hope so," she said. "And I bet Fletch is happy that you're back here."

Honestly, he'd always felt a connection to this place. "Since the army sent me packing, I need to make a living. So it's back to Texas and my business."

She nodded. "But you have family here. I learned it's not the structure that makes it a home, it's the people. My son and my sister are my family, and we added Jace and Cassie. I'm lucky to have all of them."

This discussion was getting far too involved. "Yes, you are. Look, I need to get going. Scout has been in the truck a long time."

"Oh, of course. Just tell me what you want me to do

about the table. Do you want to sell it on consignment? I'm not sure I can afford to buy it outright."

He moved the table to the end of the truck bed, then jumped down. He needed to put some distance between them. "Whatever you decide. I just need to clear out things to make room for when Fletch comes home."

Gina nodded. "How about I clean it up for you?" she suggested. "You might want to keep it. After all, it belonged to your grandmother."

"Whatever. You can go ahead and sell the trunk and rocker."

They moved the items out of the truck bed, then he helped her down. He didn't want to make a big deal about touching her, but when he put his hands on her tiny waist, his reaction became one. As hard as he tried, they ended up too close. Then their eyes met and he saw she was just as affected as he was. Great.

He placed her on the ground and she stumbled. He reached out and pulled her to him before she fell. Her softness pressed against his body was torture, the best kind.

"Ah, sorry." She regained her balance and moved back. Way back. "If you help me get these things inside, then you can be on your way."

He didn't say a word, realizing it had been a bad idea to come here in the first place. He needed to stay away from Gina Williams.

As he lifted the table off the truck, Marie came out. She called to Gina, "The school called."

"Oh, no. Did something happen with Zack?"

The blonde smiled. "No, but it seems he has a visitor. His name is Bandit."

\* \* \*

Ten minutes later Gina and Grady with Scout on a leash headed to the school office. He'd brought the dog along in case they needed some extra support to corral Bandit.

A middle-aged principal came outside to greet her. "Hello, Ms. Williams."

"Hello, Mr. Markham. This is Grady Fletcher."

"Mr. Fletcher." The principal nodded, then turned back to Gina. "It seems your son's dog came to school."

"I'm so sorry, Mr. Markham. The last I checked Bandit was in the backyard." She looked at Grady. "How could he find his way to the school?"

Grady answered, "Either he followed the scent, or the sound of the kids' voices. He has more potential than I thought."

Gina didn't care how the dog got there. Just that she had a problem if he kept getting out of the yard.

"Well according to Zack," Markham began, "Bandit is a very smart dog. Outside of a German shepherd named Scout, Bandit is the smartest dog in the whole world. And he was in the army."

"Meet Scout," Grady said and Gina noticed a hint of a smile. "I'm the one who gave Bandit to Zack. Where is the dog now?"

"Zack is with him on the playground."

Together they all walked back to the area behind the building. "Mr. Fletcher," the principal began, "Zack has told me a lot about your dogs, Beau, Rowdy and Scout. He said you're training them to be search-and-rescue dogs."

"I've only been working with Scout so far." He

glanced down at his obedient shepherd. "He's coming along. Bandit hasn't had as much training. But I'm thinking he should get a gold star for finding little boys now."

"We all hear that Scout found Zack when he was lost," the man said.

Grady nodded. "He played a big part in it."

The principal caught Gina's attention. "I know you and your son have been through a rough time this past week."

Gina hated that everyone knew what had happened. She'd hoped that she could leave her past behind in Colorado Springs. "Yes, we have. Thank you for understanding."

The man nodded. "I noticed how much Zack responded when his dog showed up today. Even though I can't have Bandit at school every day, maybe a little show-and-tell with the two dogs wouldn't hurt."

Grady hesitated, then said, "After today, I'm not sure Bandit is ready for prime time."

"Maybe in a few weeks then?"

"We'll see."

They reached the playground and found the boy and the dog along with Claire Keenan, an aid from the class.

Zack spotted her. "Mom!" he cried and came running to her. "Mom, look, Bandit found my school. He followed my scent. He came to my classroom door. He really did."

"I heard," she said, wondering how to fix this problem. She looked at Mrs. Keenan. "Claire, thank you so much for staying with them."

"Oh, I was happy to do it." She looked at Grady. "Hi, Grady. It's nice to see you again."

"Hello, ma'am."

The older woman smiled. "I just love how respectful these soldiers are. But you can just call me Claire."

He nodded then snapped a leash on Bandit. "Thanks, Claire."

Mrs. Keenan was starting to leave, then stopped. "We're having a little get-together Sunday afternoon at the inn, just family and friends. We would love it if you all would join us."

"Thank you, Claire," Gina said. "That would be nice."

The older woman looked at Grady. "You could bring Scout, and Zack can bring Bandit. There's a wooded area behind the inn—maybe you can work the dogs. The kids would love it."

Grady was barely able to keep from squirming. Great, the good citizens of Destiny were trying to bring him into the fold. "Thank you for the invitation."

"Any time. We want you to feel a part of this community."

That was the problem. He wasn't sure if he wanted to be part of anything. "I'll try and make it."

"It's an open invitation, Grady." Claire walked back into the classroom, with a promise from Gina that she'd bring Zack.

Zack's smile faded as he looked up at Grady. "Is Bandit in trouble?"

"He's your dog, son. But I suggest he has some reinforcing discipline. It sounds harsh but you don't want Bandit to get hit by a car—which he might do if he's forever wandering about the town. So it looks like you'll need to work with him. Teach him his boundaries."

Gina watched as her son leaned against the dog in question. The two were already so close.

"Will you help me, Grady?" Zack asked. "I want Bandit to be as smart as Scout."

Grady went down to Zack's level. "Then he needs *you* to teach him. You need to show him who is the leader of the pack."

"I don't know what that means."

"It means you're the boss."

Gina watched the exchange between the two. Her son was hanging on to every word Grady said. Even with Lori's husband, Jace, it had taken Zack a long time to warm up to him. Not true with this man. She wasn't sure if that was a good thing.

"Hey, Mom, I'm the boss of Bandit."

"Well, right now, I'm the boss. And you need to go back to class. So say goodbye to Bandit."

Her son hugged the dog, then stopped in front of Grady. "Will you come to my house and teach me how to be the boss?"

Gina held her breath. She didn't want to step into this, even though she knew that Grady had done so much for them. More than she could ever repay.

"How about I make sure the backyard is secured?" he told the boy. "I'll give you some exercises to help show Bandit his boundaries. But you have to do the work."

That seemed to make her son happy. "Okay."

Gina saw the change in Grady from earlier when he'd opened up to her. Were they becoming too much of a burden? Of course they were. Grady was a single man who didn't need a kid hanging on him. She kissed her son goodbye and watched him head off to class.

The ride back to her house with Grady was a silent one. When she climbed out of the truck with Bandit in tow, she expected Grady to drive off. Instead he followed them to the backyard. He searched the area until he found the hole under the fence where the dog had escaped.

"Do you have any extra wood?"

"There's some in the garage."

When he started to walk off, she tied Bandit to the post and went after Grady. "You don't have to fix it. I can do it."

"Not a problem."

She unlocked the door to the structure, turned on the light and led him to the neatly stacked boards that Jace had left after doing some house repairs.

"This is only a temporary fix," he told her.

"Then let me help," she insisted.

"There's no need." He started past her, but she refused to be ignored as she followed him.

"There's every need. I'm not helpless," she argued, then suddenly ran into the back of the man's hard body.

With a gasp, she backed away.

The wood hit the ground as Grady cursed and turned around.

His gaze met hers. "You okay?"

She nodded. "I'm sorry, I didn't know you were going to stop."

He just stood there staring at her, those dark eyes piercing.

"I don't know why, but I've made you angry."

He glanced away, then back at her. "I'm not angry at you, Gina. I'm angry with myself."

"Why?"

He took a step closer to her. "Because I can't stop thinking about doing this." He leaned down and his mouth closed over hers.

# Chapter 7

Gina jumped back quickly. "Why'd you do that?" She fought to keep her composure.

Grady shrugged. "Hell if I know."

"Well, next time try to control yourself."

"I'll be sure I do that." He turned, grabbed the long piece of wood and stalked out of the garage.

Gina sagged against the workbench and tried to slow her breathing. She ran her tongue over her lips. Oh, God. She could still taste him. Stop. It was only a kiss.

No. She wasn't going to get involved with a man. Not again. Never again. She already had the life she wanted for her and Zack. She didn't need a man in it. Besides, who would want to deal with all her hang-ups? She was so afraid of being touched, she'd never have a normal relationship.

She thought back to her old life. Eric had never treated her like anything but an object. She'd met him as a teenager when she had been so eager for attention. At that time, she'd been willing to do anything to have someone love her. Problem was, she'd confused sex with love, and had let Eric talk her into whatever he wanted. He never cared about her, only the power he had over her. And then the control had begun.

Too late, she'd realized she'd never had a voice about anything. At nearly nineteen, she'd become a bride and a mother. She knew nothing. When Eric had started pushing her around she was too ashamed to tell anyone. It had been Lori who had rescued her and Zack.

Even after counseling, she still had trouble with self-esteem, especially when it came to men. Could she handle a man's touch? She wondered if she'd ever be able to enjoy the physical part of a relationship. Could she hold the interest of a man like Grady Fletcher? As good looking as the man was, he had to be used to women's attention, experienced women. She was far from knowing how to please a man…how to keep a man.

Gina walked to the garage doorway and looked out. She saw Grady as he knelt down at the base of the fence and went to work at boarding up Bandit's escape route. Big and muscular, she had no doubt Grady was a take-charge guy. Yet, he'd never made her feel any fear. She touched her lips with her fingertips. The yearning was still there, making her want something she couldn't have. A normal relationship with a man.

Thirty minutes later Grady drove his truck along the dirt road to the cabin, still cursing his bad judgment.

Damn! Why couldn't he just keep his hands off Gina? He didn't need this complication. He'd come back here to take some time to heal and rebuild his life. He didn't need Gina Williams distracting him, making him want things again. Especially not a woman with a child reminding him of everything he'd lost.

Grady parked the truck in front of the cabin and climbed out. He got Scout from the backseat and walked up to the porch. After unlocking the door, he went inside and glanced around at Gina's handiwork.

A woman's touch. Something he'd taken for granted during his marriage. Even though he and Barbara had been together only four years, he'd got used to coming home to all the comforts. Even with the short time they'd had together as a couple, he'd missed the things that only a woman could give.

In the end, he hadn't been there enough. Okay, so she had signed on as a career army wife, but two tours of duty overseas during a marriage had taken a toll.

Although he'd warned her, Barbara still hadn't deserved the heartache. He'd given it a hundred percent when he was stateside, but that hadn't been enough to make it work. He'd learned too late—he was never the marrying kind. He should have saved them both the heartache.

He walked into the cabin's one bedroom and went to the scarred dresser, then opened the top drawer and took out a small box. The only thing he'd taken from his home after the divorce. He felt his heart begin to pound and his hands shook as he raised the lid on the treasure box he'd had since he'd been a kid. But it was what was inside that tore him apart. He looked down at the grainy photo. The only picture he had of his son.

A sonogram.

Grady sank onto the bed as he studied the image of a child that had never been born.

He took a shaky breath, wondering if this sad helpless feeling would ever leave him. The feeling that told him he'd served his country proudly, but couldn't get home to help his family. Of course, if he'd known that Barbara had been pregnant before volunteering, he might have thought twice about going back overseas. He remembered the weekly phone calls he'd made home and hearing about the pregnancy, then later when the commanding officer had given him the news that his wife was in the hospital. He'd managed to get on the first plane home. But it was too late. Worse, Barb blamed him for everything, but not nearly as much as he blamed himself.

He quickly shook away the memory.

His thoughts turned to Gina. No! He wasn't getting involved with her. She needed a man who would be there for her. A normal man without battle scars, who was able to give her what she needed. Treat her how she needed to be treated, special. Give her a home and a life of happiness.

Hell, he wasn't sure what his future would be. He had a grandfather who needed to be cared for. A cabin in the mountains that didn't even have a flushing toilet. He'd had no business kissing her. He needed to stay away from both mother and child.

Scout barked then raced out of the bedroom. Then Grady heard, "Hello, is anyone here?"

"Who the hell?" Grady quickly put the box back into the drawer and hurried through the cabin to find the intruder leaning down and petting the shepherd in the open doorway.

"Hey, Sarge, you shouldn't leave your door open," the man said.

Grady recognized the army corporal right away. Twenty-seven-year-old Josh Regan had served in his unit overseas. They'd both survived the explosion that day that had taken out two of their squad members. They'd spent time in the hospital where they'd been treated for wounds and burns. That was where they'd come up with the idea of training dogs.

"Hey, partner. What are you doing here?"

"Well, I figured I'd stop by and see how you're getting along with the dogs."

Grady couldn't help but smile. "Not too bad. I thought you were headed home to Georgia for a visit with your family and your girl."

The tall, lanky Southern boy straightened. "I've been home and discovered there isn't a girl waiting any longer." He sighed. "So after chowin' down enough of my mother's cooking, I thought I'd stop by here to see you and the dogs and firm up our plans before I headed back to Texas." Regan looked around. "So this is the place you talked about… Nice digs."

"Livable. The view is the best." He studied the kid. "I told you the last time we talked, Josh, I can't leave yet." They'd planned the partnership, but then that had been delayed when his grandfather had ended up in the hospital. "I'm not sure when I'll get back to Texas."

"I know that. I just thought I'd take a detour before

heading back to Lackland. Maybe I can hang around for a few days and we can work with the dogs."

The idea was a good one. He could get some work done on the cabin and not neglect the dogs. "I should have thought about that. We could work here for now. The cabin is short on guest quarters, but you're welcome to bunk on the sofa."

Regan seemed to relax. "You sure?"

"Wouldn't offer if I wasn't. Besides, I could use a hand with the training here, and you're the expert handler."

A big boyish grin appeared. "I've got a sleeping bag in my truck. Then I'll go visit with Beau and Rowdy."

Josh followed Grady out to the porch. He pointed over his shoulder. "I have built some makeshift kennels for now, but we might need something sturdier if we're going to work on training."

The corporal stopped and looked around at the view. "I could get used to this great view."

It was a great view, but their training facility was in Texas. "Yeah, but it's still my grandfather's cabin and he's dead set on returning here once the doctor releases him."

Josh let out a long breath. "Too bad. I could get used to the cooler weather."

Grady couldn't help but smile, too. It was good to see a familiar face. Someone who had been through the same things and understood. "Well, you're not going to get the chance to sit around and enjoy it. We'll be working."

"That's why I'm here. To help out."

And Grady was glad. They could get some things

done, and it would keep him from thinking about a pretty brunette who was too young and fragile for him. He glanced at his partner and realized Josh was better suited for Gina. Yet, he didn't want the man anywhere near her.

"Don't think I don't know what you're up to."

The next morning, Grady sat across from his grandfather at Shady Haven. "Okay, what am I up to?"

The older man glared. "You're cleaning up the cabin, then you're going to clear out as soon as I get out of this place."

Grady sighed. "You always knew I was headed back to Texas, but I'm not going to leave you until you can make it on your own. You still need rehab on your hip. That means you can't return to the cabin, especially with so much stuff crammed into the place."

"I did just fine before," Joe said, his dark eyes narrowed as he raised his large, veined hand. "I know where everything is."

"So you want me to put everything back? That might be hard to do since Gina Williams carted most of it off."

The old man frowned. "Who is Gina?"

"She runs the thrift store in town."

"You kept my bed, didn't you?"

"Didn't touch your bed. But Gina wants to know about some of Grandma's things."

Joe eyed him closely. "Seems you're spending a lot of time with this woman. Are you sweet on her?"

Grady wasn't sure how to handle this one. "No, I'm not. I don't have the time for a woman. Besides, you know I don't do so well in relationships."

"You would if you picked the right one." There was a hint of a smile. "Bring this Gina by here. And I'll tell you if she's good enough for you."

"Look, Fletch, don't you think I'm too old to have your approval on who I see."

"Ha, ha. So you are seeing her," he said, then he sobered. "Don't be too stubborn to see what's right in front of you, boy. Take it from one who knows. Time slips by fast. So make an old man happy, and bring your young lady by."

Grady knew it would be foolish if he did bring Gina here. "I'll see what I can do."

Sunday afternoon, the Keenan Inn was the place to be, especially if you liked to be around family, friends and good food.

Gina got out of the car followed by Zack just as another vehicle pulled up behind her. She immediately recognized Grady and it sent her heart racing. She'd known he was going to be here, but she still wasn't ready to see him again.

"They're here, Mom. Grady and Scout are here."

Before she could stop him, her eager son grabbed Bandit's leash and raced off toward the truck as Grady climbed out. It had been a few days since the incident in the garage, and their kiss. The feel of his firm mouth against hers, his scent stirring her emotions. It was still fresh in her mind.

The man was hard to forget. His mere size and presence demanded her attention. Yet, she'd never been frightened by him, even by those dark, piercing eyes. He looked good. She knew he was self-conscious about the scar along his neck, but she didn't even notice it anymore.

She inhaled a calming breath and walked over to him. His gaze caught hers and held, refusing to let her look away. Then finally he spoke. "Hello, Gina."

"Hi, Grady," she managed to say.

Zack caught her attention. "Mom, can I go hide some stuff so Scout and Bandit can find it?"

"In a minute," she said, noticing another man getting out of the passenger side of the truck. He was younger with dark hair that had the familiar military cut.

"Gina," Grady began, "this is Josh Regan. We served together. He's also my partner in training the dogs. He's staying with me for a while."

The younger man said, "Hello, ma'am."

"It's nice to meet you, Josh. Please call me Gina. This is my son, Zack, and Bandit."

Josh smiled. "It's good to meet you both."

"Are you in the army, too?" Zack asked.

"I was. I served under Sgt. Fletcher. I was a dog handler."

"Wow! Cool."

Grady stood back and watched how Regan's attention remained on Gina. Okay, she was pretty enough to be stared at, but not as if she was his next meal.

"Hey, Josh." Grady handed him the dog leash. "Would you mind taking Scout out back and getting the kids organized on the exercise? I'll be there in a few."

"Sure." The younger guy didn't question the order and walked off with Zack and the dogs. Grady turned back to Gina. Oh, Lord, she looked good. "How have you been?"

"I'm fine."

He watched her, seeing her cheeks redden. Was she thinking about the kiss? He quickly asked, "I meant, how have you and Zack been?"

"He's back in his own bedroom."

"That's good." Enough small talk, he needed to clear the air. "Gina, about the other day… I was out of line. I promise it won't happen again."

"Let's just say we were both caught up in the situation…" She glanced away. "I just didn't want you to get any ideas. It's not that you're not attractive. I mean, any woman would want your attention." She shook her head. "It's just I'm not ready, nor do I want to get involved with anyone."

Grady heard her words of refusal, but that didn't change the fact that he was still drawn to her. "I can understand you feeling that way, but never is a long time. You're too young, Gina. There's a guy out there for you. Not all are jerks like your ex." He turned and headed toward the backyard of the inn.

Gina released a breath. The last thing she needed was Sgt. Fletcher telling her to date. She liked her life just fine as it was. She walked up the steps at the inn. She had her son and business to concentrate on. Grady had his own work, too. They should both be able to keep out of each other's way.

Resigned to keeping her distance from the man, Gina walked through the double doors with the glass oval panels, etched with the Keenan name. Inside, she stood in the entry with the antique desk used for registering guests at the historic bed-and-breakfast.

She glanced around at the high ceiling trimmed with

crown moldings and wainscoting stained in a honey color. The walls were painted a light tan and the floors were covered in a burgundy carpet. The large polished oak staircase led to the second and third floors.

"Welcome."

Gina turned and found Tim Keenan. The handsome sixty-year-old offered her a ready smile that reached all the way to his clear blue eyes.

"Hi, Tim."

He walked up and hugged her. "Gina, so glad you could make it today. We don't see enough of you or your boy. Where is Zack?"

She stepped back. "He's headed out back with Grady and the dogs. I came in to see if I can help Claire."

"I think we have enough hands in that kitchen, but let's head back and ask them."

Tim and Gina walked through the dining room, which had several small tables for guests.

"How is Zack handling things these days?"

"Better," Gina told him. "He had a few sessions with a counselor." She smiled as they continued their journey through a butler's pantry. "I seem to be the one with the problem."

Gina was still a little overwhelmed by what had happened with the kidnapping and how close she'd come to losing her son. Yet Zack had seemed to fit right back into school and with the other kids. She was glad about that.

"I think as parents, Gina," Tim began, "we always worry about doing everything right for our kids. We can't. We just do our best and from what I see you are a great mom."

Gina felt the emotions building. "Not always. I made so many mistakes…with Eric. My son had to pay for that."

The big Irishman drew her into his arms again. "Oh, lass. You've got to forgive yourself and move on." In his tight embrace, she wondered if this was how girls felt having a father who cared about them. "You and Zack are safe here and Eric will never hurt either of you again."

"We're going to try." She pulled back, embarrassed by the tears in her eyes. "Sorry, I didn't mean to get so emotional on you."

He grinned. "Not at all. Now, our youngest, Leah, is the emotional one in the family. Always loved drama. Of course if you say anything, I'll deny it." He winked. "Come on, let's join the others."

They were greeted by the sound of voices first, then when the door opened, Gina saw several women working together in the huge kitchen, which was divided into two areas, a prep station for cooking and a dining area.

The Keenan daughters, Morgan, Paige and Leah, were helping their mother. There was a large picture window behind the table and she could see a group of kids running around the yard. The men were standing together talking as they watched the children.

Gina felt a different kind of emotion. Maybe a little panic. She'd heard from Lori that Claire Keenan had played matchmaker more than once.

They were all paired off in couples. Except her and Grady. Of course Josh made it an odd number. Good.

"Grady should open a day care," Paige said as she nodded to the group of children. "Look how he's handling those kids. They aren't moving a muscle, just glued to his every word. Who knew all that military training would come in so handy?"

Morgan stepped in. "Maybe he can share some pointers on giving orders."

Gina turned her attention to Grady Fletcher. Okay so she was drawn to the man whether she liked it or not. Big and strong, he held your attention by his mere presence. The years of military training were engrained in the man. He demanded respect and he got it. From the kids and his dogs.

"Gina! You made it."

She turned to see Claire Keenan crossing the large kitchen to greet her. After a big hug, the older woman stepped back. "You look lovely."

Gina glanced down at her dark slacks and cream-colored sweater. "Thank you."

"Since I haven't seen Bandit at school again, I guess you fixed the escape route."

Gina nodded. "Grady repaired the fence. And he gave Zack some ideas on keeping the dog home."

Claire looked out at the yard. "That man seems to have a lot of talents. We just need to convince him to stay here." The older woman looked back at Gina. "We need another nice addition to our town, like you and Zack."

"Well, we sure love it here. And Second Best is doing great."

Claire smiled. "I hear you're doing some reupholstering."

Word spread fast in Destiny. "Grady was very generous and gave me a few items from his grandfather's cabin. I'm selling some other things for him, too."

"It's about time someone cleared out some of Joe's… treasures." Claire turned to the window. "I'm also glad that Fletch has his grandson around to help with his recovery." She nodded toward the window. "It also seems he's pretty good with the kids, too. That's something special in a man."

Gina had to agree. "Yes, he is." That was all she said as she walked outside. She leaned against the railing on the deck and watched as Grady talked with Zack. She saw the happiness and respect in her child's eyes. Except for Lori's new husband, Jace, her son had never had a man to look up to.

Then Eric had found them, tried to destroy their happiness. She'd worried that Zack would pull back again, but it looked like her boy had survived, and her ex-husband hadn't won.

Best of all, with numerous charges against him, kidnapping, attempted murder and resisting arrest, he would never be a threat again. Sheriff Larkin was going to make sure that he got everything he deserved. Maybe life was turning out to be something to look forward to.

Once again, her attention went to Grady. Darn if the man wasn't one big distraction. It was a good thing his visit was temporary. Now all she had to do was stay away from him until he left town. She could do that.

# Chapter 8

Grady stood at the edge of the yard and watched as Josh took over exercising the dogs. The kids were so into it, and did exactly what they were told to do.

Scout didn't let them down after only one sniff of a small stuffed toy. Two of the older kids had been sent off to bury it, then using only their scent, Josh harnessed Scout and they went into the wooded area and soon returned with the correct items.

Morgan's husband, Justin Hilliard, came up to Grady. "I'm impressed," he told him.

Grady nodded. "Scout's been well trained."

"Does he work in snow?"

Grady continued to pet the shepherd. "Since we didn't arrive here until February, there's been limited opportunity to train, but we did a bit of tracking in the snow. I'm forever surprised how well these animals adapt to different climates."

Justin nodded. "I was surprised to hear that you're headed back to Texas."

"That's the plan." Grady glanced at Gina standing on the deck. It was tempting to stay, but a bad choice. "I'm only here until my grandfather is able to care for himself."

Hilliard let out a sigh. "I was hoping you'd think about training your dogs here."

Grady wonder what the man's point would be. "Why is that?"

"A couple of reasons. I run an extreme ski resort. People pay a hefty price to get the thrill of pushing it to the limit on the mountaintop. With that, there's always a threat of a possible avalanche. You know how critical time is in finding a buried skier and the mountain rescue squad here is one of the best. Call me a control freak if you will, but I like to have my own resources. My own qualified rescue team that I could airlift at a moment's notice."

Grady was surprised. "You want your own rescue dogs?"

Justin nodded. "Not just dogs, but I want a team with their handlers. And I'll pay well for it."

"Just for the winter?"

"Colorado has a long ski season." Hilliard went on to say, "I'm also developing mountain bike trails, with a training facility that will open in a few months. People go off the trail and get lost, even experienced hikers and bikers. I'd like to offer them that sense of security, especially since I'll be responsible for a lot of amateurs not used to the rough terrain."

Grady didn't want to be interested in the project, but he was. "You have a lot going on."

Justin nodded. "I do. I like living in a small town the size of Destiny. It's a great place to raise a family. Tourism is our main economy here." He glanced around. "This is all too beautiful to change. A lot of opportunity for someone with your talent." He handed him a business card. "If you have a chance, stop by my office at the Heritage Mountain Complex, and I'll show you my biking trails."

Grady took the card. "I can't promise anything."

"I understand, but I'd like a chance to show you what I could offer you and your partner."

Before Grady could say any more, Zack raced up to him. "Grady, look, Bandit found this." He waved the old T-shirt, but he held on to the leash with his other hand. "I buried it, and Josh took him out to search and he found it."

Justin excused himself and walked away.

Grady knelt and petted the boy's dog. "Hey, that's a good start."

The kids agreed. "And I want to train him more," Zack told him.

"It not something that's going to happen overnight, son. Scout took months and he was worked with every day."

"If you show me what to do, I'll work with Bandit every day. I promise. And my mom can bring Bandit out to you on the weekends so he can let Scout show him what to do, too."

That was the last thing Grady needed, more time with Gina. "Why don't you concentrate on Bandit being a good friend? You don't need him to be a rescue dog."

He saw the disappointment on the boy's face. Suddenly the memory of being a neglected kid with no one having time for him rushed back. "Okay, how about this?" Grady said. "What if I bring Scout into town a couple of afternoons and we'll spend time teaching Bandit a simple command?"

The boy's eyes rounded. "Really?"

"Zack, I'm willing to help, but I'm not going to be around very much longer."

The kid looked shocked and sad. "Why? Aren't you going to live in the cabin and train rescue dogs?"

"I'm only training here temporarily. I'll be going home to Texas." He hadn't had a home anywhere in a long time. "As soon as my granddad is better."

The boy's eyes lit up. "What if he doesn't get better for a long time? Can you still help me with Bandit?"

He found he would miss the boy, too. "Only if it's okay with your mother."

"If what's okay with me?"

Grady turned around to find Gina approaching them. He felt his mouth go dry, hating that she had that effect on him.

"Mom, Grady said he'll help me train Bandit. Please, can he?"

"Zack. We talked about this. You can't take up all Grady's time. He needs to work with his dogs, too."

Grady stepped in. "I wouldn't have offered if I didn't want to do it."

She didn't look convinced. "Zack... Why don't you go and get Bandit some water?"

Once the boy and dog were gone, she spoke. "Grady, you don't have to do this."

The sound of her saying his name did things to him. "It's really not a problem."

It was a problem for Gina. She didn't need to spend any more time with this man. "Still, your time is valuable."

"So is yours and you took the time to straighten up the cabin. Speaking of which, I need to ask you a favor."

What could he possibly need from her? "Sure. Whatever you need."

"My grandfather wants to talk to you about the furniture."

"Does he want it all back?" she asked. "Of course he does. I haven't sold any of it, so the sofas can go back."

She looked up to catch him smiling. "What?"

"You can't let Fletch intimidate you. That cabin was a disgrace. It's needed to be cleaned out for years. I only want you to check with him about a few of my grandmother's things."

"Of course. I'm sure you want them to stay in the family, something to hand down to the next generation."

He frowned. "That's something that isn't going to happen. The Fletcher line ends with me."

Gina watched as Grady walked off to care for the dogs. Okay, she'd said the wrong things again. Did he think he wouldn't ever marry, ever have children?

"Hey, sis," Lori called to her.

They hugged. "Hi, Lori. Glad you could make it."

She glanced at her niece, Cassie, who was already playing with the others.

"Jace had a business call." Lori looked at the group with the dogs. "Seems you got here early enough to spend time with the popular dog trainer."

"Don't get any ideas," she warned. "It was Zack who wanted to bring Bandit. Besides, I'm doing business with Grady. He's cleaning out his grandfather's cabin and the furniture is filling up the shop."

"He's also a man who spends time with your child. I'd say that's a good quality. I take it he's going to help Zack train Bandit."

"I don't know, Lori. Why don't you ask him?"

Her sister looked taken aback by her attitude. "Are you okay?"

She released a breath. "Yes. Sorry, I'm just tired of everyone asking me about Grady. Don't get me wrong. I'm so grateful the man found Zack, but that's as far as it goes. He's not my man. We're not together in any way." She took a shaky breath, unable to stop the awful memories from her marriage. "I'm not ready to be with a man, Lori.... I might never be."

"Shh. It's okay, Gina." Lori took her hand and walked away from the group for more privacy. "I'm sorry I said anything. And I promise I won't push you anymore. But be assured, when you find that right man, you'll be able to trust again."

Gina felt that familiar lonely ache that tore at her. She glanced at the good-looking ex-sergeant and a different kind of feeling washed over her.

She quickly averted her eyes away from temptation.

"What if I'm never ready, Lori? What if I can't stand to ever let a man touch me again?"

She studied her. "Are you still going to your support group?"

"As much as I can. I've been focused on Zack lately."

"You need to focus on yourself, too." She smiled. "Who knows, you might start feeling secure enough you'd trust a nice man like Grady Fletcher."

Gina started to argue and her sister stopped her by saying, "Just don't rule the man out."

Gina knew she couldn't risk it. Besides, the man wouldn't be here long enough. He was headed back to Texas and out of her life.

Two mornings later Grady pulled up behind the Second Best Thrift Shop and parked. Maybe he should have called Gina first, but it had all been a bit last-minute. Then he'd got the call from Shady Haven. His grandfather had summoned him.

He might as well get this over with so he could get back to work at the cabin. He climbed out of the truck and headed for the large back door. He opened it and peered inside. Marie was in the work area, stretching fabric over the arm of one of the sofas he'd given to Gina.

She saw him right away and stood. "Hello, Grady. What brings you here? You find more treasures?"

"What you call treasures, I call junk." He glanced around. "Is Gina here?"

Just then the woman in question walked through the door from the front showroom. She was dressed in her standard dark slacks, but today she had on a soft white-and-navy-striped blouse. It was fitted, showing off her narrow waist and nice curves. Her long dark hair was pulled back into a ponytail and hoop earrings hung from her ears.

She finally spotted him. "Oh, hi, Grady. What are you doing in town?"

He found he could easily get lost in her green eyes. "Ah, I got a call from my grandfather. He was wondering if you had time to see him today."

"I'm not sure…"

"I told him he couldn't order people around just to please himself."

Marie stood. "Gina, I can watch the shop. Sophie is here, so it's fine for me to stay."

Gina checked her watch. "Okay, but I'll have a sandwich sent over from the Silver Spoon. My treat."

"No, it'll be my treat," Grady insisted. "We'll take Fletch a piece of pie, too."

Gina couldn't think of any more excuses not to go. She went to get her purse and realized her heart was beating like a drum, hard and fast. She had to pull herself together and stop letting him get to her.

She followed him to the truck and let him help her in, and that meant he touched her. Oh, God. She felt his heat and his strength as he lifted her up into the vehicle. Once fastened in, she laid her head back and tried to relax. Grady didn't seem to be any more talkative than she. Thank goodness the trip to the restaurant was quick, then the ride outside of town only took about fifteen minutes.

Grady finally broke the silence when he announced, "We're here."

He parked in the Shady Haven lot, then they walked up to the entrance of the two-story building. "Just one thing before we go in. Don't let my grandfather get to you. He thinks because he's old he can say and do whatever he wants. If he gets too personal, tell him to back off."

"I'm sure he'll be perfectly nice," she said.

Grady wasn't sure what Joe Fletcher wanted with Gina. He figured it was because he hadn't been out for a few days, and the man was probably lonely.

They walked through the double doors of the facility. "Oh, Grady, it's lovely here."

He had to agree. "I tried to tell Fletch that he'd be more comfortable moving in here, but he misses the cabin." He went to the desk and asked the receptionist for his grandfather.

The young woman sent them into the recreation room. Grady guided her down the hall to a large area that had a huge flat-screen television. The walls were lined with bookshelves filled with books. There seemed to be a lot of activities going on, and a lot of interaction between the patients and other guests.

There were several small tables for games. That's where he found his grandfather with three women. They were playing cards.

"There he is." He put his hand against Gina's back and guided her through the room.

"Well, well, Granddad," Grady said as he stopped at the card table. "Seems you're not so lonely anymore."

Joe Fletcher glared at him. "It's a shame I need to call you to come and see me."

"I was here two days ago."

"Oh, Joe, is this your grandson?" asked one of the gray-haired women at the table. "He's just as handsome as you said."

"Grady, meet Alice, Mary Lou and Bubbles."

He nodded as they seemed to be blushing at his attention. "Ladies and Granddad, this is Gina Williams."

She stepped forward. "It's nice to meet everyone." She looked at Joe. "And especially you, Mr. Fletcher."

Joe Fletcher smiled as he looked Gina over. "Well, well, you're mighty pretty, Miss Williams. I can see why my grandson has been distracted lately."

"Granddad," Grady said in warning.

Gina blushed. "Why, thank you, Mr. Fletcher, but I think Grady's been busy with training his dogs."

"That's probably true. Sad, but true," Joe said, then excused himself from the ladies at the table. Grady took charge of Fletch's wheelchair and they crossed the room to an empty table.

"Can't wait to get out of this contraption." Joe hit the arm of the wheelchair. "I can't even go to the bathroom by myself."

Grady sat. "Fletch, you know once you finish rehab, you'll be able to walk again. All the doctors said so."

"I could be dead by then."

Gina sat across from the older man. "Mr. Fletcher, you should listen to your grandson. He's been trying to make the cabin ready for your return, but you have to do your part."

Grady bit back a grin.

Fletch finally smiled. "I like you, Gina Williams. Besides being pretty as a new spotted pup, you seem to have a head on your shoulders."

"Sometimes we learn from our mistakes." She handed him the container with the pie. "Here, Grady brought this for you."

He took the offered dessert. "Do you have a man in your life?"

Gina wasn't going to fall into this trap. "Yes, I do, as a matter of fact. And I love him to death. In fact, he and Grady are very good friends."

The thin man raised a bushy gray eyebrow. "Then he must be a good guy if Grady likes him."

"Of course. Grady even got him a dog, Bandit, and is going to help train him. Of course, we both got worried when the dog took off and followed Zack to school."

"School?" Joe wasn't dumb by any means. "Just how old is this man?"

"He's nearly eight." She glanced at Grady and felt a rush of admiration, something she didn't want to admit. "Your Grady and Scout saved my son's life." She swallowed back the emotion. "I will always be grateful."

Fletch smiled. "So it was your boy who got lost?"

"Yes. That's why I want to help to fix up the cabin. You had a lot of furniture, Mr. Fletcher. But if there's a question about anything I have in my store, of course I will return it."

The old man shrugged. "There's not much I care to save. My wife had a bunch of frilly stuff—" he glanced at Grady "—I'm sure my grandson could care less about."

Gina asked, "Is there anything you care about, Mr. Fletcher?"

He gave her a big grin. "Just my bed. I love my big brass bed."

She smiled. "Oh, I've seen it. It's lovely."

"Glad you like it. Someday Grady is going to inherit that bed."

An hour later, filled with several long stories of the past, Grady and Gina said goodbye to Fletch and walked out of Shady Haven.

Gina was quiet as she thought about Grady and his grandfather reminiscing about their past summers together. She got a sneak peak of a side to Grady she hadn't seen before, a more relaxed, a more outgoing side. She doubted that Grady had revealed it to many, and she felt lucky to get a glimpse of this man.

What she quickly discovered was that she'd like to know more about Grady. Spend more time with him, find out if he wanted more from her than just a spontaneous kiss in the garage.

She glanced at the handsome man beside her. There was a sudden tingling in her stomach, something she hadn't felt in a long time.

Was Lori right? Maybe she was ready to move on.

They reached the truck and Grady turned to her and said, "I'm sorry Fletch bored you going on and on with those stories, and the questions. You should have told him to mind his own business."

Gina smiled up at him. "Fletch is a wonderful old man. And you're pretty wonderful, too."

Grady didn't have time to react as Gina rose up, locked her hands around his neck, pulled him down and covered his mouth with a kiss. Caught off balance, he gripped the sides of her waist and just managed to hold on. As kisses went, what she lacked in experience, she made up for in enthusiasm. He could get into this. Then she quickly released him, looking shocked at her actions.

"Not that I'm complaining, but didn't I just get into trouble for doing the same thing last week?"

Her cheeks were rosy with embarrassment. "You act so big and tough. Then I see how sweet you are with kids…and how much you care for your grandfather."

He leaned against the truck and couldn't help but smile. This woman was so appealing, and so much trouble. That meant he should stay far away from her.

"Hell, if I'd known that would earn me a kiss from you, I'd have brought you here to see Fletch sooner."

"Oh, maybe I shouldn't have done that." Her face flamed even more and her gaze darted away.

He touched her chin and made her look at him. "Did you hear me complain?"

She only shook her head.

He wanted nothing more than to continue kissing her, but knew better than to go any further. That still didn't stop him from asking, "How would you like to get some lunch?"

She looked surprised at his offer. "I shouldn't. I mean, Marie is already staying later." She hesitated. "I guess I could call her."

He pulled out his phone. "What's the number?"

# Chapter 9

Twenty minutes later Grady escorted Gina into the Silver Spoon Restaurant. They walked through the glass-paneled door and were greeted by a surprised Helen Turner. The middle-aged owner was wearing jeans and a white blouse, covered by a starched apron. She also had on a big smile.

"Well, well, isn't this nice." She set down two glasses of water as they slid into a booth in front of the window. "Twice in one day."

Grady spoke up. "We took the pie out to my grand-dad and realized we hadn't eaten."

"How is Joe?" Helen asked. "Did he enjoy the pie?"

"Yes, he did. He told me to tell you it was delicious."

Helen grinned. "Well if that just doesn't make my day." She handed out the menus. "I may have to go see that old man."

After the woman walked off, Grady leaned forward. "No doubt by tonight the town will be buzzing about us being together." He looked around the room, seeing glances from the curious patrons. "They're probably wondering what an old guy like me is doing with someone as pretty as you."

"You aren't old, and thank you for saying I'm pretty."

He leaned back in the booth. "He sure did a job on you, didn't he?"

Gina didn't want to talk about her past, or her ex. "It's not something I'm proud of."

Grady wanted to set her straight, but Helen reappeared and took their order. After she left he said, "That's what you have to change, Gina. Your way of thinking that anything that bastard did was your fault." He leaned closer again, his eyes locked on hers as his voice lowered. "It wasn't, Gina. You found the courage to take your son and leave him. I'd say you're a pretty amazing woman."

Gina's heart was pounding at Grady's words. "Thank you."

"I'm speaking the truth. You're making a fresh start for yourself and Zack. You're building a business that seems to be doing well. Soon there'll be men lining up to spend time with you."

She quickly shook her head. She couldn't stop the panic she felt building up inside. "I'm not sure I can get involved with a man again."

"Why not? You managed to kiss me."

She didn't want to rehash her sudden impulsiveness. It had been so unlike her. "You're different."

He frowned. "I don't know if I like the sound of that."

She shrugged. "I've got to know you. I trust you." And she was attracted to him, she added silently. "Too bad I can't practice on you."

Grady hadn't been surprised after Gina's admission that lunch was eaten quickly and the subject had been changed to work. Twenty minutes later Grady drove Gina back to her store. He parked out back and she thanked him, then couldn't get out of the truck fast enough.

He sat there a few minutes, telling himself what Gina had said at the Silver Spoon was just joking around. He needed to let it go. So why couldn't he?

Grady climbed out of the driver's side and walked to the back door of the store. He said hi to Marie as she pushed a baby stroller out the door.

He moved into the work area and stopped, amazed to see that the old sofas were nearly finished. One was covered in a gray-and-white stripe, and the other was in a camel color. He smiled as he imagined all the work Gina and Marie had put into them.

He went down a hall past an office, then a small bathroom. He continued his journey into the main room where there was furniture arranged in groups. Against the far wall were lamps and several dining room tables and chairs. He moved toward the front and discovered a high counter. Gina stood behind it with her back to him, talking on the phone.

"Yes, Mrs. Browning, I can be out tomorrow morning." She paused. "Of course, I'll give you my price before I take anything. Okay, goodbye." She hung up and turned around.

That was when she saw him. "Grady. I thought you left."

He should have. He was crazy to be here to pursue any part of this woman. "What did you mean by saying you want to practice on me?"

Gina groaned. She was so embarrassed. "Oh, that. I was just kidding around."

He came behind the desk. "Were you joking around when you planted that kiss on me at Shady Haven?"

He wasn't going to let this go, she realized. "Gosh, you caught me. I was impulsive and talkative all in one day." She waved him off. "Just forget it happened."

He moved closer as he pushed his cowboy hat back off his forehead. "What if I don't want to forget it? What if I want to hear what you're thinking?"

Gina brushed back her hair, feeling her heart racing with him standing so close. "You've got to have better things to do than—"

"Than what?" he asked. "Show you how to kiss properly? How to feel comfortable around a man?"

She swallowed. Her throat was bone-dry. "It sounds silly to hear you say it. Besides I don't have time to date anyway. Zack needs my attention." She sighed, trying to push away the endless loneliness she always felt. "But there are times when I don't want to be alone."

"Like in the middle of the night?"

She wasn't ready to admit that yet. "More like when you get invited places and you're the fifth wheel, or everyone wants to fix you up with someone. I'm tired of the pity. The poor girl whose husband was abusive… the poor girl who had it so rough."

He reached out and touched her cheek. "First of all, you aren't a girl anymore, Gina. You're definitely a woman. A strong woman who has started a new life and is doing a good job of raising her son. Those who think differently, to hell with them."

He lowered his head and her heart began to race. "Now, as for the amount of instruction you'll need, first I'll need to sample you again."

Before she could say anything, his mouth closed over hers. It was soft, a whisper of a kiss, teasing her, making her want more.

Before she could react, Grady pulled back a little, enough for her to see his dark gaze. "Open just a little, Gina." It wasn't a demand, but a request as his thumb caressed her lower lip. "Perfect," he breathed, then went back for more. This time he added some pressure, then his hands went to her face and held her tenderly. His mouth moved over hers, tasting and caressing until she lost all track of everything except this man. *Oh, my,* she sighed in a moan as her hands came up to his chest. His tongue teased along the seam of her lips, then darted inside when she opened wider. And her own body's reaction caused an ache she'd never felt before.

He pulled back and looked down at her. She couldn't miss the desire she saw in his eyes.

She managed to speak. "How was I?"

"I think you know the answer already. I want you, Gina." He released a breath. "Does that frighten you?"

She was thrilled at his declaration, but scared to death. But knowing how much she wanted to move on, to take a chance on finding happiness. "Yes! No! I don't know, but I do trust you."

Those words seemed to bring him back to reality. He took a step back. "Don't make that mistake. You need to find a man who wants to settle down and have a family. Someone closer to your age."

She didn't remove her hands from Grady's chest. She didn't want to break the contact with him. "You have this thing about your age. You're not that much older than I am." She moved closer to him. "It didn't feel like an old man kissing me."

"You're asking for trouble."

She raised an eyebrow, going after what she wanted. To stop letting the past dictate the future. "Seems you are, too. Isn't that the reason you walked in here?"

She saw the confusion in his eyes. She forced herself to stand her ground.

"I need to go," he said, and she was a little relieved and a little disappointed when Grady turned and walked out.

It was Tuesday and Grady had promised Zack that he'd work with him after school. Since he'd walked out of Second Best four days ago he hadn't contacted Gina. He hadn't even called her, and that was for the best.

He needed time to think, needed to come to his senses. It hadn't done any good, though. The bottom line was he wanted to be with Gina Williams. And yet, he wanted more than just to spend time with her. He wanted to get her naked, to make love to her until they both couldn't think about anything else.

He released a breath. He hadn't been with any woman since his divorce. And not since he'd been burned. He touched the scar above his shirt collar and recalled Gina's hands on his chest. A portion of his upper body had been burned, too. Would the scar repulse her?

He turned down Cherry Street and found Zack was waiting for him at the curb as he got out of the vehicle.

"Hi, Grady. I've been working with Bandit every day. He's been behaving really well, too."

He retrieved Scout from the back. "Glad to hear it. Let's go see how he works today."

Grady placed his hand on the boy's shoulder as they headed to the side gate and into the backyard. Gina came out of the sliding door off the deck. He stopped cold seeing her in snug jeans and a T-shirt. Her legs might not be that long, but they were toned and shapely. Her hair was pulled back into a ponytail.

She smiled. "Hi, Grady."

"Gina."

She came down the steps and he had to stop himself from reaching for her and giving her the proper greeting he'd been aching to do since he'd left her four long days ago.

"How have you been?" he asked.

"Good." She beamed and her eyes brightened. "I sold the camelback sofa today." She giggled. "I got six hundred dollars for it."

He blinked. "Hey, that's a good profit."

"I'm glad I could give Marie a nice bonus, too. She and her husband could use the money. I feel like I should give you some, too."

He shook his head. "You did me a favor and hauled it out. I should have paid you."

"Okay, we'll call it even."

Zack came up to him. "Grady, can we start now?"

Okay, so now she was distracting him from his job. "Sure."

He walked off with Zack and for the next hour they worked Scout, all the time hoping that Bandit would follow the boy's commands, too.

Grady observed the boy and his dog. He was impressed at how well the kid handled the large animal. "Okay, tell Bandit to heel."

Zack had his dog on the leash at his left side. The twosome began walking, then Zack gave the command and Bandit obeyed. Both dogs were rewarded with some play time. They tossed tennis balls so the animals could retrieve them.

Zack came up to him. "Grady, can I ask you a question?"

He was surprised the see the serious look on the boy's face. "Sure, I'm not guaranteeing I'll have an answer."

"Does the scar on your neck hurt?"

Grady knelt and the animals came up to him. He had them sit and gave his full attention to the boy. "It used to hurt a lot," he answered honestly. "Not so much anymore."

"Did you get it when you were fighting the bad guys?"

He wasn't sure he could explain it to a seven-year-old. "Yes. There are a lot of us over there fighting."

"My teacher says you're making it safe for all of us so we can live free. And we should always thank you."

Grady nodded. "There were many soldiers who gave their lives for that freedom, too." He couldn't help but think of the men he'd lost that day. "Honor them for their sacrifice."

"I will," Zack promised. "I'm glad you came home, Grady. Really glad."

Zack smiled. "I'm glad you live in Destiny, too."

Before Grady could contradict the boy, Gina called out, "Supper's ready."

Grady glanced up, not surprised to see her curious look. He stood. "I've got to be going."

"No, please stay," Gina coaxed. "Unless you have plans."

He could lie, but Josh had gone out tonight, so he was just going to pick up a sandwich in town before heading back to the cabin. "No plans."

She smiled. "Good. I hope you like meat loaf."

What does one meal hurt? "You're talking to a man who spent twenty years in the military. We appreciate any home cooking we can get."

Leaving Scout out on the deck with Bandit, he walked into the homey kitchen. Not the most updated appliances, and the countertops were chipped, but Gina had painted the walls a soft green and added those womanly touches.

"We've got to wash up," Zack said, and took him down the hall. There was a detour into the kid's bedroom. It was blue with a lot of baseball posters on the walls.

Grady said, "I guess you like the game."

"I get to play Little League next month, but I'm not very good. Uncle Jace has been practicing with me, but I still have trouble catching."

"You'll get better with practice."

"But the other boys have been playing for two years." Zack moved his gaze away. "I didn't get to play when I lived with my dad. He didn't like me playing 'cause I couldn't do anything right."

Grady knelt down to be eye level with the sad boy. He worked to hide the anger he felt toward Lowell. "You have to know that your dad didn't treat you right. It had nothing to do with you. None of it was your fault. You can do anything you want to do. Look how much you've accomplished with Bandit."

The boy's head bobbed up and down. "And now Mommy and me don't have to be scared. I'm glad my dad went away."

So was Grady. "And he's never going to hurt either you or your mom again. Sheriff Larkin will make sure of that."

Zack threw his arms around Grady's neck. "Thanks, Grady. And I'm glad you're around, too."

There was a sudden constriction in his chest as he felt those tiny arms around him. He couldn't help but wonder if his son had survived, how close they would have been. Would they have had moments like this?

"You're welcome, kid." He stood.

After washing their hands, they went back into the hall and walked past another bedroom. No doubt it was Gina's. The walls were painted a soft yellow. It had a queen-size bed with a solid pale blue comforter, adorned with several pillows. As much as he tried to fight it, he could picture her in that big bed, with all that pretty dark hair spread out on the pillow.

He blinked away the daydream and caught up with Zack as they entered the kitchen where the food was on the table. Zack took his seat, then Gina sat. An ache filled him as he took the empty seat.

Okay, maybe he did want this. As a kid, he'd never been part of a family. The army had been the family he'd shared his life with. He looked at Gina. Why now? What was it about her that made him want something he'd already failed at miserably?

Two hours later Gina was surprised that Grady was still there. He'd insisted that he and Zack would do the dishes, then the next thing she knew, he was helping her son with his homework.

Once Zack was tucked into bed, she went in and kissed her son good-night. When she came back out to the living room she found Grady waiting by the front door, hat in hand.

"I've got to go."

She nodded. "Of course. I'm sorry, I didn't mean to take up so much of your evening."

He reached for the doorknob and stopped. "I'm not good at this, Gina. I've tried before and I made a lot of mistakes."

He must be talking about his marriage.

"I didn't mean to bring back bad memories. I'm sorry, Grady." She glanced away, feeling foolish about all those kisses they'd shared the other day. "Thank you for all your help with Zack."

She heard his curse, then he reached for her. She gasped, not from fear, but from surprise when his mouth closed over hers. She was hungry for him, praying all evening that he'd kiss her again.

He broke off the kiss. "Damn. I shouldn't have done that." His dark brooding gaze searched her face. "It's not you, Gina."

That made her angry. "Even I have heard that line

before. If you don't want to get involved with me, that's okay, but don't make up excuses."

"Dammit, I'm not a good bet." He glanced around. "My marriage was a disaster."

She wasn't sure if she wanted to know that he had loved another woman. "How long were you married?"

"Five years." He laughed. "On paper, but in reality, we weren't together much of that time. I was overseas twice. The second time was the clincher. Barbara left me."

"I'm sorry, Grady. I know that must have hurt you."

"Not as badly as I hurt her. I was never there for her. I can't blame her for ending it."

"If you were in the army when you got married, she had to know that you'd be away a lot."

"That's easier said than done. Barb asked me not to go, but I chose a unit that was going to be deployed. I chose 'the cause' over her." His pained gaze met hers. "I realized then that I could never be a permanent kind of guy. And that's exactly the type you and Zack need, a family man."

She nodded, understanding what he was trying to tell her. "Someday I want to give my son the security of a family." She hesitated, feeling her fears and emotion surface. "That's what I'm afraid of, Grady, that I never will be able to. I'd been with Eric since I was a teenager. He's been the only man I've…known. I'd never even kissed another man until you."

Grady was shocked at her confession. "Hell, Gina, there's a hell of a lot of men out there who would love the chance."

She stepped away, and he missed her closeness. "I

lost so much of my adolescence, and with my abusive marriage, I'm frightened to try another relationship." Her rich green eyes met his. "I don't know if I can ever be with a man again." Her voice lowered to a whisper. "Not intimately anyway."

He fought going to her and proving her wrong. "It'll take time, but I'm sure you'll find someone."

He watched her swallow, square her shoulders, then she asked, "Would you help me, Grady?"

Not what he expected her to say. Of course nothing had been what he'd expected since he'd met this woman. Common sense told him to leave, but that didn't stop his ache for her. His head said to run away. He didn't want to know what his heart said.

"That's the worst idea I ever heard."

"Why? I trust you."

"That's your first mistake. You shouldn't." He started to pace. "You don't want a man who will take what he wants from you then leave. And I am leaving, Gina. As soon as Fletch is well enough, I'm gone."

She nodded. "I know. That's what makes this work. You can show me how a man is supposed to treat a woman, and when it comes time for you to leave, I won't try and stop you."

"It isn't always a clean break. You could get hurt."

"I'll be sad when you leave, but if I know that it's coming, I can deal with it." She walked toward him. "I just want to know what it's like to be in a normal, healthy relationship. One where I get to be an equal partner. One where a man doesn't control me, make me do things that I don't want to do."

She blinked and glanced away. He went to her and

turned her face toward him. He saw the pain and hurt. He wanted to erase all of it.

"Hey. Shh." He bent down and brushed his mouth over hers, once, then twice, listening to her soft moans of wanting.

"You said the other day you wanted me," she said. "Have you changed your mind?"

He answered as his mouth captured hers in a hungry kiss. He drew her close, careful not to be too rough. He pressed her body against his, letting her feel his desire. "Does that answer your question?"

She was breathing hard. "Oh, yes. I want you, too, Grady Fletcher."

# Chapter 10

He was nothing but a coward.

Later the next morning Grady pulled into Shady Haven's parking lot, unable to forget how twelve hours ago, he'd run out on Gina. Facing the enemy in a foreign country had been easier than dealing with this 110-pound woman.

All night Gina had invaded his sleep, along with his peace of mind. Any rational thinking on his part had disappeared because he was actually considering her crazy idea.

Worse, it was affecting his concentration with the dogs this morning. Even Josh had noticed he'd been distracted. Finally, Grady had ended the struggle and decided to go visit his grandfather. But if the old guy brought up Gina Williams, he wasn't going to be held responsible for his actions.

Grady walked inside and the receptionist looked up and smiled, then she pointed toward the recreation room. There was no doubt his grandfather was the social one in the family. Grady headed down the hall and found Fletch sitting at his usual table with a younger woman. Lori Hutchinson Yeager.

What was she doing here?

He walked over and his grandfather smiled at him. "Hey, son, I didn't expect to see you this morning."

"Here I thought you might be lonely. I'm glad to see you're not." Grady turned his attention to Gina's pretty blond sister. "Hello, Lori."

She nodded. "Hi, Grady. I didn't mean to take up all your grandfather's time. It was important that I clear up something with Joe." She smiled at his grandfather. "We've just finished with our business."

Grady sat and asked, "And exactly what business would that be?"

His grandfather spoke up. "Watch your manners, son. Miss Lori is nice enough to come out here and correct a grave mistake she found." He nodded to Lori. "Tell my grandson, Miss Lori."

"Of course," Lori said. "Grady, I can understand your concern, but this is good. I mentioned something to you a few weeks ago about a questionable parcel of land of my great-grandfather Billy had the papers for. We discovered that he didn't really own it, at least not legally. He took it from your grandfather saying he hadn't paid the taxes. Since I took over running the bank this past year, I discovered the taxes assessed on the property were three times the normal rate." She sighed. "I'm not proud of what Billy did. So I hope after today, I've corrected the issue about the land. It will be returned to Joe."

Grady wasn't sure what was going on. "Fletch doesn't need another old abandoned mine."

"That's what is great about this, Grady," Fletch began, "It isn't a worthless mine. It's prime land just outside of Destiny. It belonged to your grandmother and now, thanks to Miss Lori, we have it back." His grandfather grinned. "And I'm going to deed it over to you."

Grady was skeptical of all this, but the look on his grandfather's face was priceless.

Lori smiled. "Well, I should get back to the bank. If it's all right with you, I'll have Paige Larkin start the paperwork."

Joe looked at his grandson. Grady nodded.

"Okay, then," Lori said. "In a few days the papers will be ready to sign."

She stood and so did Grady. That was when he noticed the roundness of her stomach. Gina's sister was expecting? "I'll walk you out," he offered.

"I'll be right back," he told Fletch, then he escorted Lori down the hall.

"I hope you'll accept my apology for the actions of my great-grandfather," Lori said. "As I told your grandfather, I've been trying to correct a lot of Billy's mistakes. Thank goodness, I'm nearly at the end of the list."

"I appreciate your efforts," Grady told her. "You've made Fletch happy. He needs something to look forward to."

Lori stopped at the building entry. "I'm glad." She hesitated. "I can't thank you for all the help you've given to my sister and nephew."

"Not a problem."

"It's still nice that you've been helping Zack with Bandit."

"And if I want to spend time with Zack's mother?"

That brought a smile to her lovely face, reminding him of Gina. "You don't strike me as the type of man who asks for permission."

Maybe he'd changed. "How about if I ask if you'll watch Zack one evening?"

"Of course I would." She grinned and headed to the door, then looked back. "He loves to sleep over at Aunt Lori's house."

It was a date. She had a date with Grady.

That was all, Gina told herself as she kept changing her outfit. She didn't exactly have many choices of what to wear.

"Here, put on these," Lori offered. She held up a pair of expensive jeans. "They'll look great with your teal sweater."

"I can't wear your pants. What if I spill something on them?"

"Come on, sis. They're a pair of jeans. I'll buy more after the baby comes." She rubbed her bottom. "That is if I ever lose the weight."

"You look great. And more importantly, your loving husband thinks so."

She held out the pair of denims to her. "Then wear them."

Gina relented and stepped into the jeans. Thank goodness the fabric had stretch in it, or she would never get them zipped. She turned from side to side to get a look. Not bad. She slipped on the sweater and put on another loan from sis, a pair of high-heeled sandals. She stood. Okay, she looked taller. What would Grady think?

Just then the doorbell sounded and her heart began to pound. "Oh, he's here."

"Slow down," her sister coaxed. "It won't hurt him to wait a few minutes. You're worth it."

Gina agreed, knowing she had to reprogram her way of thinking. From now on men were going to treat her right.

After applying lipstick, she grabbed her purse and walked out to the living room to find Grady talking with Zack.

Oh, my. He looked so…wonderful. Dressed in a burgundy Western shirt that was fitted over those broad shoulders and tucked neatly into a pair of killer black jeans.

Her son turned around. "Oh, Mom," he called. "You look so pretty."

"Thank you, Zack." She felt the heat rush to her face as she glanced at Grady. "Hello, Grady."

"Hi, Gina." His gaze was dark and intense, then he smiled as he made his way to her. "Your son's right, you do look pretty."

More heat shot to her face. "Thank you."

She managed to kiss her son goodbye before he walked out the front door with Aunt Lori.

The room grew silent as Grady stood at the closed door, his gaze moving over her body. "What you do to a pair of jeans should be outlawed."

She found she was a little breathless. "You should be happy. I can't eat much in these."

He walked to her, leaned down and brushed a soft kiss against her lips. "We'd better get out of here, or I might just decide to skip food all together."

She swallowed. "Oh, no you don't, Grady Fletcher, you promised me dinner." She grabbed his hand and hauled him toward the door and they laughed all the way to the truck.

The trip to Durango took about forty minutes. It wasn't that Grady didn't want to take Gina to dinner in Destiny. He just didn't want everyone watching them, speculating on their relationship. What they were doing or not doing was no one's business.

Damn. What was he doing? He was too old to start the dating game.

Grady parked in the public lot and escorted Gina the two blocks to Main Street and Francisco's Restaurant. Although he'd made a reservation, he took her into the bar and sat. "Would you like something to drink?"

At first she turned him down, but when the waitress suggested their famous margarita, Gina agreed to try it. Once the large glass arrived, she looked intimidated, but took a sip. "This is good."

Grady took a drink of his beer. "Just be careful. Tequila has been known to sneak up on you."

"Are you talking from experience?"

He couldn't help but smile. "Could be. In my younger and not-so-wiser days."

"I never had the chance to do much of anything. I got married when I was barely out of high school. I never went out much, or had girlfriends." She took another sip, then said, "I guess I'm overdue some experience…life."

They exchanged a glance that told him she wasn't talking just about the alcohol and his gut tightened. There was so much he wanted to share with this woman.

Finally the waitress took them to their table in a quiet corner. It was next to the fireplace and the sound of soft music filled the room. Gina sat at an angle to him. He found he liked her close, close enough to touch.

"This is lovely, Grady," she said. "Thank you for bringing me here."

It was hard to believe that she'd never been taken out to a nice meal. "You're welcome." He had to stop thinking about all the "firsts" he wanted to share with her. The waitress handed them menus and Grady opened his. "I hear the seafood is good."

Gina started to look hers over. "Oh, there's so much. Will you order for me?" she asked.

He shook his head. "Tonight, Gina, you're making your own choices."

She looked at him, her green eyes leery. She glanced over the list again. "Well, then, I'm going to have…the penne pasta and scallops." She closed the menu and handed it to the waitress.

"I'm a pretty basic meat-and-potatoes kind of guy. I'll have the rib-eye steak, medium rare."

The waitress smiled then walked away.

Gina liked that she wasn't nervous with Grady. Maybe it was the margarita that helped her relax, but she found herself at ease with him. "There's nothing basic about you, Sarge."

He gave her a stern look, then his expression softened. He reached for her hand. "I'm sure you're going to tell me why you think that."

She took another sip of her drink and said, "Maybe later. I don't think I need to inflate your ego any more."

"Wait a minute. I have an inflated ego?"

She laughed. "I was teasing. It's that you've accomplished so many things, and you've probably done everything very well."

He took a drink of his beer. "You just don't know my failures."

She studied his handsome face. "There can't be many. You had a long career in the army. I can see the respect you get from Josh. I suspect all the men in your unit felt the same about you."

It was endearing to see him blush. "Aren't you the wise one?"

Gina felt the warmth of his hand caressing hers. It sent shivers up her arm, making her aware that she was female. She glanced away and took a breath for courage before she turned back to him. She caught his gaze on her. The things this man could do to her with only a look.

She sobered. "I know a lot has changed with your accident and retiring from the military… But, Grady, you've already started a new career that you love. I'd say, all in all, you're a pretty lucky guy."

Grady didn't want to get into his past or his future. This was only about tonight. He squeezed her hand. "I feel lucky that I'm with the prettiest woman here."

She smiled at him and his gut tightened. "Thank you for saying that."

"Someone should be telling you that all the time."

He just couldn't be that guy, he added silently. "You're special, Gina."

"I guess we should start each other's fan clubs." She giggled and he found he liked the sound. That was the problem. He liked too many things about this woman.

About two hours later Grady pulled up in front of her house. He turned off the engine and sat back wondering what was going to happen next. He knew he didn't want the evening to end, but it also wouldn't be wise to stay. No matter how much he wanted Gina, he wouldn't take advantage of her. If he did take things further, it wouldn't change anything between them. In the end, he'd be leaving town.

He walked around the truck, opened the passenger-side door and helped Gina out. They made their way along the walkway and up the steps. She put the key into the lock and opened the door.

She turned back to him. "Would you like to come in for some coffee?"

With any other woman that would be a signal for something else, but with Gina, she was most likely going to fix him coffee. "Sure."

He followed her inside the dark house as she dropped her purse on the table. He stood close enough to catch her intoxicating scent, and had to fight to resist her as he followed her into the kitchen. Turning on only the under-counter lights, she busied herself filling the coffeemaker. Once finished, she turned around and looked up at him. "It'll take a few minutes to brew." She seemed nervous. "I had a good time tonight. The food was delicious."

Hell, she sounded about as unsure of this as he did. "I'm glad you enjoyed yourself."

She stepped closer. "I have you to thank for that. You made me feel…special."

"God, Gina. You have no idea how special you are." He couldn't stop himself—he pulled her into his arms and lowered his head. "Let me show you."

His lips brushed over hers and when he heard her gasp, he went back and captured her mouth. With her sweet body pressed against him, he lost any rational thoughts of going slow.

Gina followed his lead. Her arms circled his neck and she opened her mouth, allowing him to deepen the kiss. And he did. His tongue dove inside, brushing against hers, tasting and caressing. That only made him want more.

He finally tore his mouth away. "I've wanted to do that all night," he breathed, then continued the contact as he placed openmouthed kisses along her jaw, working his way to her graceful neck.

She sucked in a breath when he touched a sensitive spot. "Oh, Grady. I wanted you to kiss me, too."

"Let's see if we can keep agreeing."

He dipped his head and took her mouth again. She whimpered as he pulled her closer. The things this woman did to him made him forget everything.

Suddenly the sound of a phone startled them back to reality.

"I've got to get that." Gina pulled away and reached for the phone on the counter. "Hello?" She paused and said, "Lori, is something wrong with Zack?" She paused. "It's okay. I know you wouldn't call if it wasn't important."

Grady stepped away, trying to regain some control. Maybe letting things get this far wasn't a good idea. Gina wasn't ready.

He turned around when she ended the call. "I'm sorry, Grady. I've got to go get Zack. He's sick."

"I'll take you."

"You don't have to do that," she told him as they walked out the door. "Zack is my responsibility."

"If I drive you, then you can sit with him in the backseat."

She paused.

"Come on, Gina. You're wasting time." He guided her to his truck, realizing that the wind had picked up. There was rain in the air. "I'm a friend who wants to help you get your sick son home."

She finally smiled. "I hope you're not sorry that you volunteered."

Grady had a long list of things he was sorry about, but getting to spend more time with Gina Williams wasn't one of them.


Thirty minutes later Grady pulled up in front of Gina's house again. He got out and hurried around to the back door and opened it.

"Gina, go unlock the front door and I'll carry Zack inside."

She didn't argue and hurried up the walkway.

"Hey, Zack. Put your arms around my neck, and I'll carry you inside."

The boy groaned. "Grady, my stomach really hurts."

"It's going to be better, son. You'll be in your own bed."

No sooner had he lifted the boy out of the truck than Zack groaned, alerting Grady to what was about to happen. In a flash, Grady turned the child away as everything in his stomach came up and went all over the side of the truck and into the gutter.

"Well, that should make you feel better," he said.

Gina came running. "Grady, I'm sorry. Here, I'll take him."

"No, I got him." He took the handkerchief from his pocket, and gave it to the boy. "You finished?"

Zack managed a weak nod. "Yeah, I want to go to bed."

"You got it." Grady picked up his bundle and headed for the house. He carried him down the hall and into his bedroom. Placing him on the bunk bed, he stepped away and let Gina tend to her son.

Gina managed to help Zack into clean pajamas, get his mouth washed out and put him back into the bunk. She checked the window as she'd done every night since the kidnapping. It was starting to rain. A flash of lightning lit up the sky, reminding her that it was spring in Colorado.

"Are you going to be okay?" she asked her son.

He nodded. "I think I ate too much stuff at Aunt Lori's house."

She brushed back his hair. "Well, I'll be close by."

He snuggled under the blanket as the rain outside grew more intense, pounding against the roof. She kissed her son's head and realized he was already asleep.

She walked down the hall and into the kitchen, stopping suddenly when she saw Grady standing at the sink with his broad back to her as he washed up. In only his white T-shirt, she watched his toned muscles work across his broad shoulders and back as he washed up. Her gaze lowered to those killer black jeans that emphasized his narrow waist and hips.

She released a breath to calm her heart rate, glanced at his nice burgundy Western shirt wadded up on the table.

"I'm sorry. Is your shirt ruined?"

He turned around. "No, it just needs to be laundered."

She walked up to him. "Then I'll do it. That and apologize for Zack getting sick all over you."

"Believe me this hasn't been the first time. Through the years, I've held many a recruit's head over a latrine. Listening to them bellyache was a lot worse."

She couldn't get over this man. He took everything in his stride. "Well, as Zack's mother, I thank you for all your help."

The tension in the room was evident. Was he remembering earlier? Their kiss?

"I checked on Bandit, too," Grady told her. "He's fine, but I didn't know if he should stay in the utility room, or go to Zack's room."

"I've been trying to keep him on the porch."

"Good idea." He leaned back against the sink. "I should leave."

"But it's raining so hard."

His gaze remained on her. "If I don't, Gina—"

Suddenly lightning flashed and a loud crash of thunder sounded, then the lights flickered and went out.

"Oh, no." Instinctively, Gina started to go check on her child, but Grady stopped her.

"Bad idea to go running off without a flashlight." He felt his breath against her ear. "You have one?"

She couldn't think momentarily with him close, and touching her. "There's one in the drawer, the top one on the left."

He reached over her and his warmth seeped into her. It felt so good. Really good.

He pulled out the flashlight and turned it on. "I'll check on the boy. You stay put."

Once Grady left, Gina pulled herself together and found candles and matches. She lit them and had several arranged around the kitchen by the time Grady came back.

"Zack's sound asleep." He paused. "Looks like you're prepared."

For some things. She wasn't prepared for her feelings for him. "It's hard to tell how long the electricity will be out." She was chattering away aimlessly.

"Good idea," he told her as he made his way across the room.

Her pulse pounded in her ears, drowning out even the sound of the hard rain. She saw the smile he offered and it made her heart soar. So many emotions, she wanted to run, but she also wanted this man. "I know they might not be safe, but as long as we watch them, it should be okay."

"I'm afraid I'll be distracted," he said just as his head descended, then his lips touched hers. She sighed as the kiss deepened. She melted into him and let the sensations take over.

Grady felt an overwhelming desire as Gina moved against him. He couldn't stop feasting on her delicious mouth if his life depended on it. One kiss, two kisses weren't enough.

He tore his mouth away, then bent down and lifted Gina onto the counter. The soft glow of the candlelight only added to the intimacy.

He began raining kissing along her face to her ear. "You know where this is leading, don't you?"

She looked into his eyes and gave a nod.

"We need to *slow down*, Gina." He blew out a breath, not wanting to do anything to frighten her. "This is going too fast."

Gina wasn't sure if she knew what she was doing. She only knew that she wanted this man. "You make me feel things, Grady. Things I've never felt before."

Her hands moved up his chest over his T-shirt. She wanted so badly to touch his skin. She went to the hem of the shirt and slipped her hands underneath. The heat nearly burned through her as her fingertips made contact with his flat stomach.

For the first time she wasn't afraid of taking this next step…not with Grady. She tugged the shirt higher and leaned down to place a kiss against his skin. She felt the shiver along with his groan.

"Damn, Gina. If you are planning to drive me over the edge…"

Her own hands were trembling as she cupped his face. She leaned forward and placed a kiss against his lips. "I thought that was the point."

She went back for another kiss. She pulled the shirt higher and went for the center of his chest. Even in the candlelight, she could see the long puckered scar on his left side. It had to run from under his arm nearly to his waist.

"Oh, Grady," she cried on a whisper, feeling tears fill her eyes.

He quickly jerked down his shirt and stepped back. "Sorry, I should have warned you. It's pretty ugly."

"I'm not upset about what it looks like. Just the pain you must have endured."

He shook his head. She could see he was shutting down. "It was a long time ago." He released a breath and stepped back from her. She missed his warmth.

She got off the counter. "Grady…"

He didn't react to his name as he stood at the window. His broad shoulders were stiff, his back straight. She started toward him, but stopped, knowing the mood had changed. "Grady, I didn't mean to bring up bad memories."

"I don't have to look very far to be reminded of what happened that day."

She didn't know what to say to that, but she didn't have to—he made the choice for her.

"The rain has let up. I need to go."

She followed after him. "Grady, don't go."

He stopped at the door, but didn't turn around. "Gina, I'm not the man you need to teach you about anything. You'll need to find someone else for your next lesson."

# Chapter 11

The next day was Saturday and with Zack in tow, Gina went into the shop. While she'd felt lousy about how the date had turned out, something good had happened. Her son woke up this morning feeling great. He was also talking nonstop about Grady.

Since she hadn't slept much last night, she didn't feel much like conversing at all. She just wished she understood what had happened between her and Grady.

"Mom," Zack called to her. "Can I take Bandit for a walk?"

"Yes, but don't leave the block. Check back in twenty minutes." Old habits die hard. There was a time she wouldn't have let Zack out of her sight. Now, with Eric in jail, she knew they were safe. Plus she knew the town was filled with people who looked out for one another.

She closed the front door and turned her Open sign around and walked to the counter. Once again, her thoughts wandered back to Grady. After he had pulled back and walked out her door last night, she should have come to her senses. Besides, he wasn't going to be around much longer. How many times had he told her that? So maybe ending her crazy idea was for the best. Problem was, she wasn't interested in any man but Grady Fletcher.

The door of the shop opened and Lori walked in. "Hey, Gina," she called.

Her older sister was wearing a pair of black stretchy pants and a long pink polo shirt that showed off her blossoming pregnancy.

Gina went to greet her. "Lori. What brings you in?"

She hugged her. "I wanted to check on Zack. If he still wasn't feeling good, I'd take him off your hands. But since I ran into that happy kid outside, I see there's no reason. Cassie's helping him walk Bandit." She smiled. "Now we can talk." Her sister placed her hands on her hips. "So spill it. Is Grady Fletcher a good kisser?"

Gina felt her emotions churning inside. She shrugged as the bell over the shop door jingled and a woman walked in. Gina started to go to her, but Marie stopped her as she came in from the back and went to greet the customer.

"Come on." Lori took Gina by the arm and they headed toward the back for privacy. "You're not getting away with not telling me about your date."

Gina shrugged. "There's not much to tell. We had

a nice dinner in Durango at Francisco's. He had steak and I had—"

"Stop," her sister said. "I don't need to know the menu. I saw how the man looked at you when you both came by the house to pick up Zack. So you can't tell me that he didn't kiss you once all night?"

"I didn't say that." Tears welled in her eyes. "I just don't think he wants to kiss me again. Ever."

Gina told her sister about what happened when they got back to the house.

"He might be insecure about the scar," Lori tried to assure her. "Does it bother you?"

Gina shook her head. "Of course not. We all have our scars." Gina couldn't stop the flood of awful memories of her marriage. Would she ever forget the things that Eric had done to her? Probably not, but she wanted to replace bad times with new, happy ones.

Lori drew her attention back. "Oh, honey, I wish I could have been there to help you more. To stop Eric."

"You were there for me, Lori."

Lori hugged her sister. "Well, I'm so proud of you. And thanks to your support group you're doing a lot better. If you ever need help getting to your meetings, just call me."

Gina smiled. "Thank you. You've always been there for me. It's time I do things for myself."

"Yes, it is. And I think Grady Fletcher is just the man who can be a positive force in your life."

"I think Grady has his own demons." She released a breath, knowing it was more than his physical scars. She'd seen the pain in his eyes.

Lori studied her. "You care about him a lot, don't you?"

She sighed. "I never planned to let it happen, but I can't seem to get him out of my head. He could break my heart, Lori."

"There's always that risk, sis. But if you don't go after what you want then you'll never know how wonderful it could be."

"Spoken like a happily married woman."

Lori grinned. "Yeah, I am. And I want you to find happiness, too. You and Zack deserve that."

Yes, they did. She thought about the mess she'd made of everything last night. "I'm not very good at this dating."

"While you're figuring it out, how about if I take Zack home with me this afternoon while you work, then you can come by the house for supper?"

Gina had a funny feeling her sister was cooking up more than food. "You don't need to do that."

"I do, since I need a favor from you." She reached inside her oversize bag and pulled out a manila envelope. "These are papers for Joe Fletcher to sign. Would you give them to Grady so he can take them to him?"

Gina froze. *Go see Grady?* "Why don't you just take them to Shady Haven?"

"Because Joe asked me to give them to Grady first, so he can look them over."

"Why don't you have one of the bank employees do it?"

"I thought you were a bank employee."

"Come on, Lori. I've only staged a few bank-owned houses to sell."

Her sister shrugged. "Close enough." She walked to the door. "I'll go round up the kids and the dog. See you later." She paused at the door. "And take your time."

Great. Gina watched her sister leave. What was she going to do now? It would be a little too obvious when she showed up on Grady's doorstep.

Her assistant called to her. Marie walked over with a smile as the customer walked out the door. "You won't believe this. I just sold the Mersman pedestal table and the sideboard cabinet." She held up the credit card receipt so Gina could see the large amount charged. "Full price. She's even paying for us to deliver to Durango."

Gina glanced over the amount. "That's like two weeks' worth of sales."

"I know," Marie agreed.

Gina hated that Grady's things were disappearing from the store. "Maybe you should call Grady and let him know."

Marie shook her head. "I think for half of this amount, you need to give the news to him in person."

"Where's that pretty Gina?" Joe Fletcher asked when Grady sat at the table at Shady Haven. The day was turning out to be nice so he'd wheeled his grandfather outside into the sunshine.

"I guess she's at her store, working."

The old man studied him and leaned down to give some attention to Scout. "You'd be wise to spend a lot of time with her before another man steals your claim."

Here we go again. "I have no claim on Gina."

"But you should, son. She's a keeper. I heard she's got a boy about eight."

Grady nodded. "His name is Zack. I found him in your mine, remember?"

"That's what I mean." Fletch raised an arthritic hand. "That young boy needs someone like you in his life."

Grady already knew the kid could use a father figure. "I'm not a family man."

"Says who? That ex-wife of yours? Look, Grady, I'm not an expert by any means, but—"

Grady interrupted. "But you're going to tell me anyway."

His grandfather glared at him. "Like I was sayin', I think you've had to take the blame for a lot of things that weren't your fault. Good Lord, son, you were off fighting a war, defending our freedom."

Grady had known before he'd left on his last deployment his marriage had been on shaky ground. So the pregnancy had been a shock, but he still had wanted to be there for his child. That was what he had trouble dealing with. "Look, Granddad, could we change the subject? Talking about it isn't going to change anything."

The old man studied him for a long time, then said, "Maybe it will. I've decided to stay here to live."

"At Shady Haven?" Grady asked.

His grandfather nodded. "They have apartments for seniors."

"Why? Isn't your hip healing correctly?"

"My hip is better than ever, and I've started therapy. It's not a walk in the park, but I'm handling it."

Grady was relieved.

"Once I'm on my feet, I'll be able to take care of myself. And here there are plenty of people my own age to keep me company."

Grady still wasn't buying this. "Are you sure this is what you want?"

Fletch nodded. "Yep, I'm too old to live up on that damn mountain."

"But you love it there."

A tired-looking Fletch turned to him. "I realized something, son. I was damn lonely."

That suddenly made Grady realize he'd neglected the one person who cared about him. "Granddad, I had no idea."

"No, son. I didn't even realize it myself until I came here and made some friends. We have a lot in common." He blew out a breath. "Besides, you'll be leaving soon, right?"

Now that his grandfather wouldn't be alone or lonely anymore, that would make his decision easier. Grady thought about Gina. How much he wanted her, but he knew in his heart, he wasn't the right man for her.

He nodded slowly. "What do you plan to do with the cabin and your properties?"

Fletch shrugged. "That's not my worry anymore. I've signed most everything over to you."

Gina wanted to turn around several times during her drive up the mountain. Once she saw Grady's truck, she knew there was no going back, especially when the man came walking out from behind the cabin. He was in his usual uniform, jeans and a black Henley T-shirt that made his shoulders look massive and his arms incredibly large. He had a towel draped over his shoulder, his hair was slicked back. He must have been in the shower. God help her, she thought as she got out of her car and walked up the path.

He looked concerned. "Gina, is there something wrong?"

"No." She put on a smile, seeing the droplets of water in his hair. "Sorry, didn't mean to disturb you."

He shrugged. "Since my shower is outside, I grab it during the warmest part of the day.

The picture of Grady with water sliding over his naked body flashed in her head. Her breathing grew labored.

"Gina, what brings you out here?"

She shook away the thought. "Marie sold the pedestal table and sideboard." She reached into her purse and realized her hands were a little shaky. She managed to take out the envelope with the check inside. "Here's your share of the sale."

Grady didn't take what she offered, but instead said, "Please, come in."

She walked up the steps and into the cabin, noticing right away how he'd kept the place clean and organized. She set her purse down on the kitchen table. She needed to make this quick and leave. "We got full price for both items."

He pulled the towel from his shoulder and took the check. "This is a nice profit."

"Yes, I appreciate you letting me sell them for you."

She locked on his deep-set brown gaze and it stole her breath. Why this man? She also noticed that he looked tired. Maybe he hadn't slept any better than she had. He caught her staring and frowned. She glanced away and pulled out the manila envelope from her large purse.

"Lori asked me to give you this," she said. "It's the legal papers on your grandfather's property." She hated feeling the tension between them. "She said you needed to have Joe sign them. But he wanted you to look them over."

"All right." He didn't open it. "The next time I visit."

"Okay. I should go." She nodded and turned toward the door, but never reached her destination.

Before she got there, Grady reached for her. "Gina."

She loved his hands on her, but had to resist. "Don't, Grady." She couldn't look at him. "Please, don't say anything. I'm sorry that I upset you last night. I never meant to." She ached inside as tears gathered in her eyes. Please, she couldn't cry in front of this man.

"You didn't upset me. I did that all by myself. You did everything right. That's the problem, Gina. I keep thinking that it would be so easy to let things happen between us." He turned her around to face him. "I want you, Gina Williams. That hasn't changed, but neither has the reality that I'm leaving here."

She felt brave. "Did I ask you to stay?"

Grady released her. "No, you didn't."

"I know your life is in Texas. Mine is here with my son." She wanted him to be a part of that family, too. "For the first time in a very long time, I'm making my own decisions on what I want to do." She took a step closer. "And I wanted you to show me what it's like to make love."

Grady was a little stunned by her declaration. "Gina, you're not thinking this through."

"Oh, but I have. You've been honest with me in saying you wanted me, and I'm saying that I want you to make love to me. To show me what it's like to feel tenderness, to be cherished by a man—"

Grady stopped her words when he reached for her and his mouth closed over hers. She could only manage a weak protest as he drew her into a tight embrace.

In no time at all, she became a willing participant, slipping her arms around his neck. His tongue ran along the seam of her lips and she parted them, allowing him to delve inside to taste her.

He finally tore his mouth away. His breathing labored. "God, Gina, this isn't a good idea. You deserve to be cherished and more." Grady searched her pretty face and her thoroughly kissed mouth, wishing he could give her the world.

"Damn, you're so sweet," he breathed, then went back for more because he couldn't seem to avoid the temptation. He pulled her against him, feeling all her curves, and backed up against the table. He lifted her and sat on the edge, then pulled her between his legs.

She whimpered and he immediately pulled away. "Did I do something wrong?"

Her pretty green eyes were glassy with desire. "No, it's just I've never felt like this before." She smiled shyly. "I like your hands on me. I like it when you touch me." She took his large hand and brought it to the front of her sweater and placed it on her breast.

He cupped her weight in his palm and watched her

eyes close, but not before he saw them darken with desire. "Oh, Grady."

He kissed her again, bringing her body against him. This was quickly getting out of hand.

"Gina, we're reaching the dangerous area here. My control is only so strong."

He found himself smiling at the fact that Josh wasn't going to be home until tomorrow. Cupping her face, he zeroed in on her big green eyes. "Gina, this is your decision. If you want this to go any further, it's your choice."

She leaned forward and placed a soft kiss on the scar on his neck. "I choose you, Grady Fletcher."

He shivered at her tender gesture, causing him only to want her more. "Then I suggest we move this off the table and into the bedroom."

He captured her mouth again in a hungry kiss, then scooped her up into his arms and carried her into the bedroom. The curtains were closed, leaving the room in shadows.

"I've been aching for you since that first night you slept out on the sofa."

He set her down next to the big brass bed.

"I didn't know," she said, sounding a little breathless.

He kissed her again. "It's a good thing."

Reaching for the hem of her sweater, he swept it off over her head, revealing her ivory lacy bra that barely hid the full breasts. His heart raced as he unfastened her jeans and slid them down to display the matching scrap of material that served as panties.

"Oh, darlin', you're lucky I didn't know what you had on underneath your clothes."

"You like?"

He gave her the once-over from her shapely legs up over her trim waist and flat stomach, then to her full breasts.

He wasn't going to survive this. "You have no idea."

She smiled shyly. "I was thinking about you when I bought them."

Grady took a steadying breath. He'd never felt desire like this before. He fought to keep it light. "Why, Miss Williams, are you trying to seduce me?"

"I have no idea what I'm doing." Her voice was husky. She reached for the three buttons at his neck and managed to open them. She looked up at him. "I don't want to do anything that bothers you, Grady." Her palms rested on his chest as her emerald gaze met his. "I have scars, too. Maybe not as visible as yours, but they're there just the same. Your scars were honorably earned, Grady. They could never change how I feel about you."

He remained silent as Gina took over and tugged the shirt from his jeans, then slipped her hands underneath. He sucked in a breath as her touch began to work magic. Then she took it further as she raised the shirt and placed her lips against his hot skin.

Once, twice… Oh, God. He was barely holding on to the last of his control when he jerked off the shirt, exposing the damages of war.

She looked at the puckered skin that ran from his shoulder to nearly his waist, then up at him. He saw the tears in her eyes. "Oh, Grady." She then leaned in and kissed the puckered skin. "How you suffered."

He didn't want to think about the past. Only now, with her. "You're making it feel a lot better." He lifted her onto the bed. "But right now that's not the area of my discomfort."

She smiled up at him. "Then maybe we should re-direct our efforts."

His mouth covered hers and he kissed her as he continued to show her how much he desired her. How much he would always desire her. That was the problem. Being with her like this was only going to make it harder to walk away.

# Chapter 12

Three hours later Gina opened her eyes and discovered the sun was going down. She glanced at the clock beside the bed and saw that it was after six. And here she lay naked in bed, Grady Fletcher's arms wrapped around her waist, holding her close. She smiled, knowing she should be heading back to Destiny and dinner with Lori.

"Getting restless again?" Grady raised his head from the pillow, but didn't release her. "I thought the last time would keep you satisfied for a while."

She blushed, recalling they'd made love twice. Never had she been treated as if she were so special, so treasured. She rolled over and smiled at the sexy man.

"It was wonderful. But… I do have to pick up Zack. He's with Lori and Jace."

He frowned. "What if I won't let you go?" He pulled her close, letting her know he still desired her.

"I didn't say I wanted to leave." She cupped his face and pulled him down to meet her lips. And within seconds she let him know how much she meant those words.

He rose over her, bracing his arms on either side of her head. "That's some serious seduction tactics."

"So, Sarge, what are you going to do about it?"

Truthfully, Grady had no idea what he was going to do with her, but at this moment, he wasn't going anywhere. "My best, ma'am."

He lowered his head and kissed her, once, twice, then his mouth began to move, trailing kisses, tasting her soft skin. He worked his way down over her breasts, lower to her flat stomach. That was when he caught the nearly invisible tiny white lines. Stretch marks. The proof she'd carried a baby in her womb. He closed his eyes and tried to push away the recurring memory about his own child. He paused and Gina's hands moved to his back.

"Grady?"

He raised his head. "Sorry." He rolled away, grabbed his jeans from the floor and slipped them on. "I guess you can call it a flashback."

He turned back to see she'd covered her body with the sheet. "It's okay, Grady."

He watched her eyes shift away from his gaze. "Oh, hell." He went back to her and sat on the bed. "It's not you, Gina. I know that sounds like a line, but it isn't. I carry around a lot of baggage."

She touched the side of his face. "Is there anything I can do to help you?"

"I just need some time." That was a lie. He hadn't been able to forget the pain or the guilt over the last few years. "I'm working through some things." He got up, grabbed his shirt off the floor and walked to the doorway. "I should go check on the dogs." Then he left.

Gina sat there stunned. What had happened? Okay, she wasn't so experienced that she could drive a man wild, but she thought together they'd been pretty incredible. She climbed out of the big bed and started pulling on her underwear. After she fastened her bra, she quickly dressed in her jeans and sweater. She should be getting home anyway. Her thoughts turned to Zack. The safe way would be to forget about a relationship and focus on her life with her son. Grady Fletcher wasn't going to commit to her. She'd thought that was what she wanted until she realized how much she cared about him.

She passed the dresser and saw Grady's keys and coins tossed on the scarred surface. She also noticed the carved box and the corner of a photo hanging out. Okay, she was curious. She opened the lid and took hold of the grainy picture. A sonogram?

She looked closer and smiled seeing the familiar details of the baby. Who was this? She turned the photo over to the back and read, "Boy Fletcher" and the date. Several years ago.

She gasped. Grady had a child? She suddenly realized she wasn't alone in the room and glanced toward the doorway to find Grady.

"I'm sorry. I had no right." She put the picture back. "I should leave."

Grady came inside the room and took the picture. He wasn't sure why he was so angry. "Come on, Gina. Don't stop now. Don't you want to know who this is?"

She swallowed. "Only if you want to tell me."

His chest tightened, but he got the words out. "That's my son."

"You have a child?"

"*Had.* That's the operative word, Gina. Had."

"What happened to him?"

Here came the hard part. "My wife went into early labor…he was stillborn."

She gasped. "I'm so sorry."

"So am I. I was told that no one was to blame for what happened."

Grady remembered the two days it had taken him to get across the globe, to be there for Barb, for his son.

He couldn't look at Gina. "That's what the doctor told me once I got there two days later. I was overseas when my wife was delivering our baby."

He closed his eyes, and could see the long hospital corridors as his footsteps echoed when he ran from the elevator to the nursery, but there wasn't a Fletcher baby behind the glass. Finally the nurse sent him to see his wife in her room. He found her, all right. She was packing her clothes and about to go home with her parents. When he went to her, she pushed him away.

"You're too late, Grady," she cried. "Too late for your son. And too late for us." She'd walked out the door.

He opened his eyes and met Gina's gaze. "Don't make that mistake, Gina. Don't depend on me. I'll let you down."

"How could you know your wife was going into labor early?"

He shook his head.

"Did she keep the pregnancy from you?" she asked.

"No, but it wasn't planned, either." He sighed. "When things started to turn bad in the marriage, I chose another deployment, instead of staying and trying to work through our problems."

"The army was your job. Surely your wife knew that when she married you."

Gina went to Grady, wondering who'd been there for him to help him grieve over his child. She reached for him and felt him tense, but she ignored his resistance. She wrapped her arms around his waist and laid her head against his chest. She shed tears for the father and the child.

"I'm sorry that you never got to hold your son. That you never got to say goodbye." His grip tightened around her and she felt his tears drop against her cheek. She never dreamed she could love a man as much as she loved Grady Fletcher. She held on to him a few minutes until he finally loosened his grip and moved away.

Once he composed himself, he turned back to her. "Thank you."

"Any time."

He started to say more when his cell phone rang. He pulled it out. "Hey, Josh." He answered it as he walked away.

Gina put the treasured picture back in its special place, then pulled the bed together before she walked back into the main room.

"Okay, I'll see you back here tomorrow," Grady said into his phone. "Goodbye." He hung up.

Embarrassed that she hadn't given a thought to Grady's housemate, she blurted, "Oh, I forgot all about Josh."

"I didn't. He went to Texas to check out places for our kennel."

Suddenly reality hit her. Grady was still leaving.

He noticed her surprise, too. "I told you from the beginning, I was opening our business in Texas."

"I know, but a girl can always hope."

He came to her. "Gina. I can't tell you how special you've become to me, but... I've tried to make a go of settling down before."

She hurt a lot. "Can't say you didn't warn me." She forced a smile. "Hey, it was fun." She worked hard to hide her blush. "And this afternoon...was incredible." She glanced around for her purse and grabbed it to make her escape. "I've got to go. Maybe before you leave town you'll stop by and say goodbye."

He took her arm and stopped her. "Gina. Don't do this. You mean too much to me—"

She stopped his words of regret. "Just not enough to stay around."

"I told you before—"

"Believe me, I heard everything you said." She released a breath. "Too bad for you, Master Sergeant Fletcher, because there's a guy out there who's going to want to stick around for me."

"And that's what you deserve."

"It's something we all deserve, Grady, but first, you have to forgive yourself, realize you deserve happiness, too."

She swung around and walked out praying she could make it to her car. Once down the road, she pulled off and burst into tears. She'd lost everything she'd ever wanted in a man.

* * *

By the next morning Grady's bad mood hadn't improved at all. Even the dogs wanted no part of him. Add in no sleep and too much coffee, there was no hope that things would change anytime soon.

"Break time, boys," he called to the dogs. "Get your toys."

The shepherds took off and Scout was the first back with the yellow tennis ball. The animal dropped it on the ground and Grady threw it to the far end of the pen while he kept telling himself he'd done the right thing by letting Gina go yesterday.

He felt his chest constrict as he continued to toss the ball. She had no idea how hard it had been to lie to her, to tell her he didn't want her or her kid.

Hell, he was already involved whether he liked it or not, but she'd already had one jerk in her life—she didn't need another.

He closed his eyes and could still picture her in that big bed. Her sweetness nearly drove him over the edge. Yet, everything she did pleased him. He'd never… He shook away the wondering thought.

Damn, he had to get out of here and back to Texas.

He called to Scout, Beau and Rowdy. "Time to get to work," he told them.

He'd only been at it for about ten minutes when he saw an SUV pull up and Justin Hilliard got out.

The businessman was dressed in dark pleated trousers, a white shirt and striped tie. He walked through the rough terrain as if he had on boots instead of expensive Italian loafers.

Grady shook his hand. "Hey, Hilliard. What brings

you out to my neighborhood? Come to see how the other half lives?"

The sarcasm didn't seem to bother the visitor. "I came by to see you, Grady," he said as he stopped beside the waist-high gate. "I just finished a meeting down in Durango with my new mountain bike instructor, Brian Connelly. He's retired now from the pro circuit, so running my school is perfect for him." The man grinned. "Also he'll be designing mountain bikes which I'll be manufacturing right here in Destiny."

Grady felt extreme envy for the man who just about had everything, not his money as much as his pretty wife and children. "Seems all your dreams are coming true."

"Yeah, I've been a lucky guy. That's why I can afford to spread my good fortune around."

That piqued his interest and Hilliard saw it. "You haven't stopped by to see me, Grady."

"I've been busy. Mostly I'm not interested."

"I'm not going to let you off the hook, not until you hear me out."

Did this man ever give up? "I've already heard your spiel."

"A lot has changed since we last talked. Seems your grandfather owns some of the property I want."

Grady sent the dogs off to play as he walked out the gate to the pen. "You want this property?"

Hilliard shook his head. "The three acres just north of town. I'd planned to buy that section when Billy Hutchinson's name was on the deed, but Lorelei Yeager discovered that Joe Fletcher is the true owner. Now it seems he's transferred the title to you."

This was getting interesting. "Is that so?"

Justin nodded. "I already own the adjoining land, but I'd like to extend my trails. I want to buy your property. Question is, what's it going to cost me?"

"I haven't even had a chance to look over the land in question."

"It's definitely a prime area. I don't want to develop it, if you're worried," Justin insisted. "I want to keep the land in its natural state, except for bike trails. Do you think we could work out some kind of deal?"

A dozen things rushed though Grady's head. The sale would cut the ties here in Destiny. He could take the money for his project in Texas.

"I have another idea, Grady," Justin told him. "Since the land is a heavily wooded area, it could work for other things, too. Like training rescue dogs." He glanced around the temporary structures Grady had built. "You could build a real kennel there, too."

"That could take a lot of money."

"It's going to take money in Texas, too. It's hotter there and doesn't have these mountain views, or my offer of leasing your dogs for the winter months."

Or Gina. Grady hated that the man had him thinking of changing his plans.

Hilliard checked his watch. "Look, I've got to go now—my son has baseball tryouts." He smiled. "I can't miss it."

Another dose of envy hit Grady. "Then you should go."

"I still want to talk to you about this some more. Could you meet up later with me and Jace Yeager? Say about eight o'clock at the Rocky Top Saloon in town? We can talk over a few beers. I'm buying."

"Look, I can't promise you anything. I have a partner."

"I know." Justin began backing away. "Bring Josh along, and we'll all talk."

"Good luck to your son," Grady called.

"Thanks, I appreciate it."

Grady watched the man leave and he thought about Zack. How would he do today? He found himself putting the dogs into the kennels and heading down to town. What would it hurt just to check on the boy?

Gina walked around her empty house that evening, restless. Zack was spending the night with Ryan Hilliard. They'd been picked to be on the same baseball team today, so they were best friends now. She smiled, feeling so blessed that Tim Keenan had volunteered to be the team's coach.

She might be Zack's mother, but she had no idea how to encourage her nearly eight-year-old's new love for the game. She'd tried to help, but Zack hadn't wanted her to go, and Uncle Jace was working. She thought about Grady, but she couldn't impose on him any longer, not after yesterday. All her worries had been unfounded, though, when Zack came home beaming with news of his day. Her son's life seemed to be perfect now.

Hers was a mess. She recalled how Grady had made it clear that he didn't want her in his life. She could survive the rejection, but if he stayed in town... She blinked away threatening tears. She didn't want him to leave at all. She loved the man, and she probably would for a long, long time.

There was a knock on the door and she looked out the peephole to see her sister. She quickly let her inside.

"Lori, what are you doing here?"

"We both have the night off from kids. Zack's at a sleepover, Jace has a business meeting, and Cassie is staying with Maggie."

Gina smiled, remembering the housekeeper from Hutchinson House who'd helped raise Lori when she was a child. "How is Maggie adjusting to her new apartment?"

"She's doing fine, but I had to insist that she hire more help when the mansion is rented out for functions." Lori waved her off. "Hey, I just got a call from Paige to meet her and Morgan at the Rocky Top Saloon. You wanna come with us?"

Gina wasn't in the mood to go anywhere. "I think I'll pass."

"Why?" Her sister placed her hands on her hips. "You aren't moping around over a man, are you?"

Gina started to deny that Grady was the reason for her misery. Her sister wouldn't buy it anyway.

"Okay, give me five minutes to change."

At eight o'clock Grady and Josh walked into the Rocky Top Saloon. There was a large entry with a bar on one side and the dining room on the other. The entire place had the look of a hunting lodge with hardwood floors and open beamed ceilings, not to mention the elk and deer heads mounted on the knotty-pine-paneled walls. Country music poured out of the jukebox, but he managed to hear his name called out.

Justin stood across the room past the small dance floor toward the back. He nudged Josh and they walked over.

"Hey, glad you two could make it," Justin said.

Grady nodded as he introduced Josh.

Hilliard did more introductions. "Grady and Josh, you remember Jace, and of course, Reed. And this is Brian Connelly."

Grady shook hands all around. "Good to meet you," he said to the new guy.

Hilliard ordered another pitcher of beer as Grady sat. It was Connelly who began the conversation.

"I hear you're retired army."

Grady nodded. "Got out in December."

Josh added his similar résumé.

"Well, all I can say is thank you both for your service."

Grady nodded and took a sip of the beer that had been placed in front of him while Hilliard filled Josh in on his ideas for a kennel in Destiny.

Brian cornered Grady. "Justin told me about your dogs."

For the next twenty minutes every guy at the table was talking up all the good qualities of the town. Grady couldn't deny that Hilliard had a well-crafted plan for his biking school, riding trail and snow adventures. He put down some numbers for the property that were also impressive.

Grady leaned back in his chair. Okay, he couldn't help but think about it. Damn, it looked profitable on paper, and then he was surprised when Hilliard offered to be a silent partner in the rescue dog business.

Grady exchanged a glance with Josh. He looked curious, and Grady was once again thinking about the deal. There was only one person keeping him from signing. Gina. Could he live in this town and be around her all the time?

"Hey, Reed?" Jace called. "Did you tell our wives where we were meeting?"

Grady and all the men turned toward the door. That's where they saw four of the prettiest women in town. Morgan Hilliard, Paige Larkin, Lori Yeager and Gina.

## Chapter 13

Gina felt a warmth pulse through her as Grady's hand pressed against her waist as he escorted her to the dance floor. Silently he took her into his arms and began to move to the music. She couldn't resist and leaned into him, inhaling his scent, a mixture of soap and what she knew to be pure Grady.

She also liked the familiar feel of his body molded against hers. The heat of his skin, and the strength of his hands, hands that had touched every inch of her flesh just days ago…

She shivered.

"Are you okay?" he asked against her ear.

No! "Yes, I'm fine."

She closed her eyes, recalling the look on his face when she'd walked up to the table. He didn't want to see her here tonight. That hurt. She knew he was only her dance partner out of obligation. He hadn't been given a choice when all the other couples had got up.

"You don't have to do this, Grady." Okay, so she wanted to be in his arms, just not this way.

He pulled back. "Since I left the army, I've been pretty much making my own decisions."

She nodded, then glanced away.

He touched her chin, making her look at him. "Believe me, Gina, holding you in my arms has never been a hardship."

To prove the point, he pulled her close as George Strait sang about getting to "Amarillo by Morning." She didn't want to listen to the lyrics. Grady was leaving soon. That she had to accept, but it didn't stop the hurt.

She felt his arm tighten around her waist as he pulled her closer against him, his strength making her remember how gentle his touch could be, how loving.

The song changed to Lady Antebellum singing "Need You Now." Grady's hold tightened as their feet shuffled back and forth in the crowd of dancers. Then she felt his mouth against her ear. His warm breath caused her to shiver. Why was he doing this? Why couldn't he leave her alone?

Gina pulled back. "I can't… I've got to go." She moved through the couples dancing on the floor. Once at the table, she grabbed her purse and headed for the door.

Grady cursed, then made his way through the crowd, finally catching up with Gina at the door. With several couples nearly blocking the area, he escorted her outside and to a private spot.

"Gina, I'm sorry. I didn't know you'd be here."

She finally looked up at him. "I know. I'm sorry I spoiled your fun."

He ran fingers through his hair. "Dammit, Gina. It wasn't supposed to be fun. Justin said it was a relaxed business meeting, and then we looked up to see their wives." He met her gaze. "And you…"

"Well, I'm going home so you can go back and finish the meeting. Enjoy the evening." She took off down the street.

Grady hurried after her. "Gina, let me drive you."

She shook her head. "No, I'm not your responsibility. Besides, I can handle the short walk."

Damn stubborn woman. "I have no doubt you can, but at least let your sister know that you're going home."

He was rewarded with a furious look. "I'm not going back inside." She took out her phone and punched in the number. "Lori, I'm going home." There was a pause. "No, you stay. Grady's taking me." She ended the call and dropped it back into her purse. "Okay, you're relieved of duty," she told him and marched off.

What the hell? He went after her. "What do you think you're doing?"

"I'm walking up Main Street, then making a right on Maple, then a left on Cherry Street."

He ignored her smart answer. "So you lied to your sister."

"I don't want her to worry." They stepped off the curb and started down the next block, passing the town square and the sheriff's office. The parking lot was well lit, so was the street.

"What if something happened to you?"

She stopped and faced him. "Look, Grady, you have to quit doing this. Stop playing hero. Stop thinking you have to rescue me. I'm trying really hard to take control of my life. Do things on my own, to be independent."

He arched an eyebrow. "And I'm interfering with that?"

"Yes. You are."

"What if I just want to do the gentlemanly thing and walk a lady home?"

She threw up her arms in exasperation. "I give up."

Well, he wasn't going to and he followed her as she walked on.

Ten minutes later they ended up on her porch. "Okay, I'm home safe and sound." She slipped her key into the lock. "Good night, Grady."

"Gina," he whispered her name, hoping to get her to turn around and look at him. No such luck.

Still she faced the door. "What, Grady?"

"I'm headed for Texas in a few days."

In the soft glow of the porch light, he saw her tense. "Have a safe trip."

"Gina, it's for the best."

She swung around. "You call running away the best solution? Well then, go for it. But I think what you're doing is giving up. A second chance at a home, a family with a grandfather who loves you. But go. I hope whatever you're looking for makes you happy."

She stared at him for what seemed to be an eternity, and he couldn't stand it anymore.

He pulled her into his arms and held her. She felt so good, too good. He kissed the side of her face and quickly worked to her tempting lips.

"Grady…"

He ignored her as he covered her mouth in a heated kiss. He just needed one more taste of what he had to give up. She gave the soft moan he knew so well, but he resisted taking any more. He tore his mouth away. "Goodbye, Gina."

"Goodbye, Grady." She turned and walked inside. He just stood there, aching to go after her. Instead he started down the steps when he heard something. Moving back to the door, he recognized the sound of her crying. His chest tightened. Oh, God, he'd never wanted to hurt her. He started to knock, but paused, knowing he had too many things he had to deal with first. Instead he turned and walked away. Again.

It was a beautiful spot.

The next day Grady walked along the edge of his grandfather's property and glanced up at the picturesque San Juan Mountains. The sky was so blue it took your breath away. He also liked that so much of the area was densely wooded. He glanced at Josh and he seemed just as intrigued with it, too.

Justin caught up to them. "I can't believe you want to leave all this." The businessman shook his head. "Seems you two could have it all." He pointed off toward the woods. "What a training ground. And you can put your kennels at the base, right off the highway. You're far enough away your dogs wouldn't bother my training facility, or the guests. And we wouldn't bother your dogs."

Grady was thinking about it. "It's beautiful."

"I agree. You've got a sweet parcel of land, Grady," Hilliard told him. "Look at the spot over there." He pointed to the crest of the hill. "You could build a house there and have views all around."

With the idea of a home came thoughts of Gina. How would she like it here?

No, he had to push any thoughts of her aside, not think about what he couldn't have.

He turned to Josh. "What about you?"

"I think this is a great place," Josh said, and looked at Grady. "And it seems to me that owning the land already eliminates a big expense, and frees up more money for dogs. Maybe hire an employee to help with the upkeep. We can concentrate on the training. Whatever you decide, Sarge, I'll go along with it."

That was the lead-in Justin needed. "Look, if you're reluctant about selling any of your land to me for my training facility, how about we lease the section from you?" His hand made a sweeping motion. "And you don't lose any of this."

So tempting, Grady thought. "I need to think about it. Can you give me a few days?"

Justin nodded and walked away with Josh, leaving Grady alone with his thoughts, his dreams and what he couldn't have that kept it all from being perfect.

Little League practice was the next afternoon, and Grady found he couldn't stay away. Despite him leaving for Texas in the morning, he wanted to see how Zack was doing.

He parked on the far side of the baseball field and got out to watch the last of the practice. Tim Keenan and Jace Yeager were the coaches, but when he saw Gina's brother-in-law, he thought he'd better leave.

He headed back to the truck when he heard someone call him. He turned to see Zack running toward him.

"Grady, aren't you going to help me today?"

"Well, it looks like you have enough help already."

Tim came up to him. "We can always use another hand."

Grady looked at Jace. After a few seconds he motioned for him to join them. "Okay, what do you want me to help with?"

Tim smiled. "Jace has fielding, and I'm working with them on running the bases. So how about hitting?"

Thirty minutes later, Grady finally thought Zack was making some progress. He was a quick study.

"That's it son, keep your eye on the ball." He pitched a ball to Zack. The first one he missed, but he made contact with the second and the third. "That was great." They exchanged high fives.

The kid beamed. "You showed me real good, Grady."

He felt the pride for the boy's achievements. Finally, Tim called a halt to the practice and they finished with drinking bottles of cold water. Soon the kids went off with their parents. Zack turned to him. "I'm having my birthday party next Saturday. Will you come, Grady?"

"Oh, Zack. I'm not sure I'll be here. I have to leave town for a few days."

The boy's face dropped. "Oh, I wanted to show you some tricks I taught Bandit."

Grady knew he didn't want to encourage the boy, then have to disappoint him. "I bet they're good tricks, too. Maybe I'll stop by the house when I get back."

"So you are coming back."

With his nod, the boy said, "Okay."

Hearing Zack's name called, Grady turned to see Gina. She was walking across the field, but when she spotted him, she stopped. His gaze surveyed the petite woman in jeans and a sweater. Just like every time other time he looked at her she affected him like no other woman. How long would it take to stop wanting her? Never.

Gina raised a hand and waved to her son. "Come on, Zack," she called. "We need to get home."

"I got to go." Zack went to him and threw his arms around his waist. "Thanks for helping me today. Bye, Grady."

The boy ran off to his mother. When he reached her, Gina put her arm around her son and they walked off together. Grady had to resist running after them both. The pain in his chest spread to his heart as the two most important people walked out of his life.

"Those two are really special."

He glanced at Tim Keenan. "Yeah, they are. I need to go."

"I'll walk with you to the parking lot," Tim said. "I couldn't help but overhear you tell the boy you're leaving town."

Grady nodded. "I'm going to look at some property in San Antonio." Although he knew staying here would be better all around, he needed to make a clean break from Gina. "It's close to the base where we can get more dogs."

Tim nodded. "I guess a convenient location is important." There was a pause. "I would think staying here would be even more convenient, especially with your grandfather here and other special…friends."

Grady stopped. "Look, Tim, I know you're trying to help, but this is best for everyone."

Tim nodded toward Gina's car as it drove out of the lot. "I know there are at least two people who don't feel that way."

Later that evening Grady sat in his grandfather's room at Shady Haven.

"So you're really gonna go?" Fletch asked, not looking happy.

This wasn't getting any easier. "You knew I was leaving eventually."

"Hell, son, an old man can hope."

Grady noticed the sadness in his eyes. "I'm sorry, Granddad."

"I can deal with you leaving again, Grady, if it's for the right reasons. And if it makes you happy."

"It's for my business." God, he was a lousy liar.

"Let's at least be honest, son. My eyesight isn't so bad that I can't see you care about that pretty Gina Williams."

Damn, he didn't want to do this. "Look, Fletch, I know you want me to stay here, but…" Grady wasn't sure if he could be around Gina and Zack. "I'm not sure I fit in to all this family stuff."

Fletch looked sad as he shook his head. "I blame your parents for that. After their divorce, I wanted you to live with me permanently, not just those summers when your dad didn't have time for you."

Grady swallowed back the emotions clogging his throat. "I know."

"You always tried so hard to keep your distance,

son. You wouldn't let anyone get close." He paused. "Not all people are out to hurt you like your parents, or your ex-wife."

Grady tensed. He didn't want to rehash any of this. "I tried to play the family man before—it didn't work."

His grandfather watched him, then said, "I wish I was wise enough to give you all the right answers, son, but I can't. I lost your grandmother too soon. I didn't want to try to find someone again." Those kind hazel eyes stared at him. "That was a mistake. I was a lonely man for a lot of years."

"At least your marriage wasn't a failure. I've done so many things wrong."

"People make mistakes, son."

The pain was nearly overwhelming. "I was never home…not even when my son was born." He felt his throat closing up. "He didn't survive."

Fletch leaned forward and gripped his grandson's hand. "Oh, Grady, I'm so sorry." The old man was silent for a long time then said, "As tragic as it was to lose a child, you can't blame yourself for what you have no control over."

Grady didn't want to hear excuses. "I should have been there."

"Of course you should have been there for your wife. But, son, would it have changed the outcome?" Fletch asked.

He shook his head, unable to say the words.

"We can't live on what-ifs, son." His grip tightened. "You'll always grieve for your child, but it's time to forgive yourself, too. Let people help you," Fletch told him. "Maybe that special someone."

"Gina."

Fletcher shrugged. "I just thought that she would be someone you could build a future with. And what's not to like about a seven-year-old kid? Seems to me, that boy could use a good male role model in his life."

His heart ached. He couldn't stop himself from wanting the same thing. "I failed before."

"You weren't alone in your first marriage, so don't take all the blame." There was a long pause, then his grandfather said, "Gina's marriage was a tragic one, but she trusts you. That's because she sees what I see, a good man. Love with the right person can heal a lot of wounds," the old man added.

Grady felt a glimmer of hope. He'd never planned on another relationship, and then along came Gina and he couldn't get her out of his head, out of his heart. And she made him want to reach for that dream.

Grady thought back to the afternoon Gina had held him and cried with him for his child. How her touch had comforted him, how it had soothed his scarred body. How she had made him feel...loved. He closed his eyes and took a shaky breath. God, he loved her, and all he did was reject her. Would she ever forgive him for that? Take a chance on him?

He had to convince her. He suddenly realized how badly he wanted to make a life with her and Zack. How badly he wanted to stay right here in Destiny.

He stood and smiled at Fletch. "Do you think you could put up with me hanging around?"

The old man grinned. "Maybe if you bring Gina around to see me once in a while, and I wouldn't mind getting a great-grandkid or two out of it." He arched an eyebrow. "You need me to put in a good word for you?"

"No, I think I can handle that part," he said, though deep down he wasn't so sure. He had to repair a lot of damage.

Two days later Gina had been at work for an hour at the thrift shop. Since 7:00 a.m. She'd managed to get a lot done, too, including moving another reupholstered sofa to the display window.

"Marie, your work is incredible," Gina told her as they stood back and enjoyed the view.

"What are you talking about? You redesigned it. The sofa looks totally different."

"Well, you did most of the sewing. So why don't you take the rest of the day off?"

"Oh, no. I'm fine, really. I have a ton of work to do here."

"Not today. Take the baby to the park. You need some sunshine. Go."

The woman didn't argue, and within ten minutes Gina was alone. Oh, boy. Maybe that wasn't such a good idea. She had too much time to think.

"Do some paperwork." She went behind the counter and picked up the receipts from yesterday and started to head back to the office when the bell signaled over the front door. She glanced up to see Grady Fletcher. Her breath caught as the tall man dressed in jeans and a collared shirt walked in.

Oh, God. What was he doing here?

He looked as nervous as she felt. "Hello, Gina."

"Grady."

He shut the door and flipped the Open sign to Closed. Then he locked it before he walked over to her.

"What are you doing?"

"I'd like to talk to you. So I need a few minutes of uninterrupted time."

"And I have a business to run." She started to walk past him when he reached for her.

"Please, Gina. It's important."

Those dark eyes bored into hers. "Funny, you didn't have time for me when you needed to leave town."

"I didn't leave," he said.

She froze. "Why not?"

"I had things to do here. To settle."

She felt the imprint of his hand on her arm. She pulled away. "So when do you leave?"

"I'm not going to Texas."

Those words got her attention.

He glanced around. "Could Marie watch the shop for an hour or so? I want to show you something."

"Marie isn't here."

Then she heard the voice from the back room. "I'm here, Gina." She walked in from the back, pushing the stroller. "I returned to get my purse." She looked at Grady. "If it's for a good cause, I don't have a problem staying a few hours."

"A very good cause."

Grady turned back to Gina. She looked so pretty it took his breath away. Stay focused. He glanced over her jeans and pink blouse and tennis shoes.

"Good, you're dressed for where I have to take you."

She still resisted. "Who said I'm going anywhere?"

He stopped. "I'll make it worth your while. You can

have all the furniture in the cabin." When she still didn't move, he added, "Please, Gina. If it wasn't important, I wouldn't ask you."

"You have no idea what you're asking of me."

"I do. I'm hoping you still trust me enough to give me this chance."

She sighed. "Okay, I'll go." She glanced at Marie. "But I won't be gone long."

To Grady she said, "This had better be important."

He nodded, staring into those mesmerizing green eyes. "It's the most important thing I've ever done."

# Chapter 14

Ten minutes later they were going out of town, and at first Gina wondered if they were headed to the cabin.

No! She couldn't go back there. There were too many memories. Before she could protest, Grady drove by the turnoff. Instead they passed the new construction site that was Jace's new project.

"Isn't that the new mountain bike training center?"

"Yes. They're moving fast to complete it by mid June. Justin already has twenty students enrolled."

Gina studied the man behind the wheel. With the cowboy hat pulled low, she had trouble reading him. Why did he want her to come along? Better question, why had she consented to go with him?

He pulled off the road and into a clearing, then parked. "We're here," he announced as he climbed out and hurried around to her side. She had no choice but to take his offered hand to help her out of the truck.

"Come on." He didn't release his hold as he walked her to the edge of the hill.

She didn't want to think about the warmth of his large hand engulfing hers. How safe and utterly feminine he made her feel.

She concentrated on the beauty before her. Miles of pine and cedar trees covered the mountain range—the peaks looked as if they could touch the rich blue sky.

"It's breathtaking." That wasn't a lie, but why was she here?

He turned to her. "You really like it?"

"What's not to like?"

"This is where I'm building Sarge's Rescue Dogs and Kennel." He pointed off in the distance. "Well, it's actually going to be over there."

Her heart raced as she fought to contain her excitement. "So you decided against Texas."

"I weighed the options." His dark gaze locked on hers and held for a long time. "This is my grandfather's land. He gave it to me. Then Justin offered me a good deal to help my business—even Josh encouraged me. It seemed impractical to leave."

Well, that was just great. "Good for you. It's a lovely spot." How would she deal with Grady staying, running into him around town?

"I'm happy for you, Grady. Now, could you please take me back?" She started to leave when he stopped her.

"Not so fast. I haven't finished telling you everything."

He'd said enough. She didn't want to hear about his new life here. How he'd moved on and didn't need her in his life. "Grady. Please." She turned and marched back to the truck.

"Gina, wait," he called.

She ignored him as she reached for the passenger door, when he caught up and stopped her from opening it. He stood so close that Gina couldn't move. His breath was warm against her neck.

"You aren't even going to hear what else I have to say?"

She didn't turn around to look at him, just shook her head.

"You don't want to hear that I plan to build a place on the crest over there. How I want the whole back side of the house to be glass so you can see that view from every room."

"Sounds lovely. Can I leave now?"

"Not before I tell you—"

"Stop." Gina swung around. "I'm glad you've moved on, Grady. Okay." She hated that tears filled her eyes. "I just don't need to hear—"

Her words were smothered when his mouth closed over hers. She moaned and gripped the front of his shirt, and in her weakened state, allowed Grady to have his way. She'd missed him so much. The feelings he created in her.

He broke off the kiss. "I've missed you, Gina. God knows, I tried to stay away, tried to let you find someone who would be better for you than a set-in-his-ways ex-army guy. But I discovered that I want you, only you."

Even though his confession thrilled her, it wasn't

enough. "Grady. I can't deny I want you, too." She couldn't help but think about their little time together. "But I want more than some stolen hours."

He pulled back and his hard gaze locked on hers, then he stepped back.

"I want more, too, Gina." He still looked uneasy. "I know it's hard for you because of your bad marriage. And my track record in that department was lousy."

She frowned when he backed away. She watched as he pulled off his hat, raking fingers through his hair.

"Grady," she called to him. "Tell me why you brought me here."

He turned back to her. "I'm not good at this, Gina. In the army, you're given orders and you carry them out."

"Then consider this an order and tell me what you have to say."

Grady felt his palms sweat, his heart race. Hell, he felt like a teenager.

"I want to stay in Destiny, be close to my grandfather. Build my business here." His gaze met hers. "But most importantly, Gina, I want to build a life with you."

"But I thought you wanted to leave so badly," she finally said. "That you weren't the man for me. You couldn't give me what I needed."

He blew out a breath. So she wasn't going to make this easy. He thought about Tim Keenan's advice. He straightened and walked toward her. "That was before I realized that I could give you more than any man." His throat suddenly went dry. "Because no one could love you as much as I do."

Gina blinked, then he saw the tears in her eyes. "Oh, Grady."

He stepped closer. "Is that a good 'Oh, Grady' or a bad 'Oh, Grady'?"

She smiled. "It's good." She rushed into his arms. "I love you, too, Grady Fletcher."

He tossed his cowboy hat into the back of the truck, then reached for her. "Those are the sweetest words I ever heard," he whispered right before his mouth captured hers.

There was no way he could ever express the depth of his feelings for her, but he was going to try. He pulled her tighter against him, letting her know how much he desired her, wanted to cherish her for a lifetime.

He pulled back, but didn't let her go. He cupped her face tenderly. "I meant what I said, Gina. I want a future with you and Zack. I know you've gone through a lot. You can have all the space you need to heal, just know I'll be there. I want you to trust me that I'll never hurt you intentionally."

She kissed him sweetly. "I know that, Grady. I've known that from the first." She reached up and touched the scar on the side of his neck. "That afternoon when we made love, everything you shared with me, I know it was painful for you, both physically and emotionally." Her gaze met his, but he felt the connection deep down into his soul. "I've never felt that way…ever. Being with you was so special."

"I want to make you feel that way always," he said. "I want to marry you, Gina." He saw her surprised look. "Okay, maybe it's too early for that step. But I want to be your husband, your partner and Zack's father."

This time the tears did fall. "Oh, Grady."

He searched her face. "Again, is that good or bad?"

She nodded. "Oh, definitely good." She cupped his face. "You'll be a wonderful father… One any child would be proud of." She knew he was thinking about the son he'd lost. "Zack is going to be so lucky to have you."

"No, I'm the one who's lucky to have you both." He took a steady breath, then knelt on the ground in front of her. "Gina Williams, I love you more than I ever thought possible. Would you do me the honor to marry this old soldier? I promise to love and cherish you forever."

Her eyes widened at his proposal. "Oh, yes, Grady, I'll marry you." She leaned down and placed her mouth against his. With a groan, he stood, wrapping her in his arms and kissed her until they were both breathless.

"Oh, Grady, I'm so happy."

"Enough to play hooky with me for the rest of the day?"

Gina looked up at the handsome man who was going to be her husband. "Sounds tempting." She hesitated. "I guess I could call Marie and have her close the shop. So what do you have in mind?"

"I could lie and say we have a lot to discuss, but I have a feeling we'll get distracted the second we're alone." He grinned at her and she couldn't resist.

"So you're saying you can make it worth my while?"

"I'm a soldier, I don't back down from a challenge. Especially someone as tempting as you."

She gave him a soft kiss and turned in his arms. Together they looked at the view as she pointed toward the ridge. "You said you're building a house there?"

"Our house," he corrected. "First, though, I need to

finish the kennel for the dogs, which Jace said would be complete by summer's end." Grady smiled. "Then we can break ground on our home. We want to get as much done as we can before winter." He leaned down and kissed the side of her neck. "I want to do everything quickly so it's ready for you and Zack."

"How soon do you want to get married?"

"If it was up to me, I'd marry you this minute." He turned her around to face him. "I know you need time, Gina. I'm willing to wait until you're ready."

She felt the rush. Oh, she was so ready for this man. "Okay. We can talk about it. We need to talk to Zack, too. And your grandfather."

Grady grinned. "I can tell you Fletch wholeheartedly approves of us."

Gina smiled, too. "I love that man. Mainly because he raised you. He helped make you the man you are. The man I love."

"And you're the woman I love. The woman who saved me from loneliness. You were there for me when I didn't think I needed anyone. Gina, I need you in my life."

He paused and she knew he was thinking about his son.

"Oh, Grady. You've helped me through a lot of things, too. Mainly, I learned to trust." She slipped her arms around his waist. "How wonderful it is to be loved by a man who cherishes me. And you love my son." She smiled, realizing how lucky she was to find this man. "Zack's going to be so happy."

"I bet he's not nearly as happy as I am right now."

She nodded. "I think there's enough happiness to go around for all of us."

With Grady's arms wrapped around her, they looked out at the beautiful view, the site of their future home. Their new life. Together.

# *Epilogue*

Two days later Saturday arrived, sunny and warm and perfect for an eight-year-old boy's birthday party. Also a great day for family, new and old. Gina felt almost giddy. Grady should be here soon and then they could announce their big news.

"Mom!" Zack came running into the house. "Did you get my cake?"

"No, Aunt Lori is bringing it," she reminded him, knowing in about thirty minutes half the town would be in her backyard for the party. They'd been lucky to find so many friends since coming to Destiny.

"Oh, I forgot," Zack said.

She hugged the little boy who suddenly looked so much older. Where had her baby gone? She got a strange feeling again, thinking about Grady and starting their new life together. Having another child. She was giddy at the thought of having Grady's baby.

"Mom. When is Grady getting here?"

She brushed his dark hair from his forehead. "Soon, he's picking someone up."

She knew Zack was eager to show off Bandit's tricks. "Come on," she said. "Let's check the tables before everyone gets here."

They walked out onto the deck to view the large yard that had been decorated for the party. Several arrangements of balloons were tied to each fence post, and toward the back an obstacle course had been constructed late yesterday by one special man. Grady. She recalled last night, how she'd relayed her thanks to her man after Zack had gone to bed.

She could see Zack's excitement. "The obstacle course is so cool."

"Yes, it is. You're a lucky little boy, Zack Williams."

Gina twisted the large shiny pear-shaped diamond on her left hand. Grady had also surprised her when he'd slipped the engagement ring on her finger. In those stolen moments, her future husband had also proceeded to show her how much he loved her. Today was special for another reason. Grady wanted to ask Zack officially for his mother's hand before they made the announcement.

The yard gate opened and Grady walked in with Scout. Her breath caught at the sight of the tall man who was dressed in black jeans and a tan collared shirt. When he smiled at her, she saw the love shining in his eyes and nearly melted on the spot.

Zack spotted him, too. "Grady!" He went running off to him and greeted Scout. "I'm so glad you're here."

"I told you I'd come early." Grady smiled. "I brought another surprise. Someone who wants to meet you."

Grady winked at Gina and went outside the gate again, but soon returned pushing his grandfather in a wheelchair. "Zack, this is Joe Fletcher. Granddad, this is the special boy I've been telling you about."

Grady stood back and watched the two together. It was his grandfather who spoke first. "I hear you got lost in my old mine."

Zack nodded. "Yeah, but Scout found me."

"Maybe it's time I boarded that place up. Wouldn't want anyone else to get hurt."

"I think it's a cool place."

Fletch pursed his lips. "Maybe when I get out of this chair we can go up there together. I can show you where there's still some gold."

Zack's dark eyes lit up. "Really?"

Fletch nodded. "Say, I hear it's your birthday today. I got you something." He handed him the small box. "But you're gonna have to wait a little while to open it."

"Thank you. I'll put it with the other presents." He took off toward the table as Gina walked over and kissed Fletch on the cheek.

"Hello, Granddad Joe."

The older man grinned as they hugged. "There's my girl."

Grady raised an eyebrow. "Don't get any ideas, old man. She's spoken for."

Fletch waved him off and turned back to Gina. "Thanks for inviting me today."

"You're always included. You're family."

One of the many reasons Grady loved this woman—

her big heart. He was one lucky man. He reached down and brushed a kiss across her lips. He couldn't help but recall their time together last night. "Hello, pretty lady." He leaned close to her ear and whispered, "I can't tell you how much I hated leaving you last night."

She looked up at him with those green eyes. "Maybe we can change that…and soon."

Before he could say any more, the boy returned with Scout. Grady stepped back from temptation. "Hey, Zack, how about we run the dogs through the obstacle course for practice?"

"Okay." Zack went to get Bandit out of the kennel. Grady gripped Gina's hand, feeling the diamond, feeling her love, feeling her commitment to him. "Wish me luck."

"Always, but you don't need it. Zack already loves you as much as I do."

Grady looked down at his grandfather to see his smile. "I told you she was a keeper," Fletch said.

Grady motioned to Scout and together they walked off toward the edge of the yard where the course started. The boy met him there and gave the command for Bandit to sit, and then he unleashed him. Grady had Scout sit, too. "Could I talk to you, Zack, before we start?"

The boy looked worried, but nodded.

Grady knelt to be eye level. "I want to talk you about your mom." He released a breath. "You know I care about her."

Zack petted Bandit. "Yeah, I saw you kiss her."

"Does that bother you?"

The boy shook his head. "I just don't want you to hurt her like my daddy did. He was mean."

"No, Zack. That's a cowardly thing to do, especially to a woman or a child. There might be times when we disagree, but I'll never raise my hand to you or your mother. You have my word."

"I'm glad, 'cause Mom's happy now."

"And I want to make her even happier." This was harder than he thought. "I love your mother, and I want to marry her."

The boy's eyes lit up. "Really? You mean like Aunt Lori and Uncle Jace? We'd live together all the time?"

Grady smiled. "Yes. I'm building a big house so that will happen."

Zack's eyes grew larger.

Grady grew serious again. "Not only that, Zack. I want you to be my son."

"Really? You'll be my dad?"

He nodded, fighting for the right words. "As much as I love your mother, I also love you, too."

Before he could finish making his pitch, Zack had launched himself into his arms, nearly knocking him over. "I love you, too, Grady."

He hugged the boy, letting those sweet words sink in. That was when he saw Gina walk toward them. She hugged him, then her son. "So what do you think about us being a family?"

"It's cool!" Zack said. "Grady wants to be my dad." He petted Scout. "And we get to live with Scout and Bandit, too."

Grady suddenly realized how much he loved these two. "I think it's pretty cool, too." He hugged Gina to his side. "I get a wife and a son."

Zack grinned and looked up expectantly at his

mother. "Mom, does that mean you're going to have a baby like Aunt Lori?"

A blush crossed Gina's face as her gaze rose to his; the love shining in their depths caused his chest to tighten with longing. He could picture Gina pregnant with his child.

She smiled. "I think that's something your new dad and I need to discuss. Alone."

Grady wished they were alone right now. "Hey, I think today is someone's birthday."

With their arms intertwined and two dogs with them, they turned back toward the house and noticed the party crowd. There was Claire and Tim Keenan, Lori, Jace and their daughter, Cassie, Justin and Morgan Hilliard and their kids. So many more gathered on the deck, but they had been giving them space. Privacy.

"I think everyone's a little curious about what's going on," Gina told him. "Maybe we should tell them."

Grady smiled. "It would be my pleasure, ma'am."

Before he could make any announcement, Zack spoke up. "Mom and Grady are getting married. And he's going to be my new dad." The boy beamed up at his parents. "This is the best birthday ever."

The crowd erupted in a round of cheers. Grady looked down at Gina and saw the love in her eyes. "How did I get so lucky?"

"Me, too."

They both had to be remembering that awful day when Zack had been kidnapped. The day one strong woman had climbed into his truck and announced she was going to get her child back. "You saved my son that day," she said.

He leaned back and brushed his mouth across hers. "No, you both saved me. I'm one lucky guy."

She smiled and his heart sang. This was their new beginning, and it was only going to get better. How could it not? He finally had everything he'd ever wanted—a home here in Destiny. And his family.

\* \* \* \* \*

**Amanda Renee** was raised in the northeast and now wriggles her toes in the warm coastal Carolina sands. Her career began when she was discovered through Harlequin's So You Think You Can Write contest. When not creating stories about love and laughter, she enjoys the company of her schnoodle, Duffy, as well as camping, playing guitar and piano, photography and anything involving animals. You can visit her at amandarenee.com.

### Books by Amanda Renee

### Harlequin Western Romance

#### *Saddle Ridge, Montana*

*The Lawman's Rebel Bride*
*A Snowbound Cowboy Christmas*
*Wrangling Cupid's Cowboy*
*The Bull Rider's Baby Bombshell*

### Harlequin American Romance

#### *Welcome to Ramblewood*

*Betting on Texas*
*Home to the Cowboy*
*Blame It on the Rodeo*
*A Texan for Hire*
*Back to Texas*
*Mistletoe Rodeo*
*The Trouble with Cowgirls*
*A Bull Rider's Pride*
*Twins for Christmas*

Visit the Author Profile page
at Harlequin.com for more titles.

# BLAME IT ON THE RODEO

Amanda Renee

For Susan Gibbs Woods
Friends Forever Girlie—'Til we meet again in heaven

# Chapter 1

"Let's see if we can catch us a foal."

Sliding her arm into the sterile shoulder-length glove, Lexi Lawson slipped the neck strap over her head and faced Little Miss Confetti.

"Easy, girl." Billy Stevens led the white-and-black American Paint mare into the narrow wooden-and-metal crush and closed the front gate. The secured enclosure protected Lexi from the horse and the horse from itself during the procedure. Standing to the side, Billy whispered soothing words while gently rubbing Confetti's muzzle.

"Welcome to your first embryo transfer lesson—so come on back here for a ringside seat." Amused by Billy's stunned expression, she continued, "Equine care starts at conception, and there's more to horses than leg wraps and Coggins reports." Lexi was pleased at how proficient her protégé had become at aiding her with the standard Equine Infectious Anemia tests and the subsequent paperwork.

A year and a half ago Lexi wouldn't have considered Billy Stevens for an assistant. After escaping his abusive family, Billy ended up on the wrong side of the law when he and a few so-called friends stole some high-priced guitars from Ackerman's Music in town. A month in county lockup left him scared straight and completely alone once he was released. Never ones to turn away a person in need, the Langtry family offered him a place to live on the Bridle Dance Ranch in exchange for honest, hard work.

Cole, the oldest of the four Langtry brothers, took a shine to Billy when he noticed his interest in horses ran deeper than a paycheck. Without confidence in himself, Billy didn't believe he had a future in the veterinary field until Cole pointed him in Lexi's direction and offered to help finance some college courses this past semester. A natural, Billy instinctively sensed when a horse was even the slightest bit off.

"We'll be successful today," Ashleigh assured them.

Billy bashfully squeezed past Ashleigh and the crush. Lexi suspected he had a case of puppy love for her vet tech, but he'd soon come to realize no matter how endearing he might be, Ashleigh wasn't about to leave her husband for someone seven years her junior.

"Cole," Lexi said over her shoulder. "Have one of the grooms on standby to bring in Moonglow."

Before Cole answered, Shane Langtry cleared his

throat in the doorway of the breeding area and casually leaned against the jamb.

"I'm headed out to pick up our first official rodeo student." Shane straightened and strode over to the mare and stroked her cheek. Responding to his gentle touch, she snorted against his hand and bobbed her head.

Dressed in faded jeans and a formfitting, ab-enhancing fitted gray T-shirt, Shane shouldn't make her breath catch, but damned if he didn't, even after thirteen years. Lexi may have put his cheating ways in the past, but no one said working near the man responsible for the toughest decision of her life would be easy. Of course, she had the option to start over somewhere else, and she'd done just that for a spell.

After a year at Colorado State, Lexi transferred to Cornell University in Ithaca, New York, where she completed veterinary school and her equine internship. She'd been set to stay in the upstate area, but Joe Langtry's call six months later with a job offer and the opportunity to branch out on her own was impossible to resist. The Langtry patriarch was a true Southern charmer who had a way with words, and the money sure didn't hurt, either.

While it was an adjustment from the bone-chilling northern winters, once Lexi moved back to her family's farm, she knew Ramblewood, Texas, would always be home. Regrets were a waste of time and Lexi wasn't about to let a moment pass her by. Jumping into the swing of things with her old friends, she learned to adjust to having Shane in her life again, but it wasn't until his brother Jesse's wedding last November that she and Shane had started chipping away at the pain of the past. Some memories may have faded, but one still haunted her.

"You've been waiting for this day for a long time." Lexi smiled up at Shane. "I wish you the best."

Needing to concentrate on Little Miss Confetti, Lexi shifted her attention away from the roguish cowboy. After administering lidocaine to relax the mare's hind-quarters, Ashleigh wrapped its tail in pink, stretchy bandaging and loosely tied it to the crush's back-gate support.

"Most important—everything must be sterile," Lexi explained to Billy. In her peripheral vision, she noticed Shane still watching her, making her acutely aware how many people banked on her success today. "We don't want any unnecessary risk of infection."

"I still don't understand," Billy said. "Why are we using a surrogate if Confetti's already pregnant?"

"She's our top cutting-horse competitor," Cole said. "Eleven months is too long to keep her out of the ring, and then we'd have to retrain and get her endurance levels up to par again. When she's older and no longer competing, we'll allow her to carry."

"Plus we can get two foals from Confetti this year if we use a surrogate." Lexi had read how some veterinarians were transferring up to six embryos a year from their donor mares by constantly manipulating their heat cycles. She didn't agree with the practice and was glad the Langtrys were equally opposed to it. She only dared so much when it came to messing around with Mother Nature. "We also use surrogates if there's an injury and the horse can't carry to term, or if there are problems due to a previous pregnancy. There are many reasons, but we make sure overbreeding isn't one of them."

Billy's eyes darted between the equipment and the mare. "Will this hurt her?"

"It may feel a little strange to her, but there's no pain," Lexi reassured him. "The process goes very quickly. Mystified Moonglow is our surrogate, but we had to prepare more than one mare in case she didn't ovulate the prerequisite two days after Confetti. The ultrasound shows we're right on schedule with both horses."

Ashleigh placed a white tube in Lexi's free hand. "This is a two-way catheter," Lexi said, turning her wrist over. "Ashleigh will attach one channel to the embryo flush."

Carefully inserting the catheter, Lexi inflated the bulb inside Confetti's cervix to prevent the flush from flowing out while Ashleigh connected the saline solution with long tubing and elevated it on a modified IV stand above Confetti's backside.

"Embryo collection is always done on day seven or eight after ovulation," she explained. "At six days, it's not quite viable, and once we reach the nine-day mark, the embryo is too large and we risk damaging it. Day eight is perfect, and once we know where it is in the petri dish, it will be visible to the naked eye."

"I hope this works," Cole said. "What's the saying, third time's the charm?"

"It's also the last," Lexi stated flatly. If she failed again, she would know this wasn't meant to be, and she didn't want to tempt fate.

"This isn't foolproof. We're looking at a fifty-to-seventy percent success rate. I've always collected them on the second go-round, if we missed the first, but Confetti's been my problem child."

Lexi released a small amount of fluid through the tube and into the horse. Opening the switch between the two channels, the solution flowed through the other side of the tubing and into a filter cup that Ashleigh held.

"The trick is to always have some fluid in the cup, never allowing it to drain all the way into the bucket," Ashleigh added. "We don't want the embryo to smack hard against the side of the cup on its way out."

A few minutes later, Lexi removed the catheter and transferred the collection cup to the Langtrys' lab area. None of her other patients had their own laboratories, but then none of them owned one of the state's largest paint and quarter cutting horse ranches.

Lexi was grateful that Joe Langtry had spared no expense when he built the facility, because it allowed her greater opportunities to expand her knowledge while working in the field.

A bead of sweat traveled down between her shoulder blades in spite of the room's cool climate-controlled air. Opening a grid-lined petri dish, Lexi meticulously poured the contents of the cup into it and turned on the microscope.

"We're using the stereo microscope today." She peered into the eyepiece and adjusted the focus knob. "Examining the cells in three dimensions allows me to grade the quality of the embryo."

Slowly moving the dish under the microscope, she scanned the solution, grid by grid, hoping they wouldn't come up empty again.

"We're in luck, folks." Lexi let out the breath she'd been holding since she arrived on the Bridle Dance Ranch that morning and smiled. "Cole, can you have someone return Confetti to her stall and move Moonglow into the crush? Ashleigh will prep her.

"Take a look." Lexi slid over, making room for Billy, who hovered nearby. "We have a grade one embryo. See how the cells are compacted and all the same size? That's what we always look for."

A lot rode on this dream match between dam Little Miss Confetti and sire Dreamward Wink. The buyer, Blueford Thomas, was a longtime family friend, but Lexi had the feeling everyone was beginning to doubt her ability to get the job done, including Shane.

Seemingly satisfied, Shane turned and left the lab area without a word. Knowing full well this situation was different, Lexi couldn't help but think of the day he'd walked out on her so long ago. Ironically, an unborn child was involved, too.

"Let's transfer this baby into its new home for the next eleven months."

Shane cursed himself on his way out of the stables. Damned if the sight of her didn't still make his blood boil. It had taken a few years after she returned home for Lexi to warm up to Shane, but she still kept him at arm's length. And who'd blame her? The one time he'd cheated on her led to a two-year nightmare he'd rather forget.

A couple days before Lexi came home for winter break from Colorado State, buckle bunny Sharon Vincent knocked on his door and claimed she was five months pregnant with his kid. Their one night in Oklahoma shortly after high school graduation came back to bite him in the ass. Sharon wasn't just bad news when he met her, she was a hot mess and Shane didn't have the good sense to resist. Claiming she was on the pill, he'd learned the hard way not to trust a woman in the birth control department.

Pressured by his family to do the right thing, he immediately married Sharon, breaking Lexi's heart in the process. He'd never forget the afternoon he told Lexi the truth. Her hazel eyes flared at him like a cougar ready to attack. Only she didn't say a word. He had no choice but to walk away from her and they'd kept their distance from one another until his father enticed her to return to town permanently. Shane knew it was for his benefit. Joe Langtry loved to control situations and Shane believed his father thought he and Lexi would one day take another stab at what they'd lost.

Shane married Sharon, and for their son Dylan's sake he kept up the facade even though he didn't love his wife. Shortly after Dylan's first birthday, Tab Fanning, Shane's biggest rodeo rival, rode into town and turned his world upside down when he claimed to be Dylan's father.

Shane hadn't wanted to believe the child he'd grown to love wasn't his, and Sharon fed him lie after lie, swearing Dylan was his son. He convinced himself that it didn't matter. He loved Dylan and at this point didn't care who the father was, until a court-ordered paternity test proved otherwise. Shattered when Tab took Dylan away, Shane immediately sent Sharon packing.

Before walking out the door, Sharon admitted she

had only wanted the Langtry money and had intended to get pregnant that lone night with Shane. Her fatal flaw was sleeping with one too many cowboys around the same time. It took every ounce of Shane's strength and that of his brothers not to strangle her on the spot. From that day forward, Shane declared marriage and children off-limits.

Throwing himself into the rodeo and his work on the ranch kept his mind busy and there was no shortage of women to occupy his bed at night. His romantic relationship with Lexi was in the past but the memory of what they'd had plagued him.

They worked together, ran in the same circles and were usually found in the same places after the sun went down, but until Jesse's wedding, Shane wouldn't have even considered the possibility of a second chance. Maybe it was the clever way Miranda, Jesse's wife, paired them together during the ceremony and reception. Or, maybe it was the sight of Lexi in her beaded sage bridesmaid gown. Whatever the reason, the moment she took his arm during the wedding procession, Shane knew where his heart belonged—where it had never left.

"There's my elusive son," his mother greeted him on the dirt path leading to the stables. "I haven't seen you in two days. Thought I'd take a break from the ribbon-cutting preparations and see how Lexi made out." Kay peered up at him. "Have you heard anything yet?"

"It was a success." Shane tilted his hat back and grinned. "Had no doubt she'd get it this time."

"This whole embryo-transfer thing fascinates me. In my day, horses did their mating the old-fashioned way.

Speaking of which, how is it going between you and Lexi? I noticed you came in very late the other night. Does that mean you two had a good date?"

"I wouldn't call dinner at the Ragin' Cajun with eight other people a date, Mom." Shane had hoped to get a little alone time with Lexi that night, but they were celebrating their friend Aaron's birthday, and while Lexi had agreed to go with him, she made sure they were never truly alone. "I wish she would trust me more instead of always doing this group thing."

"Give her time, honey." Kay placed her hand over her son's heart. "It wasn't that long ago that you were chasing any female with a pulse, and some of them didn't even have that qualification."

"Ouch, Mom." While he loved his mother for always telling him how it was, her words stung. "I haven't been with anyone since the wedding and it's not for a lack of available women."

"Okay, I may love you unconditionally but that doesn't mean I want to hear about your sex life." Kay wrinkled her nose and feigned a shiver. "You keep those bits and your own bits to yourself. Do you hear me?"

"Yes, ma'am." Shane threw his arms around his mother and gave her a hug. Since his father, Joe, died last year of a sudden heart attack, he realized how short life was and how much he took for granted. He swore he wouldn't repeat past mistakes, especially when it came to family. They meant the world to him and someday he hoped to convince Lexi she did, too.

Kay Langtry was the strongest woman Shane knew. His father's will left Shane and his three brothers the business end of the ranch, while the land, houses and the winery were left to their mother. In honor of their father, and after a power struggle that almost tore the family apart, the brothers created an equine facility showcasing the spirit of the horse and the grand opening was next week. Kay ran the Dance of Hope hippotherapy facility and Shane and his brother Chase ran the Ride 'em High! Rodeo School. His brother Cole primarily focused on the Bridle Dance Ranch itself and the breeding programs with Lexi while his other brother Jesse had his own ranch to run.

Once more, his thoughts settled on the mahogany-haired bombshell inside the stables. Every day she was there and every night he tried to shake free the memories of how much he hurt her.

"Aren't you going to be late picking up Hunter?" Kay looked up at her son.

"I'm leaving now." Shane checked his watch. It took an hour and a half to drive to the airport and the flight arrived shortly after. "I love you, Mom."

Giving his mother a peck on the cheek, he hopped into his black, topless and doorless Jeep and removed the keys from the visor. He accidentally popped the clutch and shot off with a cloud of dust in his wake. He'd hear about that one later from his mother. She hated when they spun out of the parking area.

After fighting traffic the entire way to the San Antonio airport, Shane surprisingly found a parking spot close to the entrance. Inside he scanned the incoming board for Hunter's flight.

Flight 3492 11:48 a.m.—On Time

With twenty minutes to spare, he sauntered to the ticket counter and zeroed in on the fresh-faced blonde in a white long-sleeve blouse and dark, fitted vest.

"There's supposed to be a gate pass waiting for me," he drawled. "I'm picking up Hunter Rathbone."

Her brown doe eyes met his and she smiled, a slightly imperfect, yet adorable grin with one tooth barely over-lapping the other on the bottom row. Fumbling with the mouse, she inhaled nervously, causing her name tag to glint in the overhead fluorescent lights.

"I can check in to that for you." There was a hint of shyness in her voice and Shane wondered if she was new to the job. Typing in some information on the computer, she asked, "May I see your identification?"

Removing his billfold from his front pocket, he re-moved his driver's license and slid it across the counter. "Are you new here, Lily?"

When her fingers accidentally grazed his, she hesi-tated and stared down at his empty ring finger. *Why do women do that?* Tilting his head to catch her gaze, he watched Lily's cheeks turn a deep crimson when she realized she'd been caught doing the typical wedding-ring check. "I started a few weeks ago." Taking another deep breath, she tightened her grip on his license, pulled it toward her and verified his information.

"Do you like it?" Amused by her reaction, Shane decided to have a little fun and leaned on the counter, smiling easily when she swallowed hard and her pu-pils dilated.

"Yes—here's your gate pass. You'll need to go through security first then head to gate B8." She handed him his license and a map of the airport, trying to avoid any further eye contact.

Shane nodded politely, returned his wallet to his pocket and glanced at the map. "Thanks, darling." He confidently strode away from the counter knowing Lily was probably enjoying the view.

*Yep, I still got it.* He only wished Lexi thought so, too.

A couple he assumed were embarking on their honeymoon stood ahead of him at the security checkpoint, arms entwined, whispering I-love-you's to each other every few seconds. Shane fought the rude comment that teetered on the tip of his tongue, knowing it came from the hard reminder of what he'd had and lost, and wanted back with only one person.

He turned his attention to the woman in the next aisle who was balancing toddler twin boys in matching overalls on either hip. The strain of the day already evident in her face, and he sincerely hoped she was meeting someone and not heading out on a flight of her own.

He tugged off his boots, placed them on the conveyer belt and emptied his pockets into the bin. After the obligatory pat-down that left him a little uncomfortable, he hopped on one foot while he pulled on his boots.

Exiting the checkpoint at the same time, the frazzled woman struggled with her children's shoes, reminding Shane how difficult it could be to stuff a kicking foot into a tiny sneaker. Not much more than in her early twenties, she haphazardly tucked a lock of hair, which had escaped her loose ponytail, behind her ear.

"Steven, stay next to Mommy." She kneeled in front of one child, jammed his pudgy foot into the shoe and fastened the Velcro closure while looking over her shoulder at her other restless child. "Steven, come here."

The words were all it took for the child to giggle loudly and take off down the terminal. The woman stood to chase after him, catching her purse strap on the chair.

Shane ran after him, smiling at the boy's duck-waddle steps. For a moment, he felt like he'd time-warped to the days when he thought Dylan was his son. The sudden ache in his heart caught him off guard when he swung the toddler into his arms. The woman quickly caught up with him, frustration creasing her brow.

"Thank you." She reached out for the boy. "I can't believe they made me take their shoes off. Really, thanks again."

Before he responded, the woman went on her way down the terminal.

A few minutes passed once he arrived in the designated waiting area and the gate door opened. A flight attendant emerged with a lanky dark-haired, ice-blue-eyed preteen in tow. Shane approached them and gave Hunter a hug.

"It's good to see you again." Shane released him to get a better look at the soon-to-be man. "You've shot up these past few months."

Shane had met Hunter Rathbone and his parents in Denver during a high school rodeo clinic he'd led in April. Hunter raved that Shane was his idol, and when Shane mentioned he was opening the Ride 'em High! Rodeo School, Hunter practically begged his parents on the spot to let him attend the school's inaugural session. Shane kept the Rathbones apprised of the school's progress and even flew out to a couple of Hunter's events. He was drawn to the kid's talent and natural ease in the saddle. The fact that Hunter and Dylan were close to the same age caused Shane to wonder more in recent months about the child he'd lost.

Hunter beamed. "I can't believe I'm actually here with you. This is a dream of a lifetime."

"Easy, kid, you have a whole lot of living to do." Shane winked at the attractive flight attendant and handed her his license and gate pass. "Trust me when I say you have much better things to dream of when you get older."

"I wasn't sure if you were picking me up or if someone else from the school was. I'm so excited we're staying in bunkhouses. Just like real cowboys."

"You are a real cowboy." Shane tousled the boy's hair. "Half your class is coming in from out of state. You and one other are flying in, the rest are driving. And since you're our first official student, I thought I should be the one to meet you."

Shane wondered if he'd see Dylan's name on the student manifest one day. An impossible pipe dream considering Tab probably knew more about the rodeo than he did. He hadn't come across Dylan on the circuit yet, but with a bull-riding champion for a father, rodeo coursed through the boy's blood. He'd heard Tab retired, married and had more children after he gained full custody of Dylan. As far as he knew, Dylan had a good life, and in the end, that's what mattered most to Shane.

There were days he wondered if Dylan remembered their time together, and realized it was unlikely. Dylan had just turned a year old when Tab left with him, and after the way Shane had shoved Sharon out the door, he wasn't sure he wanted to be remembered for treating the child's mother that way. Not that she'd win any parent-of-the-year awards. Rumor had it she was down in Brazil trying her hand with another country's cowboys.

"I hope you're ready for a month of hard work?" Shane asked while they rode the escalator down to the baggage claim area.

"Tight!" Hunter said with enthusiasm. "I can't wait to get started."

*"Tight?"* Shane stopped walking and looked at Hunter's feet. "Are your boots pinching or something?"

"Huh?" Hunter tilted his head and slowly looked from Shane to his feet. "What are you talking about?"

"You said *tight*. What's *tight?*" Shane asked.

Hunter patted Shane on the back and urged him to walk forward before they caused a traffic jam at the bottom of the escalator. "How do I translate this for you, old man? *Tight* means the same as *cool* back in your day. You don't hang with many kids, do you?"

"No, I don't." *Old man?* Shane's ego took a bit of a hit at the comment. "And for the record, thirty-one's not old."

"In terms of a hundred being the oldest, no, you still have time. I'm sure I can teach you enough in the next month to survive the average kid. But since you're practically old enough to be my dad, it may take a little work."

"Oh, nice shot." Shane arm nudged the teen. "We'll see who teaches who this month."

His anticipation of the next four weeks began to shift, nervousness replacing his usual confidence. Maybe teenagers weren't so easy after all.

# Chapter 2

"Surprise!"

"Oh, good Lord!" Miranda wobbled backward, her hands protectively on her round belly. "Don't you people know never to startle a pregnant woman?"

"Now I told you to surprise her, not surprise the young'uns out of her." Mable's mocha cheeks flared with a hint of red. "We don't need a repeat of last year, but Tess, honey, ready the shower curtain liner, just in case." Originally, Double Trouble's house manager, Mable became a surrogate mother of sorts when Miranda moved to town and purchased the ranch. Never having had children of her own, Mable doted on Miranda as if she were her own daughter. Since Miranda's drunk of a mother had died a few years ago, Mable easily filled the void in her life.

Lexi doubted anyone would soon forget the day Vicki Slater went into labor shortly after her own baby shower ended. Miranda was right there to catch the bundle of joy in the middle of her living room. So indebted to her friend, Vicki named her daughter Randi Lynn, after Miranda.

Randi Lynn had celebrated her first birthday a few days ago and Miranda had a few weeks before she and Jesse welcomed twins. Once their honeymoon started, they immediately went to work in the baby-making department. But they weren't the only children with a birthday this time of year. One was missing. Lexi tried to push the thought from her mind.

Lexi had liked Miranda from the day she pulled into town, determined to start a new life. She'd been down that road herself and anyone with the courage to make that kind of move had her vote. Jesse couldn't have chosen a better bride—they were perfectly matched in their fire and passion.

Inside Cole and his wife Tess's newly renovated cottage, Ramblewood's women gathered, showering the latest mommy-to-be with gifts. And Jesse, the only male in the room, seemed to relish the attention. Tess and Cole's adopted daughter, Ever, helped hand Miranda her presents, although Lexi sensed she wanted to tear into each one of them herself.

"I just thought of something," Miranda said, straightening her back to rub it. "I didn't see any cars when we pulled up. Where did you all park?"

Everyone laughed.

"That was an adventure of its own," Mazie, Lexi's younger sister, giggled.

"That son of mine almost lost a few of your guests along the way," Kay said. "We had everyone park at the winery and Shane chauffeured them here in that blasted Jeep of his. Poor Bridgett almost flew out of it."

On a quarter-of-a-million-acre ranch, it was a cinch to hide a few cars. Besides being Dance of Hope's CEO, Kay oversaw the small ranch winery, and since it wasn't open on Saturdays, it was the last place Miranda would venture.

Feeling wistful, Lexi looked around the cottage at the people she considered her extended family. Lexi's parents had grown up with both Tess and Vicki's parents, and then all their kids grew up together. Now a new generation had begun and the cycle would repeat. *Minus one.*

Everyone had been surprised when Shane offered to renovate the house for Cole as a peace offering for trying to block the Dance of Hope hippotherapy facility last year. When Shane and Chase battled Cole and Jesse for control of the ranch's finances, Kay had been relegated to watching her family tear itself apart. Looking around now, Lexi admired the extensive attention to detail Shane had given the remodel.

Recently her friends' lives had changed drastically. They were married and creating families of their own. She'd wanted the same for herself thirteen years ago, if Shane hadn't cheated on her. Lexi tried not to dwell on the what-ifs, but the past still tormented her every day. Especially now that she and Shane were testing the waters again, even though she'd made it clear she wasn't sure where it would lead.

"Honey, did you see Ever's bedroom?"

"Mom…" Lexi shushed her mother. "Are you snooping?"

"No, I'm not snooping," Judy said. "I merely observed the room across the hall when I came out of the bathroom. It's adorable with purple ponies in tiaras painted on the walls. And did you see the mini hitching post out front for Ever's horse? She's one lucky little girl."

Lexi watched the five-year-old across the room. She was sitting on Tess's lap in a lilac party dress, her legs encased in braces up to her knees. Ever had a mild form of cerebral palsy, but physical therapy and daily hippotherapy sessions had increased her strength and ability to the point where she didn't rely on her crutches much anymore. Surrounded by horses her entire life, Lexi was still in awe of the therapy that utilized the animals' movements to treat people with injuries and physical disabilities.

"She certainly is," Lexi agreed. "Cole told me the day may come when she won't need the braces."

"Isn't Cole such a darling with her?" Judy asked. "All the Langtry men are angels except that Shane. He can't keep it in his pants long enough to—"

"Mom, please." Lexi held up her hand. "Let's not go down this road again. Enjoy the party and stop trying to fight my battles from years ago."

"Who's talking years? I've seen the way you two look at each other. And just the other day, Charlotte Hargrove told me—"

Not wanting to hear any more, Lexi left her mother and walked down the hallway to the bathroom, allowing herself a glance in Ever's room. Cutely decorated with its feminine frills, she remembered the animated way Shane had described the low wall-length banquette he'd built under the window so Ever could easily sit on it without assistance.

Inside the bathroom, she locked the door and rested against it. Light cornflower-blue paint decorated the upper half of the wall over white wainscoting. A tiny walker stood near the white pedestal sink. Grip bars of various heights lined the wall next to the tub so she could lift herself out without relying on someone to help her. Shane had thought of everything.

She had to hand it to him. And in his care for his little niece, Lexi knew Shane still missed Dylan, even though he refused to speak his name.

The walls suddenly seemed to close in on Lexi. Her chest tightened and she desperately needed the freedom of wide open spaces, preferably on the back of a horse. Ducking out the kitchen door, she walked to the side of the house, safely out of view.

Lexi slid to the ground and closed her eyes. Flashes from that Colorado hospital room flooded her vision and she wrapped her arms around herself. This time of year was the hardest and memories she'd rather forget invaded almost every thought.

"Lexi?" a voice called to her. "Are you all right?"

Her head shot up. Silhouetted against the sun, Shane sat astride Ransom. Shielding the light from her eyes, Lexi wasn't able to see the other riders, but she quickly made out Dream Catcher's unusual silver dappled legs and assumed their friend Clay Tanner was astride the horse. Considering the other horses she saw were under her care, the riders must be students.

"I'm fine," she said. "I pulled a muscle earlier and it's acting up—hardly worth mentioning. What are you doing here? I thought you'd want to be miles away from a house full of women and baby talk."

"Shane finally let us out of the classroom," one of the young students called out while the rest of them laughed.

Shane maneuvered his mount away from Lexi. "You'll be in the arena tomorrow. I warned you this wasn't all fun and games." Nudging the horse forward with his legs he nodded at Lexi. "Are you sure you're okay? You look awfully pale."

"Thank you, but I'm good," Lexi choked out. She wanted to forget the past and find some happiness in her life.

"See you later," the students called out.

Lexi waved, closed her eyes and wondered if her son had the rodeo bug...wherever he was.

"Who was that?" Hunter rode up alongside Shane.

"That was trouble with a capital *T*," Shane grumbled. "Let me give you some advice, kid. Don't get married."

"You and Trouble were married?" Hunter asked. "Wow, she's pretty."

"No, Trouble and I weren't married," Shane said. "And her name's Lexi. We could have been, though, if I hadn't screwed things up."

"What'd you do?"

"*I* got married." Shane looked over his shoulder. "The trail narrows up ahead when we get closer to the stream. Let the horse do the work, they know these trails."

Shane nudged his horse ahead of Hunter, ending the

conversation. He didn't want to remember what he'd lost with Lexi. The pain he'd caused reflected in her eyes whenever she looked at him, and the guilt he carried for breaking her heart was always present.

Lexi had remained close to his family, and he'd managed a friendship with her, but for the longest time, he'd vowed never to be alone with her. He didn't think either one of their hearts could take it. But once things began to change between them in recent months, Shane had allowed himself to dream of the day she'd let her guard down enough to spend time alone with him, secretly vowing to make things right between them.

At the top of his game now, Shane had a school to run with Chase and a full schedule of rodeos to ride in. The world all-around title eluded him so far and he was determined to win it before Chase did. With the help of Jesse and Cole, who filled in when needed, along with the rest of their teaching staff, he and Chase still actively competed in the rodeo and against each other. Friendly in their competition, the boys were in a tight race to bring home the grand prize. Shane wanted that championship more than anything…well, almost.

Since they'd broken ground on the new facility, Shane had found himself in Lexi's vicinity more often than not. It was all he could do to prevent her from distracting him in his quest to win that coveted belt buckle. Being able to say Ride 'em High! was owned by a world all-around champion would help make the school the best in the country. Their facility offered everything from rodeo clown bullfighting and rough-stock training to barrel racing and roping, and Shane wanted his students to walk away with the confidence and knowledge it took to best any competitor they came across. What better way to do that than with a champion as your instructor?

"How about a drink at Slater's Mill later?" Shane asked his best friend, Clay Tanner, when they arrived back at the stables. "I need some adult time, if you know what I mean."

"All right." Clay removed his saddle. "You need help returning the women to their cars?"

"Nope, Chase has those honors." Shane removed his straw Stetson and wiped his brow with the back of his arm. The last day of June meant it was the start of the sweltering season. They'd designed the new facility with an indoor arena, and divided it in half. Hippotherapy had one side of the building and the rodeo school had the other. It would allow horse and rider to work without the Texas sun exhausting them. But at Kay's insistence, until the official ribbon-cutting next week, instructors and students had to ride outside. Classes would be taught at the picnic tables near the main corral.

A few hours later, Shane made his way back to the main house for a shower and a change of clothes. After double-checking that Chase was staying in as the bunkhouse den dad for the night, Shane headed out for a kid-free evening. Slater's Mill usual Saturday night crowd gathered near the bar. Different ball games played on the screens while Elvis Watts and his band belted out a cover of "Red Solo Cup." Lifting a longneck to his mouth, he stopped midswig when he noticed a familiar sexy number shake and shimmy on the dance floor in turquoise boots and jeans so tight they must have been painted on.

Making his way through the crowd, he two-stepped next to her. "Hey, sugar britches, how's that pulled muscle?"

Lexi swung to face him, not losing rhythm with the music. "It was a polite way of saying none of your business, Shane. Don't take it personally."

Before he responded, she danced her way to the edge of the floor and dropped into the circular booth where the regulars congregated. The roster had changed over the past year. Shane's cousin Brandon and his wife Vicki had a little one to tend to at home, but Brandon still popped in from time to time to help bartend for his dad, Charlie, who owned the honky-tonk. Since adopting Ever, Cole and Tess stayed home most nights. Jesse and Miranda had two of their own on the way. The crowd had dwindled down to Bridgett, a waitress in town, Lexi, Clay and Chase. Shane wondered which of them would be the next to jump ship. At this rate, he was willing to bet he'd be the last one standing.

Placing his empty on the bar, he looked down the row of men, most sitting by themselves. Men once like him, now past their prime and alone. Was this his future? A lonely old man at a bar, night after night?

Kendra Anderson, Lexi's cousin, slipped in next to him and handed Charlie her orders.

"When do you go on break?" Shane asked the well-rounded waitress.

"In about twenty minutes." Her red tank top strained and dipped in the right places, leaving little to the imagination. "Let me guess, you're going to drill me about Lexi again?"

"I need your advice—" Shane halted at her laughter.

"Either marry her or forget her, but stop flounder-flopping about it already."

"We have a special guest singer tonight," Elvis boomed from the stage. "Let's give a big round of applause for our hometown girl, Lexi Lawson."

Lexi slinked across the stage with her arms in the air, rousing the crowd. She turned her back to the audience and picked up a vintage red Fender Telecaster, tuning it to her satisfaction. When she played a twangy, steady beat, the crowd roared, recognizing the tune. Facing her audience, she strode to the microphone, owning the stage. Looking right at him, she began singing Taylor Swift's "I Knew You Were Trouble."

Mesmerized for a moment, he felt like they were alone and she was singing only to him, even if it wasn't the nicest of songs. Breaking her gaze, Shane threw a ten on the bar and headed for the door. Her voice was as intoxicating as she was beautiful, and if he stayed a second longer, he'd wind up making a fool of himself in front of the entire town.

The crowd screaming at her feet and the blinding lights didn't block out the sight of Shane leaving. Opening a bottle of water that Bridgett handed her from the side of the stage, Lexi knew she'd probably upset Shane when she directed the song to him. Over the past few years she had watched the man drift from one woman to the next while he never cared how hard it was on her. Lexi still wasn't sure how much he'd legitimately changed, but she had noticed he wasn't catting around like he used to.

A part of her saw the old Shane she'd fallen in love

with start to reemerge, but despite his newfound loyalty to her, she also knew the man had tunnel vision when it came to winning the championship. Admittedly, Lexi wasn't sure what kind of life she'd be able to build with Shane when she was a little jealous of the dream he chased. Truth was, she blamed their demise on the rodeo.

The band invited her to sing a few more songs, and when she finally stepped off the stage with an adrenaline rush and smile of satisfaction, she searched the bar, but Shane still wasn't anywhere in sight. Not that it mattered. She was perfectly capable of having a nice evening out without Shane Langtry. She'd been doing it for years, but if she was honest with herself, she'd concede that she did enjoy having him around.

Bridgett leaned into her once she was back in the booth. "I assure you he left empty-handed tonight."

"Bridge, I'm not his keeper." Lexi pulled her hair up and off her shoulders. "He's a free man."

"Oh, please, Shane hasn't been a free man since you two broke up after high school. Someday you two will get a clue," Bridgett said.

Kendra set a folded note and two beers on the table and popped the tops off. "Compliments of the man in the tan shirt at the bar."

The three women turned to look at the stranger. He lifted a hand to wave and tipped his hat as Lexi read his scribble.

"Did you read this?" Lexi asked.

Kendra shook her head.

Lexi's eyes narrowed as she rose from the booth, grabbed both bottles and honed in on the man.

"Oh, dear, what's she going to do?" Kendra asked. "Charlie's going to be ticked off at whatever it is."

"This isn't going to be good," Bridgett replied. "I'll settle our tab because I have a feeling this night is about to end."

Weaving in and out of the crowd, Lexi approached the tawny-haired, middle-aged man with a mustache in dire need of a trim. She lifted her hands in front of her, the longnecks dangling from her fingers.

"Did you send these to my table?"

He winked. "I sure did."

"So you thought it was appropriate to ask—how was it you put it?" Lexi unfolded the note and read it aloud. "For a *redhead-and-brunette sandwich?* Honestly, if that's the extent of your creativity, I think we'd be incredibly bored."

"I, uh, I can teach you a few things." The man leered at her chest, making his greasy hair all the more obvious.

"Really? I can teach you a few things, too." Lexi winked in return.

"I bet you can." He openly gave her body a once-over while making a disgusting clicking noise with his tongue. "Where do we start?"

"Lesson one." Lexi held the beers above his crotch and poured out the contents, then slammed the bottles down on the bar. "Asking a woman and her friend for a threesome is just plain rude."

"Dammit, Lexi!" Charlie yelled from behind the bar. "Stop pouring drinks on my customers."

"Sorry, Charlie." Lexi laughed and headed toward the door.

* * *

Shane sat in his Jeep and listened to Lexi sing. Standing and staring at her in the middle of a crowded bar sure didn't do his heart any favors. No, it was safer outside where he wouldn't be tempted to rush the stage and kiss her in front of the entire town.

Lexi and Bridgett burst through Slater's double doors laughing hysterically. Unnoticed, he watched them as they walked by. The two women climbed into Lexi's black Mustang convertible and drove off, their laughter carrying across the parking lot. A man thundered out of the bar behind them, swearing at their car.

Shane ventured a guess at what had happened from the way the man wiped at his jeans. It wasn't the first time Lexi dumped a drink on someone. He wondered what the poor sap had done to warrant such a response. She had a fiery temper when it came to men and he felt he was to blame for her defensive attitude. The country girl who left for college never returned. In her place was an extremely independent woman with walls so high, no one could possibly scale them—but he would damn sure try.

"What are you doing out here? I thought we were getting a drink." Clay braced his arms on the roll bar above the Jeep's passenger seat. "I saw Lexi and Bridgett peel out of here. You look unscathed, so who was her victim?"

"Some guy." Shane shrugged. "Listen, I'm not up for another round in there tonight. Care to grab something at the Still 'n' Grill instead?"

"When are you going to admit you've never gotten over her?" Clay laughed when Shane tried to take a swing at him. "Hey, I just call 'em as I see 'em. You've had two loves in your life. Lexi and the rodeo. Swallow your pride and tell her, because you've exhausted the entire female population in town. Literally and figuratively."

"Okay, Mr. P.I." Having a private investigator for a best friend made keeping a secret next to impossible. "Here's a fact for you—she's not in love with me."

"Really? Because from where I stand, she never stopped loving you." Clay looked across the parking lot toward Shelby Street. "Why don't you go after her and end this insanity? My God, you've been celibate for how many months now and don't tell me it's because you suddenly have the urge to wait until marriage."

"I've been busy building the school."

"You've been busy pining over Lexi," Clay flatly stated. "I'm not the only one who's noticed. Just about all of Ramblewood was at Jesse and Miranda's wedding and we all saw the look on both of your faces when you escorted Lexi down that aisle."

"What do you want me do?" Shane threw his hands in the air. "Knock on her door and say, 'Hey, Lex, I love you, let's get married'? She'd annihilate me and you know it."

"This isn't an eight-second ride, Shane." Clay laughed. "You don't have to charge the woman like a bull out of the chute. But you could up the ante and do something special for her."

"Like what?" The thought of surprising Lexi piqued Shane's interest.

"You know her better than I do. You'll come up with an idea." Clay playfully punched Shane in the arm.

"Come on, let's head to the Still 'n' Grill and we'll try to come up with a plan over a beer."

Shane doubted one or two surprises would convince Lexi to trust him again, but he'd do almost anything if it meant winning her heart.

## Chapter 3

"First day of groundwork, men. I know it's early but we have a lot to cover today before the ribbon cutting." Shane led his fifteen students from the bunkhouse after a predawn workout and hearty breakfast they'd prepared together. "Some of you are more experienced than others and some of you don't have any experience. That's all right. There's no ride limit, but I don't want you to push yourself to the point of injury, either."

"These are our saddle broncs," Chase explained, taking over from Shane. "They're larger than our barebacks. I want to reiterate to everyone that we have zero tolerance for animal abuse. If we even suspect it, you are out of here. We do not condone or authorize the use of cattle prods or sharpened spurs in any rough-stock event. Before you enter any chute here on the ranch, your rowels will be checked, so if they're sharp, get them off."

When Shane and Chase designed the monthlong intensive rodeo class, they did it with serious competitors in mind. They offered two monthlong sessions for junior-rodeo children in the summer and more personalized programs for people of all ages the remainder of the year.

Stressing safety first, Ride 'em High! was one of the few schools in the country with a weeklong classroom schedule. They decided to include a grueling conditioning program to ensure the students were in top physical condition. At the ranch's small fitness center, a trainer met with the students every day and put them through rodeo boot camp to build their core muscles. When the kids left for home, the trainers recommended they join a local fitness center to maintain their strength and flexibility.

"Most of our competition broncs are six to seven years old," Shane continued. "The ones we're using today are older and not as feisty. We don't make these horses buck. It's a natural instinct and they're bred to buck. A good portion of the horses you see in competition are there because no one could ride them. Some were untrainable, others are rescues.

"Hunter, you're up." Shane waved the boy to the front. "We're starting off this morning with some saddle work."

Shane proceeded to explain the difference between saddle bronc and bareback rigging, then introduced the local college kids, home for the summer, who had volunteered to check riggings and help the students.

A saddle had been set on a large barrel attached to a wide base for training purposes. Hunter climbed on and set his boots high in the stirrups. With pointed toes, he rocked his hips slightly and squared his shoulders with the saddle. He gripped the thick braided rein and held it out over the center of the saddle swells, his other hand up in the air as if he were swearing on a stack of bibles.

"Tuck your chin a little." Shane pointed to the hole between the swells and the seat. "Look here the entire time. Visualize setting your spurs above the horse's shoulders. Raise your legs and tighten your abs."

Shane ran through the steps of riding a saddle bronc, amazed at the ease Hunter exhibited in every movement. Many of the kids reminded Shane of himself at that age. Determined, confident and willing to do anything to fulfill their dreams of turning pro. He couldn't help but wonder if this was how it would have felt training Dylan.

"My abs are about to give out!" Hunter yelled through his last mock ride.

"You're working your core." Shane placed a hand on his shoulder to still him. "This is why we're working you so hard on the stabilizing platform and the vertical leg raises. A weak core will get you thrown. Great job, Hunter. Who's next?"

"This is one of the toughest events to master," Chase said. "But I promise you, after this workout you will feel muscles you didn't think you had and you'll thank us for it."

Everyone took their turn, including Chase, who admitted he liked the barrel for an alternative abdominal workout.

"You must synchronize every moment with the horse in order to get the most fluid ride possible." Shane shrugged on his own vest. "And if you don't mark your ride, you won't receive a score. To mark, your heels must touch the horse's shoulders at the first jump from the chute."

Shane hopped the fence and made his way to the chute, where a horse waited. Measuring his hack rein over the back of the horse, he grabbed hold of the thick braided rope and slid into the saddle, placing his feet all the way into the stirrups. Lifting up his rein hand, he nodded and the gate opened.

On the saddle bronc, in the middle of the arena, was the only place he could completely forget about the past and concentrate on the moment.

Lexi awoke before the first rooster crowed. You wouldn't find anyone sleeping in at the Lawsons' house. Sixth-generation farmers, they were champing at the bit to start their day long before the sun came up. Lexi's younger brother, Nash, maintained the petting zoo animals while their father, uncle and cousins tended the fields. Her mother and aunt ran the market and gift store.

Situated right off the interstate, the 130-acre farm dated back to 1820. The original barn had been converted into a retail market and gourmet kitchen in the early fifties, catering to tourists as they drove through the state. Lexi's sister Mazie learned to cook in that kitchen, leading her to open the Bed & Biscuit in the center of town.

The Lawsons gave visitors the true farm experience,

from the petting zoo to fresh picked produce, some of which the customers were allowed to harvest themselves. Strawberry and pumpkin season filled the fields with people, but the two-acre corn maze around Halloween drew the biggest crowds.

The horses were Lexi's domain. Before showering, she headed down to the barn and fed the family's handful of horses. Once she checked her schedule for the day, she saddled Autumn's Secret and surveyed the property. Their morning and evening routine allowed Lexi to escape from the rest of the world.

Robert Smith Surtees wrote, "There is no secret so close as that between a rider and his horse." The quote had inspired the name of her mare, which she helped foal on the Langtrys' farm the first fall she returned from Cornell. Seeing how much Lexi was enamored with the horse, Joe Langtry bestowed the mare upon her—a little assurance she'd stay in town. She trained Autumn herself, and while man's best friend worked for some, horses bore Lexi's secrets, and she was confident they wouldn't be shared.

Lexi swung by the Magpie for a cup of coffee since she had to wait for the Critter Care animal hospital to open its doors. Shorted on tetanus vaccines in yesterday's shipment, she needed to borrow a few doses for the pregnant mares due to foal in the next six weeks. Lexi had had more problems of late with her supplier and needed Ashleigh to research a new one before the week's end.

"I have a bone to pick with you," Charlie Slater said from the corner table.

"Take a number," Lexi replied while Bridgett waited

for her to order, doing little to keep a straight face. "If Maggie's made any banana nut muffins today, I'll have one of those and a large coffee, extra hot in case I have to pour it on some unsuspecting patron."

"If you're going to chase my customers off, you can't come around the Mill anymore." Charlie never referred to his own last name when talking about his bar.

"Bridge, make mine to go." Pulling a few bills out of her pocket, she handed them to her friend. "I'll cover Charlie's breakfast to make up for the one, possibly two, beers that rude boy might've ordered. Oh, wait, that's right, he did order them—and wore them."

"If you don't tell Charlie what that guy wanted the other night, I will." Bridgett gave Lexi her change. "You were justified."

"I don't want you buying my breakfast." Charlie swiveled to face her. "I want you to stop assaulting people. One of these days, you're going to start a riot. That man was furious."

"Let him think what he wants." Lexi shrugged. "I'm sure there was a time or two that I dumped a drink on someone for lesser reasons. Let it go."

"If you say so." Bridgett placed a muffin in a white paper bag and handed Lexi her order. "I'll catch up with you at the ribbon cutting this afternoon."

Lexi stopped by Charlie's table on her way out. "People bought more drinks when I got on that stage than they did all night with Elvis playing the same drivel he plays every Saturday. I did you a favor, so the way I see it, we're even. Trust me when I say, you don't want his kind around there."

A few minutes later Lexi pulled into the animal hospital's parking lot. She knew Mazie probably saw her from the kitchen window of the Bed & Biscuit next door and would want to talk. When the old Victorian went up for sale a few years ago, Mazie realized its proximity to the animal hospital and the bark park would attract future clients by catering to their pets' every need.

Checking her watch, Lexi knew fifteen minutes wasn't enough time to visit with her sister. She loved Mazie, but her propensity to chat for hours wore thin when Lexi had a packed day ahead of her. Relieved when she saw Dr. Cerf park his SUV, she quickly picked up the vaccines and headed to Bridle Dance.

Lexi's cell phone rang.

"Good morning, Mazie," Lexi said without even looking at the caller ID.

"You should have stopped in. I'm pulling one of your favorites out of the oven right now. Spinach and mushroom frittata. Do you have time to turn around and have a little breakfast? We haven't had a chance to really talk in a few weeks."

"I'm sorry, my schedule is super tight today." Lexi turned off the main road. "I have a lot to do before the ribbon cutting, but I promise we'll catch up there. I love you, sis, but right now, I do have to go."

Lexi dropped the phone on the seat next to her and rolled her shoulders to ease the stress she felt starting to build. She loved her job, but some days, the constant running between ranches wore thin.

The rearing bronze horse statues at the entrance to Bridle Dance glinted in the morning light. The fully expanded foliage of the pecan trees shaded the entire length of the dirt road, while puddles of water formed near their trunks from the ranch's buried drip irrigation. Lexi's father had helped Joe Langtry design the system to maintain constant water levels during the summer dry spells.

A white canopy stood off to the side of the new equine facility in preparation for the afternoon ceremony. The massive building with beige siding sat behind a series of corrals used for the rodeo school. The rear of the building incorporated secluded pastures for hippotherapy use. In front of the double carriage-house-inspired entrance, two statues were draped in dark cloth and tied at the bottom, waiting for their unveiling in a few hours.

Local cowboys gathered around the nearest round pen. "When are you going to marry me, Lexi?" one of them called out to her.

"When you're old enough to shave," she hollered back.

"I'm twenty-one. I'm legal." The other men egged him on. "You don't know what you're missing."

"You boys go on." Nicolino waved them off. "Good morning, Lexi. Will you be at the grand opening today? Ella was talking about you this morning, saying how long it's been since she's seen you."

Shouts came from within one of the corrals. With a quick nod in her direction, Shane sat atop a bareback and raised his arm in the air to signal the chute gate to open. Bucking wildly, man and horse twisted and turned through the dust-filled eight-second ride. With all the flair and skill he'd exhibit in a competitive event, Shane grabbed his pickup man as he rode by and dismounted with the grace of a gymnast, bowing her way.

Lexi shook her head and redirected her attention to Nicolino. Starting out as a ranch hand fresh from Italy when Lexi was in grade school, the newcomer had barely spoken a word of English when Joe hired him. He'd grown to be a part of their family and married Kay's niece Ella Slater, the eldest daughter of her brother Charlie. Five kids and two loyal decades later, Cole had promoted him to general operations manager in January. Raised in the *butteri* cowboy tradition, he opted to wear heavy cotton pants and a wide-brimmed hat instead of chaps and a Stetson. The mazzarella staff he carried was used to threaten unruly teenagers more than it was to herd the horses.

"I'll be there." Lexi looked in the stalls. "I have a couple of mares to vaccinate and some paperwork to fill out here, then I'll return after making my rounds."

"Don't you want to stick around and see the show Shane's putting on for you?" Nicolino feigned shock that she'd dare leave in the middle of such an event.

"Eh, you've seen one, you've seen them all."

Nicolino's laughter followed her through the open doors.

Rivaling the size of a football field, the country French stone-and-stucco facility featured Craftsman-style windows and timber archways. A ground-level covered walkway with exposed rafters encircled the building. A large second-story cupola was perched atop the center of the sand-colored structure and housed the ranch's main office, while miniature cupolas lined the roof on either side, allowing extra light to filter through to the stalls below.

Joe Langtry had called the building his horse mansion. A better description didn't exist in Lexi's mind. Grooms and trainers hurried about, placing the finishing touches on everything before today's events.

Lexi made her way down the exposed timber interior hallway. Horse stalls with full-height mahogany-stained doors and bars prevented cribbing or chewing. Otherwise the horses could gnaw on the wood and wear down their teeth or cause colic and stomach ulcers.

Not wanting to waste time today with so much to do, she plucked her phone from her pocket and called Billy. "Vaccination lesson today. Meet me in the office so I can show you the forms and then we'll check on Crystal."

Crystal was carrying Joe Langtry's dream baby. Dam Tenny Bay and sire King's Obsession were two of the highest earners in cutting horse competition. Bridle Dance didn't own either horse, but Joe had arranged the match before his death last year. Determined to see the surrogacy all the way through, the Langtry family had continued with Joe's plans and were anxiously anticipating the foal's arrival. It was the very last project Joe set in motion, and eleven months later, the day was almost upon them.

A few hours later, Lexi gathered her bags and headed outside the stables. She loved a day without problems, especially when she finished ahead of schedule. She swung by the rodeo school and saw Kay Langtry resting her arms on the top rail of the round pen.

"You got it!" Kay shouted to one of the teens astride a bucking horse. "You boys look great out there."

Shane stood outside the pen, Ever perched on a bale of hay next to him. "Ride 'em high like Uncle Shane!"

the little girl shouted. Shane lifted her onto his shoulders, giving her a high ride of her own.

"He's really good with her and the rest of the hippotherapy kids," Kay commented, her mood pensive. "How different everything was a year ago."

Lexi draped her arm across the older woman's shoulders and rested her head against Kay's. Joe's heart attack shocked the entire community and the family infighting that ensued for months afterward had taken its toll on the Langtry matriarch, but Kay stuck with her husband's wishes and built the nonprofit hippotherapy facility. Joe wanted a place where anyone who needed help could get it, paying only what they could afford. Converted bunkhouses accommodated families from out of town during long-term therapy. After a battle with Shane and Chase that would have torn most families apart forever, everything finally came to fruition.

"I can't tell you how glad I'll be when this day is over," Kay confessed. "I know it sounds strange, but honestly, once that ribbon is cut on the front door, I'll feel like this family will finally be at peace."

A gangly boy approached Shane and handed Ever a bottle of water. Lifting her from his shoulder, Shane returned the little girl to her hay bale alongside some of the other hippotherapy kids while he watched the students and joined the boy at the rail.

Lexi smiled at his inherent teaching instincts. "I don't think I've seen Shane this content before."

"That Hunter Rathbone sure does dote on him." Kay nodded in the direction of the boy next to Shane. "I can't believe how much he acts like Shane at that age."

Hunter stood on the second rail and waved his hat in

the air to cheer on his classmate. His features no longer shadowed, Lexi saw a mop of dark brown hair, ice-blue eyes and a strong angular jaw with the hint of a cleft chin. She felt her stomach turn ever so slightly at the remarkable resemblance to Shane.

Lexi white-knuckled her grip on her satchel. "Where—where is he from?"

"Colorado," Kay replied. "Shane calls him his *Mini-Me*."

The ground beneath Lexi all but disappeared. Squatting down on the grass next to the pen, she feigned fumbling through her bag. Confident she'd regained her footing, she stood and tried to cover her bewilderment. "I must have left my camera in the truck. I—I thought the school would draw mostly a local crowd."

"Next door or the next continent, I think Hunter would follow Shane wherever he taught," Kay continued. "You should hear the child prattle on how Shane's his hero. When Hunter heard about the school, he begged his parents to send him here. Good heavens, are you all right?"

"It must be the heat." Lexi's knees betrayed her and she found herself back on the ground. "I just need a cold shower and I'll be fine."

The events vividly replayed in her mind. Years ago, in late October, Shane surprised Lexi and whisked her away for a romantic weekend at the Devil's Thumb Ranch Resort, a stone's throw from her college campus. They didn't emerge from the cabin until Monday morning, and she barely made it to her first class. Perfect in every way imaginable, their getaway reassured

Lexi that they could maintain their relationship while she continued school.

A few weeks later, when Lexi discovered she was pregnant, she rationalized that it had happened for a reason. Planning to have a family one day, Lexi wasn't sure she wanted one now. When her doctor confirmed a July due date, she put faith in perfect timing. She'd be able to continue with college in the fall without missing any classes. Not wanting to discuss it with Shane over the phone, she decided to wait and tell him in person, during winter break. Only he had a surprise of his own.

Devastated by his infidelity, Lexi was scandalized by his quick decision to marry Sharon Vincent, so she immediately returned to school. Clearly showing by spring break, Lexi lied to her family and said she'd enrolled in an internship to avoid coming home. She hated the deception, but after hearing how happy Shane was with his son, Lexi didn't want to ruin his new family. The entire town knew he didn't have an ounce of love for Sharon but Shane tolerated her for Dylan's sake and Lexi resolved that someday he'd learn to love his wife.

Determined to move forward with her career, Lexi painfully gave her baby up for adoption immediately following his birth, believing he'd have a better life with a strong, stable family. It was the hardest thing she'd ever had to do. A mother should never have to give up her child, but it was a sacrifice she willingly made for her son's future.

Not wanting to wonder if every child she saw on the street was hers, Lexi transferred to New York's Cornell University.

A day hadn't passed when she didn't think of him,

but she refused to doubt her decision. When she found out Dylan wasn't Shane's, the realization that they could have been a family if he hadn't cheated on her drove her to pieces some nights.

On her visits home, she avoided him at all costs, fearing he would know what she'd done. No one questioned her attitude, since his betrayal was public knowledge, but the guilt she felt whenever someone told her how shattered Shane was and how much he'd changed from a family man, to being wild and reckless since Tab took Dylan away, almost killed her.

Not allowing herself another glance at the boy again, Lexi took Kay's outstretched hand and managed to stand. *This can't be happening.*

"Something's wrong with Lexi." Shane started to walk toward his mother and Nicolino as they escorted Lexi to her car. "Ever, stay right there and don't go near the rails. Hunter, will you watch her for a minute?"

"Come on, bro." Chase beckoned to him from the arena. "Let's show them how it's done."

"In a minute." Shane headed in Lexi's direction until he heard her car start and saw Nicolino pat her trunk, seemingly unconcerned as she drove out of the parking area.

A few hours in this heat was enough to wear anyone out and Shane reasoned Lexi had probably overdone it, rushing around trying to be Wonder Woman. The rising temperatures were getting to all of them and Shane decided to end class early so the kids could go down to the river for a swim and cool off before they demonstrated some of their techniques for the crowd later.

Opting to stay behind, Shane had successfully avoided spending any length of time around children since he lost Dylan. One-or two-day rodeo clinics meant attachments were impossible. When Cole and Tess adopted Ever, he became an instant uncle to a precocious four-year-old. By her fifth birthday in April she'd grown to be such a part of his life, he actually sought her out every day. It pained him to think he'd once stood in the way of her progress at the ranch. In eight months, her ability to walk doubled. And with a hippotherapy facility in her own backyard, she didn't have to travel the three hours to therapy anymore.

Once Shane saw the children and adults come to Dance of Hope for therapy evaluation before the grand opening, he finally understood why this project was so dear to his father. It might be too late to apologize for trying to block the facility from being built, but it didn't mean he couldn't do everything in his power to make his family proud of him. He not only wanted their approval, but he also wanted Lexi's.

With all the children on the ranch, thoughts of Dylan had hit him harder than they had in a decade. Shane wondered if the teen ever sat in the stands during his rodeo events. There were times he caught himself checking the rider roster for Tab's name even though Shane knew he'd long since retired.

Plodding toward the small stand-alone office behind the main stables, Shane entered the air-conditioned building. A built-in table wrapped around the entire room and the computers were connected to the main office inside the barn, saving people from traipsing across the courtyard. Shane logged on to the system and opened the web browser.

Cole dropped paperwork into the inbox on the wall as he entered the office. "I'm surprised you didn't go with everyone else down to the river."

"Nah." Shane typed *Dylan Fanning* into the search engine. "I have some things to finish up."

"Don't do it, Shane." Cole stood behind him, staring down at the words on the screen. "Leave it in the past. You know he has a good life with Tab. Why are you dredging this up now?"

*Because all these kids remind me of what might have been.*

"Note to self, buy a laptop so I can have some privacy." If he knew more about Dylan, he'd have some peace and closure. Anything was better than not knowing. At the very least Shane wanted to find out if he was riding in any of the junior rodeos.

"For the little you use the internet, I'd go with an iPad," Cole said.

"You know you sound just like Dad?" Shane glanced up at his brother, wishing Cole would leave him alone. This wasn't a moment he wanted to share with anyone.

"Dad would have told you to look it up on your phone. It's capable of doing the same thing."

Shane continued to stare at his brother incredulously. Turning back toward the screen, he let his finger hover above the enter key. Shane swore silently, knowing his brother was right. He pressed and held the delete key until all the letters in Dylan's name disappeared. Annoyed with himself, he stormed from the office and went to check on Siempre, one of their newborn foals.

Animals loved you unconditionally, no matter how much of an ass you made of yourself.

Later that afternoon Mayor Darren Fox stood before a microphone in front of the equine facility, Kay by his side. "Thank you for joining us today for this momentous event. I am pleased to introduce Kay Langtry, CEO of Dance of Hope."

Applause spread throughout the ranch when Kay took her place at the microphone, the townsfolk gathered before her.

"Thank you." Pulling a tissue from her pocket, Kay looked into the crowd. "Dance of Hope was my husband's dream. A year ago, I stood by Joe's side when he started designing this facility. And though he's not with us today, I know he's up there watching.

"No amount of words can describe my gratitude to everyone who's participated in this venture. Cole, Jesse, Shane and Chase. My four boys carried out their father's dream, adding the Ride 'em High! Rodeo School to the original plans. Your father would have been so proud of you, as I am today. I love you with all my heart."

The Langtry brothers surrounded Kay, linking their arms in a protective circle around their mother.

Shane looked skyward. "I love you, Dad. This is for you."

Each brother made a brief speech of his own, splitting off to stand beside the covered statues on either side of the facility's entrance.

Jesse and Cole tugged on the cloth, revealing a life-size bronze statue of Ever atop Poncho, her hippotherapy horse, with Joe by her side.

"To say our father was smitten with my daughter is an understatement," Cole said. "She inspired him to help others and I'm grateful she had the opportunity to know her grandfather." Holding up an enlarged framed copy of the inspiration photograph for the statue, Cole continued.

"My mother took this the first time dad met Ever. The photo sat on his desk and a day didn't go by that he didn't look at it. Together, we can look upon his memory as he saw it."

Shane and Chase pulled away another cloth, uncovering a bucking horse with a younger version of Joe in the saddle, one arm in the air.

"Our father was a rancher by blood," Shane said, "but a true rodeo cowboy at heart. Back in his day, he outrode the best of them and taught all of us and many of you how to get in that saddle and stay in it." Holding up a photograph, he said, "This is our father's last competitive ride. He held on for eight seconds then walked away from the sport. The next day Cole was born and the tradition was handed down to his children."

The boys joined their mother at the entrance to the facility, the five of them reaching up to unveil the sign above the carriage house doors:

Dance of Hope & Ride 'em High!
In memory of Joseph Langtry

Lifting the oversize silver scissors, Kay cut the white ribbon spanning the facility's doors. The crowd applauded when the doors swung wide. Leading the way, Kay walked into the stone entryway that divided the two companies and hung both photographs on the awaiting wall hooks.

She turned and opened her arms to the crowd. "Welcome, Ramblewood!"

After the facility tours, the waitstaff bustled in and out of the tent while people milled about the property. Shane swore he shook hands with more people this afternoon than in his entire life.

"You had a great dad," Hunter said beside him. "I think I would have liked him."

"He'd have liked you, too." Shane ruffled the boy's hair. "Let's get something to eat."

Shane had spotted Lexi in the crowd throughout the afternoon, glad to see she felt up to attending the ceremony. Usually composed and in control, she seemed a bit harried and hung near his immediate vicinity, yet still managed to keep her distance. He resisted the urge to check on her, as he was busy with the media. The *Ramblewood Gazette* took photographs while Nola West interviewed Chase for KWTT's evening news.

"Allow me to introduce myself." A man held out his hand to Shane. "I'm Ryan Hammershimer, from Keeping it Reel Pictures, and we'd like to build a reality show around you and your rodeo school."

Shane laughed. "You want to give me a television show?" Wait until his brothers heard about this.

"What are you doing?" Mazie peered over Lexi's shoulder. "Are you taking pictures of that kid?"

"What kid?" Startled, Lexi quickly saved the photo of Hunter to her phone. "I—I'm trying to get a shot of those statues. They're truly a work of art. I can't believe they were commissioned this quickly."

"What are you hiding?" Mazie insisted. "That was no picture of a statue. What's up?"

"I'm not hiding anything, and even if I were, why would I tell you?" Lexi snapped.

"Well, thanks a lot." Mazie turned her back on Lexi and started to walk away.

"I'm sorry Mazie, I didn't mean that." Lexi caught up to her sister and grabbed her arm. "I have a foal on my mind. I truly am sorry."

"You need a vacation, sis," Mazie said. "You can't worry about work all the time."

"This coming from someone who eats, sleeps and breathes the Bed & Biscuit."

"That's different and you know it. I happen to live there. You don't live in a stable." She turned to leave. "I'm going to get you something to eat, you look like you need some sustenance."

Angling away from her sister, Lexi tried to move closer to Hunter without him noticing. When he laughed, her breath caught in her throat. *He has my laugh.* A mother dreamed of the day she heard her child's laughter for the first time. Today she heard hers.

Lexi watched Shane and Hunter pose for a series of photos for a man she'd never seen before. The stranger looked out of place in perfectly creased jeans and a snap-front shirt that was probably fresh out of the package. Side by side, Hunter looked almost identical to Shane at that age. How could someone not question this child's paternity, especially after knowing Shane's reputation when it came to women?

Lexi had lived wondering about her son for too long. She wanted proof the boy in front of her was hers, but swore it wouldn't change anything. She needed the confirmation for her own peace of mind and sanity. Nobody else needed to know. She turned and stumbled over one of the folding chairs as she tried to escape the confines of the crowd.

"Lexi?" A strong male hand lightly touched her shoulder. "Are you all right?"

Clay Tanner. It had to be fate, Lexi thought. "If I retain your services it's illegal for you to disclose my case to anyone, right?"

"Private investigators don't have that privilege in this state, but you wouldn't have to worry." Clay ushered Lexi outside the tent and away from prying ears. "You don't have to hire me, Lex. Just tell me what you need and I assure you it will remain confidential."

"Promise me, Clay," Lexi pleaded. Her heart beat wildly in her chest. Her throat began to close, tears threatening to spill with one more blink of her eyes. "I need your help."

"You have it. Sit down before you pass out and then you'll really have some explaining to do."

Lexi looked toward the facility and the people gathered around the Langtry family, Hunter still by Shane's side.

"Tell me what you need." Clay said.

Lexi breathlessly gripped her friend's arm. "I need you to find out if Hunter's my son."

# Chapter 4

"You think that boy is your son?" Clay led Lexi away from the crowd. "I think you better start from the beginning."

"I can't." Lexi frantically looked over her shoulder to double-check no one was listening. "Not here. I can't risk someone overhearing. Can we go to your place?"

Leaning into him for support, Clay protectively wrapped an arm around her and guided Lexi to her car. This was not the norm for her, Lexi thought. She prided herself on strength and perseverance no matter the obstacle. Yet twice in one day, she had found herself relying on someone else to walk her to her car. After reassuring him she was able to drive on her own, Lexi pulled out of the parking lot behind Clay's pickup.

The twenty-minute drive to Clay's gave Lexi far too much time to second-guess asking him for help. She figured shouting "Happy belated April Fool's" wouldn't fly with the detective. After keeping her secret hidden for the past thirteen years, she found the idea of unburdening it both terrifying and a relief.

Stopping behind Clay in the gravel driveway, Lexi death-gripped the steering wheel, uncertain she wanted to turn off the engine. A quick shift into Reverse seemed like a wiser option. Not giving her much of a choice, Clay strode to her car, reached across her and removed the keys from the ignition. *Damn convertibles.*

"I'm keeping these until I know you're okay." Clay sauntered to the porch. "Take your time, I'll be up here."

*You can do this. Clay's the only one who can help you.*

Lexi put all her trust and faith in her longtime friend, reasoning the former Alcohol, Tobacco and Firearms agent turned private investigator was a better choice than some stranger she found in the yellow pages. *Trust and faith.* A foreign concept that left a bad taste in her mouth. She trusted no one and the only thing she had faith in was her animals.

Blindly reaching for the handle, she swung the door wide, testing her footing for fear the earth would give way beneath her and swallow her whole. A part of her actually relished the idea of disappearing and not having to face the past. Slogging up the stairs, she joined Clay and slumped into one of the porch rockers.

"Are you all right?" Clay asked.

"Ask me that again an hour from now," Lexi muttered.

She laid her head back and squeezed her eyes tight, willing the courage to tell Clay about Colorado.

"How 'bout a beer?" Clay offered.

"Do you have anything stronger?"

Clay quietly laughed. "Just don't run off on me before I return."

"I can't, you took my keys," Lexi grumbled.

She drew her knees to her chest. She'd never thought she would have to explain giving up her son to anyone, let alone the father's best friend. This was her cross to bear alone and it should have remained that way forever. How would she tell her family?

*How will I tell Shane?*

"Lex?" Clay returned with two lowball glasses and held out one to her. "Nothing goes any further than us."

Lexi took Clay at his word. There was no other way to take him—either people confided in him with their darkest secrets or they hired him to uncover others'. But somehow, Lexi didn't think two fingers of bourbon would give her the strength she needed to come clean.

"My mom would kill me if she caught me drinking in the middle of the day." Lexi nervously laughed before tilting the glass and swallowing its contents.

"Your secret's safe with me." Unscrewing the cap, he poured her another drink before returning the bottle to the floor between them. "You realize I'm not letting you drive anytime soon."

Lexi nodded, making a mental note to call her brother Nash later and ask him to feed the horses.

"At the time I thought I was doing the responsible thing," Lexi began.

"What exactly did you do?" Clay asked.

"I had Shane's baby and gave it up for adoption."

\* \* \*

"Keeping it Reel Pictures is *the* big kahuna of reality programming," Ryan boasted, steering Shane toward one of the picnic tables. "We're offering you the chance of a lifetime."

Shane listened to Ryan while he watched Clay walk Lexi to her car. Considering her earlier episode, he figured she still didn't feel well. But he was completely unprepared when Clay followed her out of the ranch and began to wonder if there wasn't more going on between the two of them. Not that he didn't trust Clay. He knew his friend would never betray him. So why did it bother him to see his best friend and his ex-girlfriend leave at the same time and look suspiciously like they were trying not to be seen together?

"You might even end up a movie star!" Hunter exclaimed enthusiastically, redirecting Shane to the conversation.

"Smart kid. Is he yours?" Ryan continued without waiting for an answer. "Look at all the reality stars turned actors. With your rodeo following you'd start off with a large fan base."

"I'm already a star and you must be aware I have an agent, right?"

"How impersonal would it be for us to go through an agent?" Ryan draped his arm around Shane's shoulder, throwing any suggestion of professionalism he had left out the window. "This is about Shane Langtry—his life, family, girlfriends, the rodeo. How much more personal can we get. This is huge! Bigger than anything else out there, and I promise, after the end of the first season, you'll be a household name."

The man definitely had his attention. Shane loved the idea of being on the tip of everyone's tongue. Stardom aside, he'd made a commitment to his family and Ride 'em High! and he wasn't about to turn his back on any of it.

"I just opened this school, I can't leave it now."

"That's the beauty of this, Shane," Ryan crooned. "We want to shoot it here."

"Here?" Shane asked.

"Wicked!" Hunter chimed in.

"Hollywood couldn't build a set this great." Ryan swung his arms in a grand gesture. "Look at this place—it's palatial!"

"Why are you focusing on me?" Shane asked. "I mean I'm good but I haven't won the championship."

"The show will feature a few stars." Ryan drew an imaginary box with his fingers. "Picture a show like *Deadliest Catch* only with cowboys instead of Alaska fishermen. People will be on the edge of their seats watching you perform in one of America's most dangerous sports. You'll each have your own segments."

"Who else have you asked?"

"No one." Ryan shifted closer and lowered his voice. "You're our first choice and we'd like you to be the anchor of the show."

A television offer was the last thing Shane expected and one he wasn't quite certain his agent, Brock Hudson, would jump at. Why did Ryan avoid Brock, knowing he'd have to go through him at some point? With his national rodeo sponsors, Shane was already well-known, but the allure was almost impossible to resist.

"Is it true?" Tyler, one of the rodeo school kids, ran

up and breathlessly asked him. "Are you going to have your own TV show?"

"Well, that didn't take long to get out." Shane shook his head and looked down at Hunter. "What did you do, text him?"

"Nah," Hunter laughed. "Social media is the way to go nowadays. I tweeted it."

"I love this kid!" Ryan hugged the teen. "Your son's a genius! Look at the buzz he's already generated here."

"Hunter's not my son," Shane said.

"Really? Could have fooled me." Ryan shrugged. "So what do you think?"

"Excuse me, Shane," Kay interrupted. "We have someone waiting to interview us."

"Go on, I didn't mean to take up all of your time." Ryan reached out to shake Kay's hand. "That was a very moving speech up there. You raised some fine men."

"Thank you. Have we met?" Kay inquired warily.

Shane interrupted before Ryan was able to open his mouth. "I'll tell you all about it later, Mom." Shane steered Kay away from the table and nodded back to Ryan. "You'll still be around?"

"I'm not going anywhere." Ryan smiled a grin that screamed Hollywood.

"What's going on, Shane?" Kay asked. "Who was that man?"

"Mom, he could put Bridle Dance on the map."

"We are on the map—Ramblewood, Texas. There, done. Now what's this all about?"

"Here they are." An attractive brunette in jeans and red polo shirt held a microphone and directed Kay and

Shane to join his brothers. "This isn't a live segment, so please don't be nervous."

"We're used to the spotlight." Shane nodded toward some of his students, who stood by watching the interview. "It's in our blood."

"It may be in your blood but it certainly isn't in mine." Kay adjusted her blouse. "I despise TV interviews. I do wish I had a mirror so I could check my makeup. In all this heat it's probably melted off."

"You look gorgeous, Mrs. Langtry." The interviewer gave a wide, overbleached smile. Some people took teeth whitening to the extreme and it bugged the hell out of Shane. Photo ready was one thing, but there was no need to be a beacon for space ships every time you opened your mouth.

"And five, four…" The woman motioned *three, two, one* with her hand. "We're here in Ramblewood with the Langtry family for the greatly anticipated opening of the Dance of Hope hippotherapy facility and the Ride 'em High! Rodeo School."

Shane listened while his mother answered the majority of the questions like a seasoned pro. If she was the least bit nervous, she certainly didn't show it. Normally Shane and Chase handled the interviews now that Cole had stepped away from the rodeo, but today belonged to their mother and Shane loved watching her take pride in their combined venture.

The interviewer posed her final question. "And with Shane getting his own reality show, you must be excited about the national publicity you'll receive."

"Shane getting his own what?"

*So much for easing her into the idea.*

* * *

"Who else knows about this?" Clay stood in the setting sun. He was tall and tanned with a hint of sandy blond hair peeking out from under his summer Stetson. He removed his sunglasses, Caribbean-blue eyes meeting hers with all the sincerity in the world. He looked more like a movie star than a cowboy P.I.

"Only my horse, and I can trust she won't talk." Lexi attempted to laugh, rose and teetered to the porch railing that overlooked the narrow two-lane highway and emerald-green cornfields, weeks away from harvesting. It was tranquil out here, away from the bustle of her family's tourist attraction. Lexi turned to face Clay. "Now what?"

"I have to admit," Clay acknowledged, "there is a strong resemblance between the two of them, but don't jump to any conclusions until we know for certain."

"How soon can you find out?" Lexi implored, dropping back into the rocker, half the bottle gone, the effects of the bourbon beginning to take a toll. "I can't work close to him, knowing I might be inches away from my own child."

"Now that they've had the ribbon cutting, the school will do more arena work inside. It's too hot outside not to. In the meantime, I can do some digging and see what I come up with."

"And you'll find out for certain?"

"There's only one surefire way to know. You use a DNA lab for your breeding program, don't you?" Clay asked.

"Yes, but I think the Texas Veterinary Board would frown on that, let alone the ethics factor."

"Lucky for you, I don't have any ethics to worry about. I'll run the test. I can get into the bunkhouse when he's training and grab something of his."

"We're really doing this, aren't we?" Reality punched her hard in the stomach and the world began to churn in front of her.

"No more bourbon for you." Clay led Lexi inside the air-conditioned house to a couch that had seen better days. "Lay down for a while."

"My God." Lexi looked around the living room, scanning the boxes still stacked in the corners. "You've been back in town for how long and you still haven't unpacked?"

"Eh, what's another year or two?"

"Seriously." Lexi steadied herself on his arm before flopping down on the sofa, causing a small cloud of dust to rise in the air between the two of them.

"Take my bed." Clay quickly tried to hide his embarrassment. "I'm rarely home so none of this gets used very much."

"It's fine." Lexi removed her phone from her pocket and sent Nash a quick text, feigning a vet emergency. Clay ran upstairs and returned with a pillow and a sheet before she even hit *send*.

"We all have skeletons, Lexi." He helped her stand and draped the sheet across the couch before fluffing up the pillow. Lexi lowered herself back down, tucking her legs beneath her. Clay perched on the edge of the coffee table and continued. "Some greater than others but we all have one thing we don't want anyone else to know. It doesn't make you a bad person, it makes you human. My job isn't to judge you. It's to find out if Hunter really is your son."

"You'll check out his family, too?"

"If you want me to, yes."

"I need to know he's with good people." Lexi had already decided if there were any signs of abuse or neglect she'd immediately contact an attorney and fight for her son. It was an easy decision for her to make and Lexi questioned if her maternal instincts were kicking in or if it was because Hunter looked very well taken care of, and she didn't have anything to worry about. "Then I'll figure out what to do next."

"Are you going to tell Shane?"

"I'm not going to disrupt Hunter's life for selfish reasons." If he was her son and he was happy, who was she to shatter his world? "What good can come of it? Shane already lost one son, why tell him he lost another?"

"It's your call." Clay rose and tugged all the blinds closed. "Get some sleep."

"I'm really putting you in a bad spot, aren't I?" The strain she was about to cause to Shane and Clay's friendship dawned on her. "How can you keep this a secret from Shane? If he were to ever find out you knew—"

"He'd understand I was doing my job," Clay assured her. "Lexi, I can't even begin to tell you the secrets I've had to keep."

"Thank you for understanding."

"Maybe this will make you realize you're still in love with him?" Clay said from a safe distance across the room.

"What?" Lexi snorted. "No. What? Please tell me you aren't going to play matchmaker with all of this."

"My job is to state the facts, ma'am." Clay playfully tipped his hat and left the room.

Her eyes heavy with bourbon and exhaustion, she laid her head on the pillow. The hospital room once again filled her dreams. Only this time, Shane was there, cradling their son in his arms, the way it was supposed to be.

"You're planning a reality show on Bridle Dance and you didn't discuss it with me?" Kay dragged Shane into the house practically by his ear once the interview was complete. Behind them, Cole evaded any further reality show questions from the media with a firm "no comment."

"Well, technically it wasn't my idea," Shane retorted. "The show was proposed to me and it would be filmed at the school. I haven't made any decisions so I don't see what the big deal is yet." Shane gathered his arguments. "Can you imagine the volume of business we'd bring in? Just think about the attention Dance of Hope would receive. It's a nonprofit, Mom. You'd garner all sorts of donations from across the country and we could educate people about hippotherapy."

"Slow down, will you." Kay tapped her fingers wildly on the counter. "I've seen those reality shows and they'd probably wind up victimizing the people who come here for therapy and I'll be damned if I'm going to let that happen. Most of those shows are pure trash."

"Most, not all. You used to watch some of those medical reality shows and they weren't trash." Shane argued his point knowing it was futile going up against his mother. "Why does this suddenly feel like déjà vu?"

"What are you talking about?"

"This is just like last year." Shane threw his hands in the air. "You and Cole once again opposing what I want to do. I thought we got past all of this. It would be nice at least to have a conversation before you both try to shut me down but obviously things haven't changed around here."

It had been bad enough fighting almost his entire family to open the rodeo school. If Chase hadn't stood by his side, he would have felt like a complete outsider.

"This involves all of us." Cole spoke to him in his trademark annoyingly patronizing tone. "Never mind how it will affect the students. Some parents may not approve of their kids being on television. I certainly don't want Ever involved in this."

"First, I didn't say I was going ahead with it so give me a little credit," Shane argued. "And second, we mainly teach the rodeo kids in the summer and talk about an instant career boost for them. The students over eighteen can make their own decisions."

"I wasn't finished, Shane," Cole continued. "There's a major liability factor you're not seeing."

"I haven't even had a meeting with this guy to get all the facts yet." Shane's voice strained. "I'm sure the show would cover the additional insurance and the students already have to provide their own medical insurance before they even enroll. I'd never put your daughter's reputation or anyone in this family's in jeopardy."

"I don't know, Shane." Cole took a seat at the kitchen island and folded his arms across his chest.

"I don't, either." Shane sat down next to him. "Instead of judging me or the show, let's at least hear what they have to say."

Cole agreed and Shane felt his grip on his family tighten slightly. Since their father died he felt like he was always bucking against the majority. They called it obstinacy; Shane considered it thinking outside the box.

"Have you seen what they do to the families on these shows?" Kay jutted her chin and firmly placed her hands on her hips. "They'll make all of us look like a bunch of hicks. I'm not authorizing my image or likeness."

Shane shot his brother a look, and both tried to stifle a laugh.

"What are you two giggling about?"

"Listen to you with your *image-or-likeness* talk," Shane mocked. "Hollywood's already grabbed ahold of you."

"You two have five seconds to get back outside before I pummel you both."

The grown men ran to the door. Shane called to his mother, "Be careful, Mom, you wouldn't want that to be caught on film."

"Go on and get out of here." Kay turned and walked back into the kitchen.

"Mom?" Shane stood in the doorway. "I'm asking you to seriously consider the show. It doesn't have to be a bad thing and I think we have a shot of educating people on the rodeo and hippotherapy. It doesn't have to be all about me…not anymore."

# Chapter 5

Lexi awoke to the sound of her alarm. Her head pounding, she reached out to turn it off and swiftly met with the back of the couch. For a minute, she'd forgotten where she was. Fumbling in the dark, she followed the light beaming from her phone as it played a bluesy piano riff repeatedly.

Feeling her way into Clay's kitchen, Lexi swore as she stubbed her toe on one of the many boxes stacked along the wall. "Who buys a house and never unpacks?"

Patting the wall for the switch, Lexi finally managed to turn on the lights. Silently, she searched the cabinets for a bottle of aspirin. She opened the fridge to look for something to wash it down with and found an open twelve-pack of Michelob Ultra and some individually wrapped cheese slices.

"Typical bachelor." Lexi closed the door and saw Clay standing in the doorway. "Crap! Don't scare me like that. What are you doing prowling about at this hour?"

"I might ask you the same thing, but I heard your alarm go off. Oh, and thanks for the new four-letter words even I'm unfamiliar with when you crashed into whatever it was in the living room. After that greeting, I'm officially awake for the day. Coffee? Don't answer—it's obvious you need it. Just sit down and try not to kill yourself."

Lexi wasn't in the mood to argue with the man and a cup of strong black coffee was exactly what the doctor ordered after the amount of bourbon they drank. She watched Clay maneuver around the small, yet efficient kitchen. She'd only been in the house a few times when he first moved back to town. From the looks of things, that was yesterday. She knew Clay went through a rough patch a few years ago, and like he said, everyone had a secret. He hadn't shared his, not that she'd pushed. But glancing around the house, she realized she really didn't know much about the man any more other than what she saw on the surface. A hardworking cowboy turned detective.

"Yesterday was real, wasn't it?" In the recesses of her mind, Lexi had hoped that Hunter was another countless dream she'd had about the son she never met.

"You need to look at the flip side of this." Clay grabbed two stoneware mugs from the cabinet while he waited for the coffee to brew. "If Hunter is in fact your son, you must have some relief finally knowing how he turned out. He appears healthy and happy and that alone says he's been well taken care of.. You can't tell me you didn't wonder about that all these years."

"A day doesn't go by that I don't think of him." Lexi rubbed her eyes. "What am I going to do?"

"Nothing." Clay pulled up a chair in front of her, their knees touching. He took her hand in his and squeezed. "You asked me to help you and I will, but you need to stay out of it and let me do my job. Make your rounds at Bridle Dance and then leave. You don't have to go there every day anyway."

"Bridle Dance is my largest client." Lexi thought of the list of horses she had to take care of on a daily basis. "I have mares ready to foal, and they've expanded the breeding program—"

"And Ashleigh is perfectly capable of checking in at the ranch for you." Clay met her gaze and held it, giving Lexi an eerie feeling he could read her mind. "Don't make excuses to stay there, Lex. Ashleigh will let you know if something needs your attention. You have other techs that can help you."

Okay, so he did read her mind. Not that she was planning on hanging around the ranch, but the thought of her son being so close she could reach out and touch him fascinated her. She wanted to learn more about Hunter and his life in Colorado. Did he have any brothers or sisters? What were his favorite foods or favorite video games? Was he involved in any other sports? She already knew he was following in Shane's footsteps, but did he follow in hers? Did he play guitar and sing like her and did he love animals? The questions churning in Lexi's head were nothing new. She asked herself at least a dozen every day, but now with Hunter so close, her mind raced with more of them.

Those questions finally had a chance of being answered and Lexi didn't want to waste a moment. But how could she get close to Hunter without raising suspicions?

"I can't stay away, Clay." Lexi steeled herself. "I've had thirteen years of wondering. If that's my son, then he has a birthday soon and I plan on celebrating with him. One way or another I'm wishing him a happy birthday."

"I have to admit, it's nice having you home in the morning." Kay bagged two dozen freshly baked apple streusel muffins and set them on the counter. "It used to be a rare occasion to wake up and see your Jeep out there."

"Yeah," Chase added. "What's going on with you? Since the school opened, you've only gone out once."

"Let's not make a federal case out of it," Shane grumbled. "We have a bunkhouse full of kids and I think it's important to be there. In fact, I think I might stay out there with them tonight. Our instructors are pulling double duty now and it's a bit much to ask every night. I also think it would be nice to include the hippotherapy kids in our marshmallow roasts. I know their bunkhouses are a way from ours, but I think it's good for all the kids to interact with one another and— What? Why are you two staring at me like that?"

"Are you feeling all right?" Kay laughed. "I was skeptical about you opening the school and spending so much time near kids, but taking up residence with them and campfires? That doesn't sound like you. You've made a point to keep your—"

Shane raised his hand to stop his mother from continuing. He had never considered himself a kid person before his involvement with Sharon, but as soon as he had held Dylan in his arms for the first time, he quickly changed his mind. When Tab took Dylan away, remembering what he'd had and lost was too hard, so Shane distanced himself from children of all ages. The further he went in his career and the more sponsors he gained, he realized how much of a role model he had become, confirmed by the fan mail he received. He had wrestled with the idea of the rodeo school for years but didn't share it with anyone. When his father died, he finally found the courage to push forward with his idea, wanting to prove to himself and his family that he was more than just a rodeo cowboy. The kids had been more fun to work with than he'd anticipated, and when they left in a few weeks, he'd actually miss them.

From day one, Shane had picked out the school's rising stars. Everyone had potential if they stuck with the sport, but the rodeo came more easily to certain kids. Usually it was because they grew up in an environment where riding was involved on a daily basis. Hunter was one of the exceptions. His family couldn't be more removed from ranch life, yet the kid's skills rivaled those of his classmate, Tyler, whose family's cattle ranch kept him in the saddle every day.

The rodeo school kids reminded Shane so much of himself at that age. Determination was written all over their faces and nothing would stop them from achieving their goals. Shane not only wanted to witness their budding careers, but he also wanted to manage them. And in a perfect world, with more hours in the day, he would.

A kid had to be careful in this business. There was someone trying to take advantage of a rookie around every corner. Luckily for Shane and his brothers, they'd had their father managing their careers when they first started out. Once they rode the circuit for a few years, they had a good sense of who was legit and who wasn't in the industry and were able to make informed decisions with their father's guidance. These kids needed that same leadership and Shane felt he was just the man for the job. Maybe someday he'd have the time, after he won the championship.

"I need to head out and wake the troops." Shane grabbed the bag of muffins from the counter. "Thanks for making these, Mom. I know the boys will appreciate it."

"You're welcome." Kay placed a hand on Shane's arm to stop him from leaving. "Muffins and good-mornings aside, don't think I've forgotten about this reality show. I meant what I said last night—I don't want any part of it."

"Point taken. And I'd never sign a contract without running it past Brock first, although I have to admit, the deal does sound intriguing."

"Let's hear them out before we make any firm decisions, Mom," Chase added. "I'm interested in finding out more about it myself. If it's legit and they don't ridicule the rodeo, then I think it has the potential of being a good thing."

"You mean lucrative." Kay smirked.

"Last I checked, lucrative was a good thing," Shane

said. "But it's more than that, Mom. I worked hard designing this school and I'd like some recognition." He pushed through the screen door and bounded down the porch stairs. He welcomed the wall of heat that smacked him in the face because it was more bearable than the disappointed expression he saw when his mother looked at him some days. Shane was grateful the ribbon cutting was finally behind them so he could prove to her why he'd fought so hard for this school.

The rising temperatures made for some cranky kids and he was relieved to be able to work in a more controlled environment now that the indoor arena was open. It was one thing to be on the back of a bucking bronc in the heat where your attention was focused on the ride, another to be standing around in the sun waiting for your turn. He was all for working with kids, but hot, sweaty, willful kids crazed from heat—not so much. Especially since the majority of them came from northern states and weren't used to this weather.

Butch, one of the ranch's many border collies, greeted Shane on the walkway to the bunkhouses. Dropping the red tennis ball he perpetually carried around, the dog waited expectantly. Shane squatted down and scratched Butch behind the ears.

"What is it, boy?" Shane nuzzled the dog's neck. "You want some morning love? I think Mom needs a dog of her own to keep her company. What do you think?"

Butch wagged his tail and flopped onto his side, rolling onto his back. "How would you like to help me play a little joke on the kids this morning?" Shane rubbed the dog's white-and-black belly, triggering Butch's hind leg to kick in rhythm with Shane's ministrations.

Rising, Shane slinked toward the main bunkhouse. Giving Butch the down hand signal, the dog went into what Shane affectionately called *stealth mode* and belly-crawled along behind him as he crept silently across the porch. Shane eased the bunkhouse door open. Not only were his students ten toes up, but his on-duty den dad of an instructor was also out like a light. They were sleeping so peacefully, it would be a shame to wake them, but what fun.

Shane silently turned and grabbed a braided rope that hung from the rocking chair on the porch, and tiptoed back to the door. Raising his arm to bang the rope against the wall, Shane barely contained his laughter. Opening the door slowly, he peeked inside.

"Gotcha!" An arm reached out and tried to latch on to him. Shane scrambled and struggled to break free, yanking his own arm backward away from the grasp while Butch barked and spun around in a circle. The door swung wide and laughter poured out of the bunkhouse.

"What the—!" Shane steadied himself. "You scared the daylights out of me."

"That will teach you to sneak in here," Grant, one of his instructors, said. "We were waiting for you."

"That's not right," Shane grumbled good-naturedly. "Funny, but definitely not right."

"When do they start filming?" Hunter pushed past the other boys.

"Can we be in your show?" Tyler asked.

"Whoa, slow down, guys." Shane admired their enthusiasm but a few unanswered questions remained. Ryan's deal almost seemed too good to be true. And the fact he'd completely bypassed his agent caused Shane to wonder what the guy had left out of his proposal. "I haven't decided anything yet. Here are some muffins to hold you until breakfast. Now let's hit the gym."

Shane found it hard to concentrate on his workout alongside the boys. Two things filled his mind. He sensed something was troubling Lexi and that had kept him awake most of the night. Hell, Lexi was the only woman he'd ever said "I love you" to and would probably claim that honor until the day he died. Ryan's offer only added to his restless bed tossing.

"I'll meet you in the arena later," Shane said to Chase. "I want to check on the yearlings myself this morning."

He strode down the pathway leading from the bunkhouse toward the small outdoor satellite ranch office. Since running the ranch alongside his brothers for the past year, he felt guilty when he realized how much more Cole shouldered, so Shane and Chase could still compete and run the school. Shane offered to take on more responsibility, much to everyone's surprise, and was still struggling to find a balance. He was also learning the ropes on many aspects of the ranch and needed to review some of Bridle Dance's financial reports during his flight to South Dakota tomorrow morning to the Black Hills Roundup Rodeo. He hated to miss Fourth of July with his students, but when he'd signed on for the event, he'd thought it would be a great chance to escape for a few days. Have a little fun, ride hard and play a little harder.

His hand on the knob of the office door, he saw Lexi's convertible in the parking lot near the stables. Wanting to see how she was feeling, Shane searched the stables. When he found her, she looked like she'd spent the night in her clothes—*wasn't she wearing that shirt yesterday?* Shane stood in the shadows and watched Lexi come out of one of the stalls, slightly unsteady on her feet. Shane wondered how wild of a night she'd had with Clay. She didn't look sick, but she sure looked hung over.

"Looks like someone had a rough night."

Startled, Lexi wasn't used to seeing Shane in the stables this early considering he rode out to check on the yearlings most mornings or was training for his next rodeo before the work day. Plus with the school open, she expected the students would occupy his days and probably part of his nights. Surprisingly she wondered if she'd get the chance to spend much time with him this summer. Not that they'd made plans or anything, and heaven help her if she ever said the words aloud, but Lexi was beginning to enjoy Shane's company instead of always ducking and dodging him. That is until Hunter came to the ranch and reminded her of the guilt she tried so desperately to bury.

"Cole left me a message that he sold two horses during the ribbon cutting, and the buyer wants to pick them up today. I had to swing in and do their Coggins reports before they were trailered out."

Lexi liked to save the Coggins reports for when Billy was around now that he was more familiar with the testing and reporting procedures. Wanting to heed Clay's advice, she decided to hit the stables early before there was any chance of running into Hunter. Clay told her they'd meet up later, after he had the DNA kit, so he could get a cheek swab from her and she'd write him a check for his expenses.

"You look like you were ridden hard and put away wet," Shane said. "You feeling okay? I saw you leave early with Clay yesterday."

Lexi's head shot up at the declaration. She didn't know anyone had seen them leave and she certainly hoped no one overheard their conversation.

"I wasn't feeling well. My stomach's a little off, probably some type of bug." Lexi wasn't lying at this point. Her stomach felt like it could betray her at any moment. When was the last time she ate? Clay had a pizza delivered last night, but Lexi never moved from the couch, saying she wasn't hungry. She regretted it now, along with the bourbon.

"Are you sure it's nothing more?"

Oh, no—does he know? Could he possibly?

"I have to go." Lexi brushed past him. "We'll talk later."

"It will have to be a few days from now then. I'm heading to South Dakota tomorrow morning."

"Oh." Lexi didn't think Shane would leave in the middle of his first class, but then again, it was peak rodeo season, and with Shane, the rodeo came above all else. "I hope you have a nice trip. Now, if you'll excuse me."

"Look, I'm just going to come right out and ask."

Shane closed the distance between them, his eyes softening, and for a split second, Lexi thought he was going to kiss her. "Do we have a chance of a future?"

If there was any question to catch her off guard, that was the one. They'd danced around the issue since November, but never actually said the words. While the thought wasn't far from her mind, the timing was terrible.

"Shane, I—I don't know what our future holds." Lexi cleared her throat. "We just have to take things slow and see what happens."

Shane made it impossible for her to avoid meeting his gaze when he tilted her chin toward him. She'd forgotten the feel of his rough, calloused hands against her face and she'd forgotten how much she missed the way he held her and the way he would—

Shane placed both hands on either side of Lexi's face and kissed her. It was a kiss so passionate, so intense, Lexi thought she had time-warped to that fateful weekend at Devil's Thumb. Unabashed, Lexi allowed herself this one moment to remember what they'd had, to feel what they'd missed all these years.

"Don't throw away our past, Lexi."

*Past.* Lexi couldn't outrun the past any longer. It had caught up with her, and if Hunter proved to be her son—their son—the thought of lying to Shane for the rest of his life seemed a thousand times worse than not knowing who and where the child they created was.

Lexi broke the kiss and pushed Shane away. "What the hell do you think you're doing?"

"Tell me you don't still feel it, Lex." Shane tugged

her toward him. "Since you moved home, I've endured seeing you each and every day. At Jesse's wedding we agreed to make the most of our friendship and see where it led us. You and I both knew staying away from each other would be impossible."

"You can't just kiss me whenever you feel like it," Lexi hissed. "Especially when I'm working."

"Are you honestly going to deny you have feelings for me?"

Lexi did have feelings, she did still love him, and even though her heart told her it was time to give him a second chance, the strong possibility Hunter was their son negated everything.

"Listen, Shane." Lexi jabbed at his chest. "Regardless of how or what I feel, you cannot kiss me while I'm at work, even if you do own the place! Who knows who saw that kiss? I have a reputation to maintain, so I suggest you get your butt on that plane and focus on your next ride."

"After you admit you still love me." Shane leisurely leaned against the stall door.

Lexi closed the distance between them and carefully kept her tone low so no one would overhear. "You arrogant, egotistical— How can you think for one minute—we just started—"

"Yep, I knew it." Shane slapped his thigh with his hat. "Some things never change, *mi ángel de fuego*."

Lexi was taken off guard to hear Shane refer to her as his angel of fire. The last time he'd used the nickname was before they broke up. Struggling to compose herself, she stared at him, afraid to speak.

Shane didn't share her problem. "Whenever you get

riled up like this and can't finish a thought, I know I'm right and it kills you."

If he only knew how much this all really was killing her.

# *Chapter 6*

Shane replayed Lexi's colorful four-letter-word retort as his plane taxied down the runway the following morning. He expected nothing less from Lexi and was actually relieved to see her fiery passion unleashed. If she was feisty, she was okay and that was all that mattered.

*Keep telling yourself that.*

There was something definitely going on with Lexi, and as much as he hated not knowing what it was, he trusted Clay to tell him if it was serious. Trying to push all thoughts of her aside for a few hours, Shane tried to focus on the financial reports from the ranch. Truth was, he was more interested in hearing from his agent about the reality show than he was studying figures on how much grain they purchased during the second quarter of the year.

Brock told him what he knew—Keeping it Reel

Pictures tended to go for more vanity-type television shows. Shane wasn't quite sure how he should take their interest in him after hearing that.

"May I get you a drink, sir?" A flight attendant interrupted his thoughts. She was cute, petite, he'd wager a natural blonde, and Shane couldn't help but notice how she leaned in closer than she should to take his order.

"Just a bottled water, please." Shane might be the wild one of the family, but he never drank before a competition. You had to be on your game at all times in that rodeo arena. The slightest mistake could cost you your life and he wasn't willing to take the chance of even having the slightest bit of alcohol in his system.

"Are you sure there's nothing else I can get for you?" the blonde asked with some added heat to her voice and an extra button undone on her blouse, emphasizing what the good Lord gave her.

*She knows who I am.* It amazed Shane the number of people that recognized him outside Ramblewood and away from the arena. Sure, the rodeo was big, but on a commercial flight out of San Antonio, the flight attendants were rarely local. Blondie's accent leaned more toward Bostonian and there wasn't a huge following in that part of the country.

"I'm good for now." Less than a year ago, he'd have found out if she was staying in South Dakota overnight, and if she were, he'd make damn sure she saved a horse and rode a cowboy. Now, the only person he wanted to share his bed with was Lexi, and the way that was going, he'd be collecting social security before she ever even entertained the thought. Clay was right, he might as well consider himself celibate at this point.

Checking the pulse on the side of his neck, Shane confirmed he was still alive. Silently laughing, he pulled his phone from his jeans and dialed the ranch. So much for not thinking about Lexi for a few hours.

"Hello?" Chase answered.

"Hey, how's it going there?" Shane asked.

"Pretty much the same as it was when you left," Chase said. "The house is still standing, I haven't lost a kid and men from outer space haven't beamed up the ranch."

"Okay, wise-ass." Shane smirked. "I was just checking in. Have you seen Lexi this morning?"

"And there's the real reason why you're calling." Chase laughed through the phone. "I'm surprised you didn't pass her on the way in because she got here a little after you left to check in on Crystal. Looks like it will only be a few days before she foals."

"I'm hoping I'm home before then." Shane rubbed his brow. "Dad's last foal. He would have been sleeping in the barn at this stage."

"Yeah, he would have." Chase's somber tone matched his own. "He'd be out there setting up every video camera known to man trying to capture this birth. I can hear him now—'This is going to be legendary, son. When this horse makes millions you'll thank me for recording this.' He'd get so caught up in the technology side of things, he'd probably end up missing the whole event and have to play it back to see what happened."

"Ain't that the truth." Shane swallowed his laughter for fear it might turn to tears. He missed his father greatly and he'd ride this rodeo in his honor. No matter how old Shane had been, Joe had always accompanied him to the Black Hills Roundup. This was the first year he was going alone.

"I should've signed up with you this year," Chase said. "The school could have managed without us for a few days. You know Dad's there in spirit with you and he'd be proud of everything we've accomplished this past year."

"Thanks, bro." Shane swallowed, trying to clear the lump forming in his throat. "I think I really needed to hear that today. And don't sweat not being here. Those kids need you more than I do."

"Speaking of such, the boys are waiting for me," Chase said. "Enjoy your flight, don't wear out the flight attendants and call me later. Oh, that's right, you only have eyes for Lexi now. Forget about her while you're there and focus on your ride."

"Thanks, I will." Shane turned off his phone and pocketed it. Easing the seat back a little, he checked his watch.

"Your water, Mr. Langtry."

"Any idea when we'll be taking off?"

"It should only be a few more minutes. We've had some congestion this morning. Good luck on your ride tonight."

The last two words were heavy with innuendo, confirming she knew exactly who he was and hadn't just read his name on the flight manifest. Shane was flattered, but nope, still not interested. He wanted to get this show over with, meet with his sponsors and get home.

Leaving never bothered him before now. He chalked it up to Crystal's foal and the rodeo school. The boys had a lot to learn during their monthlong stay, and while he knew they were in more than capable hands with Chase, Kyle and the other instructors they'd brought in, he'd have felt better if he was there, too. Hell, even Cole had offered to throw his hat in the ring for a few sessions.

And why not? The Langtry brothers were the main draw to the Ride 'em High! Rodeo School. They were a package deal, and if someone was going to spend that amount of money for instruction, they felt better knowing a trio of rodeo champs were there to show them how it was done.

And once the reality show started taping—correction, *if* the reality show started taping—he wondered how many endorsement deals would come out of it. He'd already had a few from saddle makers, a boot company and other equipment manufacturers, but Shane wanted a nationwide truck campaign under his belt and then he could say he'd truly arrived.

Hunter was the one student he was most sure of—the boy was strong, independent and extremely competitive—and he had the drive needed to succeed. He was more mature than some of the older boys, a maturity Shane definitely didn't have at that age. The kid had the potential to go far in this business and Shane still debated whether or not to tell his agent about him. It was probably best to discuss it further with his parents when they arrived for Family Day.

"Just five more months and maybe it will all be mine."

"Excuse me?"

Shane hadn't realized he'd said the words out loud. He coolly glanced at the man across the aisle. "I'm competing in a rodeo tonight and I'm vying to win the world all-around rodeo champion title at the National Finals in December."

The man stared at him as if Shane were speaking in tongues, then turned back to his paper. *Clearly not a fan.* The plane began to move and the flight attendant picked up the in-cabin phone and began her announcements, rarely breaking eye contact with him.

Shane closed his eyes and rested his head against the seat. Lexi and yesterday's kiss came to mind. He couldn't get the woman out of his head, regardless of who he was with. For the past thirteen and a half years, whenever he closed his eyes, she was there. No one compared to Lexi, and no matter how hard he tried, no one ever would.

With Shane away, Lexi felt a little more at ease around the stables, especially since she now didn't have to worry about him kissing her randomly. She walked out of the barn and started toward her car, having avoided everyone from the rodeo school. Lexi knew she needed to keep her distance, and whether Hunter turned out to be her son or not, she had made the decision to give her child to another family a long time ago. There was no going back and Lexi was beginning to question if discovering the truth was wise.

"Done for the day, dear?" Kay asked, walking toward her on the path from Dance of Hope.

"Short list today," Lexi said. "Just an insemination— everything else looks good. Crystal's close, though. She's dripping milk this morning so I give it two days at the most."

"I never did understand this artificial insemination thing. I know it's safer for the horse, but do you ever feel like you're playing God?"

"Most definitely," Lexi agreed. "I'll breed them but I don't want to get involved in genetically altering horses. It's too risky for me."

"I wanted to talk to you for a minute. Can you come in for a cup of coffee?"

Lexi sent Ashleigh and Billy ahead to the next ranch and followed Kay into the house. Lexi adored the Langtry home, especially the kitchen. With its open floor plan and use of natural log construction, the house had a cozy atmosphere, despite its vastness. The rooms were defined with the use of oversize furniture and you felt comfortable no matter where you were.

Kay popped a couple of pods into the Keurig coffee-maker and within a minute had two piping cups of coffee. Setting the creamer out, she joined Lexi at the table.

"I just love that machine. I wish we had one when Joe was alive. That man always had to have a fresh pot of coffee. Not like he wasn't capable of making it himself, he just always had me do it. You know how men can be. Listen to me ramble on. I need a favor and I want you to keep it between us for now."

"Sure." There was no telling what the Langtry matriarch had up her sleeve. Lexi had heard stories of her wild younger years. The woman was free-spirited and gutsy, and there wasn't much she hadn't tackled in her day.

"My house is getting empty. Two of my boys are married, the other two are hardly ever home, and now that Joe's gone, I'm feeling a little lonely in this big place. Shane hinted a few times that I need a dog, although I think he's implying one of the ranch dogs. Don't get me wrong, I love border collies, but I have a particular dog in mind."

"I think that's wonderful." A dog would be the perfect companion for Kay, filling the void she must feel, always coming home to an empty house. "What breed are you considering?"

"Last week when I was in town, I saw Penny and Bella, that beautiful 'parti' poodle of hers. Those partis always remind me of our paint horses. Well, anyway, Penny told me that Bella's mom had her second litter and one of the puppies was jet-black. It was the only puppy not spoken for and, Lexi, when I stopped over and saw that little black fuzz ball, I felt this instant connection."

"A standard poodle is a lot of work with regular grooming every few weeks," Lexi said. "But you wouldn't have to worry about shedding. I'm assuming this is going to be an indoor dog."

"I already downloaded a bunch of poodle books to my computer. And Penny would be his groomer. Do you want to see a picture of him?"

Kay was adorable in her enthusiasm over the dog. If she had the patience to raise four surly cowboys and look after a husband, then owning a poodle would be a cakewalk.

"I didn't want that shedding like we had with Chinook." Kay flipped through the photos on her iPhone, finally finding the one she wanted. "Loved the dog, but I swear some nights I went to bed with fur-covered eyeballs."

Lexi fondly remembered the Langtrys' husky and Joe's best friend. "Oh, this puppy is so precious."

"I've already named him Barney, and I know you're an equine vet, but if you have a chance tonight, would you be able to go and see him with me…just to check him out and make sure he's okay? The breeder said the puppies have been weaned and some are already gone."

"I love the name Barney, and yes, I will be happy to go with you tonight. I'll give you a call after I finish my rounds and we'll head out then. But why don't you want anyone to know about it?"

"My boys will give me one hell of a ribbing when they hear I want a poodle. I'd rather wait and surprise them with it."

"I don't see why they'd tease you. They're big sturdy dogs and I can't see you being the type to have one running around in a show cut, so he'll just look like a curly-coated retriever. I think it's the perfect choice and poodles are one of the most intelligent breeds."

Lexi checked her watch. It was almost lunchtime and she needed to catch up with Ashleigh and Billy at her next appointment. Kay walked Lexi outside and the sound of laughter spilled across the road as the Ride 'em High! class ran past on the way to the bunkhouse kitchen.

Hunter's voice rose above the crowd. It wasn't because it was louder or stronger, but because Lexi instinctively tuned in to listen just for him.

"They are a proud bunch, aren't they?" Kay looked toward the crew. "Remind me so much of my boys when they were that age, running around here all full of the rodeo. And all you girls, so sweet on them."

Kay immediately looked to Lexi. "I'm sorry. Me and my big mouth."

"It was a long time ago." Lexi croaked out the words. Almost as if he read her mind, Hunter turned to look in her direction. Their eyes met and he waved.

His smile was akin to looking in a mirror. How could anyone else not see Hunter was Shane's and her child? She quickly turned to Kay, who was studying her. Did she know?

"What's bothering you, Lexi?" Kay asked. "You've been very pensive the past few days."

Lexi wanted to follow Hunter. She wanted to sit next to him at lunch and find out his favorite foods, what music he listened to, how he was doing in school, what his family was like. *Family.* He wasn't her family any-more. She made the choice to put Hunter before herself a long time ago and she didn't regret it.

Lexi looked to Kay. "Thank you for worrying about me, but I'm fine. I'll call you later and we'll go see Barney."

Lexi forced herself to walk toward her car instead of the path leading to the bunkhouses. *Don't look back.* Nothing good came from regrets except more regrets.

The weather in Belle Fourche, South Dakota, was warm but still a far cry from the sweltering heat of Ramblewood. Although it was located in the heart of the country, Belle Fourche resembled most small Texas towns. Main Street wasn't unlike Ramblewood's own and soon there would be a cattle drive coming down this one to kick off the Black Hills Roundup festivities.

Downtown, the carnival silently awaited the setting

sun, when lights would twinkle in the calliope-filled air, enticing tourists to partake in its magical charms. Cowboys and cowgirls from across the nation anxiously awaited the competition of one of the oldest outdoor rodeos. Shane could still picture his father with a foam cup of coffee in one hand and a camera in the other, photographing the entire scene. Despite the crowds, the streets seemed empty without Joe by his side.

Knowing the Black Hills Roundup was one of Tab's favorite rodeos, Shane scanned the area for Dylan as he always did at this event. Even though Tab distanced himself from the rodeo shortly after gaining full custody, Shane figured he'd still bring his son around. Years had gone by and Shane hadn't seen or heard a word about him. This event was a part of who Tab was and all fathers wanted their children to know where they came from, didn't they?

A string of Miss Rodeo South Dakota contestants posed for photos around the large stone compass marking the geographical center of the country. It always bugged his father that the true center of the country was thirteen miles north of here. Another fond memory. Belle Fourche had been their father-and-son time and the pain of his loss was more raw than Shane imagined it would be.

After checking into his hotel, he called his agent.

"Keep in mind, these are the same people who produced *Malibu Beach*," Brock said through the phone. "Yes, they took unknowns and made them millionaires, but they are also laughingstocks who no one will ever take seriously. That's not what I want for one of my clients. Money shouldn't be the driving force here. You have plenty of that. Fame, yes—go for the fame—but make sure it's the type of fame you want. And I promise you, once you sign, there will be scripts involved and some little piss-ass director telling you to pick fights with your brothers just to raise the ratings. Reality shows are anything but real and I'm advising you not to accept this offer."

Not the words Shane expected to hear from Brock, but he respected the man's honesty. He knew some of the shows were scripted and he wasn't about to let anyone treat him like a trained monkey.

"I'm not making any decisions tonight," Shane said. "I understand the impact it will have on my family and maybe it should be filmed on the road and not at Bridle Dance."

"I don't mean to sound harsh," Brock said. "But do you honestly think they'd still want you if the ranch, the school and the family weren't involved?"

"Ryan said I was the anchor of the show."

"Because you're wealthy," Brock said. "And they will find a way to use that against you. Your friends on the circuit will become your enemies when they *suddenly appear* at Ride 'em High! because the producers brought them there to create conflict. Without conflict, there's no show."

"Is there any good side to this?" Shane almost regretted asking. "If it was all bad, none of these shows would exist."

"Only the money and the fame, if you can call it that. Keeping it Reel Pictures doesn't produce quality. They're all about quantity at the cheapest cost. They can make a mint off of you and the only money you'll see is from people paying you to make appearances."

"I'm already paid to make appearances."

"And that right there is the reason they went directly to you instead of me. A show like this may not sit well with some of your sponsors and you're pulling in a nice chunk of change with them. Your popularity increased tenfold with the boot company, and if you lose a sponsorship like that, you have to carry everything on yourself. Your money isn't endless. I want the best for you, Shane, and trust me, this isn't it. I'm assuming you're still meeting with your sponsors for publicity shots tomorrow."

Shane listened to his agent for a few more minutes before ending the conversation. He promised to discuss it with his family. He needed a clear head and he needed something other than airline almonds in his stomach.

He pulled in front the Belle Inn Restaurant. It didn't look like much from the outside but the food was as close to home as he could get.

"What can I do you for, cowboy?" a waitress greeted him.

"Aw, shucks, I bet you say that to all the men around here." Normally he would have been attracted to her more-than-generous curves but women who tried too hard to be sexy no longer held any appeal. He preferred Lexi's "this is who I am, so deal with it" attitude. Hell, she'd look sexy wearing a feed bag.

"Yep, sure do," she said. "Especially when I have hundreds of them coming through the door. Now come on, hon, tell me what you want to order."

*Shot down and I wasn't even trying!*

Shane ordered and wondered how things were going at the ranch. *What is wrong with you?* This was his time away from family and work and commitments—his time to be free and do whatever he damn well pleased.

*Oh, my god! I'm homesick.*

By early evening, Lexi found herself back on the ranch, watching a black standard poodle puppy scamper across the porch.

"He's definitely going to be a big one judging by the size of his feet." Lexi tapped her fingers on the floorboards for Barney to chase. Running to Kay, he tested his strength by nibbling on her thumb. "Watch out for those needle teeth. They'll—"

"Ouch!" Kay snatched her hand away from Barney's clutches.

"—get you." Lexi watched Kay's expression light up when the puppy stretched for another go at her hands, forcing her to sit on them. "I think you two are going to be very happy together. Just don't let him near the other animals until he gets the rest of his shots."

"Can you do that?" Kay asked.

"I could, but I think you should establish a relationship with Dr. Cerf so Barney gets used to going to the vet and socializing. Plus he needs to get used to riding in the car and visiting with people off the ranch. It will be good for him."

"I think it's time for a potty break." Kay rose, swooping the puppy up in her arms. "When Chinook was a puppy I made a point of taking her out every hour and we had very few accidents. Come to think of it, the boys had more accidents than the dog did."

Lexi was sure of that. Why the woman didn't have a head of solid white hair baffled Lexi. Then again, Nice 'n Easy did amazing things. She handed Kay the leash from the porch floor, and Kay snapped it on Barney's collar and walked down the stairs. Lexi followed her into the side yard, away from the massive vegetable garden.

"Looks like we have company." Kay nodded toward the pathway.

Chase and a few of the boys walked toward them.

"What do we have here?" Chase asked, crouching down in the grass. Barney bounced straight at them.

"Meet Barney, the newest member of our family." Kay beamed.

"You got a dog?" Chase asked. "I think that's great, Mom. And isn't he a cutie. What is he?"

"He's a standard poodle," Kay replied.

Kay and Chase continued to talk but the words faded away. Hunter stood in front of Lexi, close enough for her to reach out and touch him, hug him, never let him— no! She purposely didn't hold her baby after she gave birth, knowing it would be a pain too deep to bear. Hunter squatted next to Chase and ran his hand over the puppy's head.

"I miss my dogs," Hunter said.

Lexi was unable to draw herself away from him. "How many do you have?"

"Three." Hunter's gaze never left Barney. He continued to pet and play with the dog. "Mom has a Westie, Dad has a schnauzer and me and my brother and sister have a Jack Russell named Jack." He laughed, meeting her eyes. "I know, real creative."

The words *Mom* and *Dad* stung for a moment, then

quickly passed when Lexi envisioned him with his family. Her son had siblings and pets.

"How old are your brother and sister?" Lexi knew that the couple who adopted her son didn't have any other children at the time.

"My sister's five and my brother's eleven."

They were younger—one more sign this was her child.

"We were just headed out to the store to get some s'mores fixings," Chase said.

"Can I stay?" Hunter asked, seated cross-legged in the grass with the puppy in his lap.

Chase looked to his mother for approval.

"It's fine." Kay nodded. "We'll be here when you get back."

Silently Lexi screamed for joy and prayed Chase would make this the longest grocery-store trip in history. She watched the way Hunter's hand stroked Barney's chubby puppy belly. He talked softly to the dog, welcoming him to his new home and telling him how much he'd like living there.

"I can remember when Shane was younger, he wanted to be present for every foal born on this ranch, just like his father," Kay began, reaching out and scratching Barney under the chin. "Shane and Joe sat in those stables all night long and watched the mares, not going to bed until each foal was able to stand on their own. You remind me a lot of Shane—you have that caring nature in you, too."

Lexi mentally snapped a photo of grandmother and grandson, side by side—the way it should be. The way it couldn't be.

\* \* \*

After a successful ride, Shane made it to the hotel for a hot shower followed by a couple of interviews and a meeting with one of his sponsors. His back still ached thanks to the final unanticipated twist the bronc had thrown in at the last second. Regardless, he held on to his first-place standing. He had a full schedule of events throughout the summer, and he usually looked forward to each and every one of them. This was his life, this was in his blood…this was not where he wanted to be tonight.

Stepping out into the hallway, Shane almost collided with a room service waiter. When he made his way around the cart, he got a glimpse of a tall blond cowboy turning the corner toward the elevators. *Tab Fanning?*

He ran to catch up with him before the doors closed, but by the time he reached the elevator, the cowboy was gone. As he raced down the adjacent stairwell, the leather soles of his boots almost slipped on the painted steps. At the bottom, with his heart in check, he took a deep breath before he turned the knob and walked into the lobby.

The elevator was on its way back up, meaning Tab—if it was Tab—had already gotten off. Not seeing him, Shane ran out on the sidewalk. Scanning the crowds of tourists and cowboys, he tried to spot the man he had seen only moments ago. Almost a head taller than most of the people around him, Shane spied him across the street.

"Hey, Shane, we have to meet with another sponsor." One of his teammates grabbed his arm and tried to lead him inside. "We're running behind, man, come on."

After waiting all these years to find out how Dylan was doing, he wasn't about to let the opportunity pass him by.

"Tell them I had an emergency and I'll be there soon." It was a stretch but not much of one. To Shane, this was a sanity emergency.

Down the street, the carnival was in full swing. Lights loosely hung in front of the games impossible to win. The carousel turned counterclockwise while horses and tigers slowly dipped and bobbed in time with the music. The scent of greasy funnel cakes and salty popcorn permeated the evening air. Shane once again searched the face of every man, hoping one of them was Tab. Finally he recognized the man he'd seen in the hotel. Shane ran to catch up to the cowboy and called out his name.

"Tab. Is that you?"

Time had weathered him some, but this was still the same man who had taken away the son he'd thought was his.

"Shane," Tab said flatly. "I had a feeling I might run into you here."

"The last I heard you retired." Shane looked past Tab to see if Dylan was near. "Are you alone?"

"Dylan has expressed an interest in the rodeo, more than I wanted him to. I told him he could pick one rodeo this summer and of course he had to choose one of my favorites."

"The rodeo's in his blood. Where is he?" Shane asked, eager to see the young man he'd become. "I'd love to say hello."

"Shane." Tab removed his hat and moved off the sidewalk, allowing a group of people to pass. "Dylan doesn't have any recollection of who you are. He was a baby when he left, and while I appreciate everything you did for *my son,* I think it's best to leave the past alone."

Shane knew the chances of Dylan remembering him were slim but there had always been hope. Until today.

"Honey." A gorgeous brunette approached Tab and snaked an arm around his waist. "The kids and I are getting hungry."

Behind her three kids playfully wrestled with each other as they made their way toward the adults.

"Come on, Dad." The oldest boy stood next to the woman. "There's a pizza stand over there."

"Wendy, this is an old friend of mine, Shane Langtry." Tab nodded to Shane. "Shane, this is my wife and kids, Dylan, Sandy and Will."

"Did you know my dad when he was in the rodeo?" the oldest boy asked. Dylan had grown into a fine young man—a teenager this year. Shane wouldn't have recognized him if he'd smacked into him. The chipmunk cheeks and baby pudge had been replaced by the long and lean form of his father.

"I did," Shane choked out. "He was my toughest competition. I don't want to keep you from your family. It was good seeing you, Tab…ma'am." Shane tipped his hat to Wendy and turned toward the hotel. Forcing himself not to look back, he tried to will the tears from his eyes.

*Focus, Shane. Meet with the sponsors, make your next ride and get the hell out of here.*

## Chapter 7

Miranda and Jesse's Fourth of July picnic should have been Lexi's escape, considering the amount of help Miranda needed this year. Lexi knew how difficult it was to move about once you reached the end of your pregnancy, especially in the summer. And carrying twins didn't make things any easier.

Jesse was adorable, waiting on his wife, hand and foot, making sure she didn't do anything except "sit pretty and give orders." The ornery cowboy bowing to his wife's every wish was a sight to behold. Fifty years from today, they'd probably sit on the same porch, watching their grandkids plan this picnic.

The Ride 'em High! kids and Dance of Hope hippotherapy families were some of the first people to arrive and immediately started to set up for one of their birthdays. It was nice to see the children from both facilities interact with each other. Joe would have been so proud of his boys.

Lexi hoped to spend more time around Hunter this afternoon. Yesterday had been an unexpected gift. She'd learned how much he loved his family and school, that he played football and was an Xbox addict. The more he spoke, the more she saw bits and pieces of her and Shane. Even without a DNA test, there was no doubt Hunter was her child.

She tried to convince herself not to come to the picnic. It would be best for her and Hunter if she stayed away. Clay had warned her and she should have heeded his advice. The harder she tried to keep away, the more she reasoned with herself why only one more day wouldn't hurt. One more day meant a few more questions answered. One more day became two and Lexi didn't know how she would be able to say goodbye.

Any remote possibility of telling Shane and Hunter's adoptive parents the truth was out of the question after having spoken with Hunter yesterday. He and his parents had an amazing life together and she saw no reason to disrupt it. Why hurt Shane with the truth only to have his son leave for home in a few weeks? Lexi had lived this long not knowing a single thing about her son. Now that she did, she'd have to be satisfied and let Hunter go back to his own life. With his talent, she was sure to see him again…from a distance.

"Hang in there just another few days and we'll know the truth," Clay said over her shoulder.

"When did you get his sample?" Lexi looked up at him, the hint of a summer breeze swirling the humidity around her instead of relieving the heat.

"A few days ago when you were kissing Shane in the stables."

"How did you know about that?" Lexi didn't remember seeing his truck on the ranch that day.

"Because I was there getting strands from his hairbrush and on my way out I saw you. Luckily he's still at an age where his mom—sorry, his adoptive mom—writes his name on everything. And don't look at me that way. I can get in and out of places and you'd never have a clue I was there, which apparently was the case when I swung by the ranch yesterday to see Cole and saw you and Hunter together. Lexi, you need to keep your distance from him."

"He came to me," Lexi argued.

"And your legs were broken, forcing you to stay on the ground, next to him."

"You don't have the slightest clue how it feels to be inches away from your own child—a child perpetually on your mind." The baby she ran from so many years ago had found her and there was no way in hell she was letting him go this time. It wasn't healthy and she knew it, but it felt amazing to be near him. "Once I know for certain, I'll be able to walk away."

"You're sure you'll be able to?" Clay asked.

"I never expected to see him again." Lexi watched Miranda's almost full-grown bloodhounds, Rhett and Scarlett, chase Hunter and the other boys around the field of wildflowers.

Clay eyed her suspiciously. "I have an associate in the Denver area doing recon on the Rathbones' house and so far they seem to be a normal family."

Lexi continued to observe Hunter from a distance for

the remainder of the day, choosing to stay close to her own family. Tradition dictated everyone bring a dish to share, but Mazie had brought, at last count, thirteen different offerings. When Lexi showed up empty-handed, her mother assured her she was covered.

"Okay, spill the beans." Mazie slid in next to her on the picnic bench. "Rumor has it you spent the night with Clay Tanner."

"What?"

"Don't deny it." Mazie waggled a finger at her. "Your car was there all night and into the morning."

"You told me you had an emergency." Her brother, Nash, jumped into the conversation. "You and the P.I.? Now I know what kind of undercover work he does."

"It's not what you think." On the verge of a short circuit, Lexi's brain tried to find an excuse. "I did have an emergency and then Clay called and asked me to check on Dream Catcher. We got to talking and drinking and it was just safer if I spent the night on his couch."

It was half-true, at least. Lexi wondered how many other people at the picnic were having this same conversation with Clay. Acknowledging a rumor even existed was enough to fuel it further. But this one was different. She didn't want Shane to think she'd sleep with his best friend. Lexi had had her cruel moments over the years, but crossing such a line was beneath her.

"How did his *investigation* go?" Mazie teased.

"Okay, more than I want to know." Nash made a disgusted face and stood up from the table. "At least you chose a good guy this time instead of those lowlifes you usually end up with."

"I didn't choose anyone and, Mazie, please stop

this rumor before it gets out of control. You have a big mouth, put it to good use."

"That wasn't very nice," Mazie responded with a pout.

"I didn't mean it in a bad way. But you are the gossip queen and you know it. I'm asking you to spread the word about how untrue the rumor is."

Mazie contemplated her request for a minute. "There really isn't anything going on between you two?"

Lexi shook her head. "No and there won't be."

Not wanting to be the topic of party conversation, Lexi thanked Jesse and Miranda and decided to call it a night. Elvis Watts and his band began to play another set when something caught her eye on stage.

"Hello, Ramblewood!" Elvis boomed over the microphone. "We have a young guest star up here who's going to sing us some old-school Johnny Cash."

Hunter made his way to the microphone, a Les Paul guitar in hand. Slipping the strap over his shoulder, he played the first few notes of "Folsom Prison Blues" and stopped. A crowd quickly gathered in front of the stage and cheered. Teasing them again, he played the same beginning riff.

"Who wants to hear a little Johnny tonight?" Hunter leaned into the microphone and grabbed it with one hand, angling the stand toward him. Looking to the band, he said, "Think we should give them what they want?"

Elvis laughed and nodded, obviously enjoying Hunter's showmanship.

"Let's do this." Hunter counted the band down and they began to play.

Captivated by his voice and proud of his talent, Lexi watched Hunter play until her heart was about to burst. She needed to leave before she started shouting "That's my incredible son up there!" She needed to get away and fast.

"Where are you going?" Mazie called after her.

"The fireworks are going to start soon and I want to get back home and make sure the horses aren't spooked." Many of the ranches piped music through the stables during Fourth of July celebrations to cover the cracking of the fireworks, which sounded like gunshots. Autumn wasn't a fan of loud noises and Lexi wanted to make sure someone left a radio playing before the first blast. "Tell Mom and Dad I have everything covered at the farm. There's no need for you all to miss the fireworks."

Once she arrived on the Lawson farm, Lexi ran through the barn until she reached Autumn. Wrapping her arms around the horse's neck, she wept against her mane.

"What have I done?" she asked the mare. "I gave away my child, my only child, and now I can't even tell him how proud I am of him."

Watching the fireworks from the airplane was a new experience for Shane. Still in the lead, he'd decided to cut out of the roundup early and head home. By the time morning rolled around, Shane was certain his agent would have his hide for leaving before sponsor photos were taken, but he didn't care.

He wanted to get home and tell his mom about Dylan. Despite their differences over the past year, Shane knew she'd be the one person who'd always be there for him. No matter how old he was, there were some days only a mother could make better.

When his plane touched down, there was a message from Chase telling him Crystal was beginning to foal. Shane retrieved his Jeep from the long term parking lot and sat in the holiday traffic for the next two hours before finally reaching the ranch. It was almost midnight when he pulled into the parking lot. The stables were aglow and the grounds bustled with activity in anticipation of Joe's dream foal. Why was it that a foal arriving in the middle of the night seemed more the norm than during daylight hours?

Inside the stables, his family and the rodeo school students quietly gathered outside Crystal's stall. Shane peered through the door and saw the mare lying on her side in the middle of a contraction. Ashleigh and Billy stood nearby but he didn't see Lexi.

Expecting his question, Ashleigh said, "She's on her way."

The sound of fast footfalls caused them all to turn toward Lexi running down the hallway. Even in old jeans, a T-shirt and ratty sneakers she looked beautiful.

"How are we doing?" Lexi quickly tied her hair up in a bun while she listened to Ashleigh's report. Turning to face everyone, Lexi motioned them all closer. "I need you all to join hands while we have a moment of silence to remember the man that put this foal's life in motion. Joe, I know you're watching over us."

"What are you doing home so early?" Kay hugged her son. "I thought you were staying until tomorrow."

"Change in plans." Shane caught Lexi watching him before she quickly returned her attention to the foal. Her eyes were puffy and her nose slightly red. He wondered if she'd been crying before she arrived.

After several contractions, Crystal expelled a gush of fluid. There were a few oohs and aahs, and one "wicked" that sounded like it came from Hunter. Straining to check her back end, the horse tried in vain to stand. Another contraction racked her body, and the beginnings of the sac appeared.

"I see something." Hunter pointed to the mare's raised tail.

"That's the amniotic sac," Lexi said. "It protects the foal inside the mother."

What appeared to be a white hoof and leg emerged when Crystal once again attempted to stand. Breathing heavy, the horse met Shane's eyes and held them. Lying back on her side, she grunted and pushed again, the room becoming quiet except for the mare's ragged breaths.

Another leg appeared and Lexi entered the stall, bending down to see what she could of the foal. Tearing the sac open with her hands, she grabbed hold of the pure white legs. After several minutes, she looked to Shane for help.

He noiselessly entered the stall, not wanting to startle the mare. He firmly gripped the foal's front legs and tugged while Crystal lay there motionless, letting him help her. The white head emerged and Lexi quickly cleared the sac from the foal's mouth while Shane continued to pull. When the body was halfway out, Shane tugged again on the foal's legs.

Lexi quickly checked the mare. "She's showing signs of distress. We need to get this foal out now."

"Is this a—"

"Don't, Shane." Lexi stopped him from saying the two words any breeder dreaded to hear. "On the count of three." Lexi took one of the horse's legs while Shane wrapped both hands around the other.

"One, two…" On three, the foal slid from the mare's body. Lexi pulled it slightly to the side, wanting the umbilical cord to break naturally. Shane stripped away the rest of the sac while an exhausted Crystal lifted her head to watch.

Stepping aside, they looked down at the pure white foal while it lifted its head and struggled to roll onto its chest.

Gasps came from the hallway.

"Oh, heavens, no," Kay said.

It was their greatest fear. A lethal white horse.

The barn was in a panic. Not all pure white horses with blue eyes were afflicted with lethal white syndrome and Lexi hoped this was one of those cases. When breeding American paints, there was always the risk, one Lexi tried to eliminate by always performing a detailed lineage background check and genetic testing before she bred any horse.

Shane sat on the stall floor, cradling the foal's head in his lap and wiping its nose and mouth. *Almost thirteen years ago to the day, he should have been cradling Hunter.* Lexi dressed the broken umbilical cord and they left mother and foal to bond while they cleaned themselves up. After an hour, Crystal began to show signs of rejecting her baby. Time was not in their favor. Lethal whites were born missing sections of their intestines and began to die within hours of birth. It was a painful death and one where euthanasia was the only humane option.

Thirty minutes later the foal still hadn't stood and Lexi feared the first signs of colic were beginning to appear. Ignoring the crowd that still gathered in the hallway, she gently opened the stall door and went inside. Shane joined her, and when she crouched down next to the foal, he squeezed her hand, wordlessly begging her to save the newborn.

Lexi placed her stethoscope against the horse and listened for signs of distress. He appeared weak but not in any pain, and with Shane's help, she was able to get the foal to stand. Lexi usually frowned upon most foal interference, fearing it would strain the foal's tendons or impede the important bonding time. But after a wobbly half hour, he managed to stay upright on his own.

The foal passed the usual reflex tests and Lexi wanted to see if he would nurse on his own. When Crystal became agitated and started violently kicking her baby, Lexi knew she had to separate them and asked Billy to take Crystal into a neighboring stall. Lexi ran her hands over the animal's coat and pink skin under the overhead lights. Uncertain if her eyes were playing tricks on her, Lexi swore she saw lighter patches of white within the coat. Two different shades of white would mean the horse was a dominant white, and not a lethal. Nothing would make her happier at the moment. Unless you counted reversing the hands of time and asking for a do-over.

Ashleigh prepared the milk replacer while Lexi attempted to milk Crystal without getting herself kicked. The colostrum contained the necessary antibodies to protect the foal from infection, providing the horse lived. They had an emergency reserve of frozen colostrum, but Lexi always wanted to try every option to get the mother's before she went that route.

"Let's see if we can get this boy to eat." Lexi felt all eyes were on her but she directed her words to Shane. She knew how much this horse meant to him and the rest of the Langtry family. If the foal readily accepted the milk replacer, it was another good sign. "It takes around twelve hours for the signs of lethal white syndrome to show. I'll be right here with you."

While Ashleigh fed the foal, Lexi ran outside to grab her strap-on headlamp from the car. She'd been wrestling with telling Shane the truth about their child when she received the call to come to the barn. Shocked to see him there, Lexi knew she had to push any thoughts of him and Hunter aside and focus on the potentially devastating situation inside. On the way back to the stables, Hunter met her outside the doors.

"Is he going to die?" he asked.

"I don't know." The moment felt surreal. Hunter was, in all likelihood, her son, and he was looking to her for answers about the foal. "I'm not a hundred percent sure he's a lethal white horse."

Hunter shook his head and looked at his bare feet. "Everyone was excited when he was being born. It was sick…well, kind of gross, but a sick gross. I don't understand why everyone's upset he's an albino. Why are you calling him a lethal white?"

Lexi sat on the wrought-iron bench outside the stable entrance and patted the spot next to her. Explaining the hardships of genetics and the lack of control over the situation wasn't easy with adults, even harder with children. But Hunter was almost a teenager and Lexi felt he could handle the truth. His parents might feel otherwise, but she didn't want to lie to him. She noticed Billy standing in the doorway, and while he was six years older than Hunter, this was probably confusing to him as well.

Motioning for Billy to join them, Lexi tried her best to explain the situation.

"A lethal white is different from an albino. A horse with overo lethal white syndrome usually has blue or gray eyes, but it's a genetic condition where both parents carry the defective gene. If this foal does have it, he will have an underdeveloped digestive tract and will not be able to pass anything. Surgery has never been successful, and within hours, he'll show signs of colic and cramping and will have to be put down."

"I thought we did genetic testing before we bred them," Billy said.

"We did, and these horses have been DNA tested for that gene. The problem is, American Paints are one of the breeds this syndrome runs in, and many of the Bridle Dance horses are the frame-overo color pattern, where the base is any color, but they have irregular white patches and many have bald faces. Even with testing, there is still a rare possibility that one will carry the mutation. Keep in mind this foal's parents don't belong to us, and if this is a lethal white, neither one can be bred again."

"But you said you weren't sure if this horse was a lethal white," Hunter said.

"That's why I came out to get this." Lexi held out her hand and showed Hunter the strap of her headlamp. "This will help me see his coat and skin clearer so I can get a better idea. I thought I saw a slight pattern to his coat, and if that's the case, then we may have a horse that's considered dominant white. The true test is if our foal passes the milk replacer we gave him."

Hunter nodded at her words and she knew it was a lot for him to absorb. Billy wasn't convincing in his stoicism, and she feared he might break at any given moment. She knew he had a strong love for horses, but in this field, you had to be able to take the good with the bad, or else you'd never make it.

"I think everyone should call it a night." Lexi rose, fighting the urge to wrap her arms around Hunter and tell him everything was all right. But it might not be and Lexi feared if she touched him, she wouldn't be able to let go when the time came for him to return home to his family. "Shane and I will stay with the foal all night."

"I want to stay." Billy squared his shoulders, confident and ready to assist her, but his shaky voice betrayed him.

"It's okay to be nervous." Lexi reached over and squeezed Billy's arm. "I'm nervous and this isn't my first time in this situation."

"Can I stay, too?" Hunter chewed on his bottom lip, awaiting a response.

Lexi nodded and they walked down the long corridor to the foal's stall. The barn was exceptionally quiet and Lexi eerily felt everyone's eyes were on her. She wasn't a miracle worker and she hated that everyone thought she held the power to keep this horse alive. Nothing was more out of her hands and she had to let nature take its course.

Shane sat in the corner of the stall, the foal standing in front of him, acting essentially normal. This was a better sign than a half hour ago, when it was lying on the floor. Shane rubbed his forehead. Just like his father, the wildest Langtry boy would give his life to save that of a horse. When they were kids, she always found him in the stables or riding one of the many trails. Lexi would be willing to bet his horses held as many of his secrets as her own did.

Directing her attention to the crowd in the hallway, she said, "I think it's best for everyone to go back to bed, and if anything changes, we'll let you know."

Kay agreed and ushered everyone from the barn, leaving Lexi and the three males to stay with the foal.

"Billy, come help me for a minute." Lexi placed the headlight over her hair and turned it on. "I thought I saw a pattern in the coat earlier—almost a cream color on white, but it could have been bedding dust from the pellets."

Lexi attempted to run her hand over the foal's coat. Clearly feeling better, it bounced around the stable. She hoped this wasn't a false sign. When she'd interned in New York, she'd witnessed a perfectly healthy, happy, nursing foal that was predominately white but had some darker markings suddenly turn, and within hours it had to be euthanized. An unsuspecting lethal white, and it wasn't even a pure white horse. Mother Nature was the cruelest and most unpredictable force in the world.

Billy agreed he saw some variations in the horse's shading, making them more optimistic. Hunter curled up on a hay bale near the stall door. Lexi watched him sleep, thinking about the thousands of sleeps she'd missed with him.

She looked over at Shane, who was sitting in the corner of the stall, worry and anguish across his face while he watched the foal's every move. Billy sat in the opposite corner, half-awake. She lowered herself down next to Shane, their shoulders and arms lightly touching. Lexi wanted to comfort and protect him, as she wanted to protect Hunter from the pain they might all feel shortly if the horse didn't make it.

Without hesitation, Shane lifted his arm and wrapped it around Lexi's shoulder, allowing her to settle against his chest. Inhaling his scent of hay and horse, Lexi almost laughed at the irony of him trying to protect her. There were no words between them, no fleeting looks, just a silent understanding and a common hope.

Holding Lexi temporarily erased the pain of the past. He'd forgotten how much he needed her until he felt her body next to him again. Hating to see any animal suffer, Shane wished there was more he could do to help the foal. There was some comfort knowing Lexi had done everything possible, but now they had to watch the clock painfully tick by.

Shane smiled when Hunter shifted in his sleep. All the kids had grown on him, something he never thought possible. Looking down at Lexi, he wondered if they had a chance of having children someday.

"I saw Dylan last night in Belle Fourche." Shane

wasn't sure if Lexi wanted to hear about the child that tore them apart but he needed to let her know that chapter of his life was finally closed.

Lexi stiffened slightly before she spoke. "You finally found him after all these years. How did it go?"

"Tab told me Dylan didn't remember me." Shane sighed and rested his head against Lexi's. "He has a brother and a sister, a new mom and what looked like a really nice family."

"You're okay with that?" Lexi asked. "With letting go of him?"

Shane laughed. "What choice do I have? I've wanted to see the kid for the longest time, and when I did, he didn't have a clue who I was. In the back of my mind, I knew he wouldn't. Of course, I hoped he would, but it's better this way. He's happy and that's what really matters."

"Sometimes they're better without us," Lexi said.

"Us?" Shane asked.

Lexi sat up, rolling her shoulders. "It's just a figure of speech. I was generalizing."

Shane felt there was more to it than that but he also knew not to push Lexi. He enjoyed her presence around the ranch and he didn't want to push his luck, although the kiss the other day probably didn't help. Hunter woke and groggily made his way over to them. The foal was curious and sniffed at him. Ramrod-still, Hunter allowed the horse to take inventory before it was seemingly satisfied and walked away.

Weary, Hunter sat down next to Lexi and rested his head against hers. Shane saw Lexi's face go from pink to pale in under a second, her hand frozen in midair as if she didn't know what to do.

"He doesn't bite, Lexi," Shane whispered, trying to recall if he'd seen her with kids before. When the schools did their "visit a profession" day, usually Ashleigh led the groups around and had the most contact with the kids. Lexi gave her speech and that was it.

The foal bounced across the stall, trying out his newly discovered legs, stopping only to urinate, and even then, it was a bouncy event. A few minutes later, he attempted to lie down, bending his front knees and then standing back up, uncertain of the process. Finally finding his coordination, the foal gracefully lowered himself to the ground. Shane saw Lexi place her hand over Hunter's and squeeze gently to reassure him this was normal behavior. Shane had seen a foal's awkwardness a thousand times but they hadn't had a horse this unusual before.

"He seems like every other foal I've seen here, except for his color," Billy said from his corner, startling Lexi. She immediately broke contact with Hunter. "Sorry, I didn't want to interrupt you guys, but are you getting any sign one way or another?"

"I'll feel better when he gets back up on his own," Lexi told him. "He should only be down for about thirty minutes, give or take."

It had been a few hours since the foal's birth and they anxiously awaited the horse to do its business. It wasn't what Shane called a date by any means, especially with Billy and Hunter as chaperones, but sitting there, on a stall floor in the middle of the night with Lexi, was pure and real. They had their differences, but horses were the one constant between them and Shane thanked his father every day for bringing Lexi home. He wished he had told Joe that while he was still alive instead of always giving his dad a hard time over one thing or another.

Lexi looked at Shane, and he wondered if she could read his thoughts. Half smiling, she gave him her full attention. "All right, tell me more about Dylan."

Shane bit back the sob that almost broke through. The one he'd been holding since the child he'd loved all these years, the child that he'd sworn to protect and take care of the first year of his life, didn't know who he was. That hurt like hell. He appreciated Lexi wanting to hear more, knowing the mention of Dylan was a reminder of his infidelity.

"He was taller than Hunter, but had the same build," Shane said. "Definite resemblance to Tab, but mostly he favors his mother. I'd stare at Dylan in his crib, trying to find even a little part of him that looked like me. Maybe I knew he wasn't mine, but once I held him all bets were off and I loved that kid. God, I miss him."

"Hunter told me the other night that he has a birthday in a few days." Lexi absently rested her hand on Hunter's shoulder. The boy had fallen asleep with his head on her lap. "I'm assuming you're having a little party for him like Dance of Hope did for Josh's birthday." Recovering from a traumatic brain injury, Josh had turned seven last week and the entire ranch was there to celebrate the occasion with him.

"You're welcome to join us," Shane said. "You know kids—thirteen's a big deal. He's officially a teenager."

"Are his parents flying in?" Lexi asked.

"They're coming at the end of the month for Family Day," Shane said. "They sent a package down that I'm holding in the house for him."

"Family Day?"

Shane felt Lexi stiffen and wrapped his arm around her tighter. "Just like when we were in sleepaway camp. Are you all right?"

Lexi nodded, but Shane once again sensed there was more than she let on. At first he'd dismissed her interest in the school, thinking it was a curiosity, but she seemed to be spending more time around the kids lately, and Shane wondered if her biological clock was kicking in. *I'd love to be the one to stop that clock.*

Taking a chance, he threw the words out there. "Do you ever think about having kids?"

Judging by the look on her face, Shane thought she was about to haul off and slug him. The foal moved and quickly leapt to its feet. Billy slid across the wall to Lexi, causing Hunter to stir awake. Lexi reached out and they all joined hands, anxiously awaiting its next move, all wishing for the same thing. The four of them huddled in the corner of the stall, one white foal staring back at them.

"You should name him Apollo," Hunter whispered.

"Apollo?" He hadn't considered that name before. Regardless of which way this went, the animal deserved to have a name.

"I learned about him in mythology. He was the Greek god of the sun and light and you can't get any lighter than that."

They all laughed. "No, you can't."

The horse moved to the center of the stall and stood

still, its tail raised in the air. Shane shut his eyes and said a prayer under his breath. Lexi tightened her grip on his hand.

And there it was. The dark, tarlike meconium that accumulated when the horse fed in the womb. It was the sign they were waiting for.

"Oh, that's gross." Hunter stood and covered his nose.

"That is the most beautiful thing in the world right now." Lexi rose and dusted off her jeans.

"Almost the most beautiful." Shane pulled Lexi in for a hug. "Thank you for being here," he whispered against her hair.

"I'm just doing what you pay me to do." Lexi pulled back, looking him in the eyes.

The tension between them gone, Shane brushed an errant lock of hair out of her face. The feel of her body next to him, touching him, confirmed what he'd known all along. He loved the woman standing before him and no amount of time in the world would change that.

"Are you two going to kiss?" Hunter asked, breaking the moment.

"Come on, kid." Billy ushered him out of the stall. "Let's get some fresh bedding for—are you going to name him Apollo?"

Shane reluctantly stepped away from Lexi, leaving her obviously flustered and blushing.

"I think Apollo's a perfect name," he said.

Hunter smiled and left them alone.

"What do you think, doc?"

"I think we have a dominant white but I'm still going to run a homozygous test for a genetic abnormality. And

I'm definitely going to have both parents' stables run further testing—"

Shane placed a finger on her lips to silence her. Closing her eyes, she lowered her head before he had a chance to kiss her.

"Shane." Her voice was barely a whisper. "We can't."

"We can if you let it happen." His breath was warm against her cheek.

She wanted it to happen. She enjoyed the way his arms felt around her body. She missed his scent and most of all she missed his taste.

Reaching up toward him, Lexi laced her fingers behind his neck and drew him in for a kiss. Their tongues met with the sensual familiarity of two longtime lovers. Maybe it was because she'd spent the last few hours with Shane and Hunter. A secret family that no one knew about and a dream fulfilled she'd never thought possible. This was theirs, this was the life she'd wanted all along—the one she deserved. This was—wrong.

Lexi broke their kiss and pushed Shane away. Breathlessly they stared at each other.

"What the hell was that? I think we're getting closer and you pull away again. I can't keep doing this, Lexi."

"Uh-oh," Hunter said from the stall door. "Trouble."

Lexi saw half the ranch standing in the hallway watching their exchange.

"I'm sorry," Billy said. "I thought everyone would want to know the good news."

Flustered, Lexi inhaled sharply. "It's okay." She walked to the stall door, not daring a glance back. "We need to clean this stall and I want to try nursing again.

If we can't then I'll try another mare. Some of the foals are weaning so we should be fine."

"Ashleigh's on her way in." Billy moved aside to let her pass. Shane made no move to follow.

"Thank you." Lexi squeezed Billy's arm and looked down at Hunter, who stood next to him. This time next year he'd probably be taller than she was. Such a strong man in the making. "I'm so proud of you both. That was pretty intense in there and you held up great."

"Thanks." Hunter smiled at her—the pain tugging at her heart almost unbearable. She wanted—she needed—to hug the child she thought was her son and show him how much she loved him.

*And his father, too.*

# Chapter 8

Lexi swung the stable doors wide with such force she was surprised they remained on their hinges. Thick middle-of-the-night, humidity-laden air made it even harder for her to breathe. She needed to know for certain that was her son who had fallen asleep on her lap. And Shane had kissed her. Why was this happening now?

Knowing she couldn't let this go any further, she had to finish up tonight and keep her distance, even if it meant leaving town until Hunter returned to Colorado. Lexi had a standby large-animal veterinarian she referred people to if she wasn't available. She had faith he'd be able to cover her emergencies.

Steadying herself, she headed back into the stables and peeked at Apollo. He stood there, looking at all the people staring at him as if to say, "What's the big deal?"

"Come on, guys." Chase rounded up his students and led them toward the door. "Time for bed…again."

"Would you like some coffee, dear?" Kay asked while soothingly rubbing Lexi's back. "You look exhausted."

"I would, but I have appointments I need to keep today." Lexi wanted to find Ashleigh and give her a list of things to handle in the morning.

"Take a break and come upstairs with me," Kay gently demanded. "I'm not taking no for an answer. You look like you're ready to collapse."

Left with no choice and in desperate need of a mini-break, Lexi followed Kay toward the office stairs in the center of the stables.

"If you didn't still have work to do I'd pour you a brandy," Kay whispered from the step above her. "A kiss like that warrants a drink."

No sense wondering if anyone saw them anymore. Soon, the entire town would be chattering about her and Shane's kiss. At least it would take people's minds off the supposed one-nighter she had with Clay.

Upstairs, away from the commotion below, Kay fixed Lexi a cup of coffee and motioned for her to take a seat. The office sat above the stables, with Craftsman-style windows encircling the room, allowing for a 360-degree view. In the moonlight, the ranch had a fairy-tale luminescence to it. In a way, her fairy tale did come true tonight, if only for a little while. The family Lexi thought she'd never have was hers for a few fleeting hours. Then like most dreams, she awoke and it was over.

"Get your bearings about you and then you can get

back to work." Kay mothered her like one of her own. She was a kindhearted, hardworking woman who had a grandson a few feet away and Lexi didn't have the guts to tell her the truth.

Lexi rubbed her eyes with the heels of her hands, trying to find relief from the hay dust irritating them. "A part of me could curl up and sleep for hours, the other part is too full of adrenaline."

"It's been a long night," Kay said. "Did something happen before you got here? You seemed upset when you came in."

"No," Lexi said. "I was just going to bed when the phone rang." More like she was going to cry herself to sleep like she had so many other nights.

"When are you going to tell him the truth?"

Knocking her coffee onto the floor, Lexi cursed under her breath. *How does she know?*

"This is exactly what I mean." Kay handed her a roll of paper towels. "You're overly tired, clumsy and you're obviously still in love with my son."

"Wh-what?"

"He hasn't stopped loving you and he does every foolhardy thing there is to forget you, only he knows he can't. We all see it. Why can't you both admit it to each other and get on with it?"

"It's complicated." Lexi wiped up the floor and tried to remain calm. *She doesn't know.*

"Because you both make it complicated," Kay said. "Far be it from me to interfere, but let me say this…you two have wasted so much precious time sidestepping each other it's like watching the world's longest waltz."

Lexi laughed at the picture she painted. "I love you,

Kay. Thank you for the coffee, or what I had of it, but I need to finish up down there before my next appointment."

After Ashleigh told her that Crystal still wouldn't allow Apollo to nurse, they brought in Delilah as a surrogate mother. Delilah's foal had completely weaned a day ago and the mare was still producing milk. Apollo instantly took to her and Lexi felt better about the foal getting the proper nutrients.

Placing Apollo and Delilah in an adjacent stall to Crystal's, Lexi hoped Crystal's attitude toward her baby would change. In the meantime, she'd treat both mares as if they were nursing, increasing the food and nutrient intakes.

Before leaving the ranch, Lexi gave Crystal a thorough postfoal exam and then checked on Apollo one last time to ensure he was in fact a normal, healthy foal. Standing alongside his surrogate mom, the white foal looked up at Lexi with his blue eyes, not a care in the world.

*Oh, to be a horse.*

Lexi sent Ashleigh and Billy home for a few hours, then managed to leave herself without running into Shane again. She was barely able to keep her eyes open when she pulled into her driveway. Resting her head against the steering wheel, she willed herself the strength to get out of the car.

*Please let tonight be a dream.*

Shane walked with Hunter to the bunkhouse, downright confused after that kiss. It was as unexpected as it was natural, and it was perfect until Lexi pushed him away.

"You really like Trouble, don't you?" Hunter asked.

Shane laughed. "What did I tell you about calling her that?"

"Hey, I'm just repeating what you told me the day I met her." They stopped on the bunkhouse steps. "I'm not tired and the sun's going to be up in a few anyway. Do I have to go back to bed?"

The sky to the east showed a hint of light gray and the stars were beginning to fade. The evening crickets had long since tucked up their legs and called it a night while the birds had begun their morning song.

"The Magpie opens in a bit. Think you can manage to quietly grab some clothes from inside?" Shane looked down at Hunter's bare feet. "And boots?"

Hunter snuck into the dark bunkhouse. It reminded him of when Shane and his brothers were kids and Jesse would sneak into the bunkhouse trying to steal the ranch hands' boots. Jesse was always the prankster, and Shane was surprised his brother didn't get himself shot with half his shenanigans. He missed those days, when life wasn't so complicated.

Minutes later, Hunter eased the door closed and they headed up to the main house. Barely containing his amazement, Hunter walked into the Langtrys' kitchen overlooking the great room.

"Wow!" The moon shone through the large skylight, highlighting the rustic log walls. Shane's father had taken great care choosing hand-hewn beams instead of machined lumber. His mother's respect for the local Native American Kickapoo tribe was evident in the beaded artwork that adorned the walls. But Shane's favorite part of the house was always the monumental, floor-to-ceiling river-rock fireplace.

"Come on." Shane led the way up the stairs to the loft, making the room below appear even grander. "You can shower down the hall and I'll meet you out here in a few."

Unable to tear himself away from the railing, Hunter looked around the golden-timbered space. "This is even bigger than the lodge my family goes to in Aspen. You must be mega-rich."

Shane grinned at the boy's innocence. Most days he forgot how privileged he'd had it growing up. He didn't know much about Hunter's parents, aside from rodeo, and even then, they seemed a little out of their element. They were more the nine-to-five desk-job type, whose idea of a vacation was a spa retreat instead of a camping trip.

"Take your shower so we can eat and be back before the rest of your class wakes up."

The cold shower did nothing to quell his thoughts of Lexi. The same passion had still coursed through their bodies when they'd kissed. Shane thought it would feel like it used to, but instead there'd been something unfamiliar and much more personal than in any kiss they'd ever shared before. Longing and need coupled with a raw and complete devotion he couldn't explain. He needed to have her back in his arms, his bed and his life because tonight confirmed it—she'd never left his heart.

"Lexi!" A loud banging surrounded her. She tried to move and her back ached like hell. "Lexi, open the damn door before I rip the roof off."

"Daddy?" Lexi opened her eyes. She was still in her car, in the driveway, and her father was pounding on the side window. Reaching for the door, she flicked the power lock button.

"Are you sick?" Jim Lawson pulled her from the car. "I heard you pull in but when you didn't get out of the car I began to wonder."

"I'm just tired," Lexi said. "I had a long night."

"You better not be drunk." Jim turned her to look at him. "Are you?"

Lexi shrugged out of his grasp. "I haven't come home drunk since I was in college."

"Where were you all night?"

"The fifth degree, Dad? Really?" Lexi trudged to the side door of the house, leaving her boots in the mudroom. "You know I'm on call twenty-four hours a day."

"I'm usually asleep when you're on call." Her dad harrumphed and sat down at the small table against the kitchen wall. "Was it an emergency or a foal?"

"Both." Lexi opened the refrigerator and grabbed a can of Diet Coke, popping the top. "What on earth are you wearing?"

Jim's tattered, flannel bathrobe, which he refused to throw out, barely covered his bright blue, cartoon-cow boxers and a white, sleeveless undershirt.

"I was worried." Jim looked down at the stain on his shirt and scratched at it. "Hmm, wonder where that came from."

"I'm fine, and I'll tell you about it after I clean up and get into some fresh clothes." She checked her watch. "I suggest you do the same. I guess it's morning anyway."

In the safety of the bathroom, Lexi locked the door

and took a quick shower. She didn't want to stop moving and she certainly didn't want to think. People and animals relied on her and there was no room for emotion in her work.

Lexi went out to check on her own horses before she left, when someone cleared their throat at the other end of the barn.

"Hello?" Lexi called out.

"Heard you had quite a night." Clay strode to the stall door.

"Sure did. Got to spend most of it in extremely close quarters with Hunter." Lexi wiped at her eyes, and grabbed a rubber curry comb from the shelf. Grooming Autumn calmed her nerves and the horse loved the attention. "I'm assuming you're here because you have the test results."

"He's your son, Lexi."

Lexi froze midstroke, bracing herself against Autumn. "Thank you. Let me know how much I owe you for everything."

Clay unlatched the stall door, but didn't open it. "Come out here, Lex, so we can talk."

Ignoring him, she continued her circular motions on the horse's body.

"And his family?"

"Lexi?" Clay hesitated. "I wish you'd—"

*"And his family?"* Lexi said through gritted teeth.

"Soccer mom, business dad, no debts, no criminal charges, not even a speeding ticket. You chose a good family, Lexi, and you did right by your son. Don't beat yourself up over this."

"I'll be fine." Lexi placed the comb on the shelf and

walked out of the stall. "It's not like I didn't already know it. I just need a few minutes to let it sink in then I have to get back to work."

"Not until I make sure you're all right. When was the last time you ate?"

"Yesterday at the picnic, I guess." Food was the last thing on her mind.

"Well, I certainly didn't see you eat and you left early. Come on, we're getting breakfast. We don't have to talk but I'm not leaving you like this and that's final."

"Fine." Lexi didn't want to argue, she didn't want to think, either. The more she thought, the more she felt. She just wanted to work and keep her mind occupied. There was always safety in keeping busy. "My car... I'll drive."

"Considering the front seat of my truck is loaded with crap we have no other choice, but Lexi, I'm driving."

Being a passenger in her own car felt foreign to her. At least when she drove she had control, and right now her life was spinning out of control.

"Hunter's parents are coming to town for Family Day at the end of the month and I don't know how to handle it."

Clay pulled the car off to the side of the road and faced Lexi. "You need to decide once and for all if you're really going to keep this from Shane and Hunter. I know you said there's no point in telling them, but you need to look at this from all angles."

"Meaning if they found out later on." Lexi knew the obvious answer was to come clean to everyone and let the chips fall where they may. The logical side of her reasoned that what they didn't know couldn't hurt them, and if their relationship were only a temporary one, she might be able to get away with it. Shane had already traveled to a few of Hunter's events and Lexi was certain there were more to come. If their resemblance increased, someone was bound to ask questions. With Shane's wild history, a paternity test wouldn't be that far off-base, but once you did the math, she was the only possibility as Hunter's mother.

"Are you prepared to keep this secret from Shane forever?" Clay asked. "You two have gotten closer recently. Can you live with this?"

"I've lived with it all these years." Lexi shrugged. "This isn't much different."

"It's a lot different, Lex. You didn't know where or who he was. Now you do and he has an ongoing relationship with his father."

Lexi laid her head against the car seat and closed her eyes. "I have to do what's best for Hunter and that would be not to disrupt his life. I can handle the guilt and the pain. I've been handling it all along. No one needs or deserves to get hurt, Clay. We need to let it rest."

The conversation over, Clay continued to drive to the Magpie. Lexi agreed to a quick bite and then she'd start her rounds. She needed to call Ashleigh and have her keep an eye on the horses at Bridle Dance. Determined to keep her distance this time, Lexi wasn't taking any more chances around Hunter and Shane. She knew the truth. She'd made her decision years ago and that was that. Nothing was going to change.

"Isn't that her car?" Hunter asked when they parked in front of the Magpie. "I thought horse vets drove trucks."

"She has a Ram 3500 Dually she uses for trailering horses," Shane said. "But it's easier and cheaper to use her car for typical ranch calls."

Lexi's mud-covered Mustang sat in front of the luncheonette, in desperate need of a wash and wax. Clay had told him to surprise her if he wanted to win her back, and he knew Lexi definitely wasn't the traditional-gift type. Shane tried to think of a way he could get her car detailed without her knowledge. In high school, she'd stolen his filthy white pickup and detailed it when he was away at a weekend rodeo. When he returned he didn't even recognize the truck was his. It was a sweet gesture he'd never had the chance to return.

"How are you at stealing cars?" Shane asked.

Hunter's head shot up. "We're going to steal her car?"

"In a manner of speaking and I need your help."

Shane told Hunter his plan, but they needed a way to see it through. Figuring she'd be at the ranch later, they decided that if Hunter kept her occupied, Shane would have a golden opportunity, with a limited amount of time.

Bells above the door jingled as they entered the cozy luncheonette. The handful of Formica-and-chrome tables were already filled to capacity but one booth was still empty—right behind Lexi's spot at the counter. Nerves began to hitch a ride to his palms and he wiped the sweat on his jeans. A seasoned pro at women, Shane knew his typical charm was out of the question.

Hunter nudged him. "Just say hi," he whispered. "Keep it simple."

Shane looked down at the kid in annoyance. "Oh, okay, coach." His sarcasm was thick.

"It's better than standing here," Hunter retorted. "Just sayin'."

Shane tapped Lexi on the shoulder. "Hi." The word came out slow, mumbled like he had a mouthful of marbles. Hunter rolled his eyes and squeezed in on the other side of Lexi, almost causing her to fly off the stool.

*Great team we make, kid.*

"What are you two doing here?" Lexi's eyes darted from one to the other. "Don't the students eat at the ranch?"

The harshness of her tone made Hunter retreat toward the booth. He sat down and removed a menu from behind the napkin holder, ignoring them. Either he was giving them a moment to talk or she'd hurt his feelings. Shane was pissed.

"Attitude check?" Shane said to Lexi. "You want to be mad at me for a kiss? Fine, but don't take it out on him."

Lexi looked around the luncheonette, checking to see if the other customers had overheard. Their immediate downward glances confirmed they had and Lexi laid her fork on her empty plate and stood. Leaving a twenty on the counter, she walked out the door, leaving him to stand in the middle of the Magpie with his hat in his hand.

Clay strode from the bathroom and motioned toward the counter. "Hey, man, where'd she run off to?"

"She just left," Shane said. "Did you two come together?"

He knew there was a rumor going around town about Clay and Lexi, and naturally he blew it off. But seeing them together in the morning made him wonder.

"We did but it's not what you think. Nash is taking a look at my truck and Lexi and I decided to grab a bite to eat while I waited. I'd better catch up to her before she leaves me here. I'll call you later."

Shane slid into the booth across from Hunter. "I'm sorry she treated you that way. She was out of line."

"Forget about it. What the hell was that *hhhiii* business?" Hunter set his menu on the table and stared at him. "Did someone set your mouth on hot and it ran?"

"Watch your tone, and that's what you told me to say." The little man had a set. Shane opened his menu, although he knew the thing by heart. "What do you want to order?"

"I didn't tell you to say it like that." Hunter reached across the table and pulled Shane's menu down. "It sounded like you had a mouthful of molasses."

"You're going to give me advice on women?" Shane laughed.

"Yeah, I think I should," Hunter asserted. "I do pretty well myself at home."

"Oh, you do?"

"Running off my customers so early in the morning?" Bridgett stood at their table with her short pink uniform and white apron. "What can I get you two?"

Hunter mouthed "watch this" to Shane and turned his body toward the waitress.

"Your hair reminds me of a warm summer day at sunset."

*Oh, no, he didn't.* Bridgett smiled, color rising to her cheeks. "Aren't you just the sweetest thing. Do you like pancakes, because we make the best chocolate chip pancakes in the world."

"I'd love some." Hunter beamed, clearly proud of himself.

"And you?" Bridgett asked Shane with far less enthusiasm, almost bordering on disdain. "Your typical—I mean your usual?"

Shane nodded and Hunter almost fell out of the booth laughing at him. "She likes me better than you," he mocked.

"I have to admit, that was a good pickup line." Shane laughed. "I guess I did ruffle a few feathers this morning."

"We only talked to two women this morning and they're both mad at you." Hunter looked toward Bridgett and waved. "What's the deal with the redhead? Why does she hate you?"

"Bridgett happens to be Lexi's best friend. So if Lexi is ticked at me, so's Bridgett."

"Nah, I'll soften her up for you," Hunter said. "Are you going to let me have a cup of coffee or are you going to tell me it will stunt my growth like my parents do?"

"Go right ahead." Shane couldn't remember ever not drinking coffee. "You'll need it today."

"I hear we have a little heartbreaker in our midst." Maggie Dalton turned their cups over and filled them both with coffee.

"Maggie…" Shane began before Hunter could work his charms on the woman. "This is Hunter Rathbone, one of my students. Hunter, this is Cole's wife Tess's mother, Maggie."

"It's a real pleasure to meet you, ma'am." Hunter grinned innocently. "I can see why Tess is so beautiful."

*Not again.*

"Aren't you cuter than a kitten in pajamas!" Maggie turned to Shane. "He reminds me of you when you were that age."

"Thanks." Shane smiled. *At least someone noticed me.*

"Listen." Maggie leaned into Hunter. "Don't take any advice about women from this one here, trust me."

She winked and walked away.

"You must be some dog." Hunter tugged a napkin out of the dispenser. "The things you can learn from me."

"Oh, that will be the day." Shane smirked.

"What did you do to her anyway? You said something about getting married the other day."

"I was supposed to marry Lexi and ended up marrying someone else."

"Knocked a chick up, huh?"

Shane almost choked on his coffee. "Precocious, aren't you? And yes and no. The kid turned out not to be mine."

"Gold digger or just a tramp?" Hunter said so matter-of-factly Shane didn't believe he was talking to a kid.

"Both, and you ask too many questions."

"Do you want my help with Lexi or not?" Hunter asked. "At the rate you're going, every female in town will be throwing eggs at you by sundown."

"Here you go, honey." Bridgett set Hunter's pancakes down in front of him, complete with a giant whipped cream heart on top of them. She gave Shane his order without a word and walked away.

"All right, you win. I need your help."

# Chapter 9

"Where are you off to in a hurry?" Clay tried to stop Lexi from leaving without him

"Hop in and I'll drop you off at your truck." Lexi stepped on the gas before Clay even closed the door. "I appreciate your help, but it's over with now. I'm taking your advice and steering clear of them. While they're eating it gives me a chance to check in at the ranch and head out before they return."

"My advice was *before* you found out, not after." Clay held on to the dashboard while Lexi turned off Main Street. "Follow your heart, Lexi, but try not to kill us in the process."

"No, absolutely not." Following her heart was selfish. "This isn't about what I want. I take that back… yes, it is. I want Hunter to be healthy and happy and he is. He doesn't need to know I'm his biological mother."

Minutes later they were in her driveway, behind his truck. Clay stepped from the Mustang and before he could say another word, Lexi threw the car in Reverse and left Clay with no other option than to close the door and let her leave. Her feelings weren't important and she'd known that the day she decided to bring a child into this world. Giving him up for adoption was painful, but the more Lexi thought about it, it wasn't the most painful thing in the world. Seeing hurt and distrust on Hunter's face would be, and she wouldn't be able to live with that.

At the ranch, Apollo and Crystal both checked out perfectly. Ashleigh had tried unsuccessfully once again to introduce mother and baby without any luck. Not willing to push the matter any further, Lexi resolved that Delilah would be Apollo's new mother since they appeared to be forming a bond. The animal world and human world weren't that different after all.

By the time she finished on the ranch, Shane and Hunter were driving in, passing her on the main road. She didn't wave and she didn't even look in their direction. Keeping her eyes straight ahead, Lexi gripped the wheel and headed home.

It was later than usual for Autumn's morning ride, but Lexi would rather go out late than miss their alone time. Opting to ride bareback today, she directed Autumn to the trail behind the crops. Nowhere near the size of Bridle Dance, the Lawson farm had a modest amount of acreage and enough land to ride multiple trails and not get bored.

The reins loose in her hand, Lexi allowed Autumn to choose their destination. Figuring the horse would pick her favorite spot near the small fishing pond, they instead made their way toward the north end of Cooter Creek, where it first entered Ramblewood. Autumn languidly walked along the water's edge and Lexi knew her horse sensed her tension and was allowing her the time to unwind.

Horses amazed her the way they noticed your every emotion. It was one of the reasons she loved to ride without a saddle. She felt more connected with the animal and she trusted Autumn completely.

Taking longer than expected, she called from the trail to check in with Ashleigh. The Lawsons' market and gift shop had a separate back area with its own outside entrance that Lexi had converted into her office. She needed to send out some invoices and check her patient vaccination schedules. They would have to get a start on the next round of West Nile within the coming week.

"Hello?" Ashleigh said.

"It's me. Are you in the office yet?"

"I'm here with Billy and Michelle starting the West Nile and influenza schedule."

Michelle was one of their summer techs home from college. She was two years away from her bachelor's then she was off to veterinary school. Once again, Lexi's techs were one step ahead of her.

"Well, that takes care of the reason I was calling." Lexi lifted her face toward the sun. "I'm out on Autumn but I'll be in before my next appointment."

She had a follow-up with a show jumper in the afternoon, leaving her with the rest of the morning for herself. Lexi hopped off and led Autumn to the water to drink. When she was finished, Lexi wound her arms around the mare's neck, and Autumn lifted her front leg and wrapped it around Lexi's waist. It was a trick Jesse trained his horses to do, and one she taught Autumn when she was a yearling.

Thinking about Jesse made her wonder about Miranda. When she'd left the picnic the poor woman looked like she was about to pop. She wasn't due for another three weeks but the doctor told her it could be sooner, especially when carrying twins.

There it was…once again she was thinking about Hunter. Placing both hands on Autumn's back, she hopped and swung her leg over.

*Maybe it's time I moved on from Ramblewood.*

Shane hadn't seen Lexi in three days and there was no doubt in his mind she was avoiding him. She came in early the first day, so he thought he'd catch her on the second. That morning she sent Ashleigh instead and showed up when he was teaching class. Thinking he'd outsmart her, today he held class outside since a slight cool front had come through, but she didn't show at all.

He called Clay before the afternoon class began and asked if he'd heard from her.

"I haven't seen her, either," Clay said. "Have you tried her office or her house?"

"Every time I step foot on their land one of her kin threatens to shoot me," Shane groaned. "I'm not exactly the Lawsons' favorite person."

"Give her some time, she'll come around."

"Time for what?" Shane pinched the bridge of his nose. "Do you know something you're not telling me?"

"You've been a little pushy lately," Clay laughed.

"You went from patiently waiting for her to let you back in to shoving your tongue down her throat in the middle of the stables."

"I'll have you know she kissed me," Shane said indignantly.

"I'm talking about last week, not the other day."

"How the hell do you know about that?" Shane demanded.

"You kissed her in a public place," Clay said. "Do you realize how many employees you have working for you? People talk, man."

"Will you call her for me?" Shane hated to ask his friend to get in the middle of things, but Lexi wasn't making the situation easy and he wasn't going to give up on her.

"I can try. Any particular message you want me to tell her? Maybe three little words?"

"Don't you dare," Shane threatened. "Just, I don't know, have her call me and mention Hunter's birthday party. She knows about it, but she may have forgotten."

Shane pocketed his phone and headed toward the arena.

"Any luck?" Chase called out when he opened the gate.

"Clay's going to try to reach her." Shane double-checked some of the rigging hanging on the rails. "I'm supposed to ride in Tennessee this week."

"You going to go?" Chase removed one of the hack reins for a closer inspection.

"I should." Shane exhaled slowly. "I hate leaving this all on you."

"No bother." Chase smiled, placed the rein back on

the fence and continued on to the saddle rigging. "I'm not going to think twice when I do it to you next month. Don't blame not going on the rodeo school, Shane. If you want to stay because of whatever is going on between you and Lexi, then stay and tell her why you're staying."

"I would if she'd talk to me." Shane adjusted his chaps and the class started to file in.

"If it were me, I'd go to Tennessee for a chance to clear your head," Chase said. "It's two days, it's not like she's going anywhere. All right, class, let's—"

"Shane! Chase!" His mother screamed across the parking lot. "They're coming!"

Hopping the fence, Shane grabbed his mother before she fainted. "Calm down. Who's coming?"

"The babies!" She fanned her face. "We have to go."

"You're not driving anywhere." Chase ushered his mom toward the door. "Are Miranda and Jesse at the hospital?"

"On their way." Kay's voice was ragged. "You drive then."

"You coming?" Chase called over his shoulder.

"Kyle, you got this?" Shane asked.

"I'm good. Just go." Kyle waved him out. "Give them my best."

"I'm not going in that doorless thing," Kay said as she pointed at Shane's Jeep.

"We're taking your car, Mom." Chase held the door open for her before she pushed it closed.

"Not like that you aren't. You're not getting my Mercedes dirty—go get changed."

"I thought you wanted to leave now?" Shane asked.

"No sons of mine are going to the hospital with dirt on their faces and heaven only knows what under their nails."

"We've certainly gone looking worse." Shane nudged Chase.

"I meant the maternity ward. Oh, shit." Kay fumbled for her phone. "I forgot to call Tess. Where's Cole?"

Shane and Chase laughed at their mother's infrequent swearword and scrambled into the house to make themselves more hospital presentable. By the time they arrived, the rest of the family was in the waiting room along with Mable and Lexi.

"I'm just glad we got her here before she birthed those babies on my clean floor," Mable said.

Animated as usual, the woman filled in everyone who entered the immediate vicinity. Strangers and all. "Can you imagine the handful these young'uns are going to be with those two as parents? Stubborn, I'll tell you that much. I just wish I knew what they were."

"We all do," Kay said. "I'm so tired of knitting yellow or green. Leave it to them to make it difficult on us and wait until they're born to find out the sex."

Shane wrinkled his nose at the antiseptic smell of the hospital. He crossed the room toward Lexi, and she squared her shoulders as he drew near. He wondered if she'd bolt at any second.

"I get the distinct impression you've been avoiding me." Shane sat in the chair next to her.

Lexi loudly sighed and slumped in the chair. "I've had quarterly West Nile vaccines to administer around the county, plus six-month influenza for all the yearlings." She rose to leave and Shane grabbed her hand. Her fingers were cold and stiff, like icicles.

"Please don't go," Shane implored. "How did you hear about Miranda so fast?"

"I was the driver," Lexi grumbled, lowering herself back down into the chair.

"What?" Shane chuckled. "How did that happen?"

"I was vaccinating Jesse's horses when Miranda went into labor. Can you imagine Mable or Jesse driving here?"

"Please tell me you didn't squeeze them all in your Mustang." Shane didn't even want to imagine it.

"Didn't I?" Lexi's brows rose. "I had no choice. Mable's car is a scary-ass bucket of bolts and there was no way Miranda was getting her baby belly up and into a truck. They seriously need to rethink the vehicle situation over there. So, Miranda rode up front with me and I squeezed Mable and Jesse in the back."

Shane laughed. "Was the top up, at least?"

"Heavens, no." Lexi started to laugh. "There is no way Jesse would fit in that backseat if it was."

"Mable must have loved that."

"That woman screamed the entire way here like a damn police siren." Tears trailed down Lexi's face. "Believe me when I tell you, they heard us coming."

Shane howled. "My poor brother."

"My poor ears! Miranda was the easiest one of the bunch and she was in labor."

Shane swiped his eyes with the back of his hand. "I think you deserve a medal."

"Screw that," Lexi said. "I want a trophy."

It felt good to laugh, especially with Lexi. The tension was gone, at least for a few moments while they waited for the next Langtry generation to arrive.

"There's something I've wanted to tell you for a few days now," Shane began.

"Should I be worried?" Lexi said. "You're not pregnant, are you?"

Shane bit his bottom lip, not sure how to respond. "At least we can joke about it."

"It's either laugh or cry and I prefer laughter."

"Well, this will really make you laugh." Shane's excitement rose at the idea of his television show. "I was approached at the ribbon cutting to do a reality show centering on me and the school."

"Someone wants you as their reality?" Lexi giggled. "Now that's funny."

Feeling a bit wounded, Shane didn't respond.

"You're serious?" Lexi asked. "I heard rumblings about it but I thought it was a story one of the local news stations was running on the school. I'm sorry—continue."

"They're choosing a few rodeo cowboys and shooting the segments all over the country. Of course, they want us to meet up at the same rodeo events so we can have on-screen time together, but they want me and Ride 'em High! as the show's anchor."

"What about Chase?" Lexi asked. "The school is half his."

"It's all still up in the air and we haven't had a chance to sit down with anyone from the show yet." Even though he and Chase hadn't agreed to do the show, they still wanted to send a production crew out to look around. "They want to take some test shots this week, but if we do go through with it, they'll probably ask you to sign a waiver of some sort."

"Me?" Lexi asked. "How do I fit into all of this?"

"Everyone does. They'll film in and around the ranch, plus in town. I'll have a camera crew following me."

"Count me out, cowboy." Lexi shook her head. "I don't want any part of that."

"Now you sound like my mom and Cole."

"Keep them the hell away from me, Shane." Lexi stood and walked outside before he could stop her.

"Please answer, please answer, please answer." Lexi spoke into the phone while she paced in front of the hospital.

"You've reached CT Investigations. I'm unavailable at this time. Please leave a message and I'll return your call shortly."

"It's Lexi. I need to talk to you right away. It's urgent."

"So start talking." Clay appeared between two parked cars.

"Don't do that!"

"I told you I can get in and out undetected," Clay joked. "Is everything okay with the babies?"

"Everything's fine." Lexi dragged him away from the hospital entrance. "Did you know someone asked Shane to do a reality show here in Ramblewood?"

"He told me the other day, I tried to talk to you about it but you haven't returned any of my calls." Clay relaxed on a brick parking lot break wall. "You can't be anywhere near that show."

"No kidding!" Lexi began to panic. *This can't be happening.* "But how can I avoid it if they're filming everywhere? Especially if they look into his past, they'll find me."

"When you gave your son up for adoption, did you use your real name in the hospital?" Clay asked.

"Was there another way? Because I wasn't given any options." Lexi wildly threw her arms in the air. "That's bad, isn't it?"

"Who paid your hospital bills?" Clay asked.

"The agency handled everything." Lexi stared at him. "It was part of the adoption."

"And you've checked your credit report to make sure nothing from back then has shown up? Nothing was past due or went into collections?"

"No, but that was almost thirteen years ago." Lexi dismissed the idea. "Even if there was, they'd have dropped off my credit report after seven years."

"Not if the account was sold." Clay had her attention and realization started to set in. "Each time an account is sold, it goes on your credit report and then it remains for seven years."

"What?" Lexi sat on the wall next to Clay. "How can I get a copy and check?"

"Normally you would check these things every year online but I'll do it and I'll run an extensive background check on you to see if there are any surprises lurking out there. Keep in mind, I'm not the only investigator out there and these shows love to dig up dirt. If someone finds out you went to school out there and combines that with Hunter living in Denver and then you factor in the resemblance thing and your reluctance to be on the show, you'll be in trouble."

"And if they find out…" Lexi didn't need to finish the sentence. She knew she had to tell Shane the truth.

Clay entered the waiting area with Lexi close behind.

"Look who I found in the parking lot?" She sat down on the opposite side of the room and nervously bounced her leg up and down.

Clay made his way around the room, asking for the latest update before he took a seat next to Shane.

"What's up with her?" Shane nodded toward Lexi. "Did she tell you she raised Cain over just the thought of being on the show?"

"Are you sure you want to do this thing?" Clay asked. "You're facing some pretty tough opposition. The only people on your side are Chase and your students, and you need to make the parents aware there's a production crew coming, even for test shots of the grounds."

"Not you, too?"

Shane was about to argue when a nurse appeared. "Langtry family?" Everyone said yes in unison. "Both Mommy and babies are doing fine. Daddy not so much."

"What happened to my son?" Kay asked. "All he had to do was stand there!"

"Well, Mr. Langtry had a little problem in that department. It's not unusual, but we stitched him up."

"Stitched?" Shane snickered.

"He hit his head when he passed out," the nurse said.

"Fool child," Mable said. "Can you tell us the sex of the babies?"

"Two boys." The woman smiled. "Congratulations, Grandmas."

"Grandmas?" Mable repeated. "I'm not the babies' grandma."

"On the contrary. Two visitors may go in and Miranda asked for both grandmothers."

"Oh, dearest me." Mable's eyes began to well with tears. "I'm a grandma too, Kay! We're both grandmas!"

Everyone laughed, everyone except Shane. Dylan was born in this very hospital, with the entire family gathered around. He understood why his brother passed out. A birth wasn't something you wanted to watch every day, but you couldn't tear yourself away when it was your own child. The child you helped to create, or at least thought you did.

"How are you doing?" Lexi asked. "I know this must bring back some memories."

"I still can't believe Sharon let me believe Dylan was my son for an entire year. It was cruel."

"Mmm, I was never convinced she knew who the father was," Lexi said. "I think she chose the one with the most money."

"I wish she hadn't and we'd still be together." Shane searched her eyes for some recognition in return.

"It doesn't change the fact that you cheated on me, and honestly, I don't want to rehash that. But we do need to talk."

"We do, and there's something I need to tell you, too, but not here." Shane looked around the waiting room. "Let's grab a cup of coffee."

The only choice in the cafeteria this late was coffee or soda and snack crackers. Sitting across from her,

Shane tried to find the nerve to tell Lexi he loved her and that he'd never stopped.

She looked tired and withdrawn and he wondered what she wanted to tell him. There was a nagging feeling in the pit of his stomach that she was about to announce that she and Clay were together, despite both of their denials. Shane didn't want to give her the chance to say the words. She needed to hear how he felt first and maybe...

"Lexi," he began. "I—I want a second chance."

Okay, so it wasn't exactly how he planned it but it was close enough. He'd made a direct declaration of his...of his what? *Attraction?*

"I mean, you and I have a past." *Spit it out already.* "And I think we can have a future together and I—"

"There you are," Clay interrupted. "Your brother's asking for you."

Shane exhaled the words *love you,* under his breath but she didn't hear him. "Which brother?"

"The one that just became a father." Clay looked incredulously at Shane and then at Lexi. "Bad timing?"

His friend just stopped him from making a fool out of himself.

"Nope, you're right on schedule."

"Were you about to tell him?" Clay asked after Shane left the cafeteria.

"Yes!" Lexi ran a hand through her hair and looked up toward the fluorescent lights. "For a detective, this here—" Lexi waved her fingers around the empty room "—should have been your first clue. Quiet, out-of-the-way place. The two of us alone. Are you picking up what I'm putting down, Magnum?"

"I didn't think you'd do it right now!" Clay huffed.

"Why not?" Lexi stood. "There's no good time."

Lexi returned to the waiting room when Vicki arrived. "We couldn't get a sitter this late so I finally told Brandon to stay home with Randi Lynn and I came on my own. She really had a short labor, huh?"

Lexi had been in labor for twenty-two hours with Hunter. Several epidurals didn't completely kill the pain and she understood why some people wanted to be unconscious. Then there were people like Vicki, who got overexcited at a baby shower and gave birth in a matter of minutes. Easy peasy and call it a day.

"Lexi, you can go in and see her now." Kay ushered Lexi towards the hallway.

"Vicki's here, she can go before me." Lexi knew Shane was still in there and a hospital room with a baby was the last place she wanted to be.

"You go on," Vicki insisted. "You drove her here. You deserve to go in first."

"Room 226 on the left." Kay pointed down the corridor.

The cream-colored walls seemed to close in on Lexi while she trekked down the hallway, painfully taking her time, hoping Shane would appear and return to the waiting area.

Room 226. There it was. Miranda, Jesse and the babies were on the other side of that door. And so was Shane. She inhaled deeply and let out a long slow breath. Knocking lightly, she gingerly pushed the door open and peeked inside.

Jesse opened the door the rest of the way. "They just fell asleep. Come on in."

Lexi tried not to stare at the bandage on his forehead when she hugged her old friend.

"Congratulations," she whispered.

Shane sat in the recliner cradling one of the boys, rocking slowly and staring intently into the infant's face. Lexi was unable to choke back the tears she'd been holding the moment she walked in the room, and let them spill over. Shifting focus, she looked at Miranda holding a tiny wrapped bundle.

"I'm so happy for you." Lexi squeezed her free hand.

"Thank you," Miranda softly said. "This is Jackson and that's Slade."

"They are so precious." Lexi didn't dare gaze in Shane's direction. "I love their names."

"Here," Shane said behind her. "You can hold him. Slade, meet Lexi."

Their bodies touched as Shane placed Slade in her arms. Unable to control herself, she looked into his eyes. Now she knew. She knew exactly how it would have felt if Shane was there when Hunter was born.

Holding Slade in her arms, she sat down in the chair and cried.

# Chapter 10

After her emotional breakdown at the hospital, Lexi managed to limit her time on the ranch. She was thrilled to hear Shane had gone to Tennessee for a few days, and when he came back, she made herself nonexistent. Despite swearing she'd keep her distance, at the last minute she decided there was no way she'd miss her son's birthday. Shane and Clay had both called that morning to remind her she was invited to the party they'd planned for that afternoon, reassuring Lexi that the reality show had finished taping. This was her first and last birthday with her son and she was determined to enjoy every second of it.

The barbecue pits were located near the bunkhouse and Lexi was glad she wore a pair of old sneakers to walk up the hill. She had her bathing suit on under her shorts and tank top in case everyone decided to go swimming.

Lexi loved the family atmosphere of the ranch birthday parties. Kay knew it was hard for the resident hippotherapy kids to be away from home and friends on their birthdays, so she'd decided to throw a party for each of them when their birthdays rolled around. Shane and Chase followed suit with Ride 'em High! and between both facilities, this was the second birthday this month.

After a lunch of barbecued hamburgers, hot dogs and corn on the cob, Shane and Chase carried out a huge sheet cake with a cartoon version of Hunter on top of a bucking bareback.

"Tight!" Hunter shouted.

Since it was Sunday and they didn't have classes today, they rode four-wheelers down to the river for a swim. Thanks to Hunter's machinations, Lexi ended up on the back of Shane's ATV and had to hold on to his waist for dear life. He drove the blasted quad the way he drove that Jeep of his, wide open all the way.

It had been years since she'd swung on a rope swing and Lexi wasn't sure she trusted anything that hung from a tree since grade school. "You're up, babe." Shane handed her the rope.

"I don't think so, babe." She didn't need to swing out over the water and lose half of her bathing suit. What possessed her to wear a red bikini to a birthday party anyway? *Because you knew Shane would like it.* But like it or not, she was not taking her tank top off.

As she waded into the water, someone came up behind her and pushed her under. Resurfacing, she looked around to see Hunter laughing hysterically.

"You are asking for it." Lexi splashed water in his direction.

"Uh-huh." Hunter nodded. "But you have to catch me first."

Lexi dived under the water and swam toward him. He may have had the element of surprise but she had speed on her side. Especially since she was on the swim team in high school. Within seconds she was upon him. Grabbing hold of his foot, she tugged him under the water.

Both came up for air at the same time.

"What was that you were saying?" Lexi asked.

"That's not fair." Hunter splashed her. "I didn't know you were that fast."

Lexi laughed. "You're the one who asked for it."

Hunter starting laughing again.

"What's so—" Lexi felt herself rise out of the water and fly through the air. "Shane!"

Lexi jumped on his back and unsuccessfully tried to push him under. Seeing her struggle, Hunter joined her and together they were able to take him down.

"Who said anything about tag teams?" Shane pushed his hair back from his face, water dripping from his nose. "You two cheat and you know what happens to cheaters?"

Shane scooped her up in one arm and Hunter in the other, not letting either of them go. For the moment, Lexi allowed herself to enjoy what a summer day would have been like if she hadn't give her son up for adoption.

"Thank you for coming today," Shane said later as

he sat down next to her in one of the Adirondack chairs. "I think this was the most fun we've had together since we were kids celebrating our own birthdays."

"I'm glad I came." Lexi admired the man beside her. "You've changed since you built the school. Do I dare say you're tamer and more enjoyable to be around?"

"I know, it's so strange," Shane agreed. "I thought by the end of each day I'd be champing at the bit to get out of here, but I'm not. I'm actually going to miss these guys when they leave. Spending time with these kids has really made me rethink my life."

"You won't have time to miss them with your next class in August and your reality show." Lexi bit back the bile on that last part.

"The show's not a definite. *Nothing's* definite and my agent's not a fan of the idea. Plus I noticed you weren't thrilled with the idea."

After Clay ran a background check on her and didn't come up with anything linking her to Hunter, she felt more secure, but that didn't mean she was willing to take the chance.

"I told you how I felt about that, Shane. I'm not going to change my mind."

"What about us? Think you can change your mind about that?"

"I think we can discuss it, but I'm not making any promises." Lexi knew she shouldn't lead him on. She knew a relationship was impossible with a secret this deep. And if he did the reality show, there was definitely no way they'd be together, but the word *no* wouldn't come out of her mouth. She wanted another chance at happiness with Shane in spite of it all.

"Do you want to open up the gift your parents sent down?" Shane stood when Hunter walked over to them.

Kay and Lexi joined Shane and Hunter at the picnic table while the teen eagerly tore at the silver gift wrap. Inside, one of a cowboy's favorite items appeared.

"Now I have one just like you." Hunter placed the straw Stetson on his head and tipped it forward slightly to match Shane's.

"That's sharp-looking," Kay said, while Barney tried to squirm out of her arms. "You can even wear that with your Sunday jeans."

"Don't forget the card." Lexi handed Hunter the envelope attached to the torn wrapping paper.

Hunter read the card to himself and his eyes began to fill with tears.

"What's wrong, honey?" Lexi wrapped her arm protectively around his shoulder. "Why are you upset?"

"I've never been away from my family on my birthday before and I miss them," Hunter confessed. "Plus they call this my Gotcha Day."

"Your Gotcha Day?" Shane asked.

"It's the day they adopted me. My brother and sister are adopted, too."

Hunter's indifference surprised Lexi. She was also surprised Clay hadn't uncovered the other adoptions. He might have if she'd given him the go-ahead to keep digging.

No one asked any questions and Hunter didn't expand any further. He was a normal, well-adjusted kid with a loving family and that was the best gift she could give to her child.

\* \* \*

"Now's your chance to get her car," Hunter whispered to Shane when Lexi started to clean up the picnic table. "I can keep her busy."

"I don't want to leave in the middle of your party."

"I'm a man now, I can take care of myself," Hunter drawled. "And this is a get-together. I'm too old for parties. She still has her bathing suit on so I'll ask her to go swimming again in the river."

Sneaking across the corral, ducking behind horses, Shane hoped no one noticed the extra set of legs running by. He knew Lexi always left the keys under the seat in case she had an emergency and had to leave quickly. He didn't have time to wash and wax it himself, but he did have time to drive down the highway to Bubba's Bubbles and get it detailed.

The line for the car wash started all the way down the street. If Shane had any chance of getting Lexi's car back soon, this wasn't going to cut it. He dialed the number on the sign, and a woman answered.

"Darla? It's Shane Langtry. Do you think that husband of yours can do me a favor?"

Two hours later, he was back on the road. Hunter had texted him thirty minutes ago that Lexi was receiving some business phone calls but so far none of them were emergencies. This was a good thing considering he had her medical bags in the car with him. Hopefully he'd return before she missed them. He had to give Hunter credit, the kid was a good partner in crime.

He glanced at the glove box and wondered what else she might have in the car. Reaching over he tried the latch but it was locked. Looking at the steering column, he saw the key on her key ring. If he pulled off the road and opened the lock, he'd learn what she had not so successfully been hiding. *And he'd be a first-class jackass.*

Shane caught a woman going through his phone once and that was enough for him to kick her to the curb. Curiosity was one thing, but respect was another and he wasn't going to violate Lexi's trust that way. Then again, he was driving around in a car he'd technically stolen so that didn't say much about him.

Stopping at the ranch entrance, he texted Hunter to make sure Lexi couldn't see the main drive or parking area. Pulling into the same spot she'd parked in, he tossed her keys under the seat and snuck back toward the barbecue pits.

"Where on earth have you been?" Kay grabbed hold of him behind the bunkhouse. "How dare you sneak out of here when this was your idea."

"I took Lexi's car to get detailed." Shane loved the shocked expression on his mother's face. "Hunter was in on it, too. Do me a favor and tell Lexi one of the grooms noticed she has a flat tire."

Shane crept through the bushes on the other side of the pits so he'd be able to saunter in inconspicuously.

"Really?" Lexi listened to Kay and sighed. "Those are fairly new tires."

"What's wrong?" Shane slipped in beside her, signaling to Hunter, who was standing nearby with some of the other students.

"Where'd you come from?" Lexi looked around. "Never mind, someone told your mom I have a flat tire and I was going down to check it out."

"Hunter and I can change it for you," Shane offered. "Isn't that right?"

"You can change it, I'll supervise." Hunter grinned. "It's my birthday."

"Thanks, kid." Shane appreciated the added cover.

They hiked down to the parking area and Lexi walked all around her car, looking at each tire. "I don't see a flat, do you?"

"Are you sure that's your car?" Shane asked, trying not to laugh.

"Yeah, it looks too clean to be yours," Hunter added.

"Of course this is—how did my car get so clean?" Lexi ran her hand over the trunk. "Waxed, too?"

"Must have been the car fairy." Hunter peered in the windows. "Even the inside's clean."

"Did you do this?" Lexi poked Shane in the chest. "Is that where you've been?"

Shane sheepishly nodded, not sure if she was pleased or mad. "I'm repaying you for when you did mine."

"Well, it sure took you long enough." Lexi reached up and kissed him on the cheek while Hunter gave him the thumbs-up from the other side of the car. "Thank you."

"I'd do anything to see you smile," Shane said. "Someday I'll prove just how much you mean to me, and when I do, you'll finally understand we were meant to be together."

Family Day was in full swing at the Ride 'em High! Rodeo School when Lexi drove into the ranch. She'd made the decision last night to stay away because she didn't want the pain of seeing her son with his adopted family. Curiosity got the best of her somewhere between "don't do it" and "just a peek won't hurt."

A peek it was. Grabbing her medical bag from the back of the car, she had the excuse to be there without looking suspicious. Not that she'd ever look suspicious at Bridle Dance, but she was overly paranoid and hoped no one caught on to her fear.

Walking through the stables, she turned the corner and faced Shane, Hunter and his family looking in at Apollo. Immediately regretting her decision, Lexi spun on her heels and tried to retreat before anyone saw her.

"Lexi, wait!" Hunter called out to her. "I want you to meet my parents."

Lexi took a deep breath and slowly turned to meet the Rathbones…the people raising her son. She had opted for a closed adoption but she couldn't be certain what the Rathbones knew about her. Slowly she reached out for what seemed like an eternity and shook the hand of the woman her son called Mom.

"It's nice to meet you," Lexi said.

The woman's head tilted slightly and the handshake lingered longer than it should have, making Lexi increasingly nervous.

"*Our* son tells us you're a veterinarian," Mrs. Rathbone said.

Paranoia be damned, there was a definite emphasis on the word *our*. Lexi didn't know how but she was almost certain the woman knew who she was. Maybe it was intuition, maybe the adoption agency revealed more about her than they should have, but the fear and anger in the woman's eyes told Lexi she needed to get the hell out of there.

"I'm sorry, I have an emergency." Lexi made a bee-line for the side door and sprinted past two corrals to her car. Fumbling with the key, she started the engine and peeled out of there before anyone caught up with her.

She dialed Clay's number and he answered on the second ring.

"They know." Lexi began to hyperventilate and forced herself to pull down a side road and stop the car.

"Who knows?" Clay asked.

Lexi tried to calm her ragged breaths.

"Breathe, Lexi," Clay soothed. "Are you home?"

"No." *Breathe in, breathe out.*

"Are you at the ranch?"

"No, I left," she croaked. "The Rathbones are here."

"For Family Day, right?" he asked. "I'm not even going to ask why you went there. I probably would have done the same thing. Did you tell them or did they figure it out?"

"When she heard my name," Lexi sobbed. "She knew. What have I done?"

"Don't jump to any conclusions, Lex. How far are you from home?"

"Ten minutes."

"I'll meet you there," Clay said. "Can you manage to drive there?"

"Y-yes. I'll be in the stables."

"Sit tight, Lex. I'm on my way."

Lexi led Autumn into the barn and started to brush her. She thanked the stars that she usually had the stables to herself with the exception of Nash when he wanted to ride. She didn't have to worry about anyone invading her space and she could breathe a little easier.

She heard Clay's truck roll in and she was glad she had him to confide in.

"I see you got here in one piece." Clay smiled but Lexi didn't have it in her to return the smile.

"They're probably telling Shane right now."

"Even if they know who you are they have no way of knowing he's Hunter's father."

"They know." Lexi stopped brushing Autumn and closed her eyes. "Because they just pulled in the driveway."

"That was a blast today." Shane sauntered into the kitchen and popped a pod in the coffee machine. "I think I'm really cut out for this whole teaching gig."

"You certainly surprised me." Kay held Barney out in front of her and started talking to him. "I didn't think he'd have the patience. Did you? No, you didn't."

"Yup, she's lost it." Shane laughed.

"I know I fought you and Chase on this, but I'm proud of you two." Cole joined Chase at the counter. "You've impressed me."

"Thanks, I think." Shane took a sip of coffee. "Has anyone heard from Lexi? She said she had an emergency and tore out of here."

"I hope it was nothing too bad," Tess said. "Although it wouldn't be an emergency if it wasn't serious."

"I might call her in a few if I don't hear anything," Shane said. "I can't tell you how many people told me today that Hunter and I look alike. The kid definitely has potential on the circuit. After I speak to his parents,

I'm going to see if Brock wants to rep him. They seem like nice people but they're completely clueless when it comes to the rodeo."

"Have you stopped to think about why Hunter might look and act so much like you?" his mother asked.

"The kid idolizes me," Shane bragged. "I'm sure he picked up my mannerisms along the way."

"I think he did, too, but I don't believe it came from watching you," Kay said.

"I've been thinking the same thing," Cole added. "I think he comes by them naturally."

Shane laughed. "What are you implying? That Hunter's my kid? I was married to Sharon and I assure you, I didn't touch anyone while we were married, including Sharon."

"You weren't married to her nine months before Hunter was born. You married Sharon in November," Cole said.

"Hunter would have been conceived in October," Kay added.

"Okay, so I was with Lexi." Shane thought back to the month before he married Sharon. To the weekend he spent with Lexi at Devil's Thumb…when Lexi attended Colorado State.

"What are you saying?" Tess laughed. "We—or someone—certainly would have noticed if Lexi was pregnant when she came home from school for the holidays, at least by spring break and definitely by the summer."

"She didn't come home," Shane mumbled.

"What did you say, Shane?" Cole asked. "I didn't hear you."

"She didn't come home until August, right before she transferred to Cornell."

"Can I help you?" Clay called out from the barn door.

"Is Lexi here?" the man asked. "That is her car, isn't it?"

"We need to talk to her," the woman said.

Clay looked toward Lexi in the shadows. "Your call."

Lexi exhaled sharply. "Let's get this over with."

Clay stepped aside so Mr. and Mrs. Rathbone were able to see her. They walked across the yard toward her and then just stopped and stared.

"I'm Clay." At least someone broke the ice.

"I'm Dennis and this is my wife, Melissa. We're Hunter's parents."

Lexi stiffened at the word but forced herself to meet their gaze. "How did you figure it out?"

"We didn't know much concerning Hunter's biological mother but we did know her name was Alexis," Melissa said. "That she was from Texas and studying to be a veterinarian. All this time Hunter was telling us about a vet named Lexi and it didn't dawn on me that you were Alexis until I saw him next to you. I immediately saw you in him and I knew."

"I promise I won't interfere in his life," Lexi said. "I had no idea he was coming here. This was as much a shock to me as it was to you."

"So this wasn't your and Shane's plan?" Melissa spat. "Because I'm assuming he's the father now that I've seen the three of you together. How was this going to work? You get him down here for a month and try to take him from us?"

"Definitely not. I wasn't even sure he was my son. I had to hire Clay to find out."

"Hire him?" Dennis asked. "What are you?"

"I'm a private investigator, sir, and I can assure you, Lexi did not plan this. She's been agonizing over this for weeks and she had decided not to say a word to anyone about it."

"Oh, sure." Melissa rolled her eyes and folded her arms across her chest. "You don't think we honestly believe that?"

"The reason I gave you my son, and yes, I *gave you my son,* was because I wanted a better life for him. I want him to be happy and I'm not going to do anything to jeopardize that."

"At least now it makes sense why Shane's taken such an interest in Hunter," Dennis said, fuming at Lexi. "Does he even think he has any talent or was this just to get close to him?"

"I didn't even know Hunter was mine and Shane didn't, either. He still doesn't know he has a son."

Her confession brought immediate silence.

"Yes, I'm the horrible woman who gave her son up for adoption and didn't even tell the father she was pregnant. I had my reasons and I stand by them today. He's your son. I won't do anything to change that."

"It's not that simple," Melissa said. "All of our kids are adopted and we have a no-secret policy in our family. We told them if their parents ever surfaced, we wouldn't keep it from them. I'm not going to break that promise to Hunter. He has a right to choose if he wants a relationship with you and Shane. We're not going to make that choice for him."

"I admire your decision, but please give me some time to tell Shane."

"We'll give you a few hours," Melissa said.

"What?" Lexi sputtered.

"What's the rush?" Clay asked. "Why can't you give her a few days?"

"We get on a plane to go home tomorrow," Dennis said. "We need to give Hunter some time to decide if he wants to get on that plane with us."

"Do you have a number where I can reach you?" Lexi's hands shook as she removed her business card out of her wallet and handed it to them. "My mobile number is on the bottom."

"I think I should drive you to the ranch," Clay said after the Rathbones left.

Lexi shook her head and calmly sat down on the hay bale near Autumn's stall. Covering her eyes, she cried.

"I lied to both of them," she sobbed. "And now I have to break Shane's heart. I never wanted to hurt anyone. I just wanted my son to be happy."

"I was just about to call and check up on you," Shane said when he saw Lexi walk up to the corral where the boys practiced roping. "They're really good. Hunter and Tyler show the most potential. What do you think?"

Shane glanced sideways at Lexi when she didn't respond. Sunglasses covering her eyes, she stood and watched.

"Everything all right with your emergency?" Shane had a strong suspicion what that emergency was, considering the Rathbones left shortly after she did.

Lexi nodded. "Um, I don't know yet."

"You know how everyone keeps saying how much Hunter looks like me?" Shane turned his back toward the corral fence, placed a booted foot on the bottom rail and hoisted himself to sit on the top. "You're going to love this—my mom and Cole have this wild idea that you had a secret kid when you were away at Colorado State. Isn't that a hoot?" He quickly glanced down at Lexi, but she only stared out into the corral. "I did the math, and that meant you would have been pregnant when I married Sharon and I told them there was no way in hell you'd have allowed that to happen if you were carrying my child. That's insane, right, Lexi? You'd never do something that horrible to me, would you?"

"It's not insane, Shane."

Seething, he said, "Just say it!"

"Hunter is your son." Lexi shook her head. "He's our son."

Shane hopped off the fence and turned her to face him.

"I have a son and you kept it from me for thirteen years?" Confirming what he already knew made the situation that much more painful. "I was wrong. There is someone worse than Sharon—you."

# Chapter 11

Shane gripped Lexi by the arm and led her away from the round pen and toward the parking area. The last person he wanted to overhear the conversation about his real parents was Hunter since it was obvious the kid had no idea he was his father.

"How could you do this to me?" Shane growled, still holding on to her arm. "What right did you have to take my child away from me?"

"I was eighteen." Lexi pulled away from him. "I came home to tell you but before I opened my mouth you told me you cheated on me, got Sharon pregnant and oh, by the way, we're getting married in a few days. Happy Thanksgiving to me!"

"That doesn't excuse what you did." He couldn't believe she was trying to talk her way out of this.

"You made it very clear to me that day that you and I were no longer together. That you had a responsibility to your child and you were going to see it through. Think back to that afternoon, Shane. What did I say to you? Nothing! You wouldn't even let me speak. Once again, it was the *Shane Show* and it was all about you and the damn rodeo. News flash—I made it about our son and did what was right for him."

"By keeping him from me?" Shane removed his hat and waved it in the air. "How was that the right thing to do?"

"I couldn't raise him on my own. I was in school and I was staying in school."

"You were selfish," Shane spat. "You thought only about yourself. Don't you dare say you did this for Hunter."

"I was selfish?" Lexi laughed. "Who couldn't keep it in his pants? Hmm, I think that was pretty selfish on your part. And who couldn't use birth control? Ding, ding, ding, right again. So don't give me the 'I'm selfish' crap."

Shane didn't believe the words coming out of her mouth. He made a mistake, but it didn't justify giving their son up for adoption. Not when he was willing to be a parent.

"I would have raised him if you were so dead set on going to school."

"Now that's funny. Sometimes I have to laugh at all these recollections you seem to have of Dylan because you were never around. You were constantly on the road plus you had your hands full with a buckle-bunny tramp of a wife. You barely handled that. There was no way you'd be able to deal with another child."

"I was there for Dylan." How dare she say he wasn't. He'd loved that child more than he loved anyone. It was a different love than what he'd felt for Lexi, which was nonexistent now.

"I was even thinking about this at the Fourth of July picnic," Lexi went on, "and how once again you weren't around. You've never been around longer than a few weeks in a row and even that's a stretch. So don't you dare accuse me of being selfish and for wanting to stay in school. You were born rich and you'll die rich, but in the end you're a rodeo cowboy in his thirties who doesn't give a crap about anyone else except himself."

"Now I've lost two kids."

"Blame yourself for that." Lexi walked toward her car. "Tell me, what would you have changed about your life, if you had known about Hunter?"

Shane slapped his hat against his thigh as he tried to come up with an answer. He knew many rodeo cowboys with families at home and he also knew many that retired early to be with their families.

"I would have made it work." Shane sat on the tree stump in front of Lexi's car. The cut was fresh, but he didn't remember when the tree was taken down. *It must have happened when I was...away.* "I'm not gone *all* the time, but yes, I'm on the road a lot. How else am I going to win the championship?"

"I, I, I!" Lexi stomped her foot for emphasis. "Listen to yourself. It's all about you and the rodeo—what you want, what you need, what makes Shane happy. You say you've changed, but you haven't. No one wants this stupid rodeo reality show and yet you're shoving it down everyone's throats. Why? Because Shane Langtry has to be in the spotlight all the time."

"That's not true." Shane jumped to his feet.

"Really?" Lexi stepped toward him, inches from his face. "Where's Chase in all the talk about the TV show? You never mention him."

Shane felt his blood pressure skyrocket. He'd been furious with Sharon, but it was nothing compared to the anger he felt toward Lexi. The one woman he loved, the one person he trusted, and she'd betrayed him. *You betrayed her first.*

He needed to get away from her before he did something they'd both regret.

"Get out of here," Shane snarled. "I don't want to see you here again. You're fired."

"Oh, please. Is that your reality-show training kicking in? You can't fire me because I don't work for you. I own my own practice and if your family chooses not to use me again, then so be it. But just so you know, the Rathbones are on their way to tell Hunter."

"They're coming now?" Shane looked toward their son, who was laughing and swinging his rope high in the air.

"Yes."

"Unbelievable." Shane thought she'd done the worst to him. This just confirmed it. "You're only telling me because you got caught."

Lexi nodded. "You're right. If they hadn't found out, I wouldn't have told you. I was not going to disrupt his life, and he has a great life, with a wonderful family, which is more than we would have been able to give him."

"I never had the chance."

"Neither did I," Lexi thundered. "You took my chance away the night you cheated on me, only I didn't know it then. Instead, you let me live a lie and then shattered my world when you told me you created a family with someone else. What I did was never about another man. It was about an innocent child that didn't deserve to be brought up in the middle of a battlefield."

"You can't even say you're sorry, can you?"

Lexi shook her head. "I stand by what I did and I make no apologies for it."

A tan SUV parked in front of the rodeo school. The Rathbones remained in the car, watching their son practice. *Their son.* Shane's parental rights had been stripped from him without his knowledge and he had to accept it. Even he knew no judge worth his salt would give Shane back his son, and even if that happened, Hunter would resent Shane. There was literally nothing he could do about any of it.

"I'm sure you want to talk to the Rathbones." Lexi slid behind the wheel of her convertible. "They're good people, Shane. I had them background-checked and their first priority is—"

Shane raised his hand to stop her from speaking. "You had them background-checked? When? Then or recently?"

He watched Lexi swallow hard, knowing she'd said more than she had intended to. "That SOB." Shane tightened his hands into a first. "My best friend knew Hunter was my son and didn't tell me?"

Lexi slowly nodded. "I had to be certain."

"And like you said, if you hadn't been caught, you wouldn't have told me, right?"

"Right." Lexi didn't blink. She just stared at him, devoid of all emotion. He had to hand it to her, she'd mastered the doctor's "I have bad news" expression perfectly.

"You asked Clay to lie to me?"

"I asked Clay to do a job for me, and yes, I wondered how you'd react if you found out. Clay said you'd understand it was his job. That's how much faith he put in the strength of your relationship."

"Stop trying to sugarcoat it." Shane stepped away from her car. "You both betrayed me. I'm such a fool— here I thought maybe you were sleeping together, not keeping my child from me."

Lexi was right. Shane hated her for giving up their son and she'd broken his heart. She didn't mean for it to happen that way, but it was the right decision at the time.

Upon seeing the Rathbones drive onto the ranch, Lexi decided it was best to leave them alone to talk, without her. She called Ashleigh and told her to check on Bridle Dance's horses and to call her if there were any problems. Come tomorrow the Langtrys would probably have another equine vet and she'd have to live with it.

She needed to get past today, and if telling Shane was hard, telling her family might be worse. Parking behind the Bed & Biscuit, she started to climb the Victorian's back stairs.

"Lexi?" A woman's voice called her name. "Over here, at the vet's office."

Lexi squinted across Mazie's backyard and saw Kay standing next to her Mercedes with Barney in her arms. Bracing herself for another onslaught, Lexi negotiated her sister's agility obstacle course for dogs, unlatched the gate and stepped into Dr. Cerf's parking lot.

"Hello, Kay." Lexi reached out and scratched Barney under the chin. "Hello, Barney."

"We had a great vet visit today." Kay kissed the poodle pup on the top of the head. "He got another shot and he's up to twelve pounds."

"That's great." Lexi was surprised at Kay's nonchalance, considering Shane told her his mother and Cole had figured out the truth. "How did you know?"

"He told you, huh?" Kay shifted Barney in her arms. "Can I put him down?"

"I wouldn't." Lexi shook her head. "Sick animals come to a vet's and you don't want a puppy that's not fully immunized to touch the grounds or the floor inside."

"So it's true, then?" Kay's tone was surprisingly unaccusatory while she transferred the puppy from one arm to the other.

"It is and I'm sure you have plenty of questions." Lexi steeled herself once more, ready to hear how ungrateful she was when Joe gave her the gift of a lifetime by bringing her home and setting up her lab. Or how her husband died without knowing his grandson. But Kay didn't say anything.

The woman reached up and gave Lexi a hug, Barney between them, licking at her.

"Being a mother is the toughest job in the world." Kay drew back and held Lexi's chin. "I know you did what you thought was best for Hunter. Shane made a mess of things and his father and I only added to it when we told him he needed to do right by Sharon and marry her. We never should have forced that issue."

"I can't believe I'm hearing this." Tears welled in Lexi's eyes.

"Don't get me wrong, Lexi," Kay warned. "I'm not excusing you for not coming to Shane and discussing this, but I do understand why you didn't. You made a good choice for Hunter. I can't tell you it was the best choice because no one knows that, but you put his needs before your own and he seems very well-adjusted."

"Giving him up was the hardest thing I ever had to do, and please understand I didn't just keep this from your family. My family doesn't know either and I need to tell them today. The sooner the better, considering the Rathbones are with Shane now and they plan on telling Hunter everything."

"I should be getting home then." Kay opened her car door, fanning the inside. "Oh, it's hot in there. Call me if you need my help and remember, Lexi, we love you."

"Even after all this?" Lexi asked.

Kay smiled. "Remind me one day to tell you some of the crap Joe pulled for love. Give Shane some time, he'll come around… I promise."

That definitely wasn't the conversation she expected to have with Kay. Two down, many more to go, but Lexi didn't think her heart could handle another one-on-one confession. She needed to round up her entire family, tell them all together and pull the Band-Aid off in one fell swoop.

Letting herself in Mazie's back door, she found her sister in the kitchen, baking as usual. Forever taking care of everyone else. Lexi wondered what her sister would have done if it had been her instead of Lexi. Knowing Mazie, she would have strapped the kid on her back and gone about her daily routine. Domestication suited her perfectly, just like it did Vicki Slater and now Miranda. And maybe if it had happened to Lexi at this age, things might have turned out differently, but at eighteen she wasn't ready for anything more serious than a textbook.

"Are you all right?" her sister asked while rolling out a pie crust, not bothering to look up. "Your conversation with Kay seemed pretty intense out there."

"Can you come to the farm tonight around nine? I need to call a family meeting."

Mazie stopped rolling and met her gaze. "Lexi, what's wrong?" Mazie wiped her hands on a nearby dish towel. "You look terrible."

"Trust me when I say I feel even worse."

"Are you sick?" Mazie ushered Lexi toward a chair and forced her to sit down, quickly testing her cheek with the back of her hand to see if she had a temperature. "Whatever it is, we'll find you the best doctors."

"Mazie." Lexi grabbed her sister's hands. "My overly dramatic little sister, I'm not sick. I do need to tell everyone something tonight and I need your help. Do you think you can do that without asking too many questions?"

"I—I guess." Mazie sat down at the table. "Why are you being so cryptic?"

Lexi laughed. "And the questions already begin. Maybe I should have gone to Nash."

"No, don't—I'm sorry," Mazie said. "What am I saying, I'm not sorry. You're my sister, something's obviously wrong and I've been worried about you lately. Ever since that rodeo school opened, you've been distant and kind of bitchy." Mazie's hand flew to her mouth. "It's that kid, isn't it? The one that looks so much like Shane. Don't tell me—he had another affair while you two were together, didn't he? There's been talk around town that Hunter was his long lost son. Who is she? Is it someone we know?"

"Yes…very well."

"I'm sure you understand we have questions," Dennis Rathbone said to Shane outside the rodeo school entrance. "After we tell Hunter, Melissa and I are going to want to sit down with both you and Lexi to sort this mess out. I can't begin to tell you how distrustful we are of this situation."

"So you already have a judgment about who I am?" Shane thought he'd at least have a chance to tell them his side of the story before they took Hunter back to the hotel. He guessed he should be thankful they hadn't packed Hunter's belongings yet. Shane wanted to consider the fact that they left their two younger kids at the ranch with Hunter while they tracked down Lexi as a sign they had some trust in him. "This doesn't paint me in a good light considering I was the one Lexi kept this from all these years. I'm not some horrible monster of a parent."

"We don't know what to think or believe and I don't feel comfortable leaving Hunter here with you until we know more," Melissa said, her anger obvious. "You have to admit, this doesn't look good for either one of you. And that private investigator she hired. What's to say she didn't hire him to find Hunter? You could both be in on this."

"Then get all the facts," Shane pleaded. "I was married to someone else when Hunter was born. Lexi went away to school and stayed away until after she gave him up for adoption. I didn't know she was pregnant. No one did."

Melissa and Dennis regarded him for a while before Melissa finally spoke. "Lexi disappears for nine months and no one suspects anything?"

"It's not as simple as you're making it out to be." Shane wanted a chance to know his son, to spend more time with him. He'd go to hell and back not to get shut out again.

"We're going to tell Hunter the truth first," Dennis said. "And then we'll let him decide if he wants a relationship with you and Lexi. This is his choice alone, but we will supervise any communication and we have the final say if something seems even remotely off."

"Fair enough," Shane agreed. "Thank you. Not just for this, but for raising an incredible kid. Excuse me."

Shane didn't want to see Hunter walk away knowing he might never see him again. He'd already lived that pain once. He heard footsteps behind and turned, hoping to see Hunter chasing after him.

"What's going on?" Chase asked. "Why were you and Lexi arguing and why are you so upset?"

"Because that kid…" Shane saw Hunter meet the Rathbones at the fence rail. "The kid that looks so much like me…*is my son*. And there isn't a damn thing I can do about it."

"You have to be joking." Chase looked from Hunter to Shane. "Aren't those his parents?"

"Guess you weren't there when he told us he was adopted during his birthday get-together. None of this makes any sense. The night Apollo was born she was scared to death to touch Hunter."

"You're losing me." Chase placed his hands on Shane's shoulders. "Is Ashleigh his mother? Wow, she had to be his age when she had him. How could you?"

"What?" Shane pulled away from Chase. "Not Ashleigh—Lexi. Lexi is Hunter's mother."

"But how? She was never pregnant."

"Well, apparently she was, because she gave birth to him when she was still at Colorado State and the Rathbones adopted him. She kept one hell of a secret from me. Never in a million years would I have guessed this one."

"I can't believe it." Chase removed his hat and scratched his head. "Hunter's really yours and Lexi's."

"It's so crazy even I don't believe it," Shane said. "But there's more. Someone else knew about it and didn't tell me."

"Who?"

"Clay." Shane wanted to wring the man's neck. "Some friend, huh? Turns out he's been helping her."

"Helping her do what?" Chase asked.

"To cover it up, I guess." Shane paced back and forth on the walkway. "I haven't spoken to Clay yet."

"That doesn't sound like him at all." Chase put his arm around Shane's shoulder and led him toward the parking area. "Clay uncovers things, not hides them."

"Lexi said he helped her confirm Hunter's paternity."

"Now that makes more sense," Chase agreed. "I think you need to stop jumping to conclusions and speak with Clay."

A car started and Shane and Chase watched the Rathbones rental SUV drive out of the parking lot. A piece of his heart felt like it had just been torn from his body.

"Where are they going?"

"Back to their hotel, where they can tell Hunter that we are his biological parents and then he will decide if he wants further contact with us. How could she do this to me?"

Shane knew his brother was right. He had to talk to Clay and hear his side of the story the same way he'd asked the Rathbones to listen to his. But his best friend? He could have overlooked almost anything but keeping his kid from him…that was unforgivable.

Twenty minutes later, Shane found himself knocking on Clay's front door.

"Hey, man," Clay greeted him. "Since when do you knock or come in the front door?"

"How long have you known Hunter is my son?"

"I wondered when you were going to show up." Clay held the door open for Shane. "I got the DNA results before Hunter's birthday."

"You DNA tested my son?" Shane snorted. "Why didn't you tell me?"

"Because it wasn't my place. Lexi hired me to do a job, Shane. It was never about you."

"How can you say that?" Shane yelled. "Now you sound like Lexi."

"Because it's the truth. Lexi came to me the day she first saw Hunter. She wasn't going to say anything to anyone until she knew for sure, and honestly, Shane, Lexi thought she was doing what was best for Hunter."

Clay walked into the kitchen and took two beers out of the fridge.

"Enough with the stall tactics, please. Lexi isn't going to miraculously appear and save you." Unless Clay was waiting for her to show up. "Let me guess, she's on her way."

"She might be." Clay shrugged, twisted the top off his beer and handed one to Shane. "I don't know where she is or where she's going. I haven't spoken to or seen her since the Rathbones confronted her at her house. I'm still trying to figure out who told them where she lived."

"What did her family have to say about this? Or, did they know from the get-go? Is that why they hate me so much? Did they keep her away while she was pregnant and then force her to give the baby up because it was mine?"

"Listen to you," Clay laughed. "Quite a conspiracy theory you have going on there. Her parents hate you because you were a dog and hurt their daughter when you married your pregnant one-night stand. They didn't know then and they don't know now. Well, they might now if she came clean to them after she told you."

"Then tell me what I'm missing." Shane placed the

unopened beer on the coffee table and sat down on the couch. "Be my friend and tell me."

"There's nothing left to tell you." Clay stood firm. "There was no plot against you. She didn't know what to do with the information. She was scared and alone and I was the one she turned to. I was also the furthest removed from the situation. If that bothers you, I'm sorry, but at least it was me and not someone else. I would never betray either one of you."

"I have to ask you this and I hate like hell that I do." Shane had heard the rumors around town that Lexi spent the night with Clay and now he needed to hear the truth for himself. "Please be straight with me. Did you sleep with Lexi?"

"How can you even ask me that?" Clay's wounded expression made Shane feel like a first-class jerk.

Soon, Shane found himself driving east on the interstate, wanting to put as many miles between him and Ramblewood as possible. An hour later, he pulled into a truck stop to refuel and think. He ordered a burger and Coke but hardly touched either one. Watching the cars and trucks barrel down the highway, Shane remembered the first time he got the bug.

He and his family were sitting in a roadside restaurant, not unlike this one, somewhere in Louisiana. They were on the way back from one of their vacations and Shane stared out the window wondering where everyone was going. He wanted to travel and see the country and the rodeo would definitely take him there.

It had its up and downs, but in the end he'd accomplished everything he set out to do, except win the world all-around title. This year he had a solid chance and he wasn't going to let anyone stand in his way.

*What about Hunter?*

What was he going to do if Hunter said he wanted a relationship with him? Denver was only a two-hour flight away, so it would be feasible to be present for all Hunter's events. Besides that, Shane had contemplated representing Hunter, being his agent. But that also would entail scaling back his own rodeo time and he wanted that championship so bad he could taste it. The world all-around title had been his dream since he first sat on a horse. He'd be the first Langtry to win the title and Chase was right there beside him in the standings. Shane had to get there first, then Chase could win it ten times over, but he had to be first.

*And this was what Lexi meant.*

"Dammit!" Shane slammed his fist on the table.

"I'm sorry, is there something wrong with your food, sir?" the waitress asked.

Embarrassed, Shane glanced around the restaurant and realized he had an audience. He lowered his head and tried to sink down in the booth. "No, ma'am. My apologies, I'm just having a rough day. May I have my check?"

Leaving the woman a generous tip, Shane drove back to Ramblewood and asked Lexi to meet with him. Reluctantly she agreed on the condition they talk and not yell at each other.

Shane wanted to hear about her pregnancy, Hunter's birth, everything on the background check. He needed to know all he could about *his son.* The question was, would she talk to him after the way he treated her?

* * *

Lexi waited in the car for Shane, choosing the ball field as a neutral location. She had two hours before she faced her family.

Shane parked next to her and they both got out of their cars.

"Thanks for meeting me," Shane said. "Have you heard anything?"

"No." Lexi wondered if he had, and if he'd even tell her. "You?"

Shane shook his head and started to walk. She joined him, and the sounds of baseball bats striking balls and kids' laughter made Lexi second-guess her choice of locations.

"Was it a difficult pregnancy?" Shane asked.

Surprised at the question, she thought back to the days she tried so hard to forget. "Uncomfortable when it got warmer, but other than that I still went to class every day and continued working. Twenty-two hours of labor, that was a different story altogether."

Shane couldn't even imagine what that was like. "What did you do with all the ultrasound pictures from your appointments?"

"I didn't have any."

"What?" Shane stopped her. "You didn't go to the doctor?"

Lexi shook her head and continued to walk. "I mean I didn't have any photos." Lexi didn't want to see her baby before or after it was born. "The doctors knew I was giving him up for adoption so I chose not to see him. I heard the heartbeat and I knew it was a boy when he was born, but that was it. I never laid eyes on Hunter until a few weeks ago."

"How did you know it was him?"

"The resemblance to you was uncanny, and then when your mom told me he was from Colorado I started to ask more questions, then I begged Clay to find out for sure."

When Shane didn't comment, Lexi braved a glance at him. His jaw tight, she knew he wanted to say more and didn't.

"I put Clay in that position, so if you're going to be mad at someone, make it me, not him."

"I'm not mad." Shane stopped walking and looked toward the softball game. "I'm disappointed that you thought so little of me that you had to hide our son."

"And I'm disappointed in how you handled it, but what good does that do us today?" Lexi turned to walk back toward her car. "I'm not going to play the 'blame game' again."

"How am I supposed to react?" Shane asked. "Please tell me so I can get something right this time."

"I don't know what to tell you."

Lexi's phone vibrated in her pocket. She mouthed "it's them" as she answered the phone.

"Hello."

"Lexi, it's Melissa."

"How are you?" Lexi asked, knowing they were probably anxious as well.

"We're still trying to understand the chain of events." Melissa's tone was curt. "We weren't expecting to ever meet Hunter's parents. Honestly, he's never expressed an interest in knowing who you are."

"Oh." The words stung. Shane stood in front of her, trying to read her expressions.

"I'm sorry." Melissa sighed. "I don't mean to hurt you, but we have a fairly normal life and this took us by surprise."

"Us, too." Lexi wasn't sure where the conversation was leading. Afraid to ask any questions for fear she'd chase off Melissa, Lexi allowed the other woman to steer the conversation.

"We've spoken with Hunter and told him you and Shane are his biological parents, and if you agree, he would like to have some form of a relationship with you."

"Yes!" Lexi kneeled to the ground, looking up with tears spilling onto her cheeks. "Yes, it's more than okay. We'd love to have a relationship with him."

# Chapter 12

"So you're my dad?" Hunter said, sizing up Shane across the table. "Now you know where you get your good looks from."

Shane laughed. "That I do."

The Rathbones reluctantly agreed to allow Hunter to finish out the rodeo program, but only if they were all able to sit down in the morning and discuss the situation. Until their meeting, they wanted Hunter to stay with them at the hotel. Lexi and Shane agreed, but Shane asked if he could meet with Hunter for a few minutes tonight.

Sitting a couple of tables away in the hotel restaurant, Dennis and Melissa protectively watched Shane's interaction with their son. Lexi wanted to join them but explained to Hunter that she had to make things right with her own family and promised to see him tomorrow. Hunter must have inherited his maturity from Lexi because the boy had twice the amount at thirteen that Shane had at that age.

"I can't wait to go back to school and tell all my friends who you are," Hunter said.

"Your mom and dad are okay with you telling people about me?" With his reputation, he was surprised the Rathbones didn't grab Hunter and run in the opposite direction. He hadn't exactly been an angel, but to people outside of the rodeo circuit, he was just another Texas cowboy.

"Oh, yeah." Hunter looked over to them and waved. "I know they look uptight, but they're really not. I mean we can't get away with cutting school or eating pizza for dinner every night, but I know I can talk to them about anything. My sister, Amelia, has known her mom since she was born. She even comes to holiday dinners."

"Really?" Shane was amazed at how casually they took adoption. "If she's still that involved, why didn't she just raise your sister?"

"Adults make things too complicated." Hunter twisted his straw wrapper. "Amelia's mom was seventeen when my sister was born. She wanted to graduate and go on to college—kind of like Lexi. Her parents got a lawyer who told my parents they could adopt Amelia but her mom wanted her to know who she was. I think they call it an open adoption. So my sister has our mom and she has her bonus mom. Now I'll have a bonus mom, too."

"You're amazing." Shane almost found it impossible to take his eyes off his son. "How'd you get so smart?"

"It's in my genes. My mom's a doctor, ya know."

Hunter smiled. "She's telling her family about me to-night, huh? Do you think they'll like me?"

"Are you kidding me? They'll love you," Shane re-assured him. "Lexi's family lives on a farm and they have a big country store and a petting zoo."

"Are they going to be mad?" Hunter furrowed his brow. "Lexi's parents?"

"Mmm, I'm not sure how they're going to react." Shane checked his watch. It was quarter to nine and he knew she must be nervous.

"Maybe you should be there," Hunter said. "You're kinda responsible for the situation."

"Yeah." Shane wrinkled his nose. "I kinda was."

Lexi's entire family sat in the living room, curious as to what the emergency meeting that Mazie called to order was about.

"There's something I need to tell all of you so I'm just going to say it." Lexi inhaled and let out a long slow breath. "I had a baby when I was eighteen and gave it up for adoption."

*There. Band-Aid off.*

"You did what?" Judy Lawson approached her daughter. "You had a baby?"

Lexi backed away from her mother. Okay, so maybe this wasn't the best approach.

"Mom." Nash stepped between the two of them. "Sit down and let Lexi explain." He turned to look at her. "You are going to explain, right?"

"There's not a whole to say and getting mad at me isn't going to solve anything, either."

"Is this one of those 'I didn't know I was pregnant'

stories?" her aunt Heidi asked. "I never did understand how that was possible."

"I knew I was pregnant all along and I had planned on telling Shane."

"Shane?" everyone said in unison.

"Well, yes, who else would it have been?"

"That makes it even worse," her father said.

"Why didn't you tell me?" Mazie scolded. "I would have been there for you."

"Because you were sixteen."

"I knew she shouldn't have gone away to school," her Uncle Ed said. "There were perfectly fine schools here."

"Did he make you keep this a secret?" her mother asked.

"No, of course not." These were the hundred questions she didn't want to face. "He didn't know because I didn't tell him."

Everyone started talking and yelling at once, making Lexi want to crawl into a hole and hibernate. She'd known this wasn't going to be easy, but a free-for-all wasn't what she'd expected, either.

"What the hell are you doing here?" Lexi heard Nash say behind her. Turning, she saw Shane standing by the front door.

"I tried the bell, but I guess no one heard me," Shane said, the room becoming deathly silent. "I take it you told them."

"You knocked up my sister?" Nash stood an inch shorter than Shane but carried slightly more muscle from working on the farm. "Answer me, Langtry."

"I did but—"

Those were the only words Nash needed to hear before he punched Shane in the face, knocking him into the door.

"Nash, what are you doing?" Lexi rushed to Shane's side, blocking her brother from hitting him again. "Are you okay?"

"Oh, that's going to leave a mark." Shane touched the side of his face. "I'd expect no less from you, Nash. I would have done the same thing."

"Get out of this house," Nash growled, pushing Shane through the doorway.

"You get your butt over here." Her mother yanked Shane into the living room. "I want to see the both of you in the kitchen."

Shane leaned into Lexi as they hurriedly walked through the dining room. "You do have ice in there, right?"

Lexi smiled. Levity after being punched in the face was either brave or incredibly stupid and she hadn't quite figured out which one Shane was yet. She was also surprised to see him.

"I don't need help, Nash." Judy swatted behind her. "But good punch, son. As for you two…" Lexi's mother closed the kitchen door. "Sit down."

"I just want to get Shane some—"

"Lexi, sit," Judy ordered. She roughly grabbed hold of Shane's chin and turned his head to the side. "I've seen worse. You'll live…for now."

Removing a small plastic bag from the drawer, Judy filled it with ice, knotted it closed and shoved it at Shane.

"Start from the beginning."

Lexi took a deep breath and felt Shane's fingers intertwine with hers. Somewhere over the past few hours a change of heart had occurred with him and she wasn't about to look a gift horse in the mouth.

Her mother stared at her disbelievingly when she finished her story.

"Will I be able to meet him?" Judy asked. "And be a part of his life?"

"I don't know." Lexi shrugged. "We have to work that out with the Rathbones. Hunter is their child now and we have to play by their rules."

"Don't I have grandparents' rights? I've heard about cases like that."

"So you're planning on suing them?" Lexi smirked. "No judge would try that case, Mom, and I severed all rights when I gave him up. It's not up to us."

"Do you want a relationship with him now?" her mother asked.

"I would like to get to know him better," Lexi admitted. "Do I want to take him away from the only family he knows and loves? Absolutely not."

"I still don't understand why you didn't come to us," Judy said. "We would have helped you. It takes a village to raise a child and the Lawson farm is a small village."

Lexi smiled at her mother's analogy. She knew her mother was right. If she'd told them, she'd have had the baby and they'd have raised it for her, until the Langtrys came in and sued her for custody. There was no way they would have allowed Lexi's parents to raise her child when the father was very much in the picture. It was a scenario she'd considered, but the thought of Sharon anywhere near her child gave her fits of terror. She didn't trust the woman not to harm their baby and

Lexi was relieved when Tab won sole custody of Dylan once the paternity results were revealed. Sharon was the type of gold digger you saw on Jerry Springer.

"What about you?" Judy said to Shane. "What do you have to say for yourself?"

"It's brand-new to me, too," Shane said. "I'm hearing this for the first time just like you are."

"You realize if you hadn't screwed up so bad you and my daughter would have raised Hunter together."

"Mother!" Lexi knew her mother was upset with her, but she hadn't expected the cruelty.

"I know I'm responsible, Mrs. Lawson," Shane acknowledged. "I understand now why Lexi did it and I hope I get the opportunity to spend more time with my son."

"I don't know what's going on between you two again, but let me make myself perfectly clear." Judy leaned over Shane and braced herself on the arm rails of the chair, inches from him. "If you break her heart again, I'll break something of yours and I can promise you it will be more near and dear to you than your heart."

By midnight, they had thoroughly answered all the questions put forth by the Lawson inquisition. Even though she was exhausted, Lexi wanted time alone with Shane to learn more about his meeting with Hunter. He'd mentioned some of it to her mother but she wanted to hear every detail of what their son had to say.

"I guess you need to get home, huh?" Lexi walked Shane out on the front porch.

"Not necessarily. I'm tired and sore." Shane rubbed his jaw. "But I think I'm too wired to sleep at this point."

"I'd ask you to stay here and talk but I'm afraid Nash might shoot you." Lexi feared it was a real possibility. "There's a twenty-four-hour Dunkin' Donuts near the Rathbones' hotel."

"Sure, but we'll take my Jeep." Shane held the door open for her. "No offense but I don't trust your family not to cut my brake lines."

"Good call," Lexi agreed. "Are you okay to drive?"

"You can drive." Shane tossed her the keys.

Lexi had learned not to talk when driving a convertible. The passenger couldn't hear you and you never knew when something was going to fly over the windshield and end up in your mouth. She'd swallowed a fly like that one time. The Jeep was no exception and their ride was silent.

Parking, she pulled the key out of the ignition but made no move to get out. Hunter's hotel was yards away. Inside their son was sleeping. *Their son.*

"Come on," Shane said. "We'll see him in a few hours."

They both ordered coffee and decided to split a small box of Munchkins. At a corner table, they finally had the chance to sit down and absorb the situation.

"Long day?" Shane joked.

"That's putting it mildly," Lexi said. "It's really happening, isn't it?"

Their eyes met and Shane nodded, then reached for her hands. For the second time that night, they linked them together and Lexi started to cry.

"Dammit." She tried to turn her head away from him but he caught her chin. "I never cry. And today I'm all over the map. I'm not saying I regret today because I am so glad it happened, but I keep thinking if I had just stayed away from Family Day this morning, like my gut told me to, none of this would have happened and we'd never have this chance. In a little while Hunter would have returned to Denver and nothing would have changed."

"Well, maybe not for me." Shane wiped the tears from her face. "Could you really have let Hunter go, knowing he was ours?"

Lexi nodded. "I didn't want to hurt or confuse him. I didn't expect his parents to be open to the idea of us spending time with him. Believe it or not, I never wanted to hurt you, either. This wasn't revenge for you cheating on me."

"Hunter told me that his little sister's biological mother…oh, wait, what does he call her? Bonus mom— his sister's bonus mom has been in touch with her since day one."

"Really?" That gave Lexi hope of a future with Hunter. "How does that work?"

"It was an open adoption. They had agreed to her being a part of Amelia's life from the start and they were fine with it. You're right, they are good people. A little mistrusting of us at the moment, but hopefully after today, they'll realize we had no idea Hunter was ours."

"That's my fault." Lexi pulled apart a chocolate Munchkin and popped half of it in her mouth. "Once I realized who they were, I should have called and told them the truth."

"I tried putting myself in your shoes, and it's difficult to do—being a man and the whole pregnancy thing— you deserved so much better than what I did to you."

"Really?" Lexi was surprised to hear his admission. "I thought you'd always hate me."

"I love you, Lexi," Shane admitted. "I may get mad at you and I can definitely say no woman has ever made me feel shame like you do, but I could never hate you."

Lexi wasn't sure if his words were meant as a friendship "I love you" or if he meant more by the declaration. Tonight it didn't matter. If it was more, she'd hear the words again. If it wasn't, then so be it. This morning she'd lived in fear and under a cloud of secrecy. Tonight, she'd never felt more at peace.

"He asked about your family," Shane said. Although after tonight's melee, he wasn't sure how much Hunter should be around the Lawsons. They'd probably poison Hunter against him.

"I can just imagine what you told him. My mother hasn't been too nice to you through the years."

"She's just protecting her baby. I understand that." He'd let Judy off the hook for hating him years ago. Once he married Sharon, the woman had every right to hate him. "I told him about the farm and the store, but he's really excited to see the petting zoo."

"He definitely loves animals," Lexi said. "The night your mom and I picked up Barney, he told me he has dogs back home."

"Maybe he'll become a veterinarian when he grows up." Shane smiled, imagining what it would be like to have a doctor for a son.

"I thought you wanted him to ride."

"I do. Hey, he could always be a rodeo vet," Shane laughed. "They do have them, you know."

"I'm well aware of their vet practices, thank you."

"He definitely has your tongue, Sassy Lawson." Shane playfully nudged her arm.

It was nice being able to share something this intimate with Lexi again. Shane wasn't sure how the visitation would work out but he was willing to take anything tossed his way, especially if it meant spending more time with Hunter. Only one week left in class and then their time would end. Shane hoped it wouldn't be long before his son saw him again.

Lexi slid a penny across the table to him and tapped it. He'd forgotten their "penny for your thoughts" game from when they were kids.

"I was just thinking how much I'm going to miss him when he leaves next week. I guess it's really not fair to you."

"What's not?" Lexi asked.

"I get to spend twenty-four hours a day with him and you just see him here and there."

"My punishment, I guess." Lexi smiled. "I'll be fine."

"Aww, don't say that," Shane said. "Maybe we can take a vacation together? All of us, including the Rathbones and their other kids, as a 'getting to know you' type trip. Maybe a cruise?"

"I think the kids would love that," Lexi said. "Maybe we can mention it to them in the morning unless... Do you think they'll think we're trying to buy Hunter's affections?"

"It's a fine line we'll have to be aware of, but I think we can bring it up tactfully."

A few hours and multiple coffees later, they drove

out of the parking lot and headed home. Still in the previous day's clothes, they both were in need of showers.

"I'll pick you up around a quarter to eight?" Shane pulled into Lexi's driveway, noticing the curtains in the front window fluttered as he cut the engine. "That gives us a little over two hours."

"That sounds good. Gives me a chance to clean up."

"Let me walk you to the door." Shane unbuckled his seat belt.

Lexi reached out and grabbed his arm. "I wouldn't do that if I were you. Until I talk to Nash, I think you need to stay in the safety of your vehicle, although this thing doesn't offer you much protection."

They both laughed at the thought while keeping an eye out for long barrel shotguns.

"Just for the record, I'm glad this is all out in the open now," Lexi confessed, not releasing her grip on his arm. "It was painfully hard to keep that secret."

"I can imagine it was," Shane said. "No matter what's going on in your life, Lexi, you can always come to me, even if it involves me. I'm sorry for the horrible way I treated you earlier."

Their face inches apart, Shane ran his thumb across Lexi's bottom lip. Her tongue darted out to moisten them. He couldn't resist any longer—overprotective brother be damned, he wanted to kiss her and he *was* going to kiss her.

Cupping her face with one hand, Shane gently tugged her toward him, a barely noticeable effort thanks to her willingness. She reached for his face, carefully avoiding Nash's handiwork. He tasted her gently at first, then quickly she became a need he found almost impossible to resist.

He heard Lexi's breath quicken with each kiss. Every tongue stroke sent his mind in one direction that led south of her border. He forced himself to remember where he was—in front of her house, with her family inside. He had disrespected her once by cheating on her. He wasn't going to do it again by taking things too far in her driveway for her family to see.

Breaking the kiss, he made himself pull away from her. "Not here," he whispered. "I'll be with you anytime, anyplace, but definitely not here."

Lexi nodded and gave him one last lingering kiss goodbye before she jumped from the Jeep and bounded up the porch stairs.

It turned out to be a good night and he had a feeling it was going to be an even better tomorrow.

Lexi quickly locked the front door behind her and ran up the staircase to her bedroom, ignoring the sulking form that sat on the couch waiting up for her. If her mother wanted to sit there in the dark, that was her business, but it didn't mean she had to explain anything. Lexi lived at home out of convenience. Her office and stables were only a few feet away, but whatever happened next with Shane would have to be accepted or she'd find a new place to hang her hat and shingle.

Lexi leisurely showered, washing away the stress of yesterday. She was horrified when she saw her reflection in the mirror and could only imagine what the Rathbones thought of her based on first appearances. Today was a fresh start with Hunter and Shane. She hoped Hunter's parents approved of their cruise idea, but she prepared herself in case they didn't. She expected nothing and was grateful for each and every moment the Rathbones would allow.

The ragtop and doors were on the Jeep when Shane picked her up a few hours later.

"It's an important meeting and I figured you didn't want your hair blowing all over the place. I even cleaned the seats. You look beautiful, by the way."

"Thank you." Lexi loved that Shane remembered how much she hated flowers, candy or anything remotely resembling sappy. His consideration for her hair and her clean seats meant more to her.

"You nervous?" he asked. "Because I sure am. The bruise on the side of my face isn't helping matters."

"I'm definitely nervous," Lexi confessed. So nervous she'd tried on twenty different outfits before settling on a simple coral skirt and a beige fitted T-shirt. "I had a talk with Nash and he promised not to hit you again."

"Does that go for any other weapons or just fists?" Shane joked.

"I think you're safe."

Within minutes, they were in the hotel lobby, waiting for the Rathbones to come down with Hunter. When the elevator finally opened, Dennis and Melissa appeared but Hunter wasn't with them.

Lexi grabbed Shane's hand and squeezed it. Why wasn't he with them? Had they changed their minds?

It seemed like hours before the couple crossed the room to Lexi and Shane, and Lexi swore she held her breath the entire time.

"We thought we could talk to you both before Hunter

came down," Melissa said, zeroing in on their linked hands. "Plus we don't have a babysitter up there for our other two."

Exhaling a sigh of relief, Lexi and Shane followed the Rathbones into the hotel restaurant. This had to be difficult for them, too.

"I see you had a run-in with someone's fist," Dennis said to Shane.

"My brother kind of let him have it last night," Lexi answered for him, knowing no man liked to admit he got his butt kicked.

"You two seem different today." Melissa's tone almost bordered on accusatory. "More couple-like. I didn't get that impression yesterday."

Shane placed his hand over Lexi's on the table. "We're taking things day by day. It's been a whirlwind for us, as I'm sure it has for you and your family."

"It has," Melissa said. "But we're not entirely foreign to this concept. Hunter told us that he explained Amelia's relationship with her birth mother."

"He did and I admire you for supporting that." Shane glanced at Lexi. "We hope someday you will feel the same about us."

"That's what we wanted to discuss," Dennis began, and Lexi feared they had thought things over and decided not to allow Hunter to see them. "We've heard through others that Hunter has some real talent and we concede to knowing zilch about the rodeo. We're not fans of the sport, so let's get that out of the way. We think it's dangerous and it scares us to death but it's in Hunter's blood, and if this is what he chooses then we're not going to stop him."

"Hunter has expressed interest in attending your next class in August," Melissa said. "And while we would like him home for the second half of the summer, we feel it's important for him to get to know the both of you."

Lexi's mouth dropped open, but she was unable to speak. She looked at Shane, who put his hands over his eyes and half laughed, half cried.

"That's if you have room for him in your next class," Dennis added. "We told him we would check with you first."

"I don't know what to say." Lexi leaned into Shane, resting her head lightly on his shoulder and smiling. "We had something we wanted to run past you."

"First, there is always room for Hunter in any of my classes." Shane looked at Lexi and she nodded, giving him the go-ahead. "I think we might have an idea that would suit everyone's needs. How would you, Hunter and your other children feel about going on a cruise with us before the summer's out? It's our invite, we'd cover all your expenses. And you can even bring Amelia's bonus mom."

"Now I'm the speechless one." Melissa softened slightly, tears in her own eyes. "Honey, we were planning on taking a family trip anyway. What do you think?"

"I think it sounds like a wonderful idea," Dennis said. "But I think Melissa and I need to discuss it further. We're going to go up and get Hunter, and we'll see about the trip."

After spending the next hour talking with Hunter alone, the Rathbones rejoined them and announced they'd decided the trip would be a great way to get to know one another. Lexi was introduced to their other two children and they ate brunch together while they told the kids about the upcoming vacation. Lexi loved the way all three children's faces lit up as they planned the excursions they wanted go on.

The four of them discussed travel plans over coffee and the Rathbones decided since Hunter was staying with Shane on the ranch until the second week in August, they would meet in Walt Disney World for a few days before a ten-day Caribbean cruise.

Hunter rode home with Lexi and Shane, saying goodbye to his parents at the hotel. Lexi gave them a lot of credit. It couldn't have been easy for them to leave their son behind with his biological parents, especially when they had so many unanswered questions.

"You guys are the best!" Hunter said when he climbed in the backseat of the Jeep.

"We think you're pretty special, too," Lexi said.

She felt herself relax for the first time in days. They arrived this morning not knowing how much of their son they would be able to see. They left as a family planning a vacation together. As Hunter would say, *tight!*

# Chapter 13

"Lexi!" Shane shouted. "We're going to be late."

Lexi's bedroom window flew open and she popped her head out. "One minute!" She waved to Hunter, who was leaning out of the Lincoln Navigator's side window.

"Don't encourage her, Hunter," Shane chastised. The teen giggled and sat back down in his seat.

"I'm coming, I'm coming." Lexi pushed her way out the front door with two suitcases in tow. "Okay, Mom, I'm leaving," Lexi shouted through the door.

"Have a great time, dear." Judy stepped out on the porch and gave Lexi a hug. Shane loaded the suitcases in the SUV, while Judy said hello to her grandson. "You make sure she behaves, Hunter."

"I will."

"And you." Judy addressed Shane. He guessed it

could have been worse. At least she was down to three-letter words instead of four. "Try not to do anything stupid."

"Yes, Mrs. Lawson." Shane struggled not to crack a smile. *Now that would have been stupid.*

"Oh, hello, Chase," Judy said. "I didn't see you there. You drive safely."

Shane held the back door open for Lexi to sit next to Hunter while he sat up front with his brother.

"Judy just loves you to death, doesn't she?" Chase snickered.

"Shut up and drive." Shane laughed.

"Oh, wait!" Lexi called out. "Stop for Nash."

Nash leaned in the window and gave his sister a hug. "Don't worry, I have everything covered here. Enjoy your vacation, sis. I can't remember you ever taking one."

They made it to the airport with only minutes to spare. After saying goodbye to Chase and getting one last reassurance that the school was covered, Shane allowed the excitement of their trip to set in. Despite his extensive traveling, he couldn't remember the last time he went on a nonworking vacation. This was a real treat.

Ironically, the same woman he'd flirted with the day he picked up Hunter waited on them at the ticket counter. He smiled sheepishly, wondering what she thought today as he stood in front of her with a woman and kid. Whatever it was, she only shook her head and they were on their way.

"She seemed to recognize you," Lexi said.

"She gave me a hard time when I picked up Hunter last month." So it was a little white lie.

They boarded the plane moments later.

"Wow, first class!" Hunter exclaimed.

"You are definitely spoiling him." Lexi leaned across the aisle toward Shane's seat. "Me, too, but this time I'll let it go. Just remember, he has another family with a much more modest lifestyle," she added quietly.

"They're flying to Florida first class, too." Shane smiled. "Stop looking at me like that. It was the least I could do considering everything they've done for us."

"That's all fine and good, but I'm serious, Shane. After this trip, no more extravagances. The Rathbones will end up resenting us."

"Yes, dear."

Shane hated to leave before the August kids completed class. By the time they returned from vacation, his students would be gone. Having to say goodbye to his first class had come with some unexpected emotions. Originally he'd started the rodeo school for profit, but was surprised at how much he enjoyed teaching and being around kids. Even more, he was surprised at how attached he'd grown to each one of them.

While he still wasn't sure where his relationship with Lexi was going, he definitely enjoyed the direction it had begun to take. He'd love to have the chance of children in their future, but today, he was very content with the one they had.

The beginning of this trip was bittersweet. The countdown to when they had to say goodbye to Hunter had officially started. They had two weeks left together and Shane was determined to make the most out of every fun-packed moment. He knew Lexi didn't want to spoil Hunter, but this was a once-in-a-lifetime trip for both families, and their wish was his command. Nothing was off limits.

Lexi swore they rode every ride at Disney World, Sea World and Universal Studios in three whirlwind days. As kids, she and her siblings always wanted to go to Disney World, but as a farming family, they couldn't afford the trip. The Rathbones, their children and Amelia's bonus mom, Bethany, traveled like normal families on vacation, and with Shane and Lexi, they defined the term *blended family*.

Their ten-day cruise to the Caribbean was breathtaking, and Lexi fulfilled another lifelong dream when she swam with the dolphins during their excursion to Atlantis. Sharing the experience with the two men in her life made it all the more special. And somewhere between Jamaica and St. Martin's, she realized Shane was the man she wanted to spend the rest of her life with.

During their vacation, Lexi and Shane had an opportunity to witness the Rathbones' parenting style. Choosing to leave all discipline up to them, Lexi appreciated their fairness. For the most part, they allowed their children to make their own decisions, within reason.

Melissa presented them with a very liberal holiday schedule, allowing Lexi and Shane to rotate the holidays with them. This year, Hunter would visit them for Thanksgiving and next year for Christmas. Summers were open, allowing Hunter to choose his destination. Melissa and Dennis were being more than generous, and Lexi felt she'd made the right decision thirteen years ago.

Then the day Lexi dreaded had finally arrived.

Hunter was flying to Colorado with his family and she was heartbroken. She'd never imagined saying goodbye this time around would hurt this much.

"I had a great time this summer." Hunter fought to hold back his tears. "It was more than I expected. Thank you."

Unable to hold back her own emotion any longer, Lexi cried when she hugged him goodbye. "You are the greatest gift in the world."

"Don't cry, Mom." Hunter wiped her cheeks.

The word she never thought she'd hear was pure heaven. "I've loved you from the moment I knew I was pregnant with you. Please always know that. I love you, Hunter."

"I love you, too. I've had a wonderful life. I wouldn't trade it in for anything and I have you to thank for that."

Hugging her son one last time, she kissed him on the cheek and walked him the final length to the security check point where Shane and the Rathbones waited.

"Thank you for allowing me that time alone with him," Lexi said to Melissa. "I will always be grateful."

Lexi hugged Melissa and the rest of the family before they said their final goodbyes.

"We promise to come see you ride soon," Shane said, clearly not sure if he should hug or shake his son's hand. Hunter made the decision for him when he threw himself into Shane's arms.

"I love you, Dad."

"I love you, too, son."

Lexi slept most of their flight home. Shane asked her to stay at the ranch at least for the night, but Lexi said she wanted to sleep in her own bed after sleeping in a strange one for the past two weeks. He knew how much she missed Hunter, because he missed him just as much. What surprised him was Judy's attitude toward him when he dropped Lexi off at the house. She was borderline cordial and Shane wondered if hell had frozen over.

Back home, he walked down the eerily quiet path toward the bunkhouse. The second monthlong class had ended a few days ago and the outbuildings were once again vacant. The ranch seemed empty without the sound of Hunter's laughter and Shane swore if he closed his eyes and listened really carefully, he could still hear his son's voice.

The kid had grown on him even before Shane knew he was his son. He was so proud of him. In two months, Hunter had improved his riding and was ready for the junior rodeo. Shane swore he saw the kid shoot up two inches over the summer. The Rathbones agreed to allow Shane to manage Hunter's career and that guaranteed his rodeo schedule wouldn't be overbooked. He wasn't going to watch Hunter burn out as he'd witnessed so many times with other young rodeo talents. Tomorrow he wanted to start planning some fall events, and Shane planned on being there for every one of them. He knew Lexi's schedule was tight, but he hoped she'd be able to join them on most trips.

When Lexi arrived at the ranch the next morning, Shane noticed she was more quiet than usual, feeling Hunter's absence, too. Shane always thought life was exciting on Bridle Dance, but without the laughter of children, there was no joy in it. He'd make a point to spend extra time with Cole and Tess's daughter, Ever, when she came home from school, and soon Miranda and Jesse's twins would start coming for visits.

The rodeo classes were scheduled for after-school hours and weekends with a few weeklong clinics here and there. Since there were so few people coming and going on the ranch, Shane told Kay to have the Dance of Hope therapists use the front corrals instead of the secluded ones behind the building. It helped hearing children's voices again, but no child could replace his own.

Searching the stables for Lexi, he found her inside Apollo's stall. Now six weeks old, the colt was frisky and playful and did not appreciate a vet exam. Outwitting Lexi and Ashleigh, Apollo wouldn't allow them to catch him.

"How about you have dinner with me later?" Shane asked.

Ashleigh stopped and wiped the sweat from her face. "I'm sorry, I'm married."

"Just my luck," Shane laughed. "What do you say, doc? The Whole Enchilada for dinner?"

"Ooh, fancy." Lexi nodded. "That actually involves me taking a shower."

Lexi was looking forward to a night out even though she was still drained from their trip. The thought of hanging around the house or the ranch doing nothing made her miss Hunter even more. He had video-chatted with her last night when he arrived home, thanking her again for everything. The kid was amazing. Lexi gave him away and he thanked her for it because he loved his life that much.

Now that they were on dry land, the romance of the sea and Hunter gone, Lexi wondered where her relationship with Shane would lead next. The old Shane, the kind and generous one she fell in love with in high school, had reappeared and she hoped he stayed.

Lexi still took Autumn for her afternoon rides, but they were no longer pensive and wrought with angst. Autumn sensed her mood change and began to take more liberties during their outings. Taking off and galloping around the fishing pond had been her latest. Lexi felt good and so did her horse.

She was eager to talk to Shane tonight about a business proposition she'd received this morning from the large animal vet who usually covered her emergency calls. Dr. Rhodes wanted to know if she'd be interested in combining their practices. While she specialized in equine internal health and reproduction, Dr. Rhodes's practice included livestock as well as equine care. There were pros and cons but ultimately it would free up some of her time and allow her to visit Hunter's rodeo events with Shane.

After Lexi showered and changed for her date with Shane, she joined her mother in the kitchen while she prepared the family's dinner.

"How are you doing, Mom?" Lexi gave her a kiss on the cheek.

"Don't you look pretty." Judy motioned for her to spin around. "Night out with the girls?"

Lexi laughed. "You know I'm going to dinner with Shane. I have a few minutes before I have to head over there and I thought I'd spend them with you."

"It's sinful that he doesn't pick you up like a proper lady."

'Well, considering I had his kid out of wedlock at eighteen, I think that negates the whole 'proper lady' thing and Shane doesn't exactly get a warm welcome when he comes here."

"I was very well-behaved yesterday when he dropped you off, wasn't I?"

"I'm still trying to figure that one out." Lexi squinted at her mother. "Either you really missed me or you got into my horse tranquilizers."

"Now, now, respect your elders," Judy said. "Do you think Hunter would mind if I sent him a letter?"

"I think he'd love it, but you'll get better results with an email instead. And then he can write you back easily. You can call him on video chat if you'd like. I can set you up on the computer or you can use my phone."

"Really, I can see and talk to him?"

"Here, what time is it? He's an hour behind us but he's out of school by now." Lexi pressed the video-chat button on her phone and Hunter's number appeared. "You ready, Mom?"

"What do I do?"

"Hold the phone up in front of you, like this." Lexi held her phone a foot in front of her face and handed it back to her mother. "Are you ready to call him?"

Judy eagerly nodded, her excitement evident.

"Press this button." Lexi pointed to the big green *send.*

After two rings, Hunter answered, his beautiful blue eyes looking back at them.

"Hi." Hunter waved.

"He waved…did you see that?"

"Yes, Mom, I saw. It's on speakerphone. Talk to him, not me."

"Hey, Mom, where are you?" Hunter asked.

"I'm here, honey. Trying to teach this one how to video-chat."

"Wicked," Hunter said.

"How was your first day of school?" Judy asked.

"It was all right. I'm in a new school this year so I have to learn where everything is."

"Why is he in a new school?" Judy asked Lexi.

"Because he's in eighth grade." Lexi pointed to the screen. "Ask Hunter, not me. He sees you talking to me."

"Oh." Judy looked back at the phone. "You know, Hunter, I've never been to Colorado. Maybe I can fly out and see one of your events with Lexi and Shane. Would that be okay?"

"That would be awesome. Is Grandpa Jim going to come, too?"

"Oh, you want him there?" Judy frowned. "I kind of wanted to leave him home."

"Mother." Lexi swatted her. "Let me talk to him." She took the phone from Judy. "Hey, sweetie. Did your first day really go okay? You seem down."

"Yeah, I just hate being in the youngest class." Hunter made a face. "We're the babies. You look real pretty. Are you going out?"

"Shane's taking me to dinner at the Whole Enchilada."

"You know he's in love with you, don't you?"

"How do you know that?" Lexi asked, wondering

if her mother overheard his comment. Glancing back, Lexi saw she had returned to cooking dinner.

"A man senses these things about another man."

"Does he?" Lexi smiled, loving every moment she could talk to her son whether on a tiny screen or in person.

"Yeah, well, that and the fact he talks about you nonstop. I'm surprised he didn't drown when we were snorkeling because he rambled on so much."

"You're making that up."

"Maybe the drowning part but not the rest," Hunter said. "I like seeing you two together. He was grumpy without you."

"That's what people said about me," Lexi added.

"I know." Hunter giggled. "I always heard that Lexi Lawson is the grumpiest person around."

"You are so going to get it." Lexi laughed.

Shane's phone rang while he waited for Lexi to arrive that evening. His agent's name appeared on the display.

"Give me the good news," Shane said.

"You got it," Brock said, sounding less than enthused

"Woo-hoo!" Shane shouted.

"The network wants to buy it and start filming next month. They chose five rodeo cowboys but I don't know who the others are. We may not find out until after they start filming. Adds the element of reality TV surprise."

"Before you go any further," Shane began. "Hold up for a minute. There's something I want to tell you. Brock, you're never going to believe this, but I have a son."

"Is that why you've been unreachable for the past few weeks? You really should keep your agent in the loop, so I don't keep telling people I *might* be able to book you for an appearance. Who'd you knock up this time?"

"Hey, now, it's not like that and that wasn't even true back then," Shane argued. "Well, actually it was but I didn't know it."

"Dylan's really your son?"

"Not Dylan." Shane stepped out on the front porch overlooking the walnut trees lining the main entrance. "Hunter Rathbone. Remember that name because this kid is going to be a megastar. He has all my talent and his mother's brains—"

"How old is this kid that he's so talented?" Brock interrupted.

"He just turned thirteen." Shane saw Lexi's black Mustang convertible turn down the road, clouds of dust kicking up behind her. He walked back into the house to grab the junior rodeo schedule printouts.

"You're not thinking about putting him on the show, are you?" Brock asked. "Because I don't think that's the *adult* angle they're going for."

"Adult?" Shane asked. "What are you talking about? This is something my kid can watch, isn't it?"

"Of course, although I'm still baffled by this kid thing. It won't be X-rated, but I warned you about these types of shows, especially with Keeping it Reel Pictures. Sex sells and I'm sure they'll plant groupies for your viewing pleasure."

Lexi walked through the side door. She was gorgeous in her denim shorts and mile-long legs still tan from their cruise. Normally in boots or sneakers, she wore wedge-heeled sandals that tied at the ankle and a white flowing short-sleeve shirt. Her dark mahogany hair fell in long, loose waves down her back. When she removed her sunglasses, her eyes met his and she smiled. He'd waited a lifetime for that smile and now it was his. This was his viewing pleasure.

"It's not going to work," Shane said to Brock.

"What's not going to work? Are you talking to me or someone else?"

"I'm talking to you. Please tell them thanks, but no thanks."

Before Brock could argue, Shane disconnected the call and crossed the room to Lexi.

"What was that all about?" Lexi said, looking down on the counter. "Are these Hunter's upcoming rodeo dates?"

"Mmm-hmm." Shane wrapped his arms around Lexi and pulled her body against his. "And that was Brock telling me the network wants to buy the show and start filming next month."

"I don't understand. I heard you say 'no thanks.'" Lexi's confusion was evident in her furrowed brow and wrinkled nose. "I thought this is what you wanted."

"You're right." Shane spread his legs slightly, fitting her tighter to him. "*This* is what I want. You, right here in front of me."

Shane took her mouth with his. There was no pretense, no gentleness. It was a kiss meant to speak for him. A strong, passionate kiss that she relented to and responded in kind. Cupping her bottom, he lifted her as she wrapped her legs around his waist. Carrying her upstairs and into his bedroom, he kicked the door closed with his foot.

Laying her on the bed, he stepped away and moved toward the window, leaving her to whimper.

"I told Brock no," Shane said.

Dazed, her lips swollen from his kisses, she propped herself up on her elbows.

"You told who, what?"

He crossed the room and stood at the foot of the bed. The woman he loved was ready and willing for him. A more beautiful sight didn't exist. He wanted to kiss her and make love to her, but he had something more important to tell her first.

"I told Brock that I'm not doing the reality show." Shane reached for her hand, pulling her into an upright position. "I realized it doesn't mean the same to me anymore."

"Why the change of heart?" Lexi asked.

"Our son and you." Shane held her hand in his. "I don't want to do it anymore. I'd rather focus on us, the school and the ranch, and honestly, being the center of attention is really draining."

"What about the rodeo?" Lexi questioned.

"I'll still ride in some events but I'm going to scale way back. Let this be Chase's year." Cutting back wasn't part of the plan until he won the championship. "He doesn't have the commitments I do and this leaves a lot more time open for me to see Hunter."

"I can't believe what I'm hearing," Lexi said. "Dr. Rhodes asked me if I wanted to combine practices. I haven't decided one way or the other, but it would free me up more, too."

"That would be incredible," Shane said. He leaned in for a kiss and tugged her to the edge of the bed so her legs hung off the edge. "There's something I want to talk to you about."

"Should I be worried?" Lexi grimaced.

"I hope not," Shane said. "Let me ask you this— where do you see us going?"

"I'm not sure," Lexi admitted. "I love being with you and I love being with our son. These past two months have been wild and crazy and they define us perfectly. Why?"

"The way I see it, you and I are meant to be." Shane lowered himself on one knee. "We had a rough go of it no thanks to me, but our love for one another created a pretty incredible kid."

"Shane, what are you doing?"

"We are always going to be a part of one another's lives and I can't think of another woman I'd want to share my life with. I've done a lot of thinking, I know you're not the ring kind of girl, especially with where you stick your hands, and my job's no better in that regard. So, I say we screw tradition, get ourselves hitched, tattoo a couple of wedding rings on our fingers and do this. What do you say? Will you marry me?"

If that wasn't the most unorthodox proposal she ever heard, Lexi didn't know what was. But it was honest and was Shane being true to himself, and that meant something to her. The past was unchangeable, but the future was wide-open. They had already become an unconventional family thanks to the Rathbones' generosity.

There was no further doubt in her mind—Shane Langtry, the wild rebel of Ramblewood, finally had his own legacy in his son.

"Yes," Lexi laughed. "Now let's do this thing before

someone gets wind of it and tries to stop it, namely my brother."

By sunrise, Lexi found herself seated next to Shane on a plane to Las Vegas with Bridgett and Clay across the aisle from them. She didn't think she'd ever get through the ceremony without dying of laughter when an Elvis impersonator at the Graceland Chapel officiated their wedding.

Lexi knew neither family would bat an eye at their elopement. This was their style, and when she looked into Shane's eyes while a burly woman named Wild Jill tattooed a simple band around her ring finger, she knew it was all meant to be.

Shane Langtry was officially a marked man—her man.

\* \* \* \* \*

# WE HOPE YOU ENJOYED
# THIS BOOK FROM

## HARLEQUIN
## SPECIAL
## EDITION

*Believe in love. Overcome obstacles. Find happiness.*

Relate to finding comfort and strength in the
support of loved ones and enjoy the journey
no matter what life throws your way.

**6 NEW BOOKS AVAILABLE EVERY MONTH!**

"We need to get our story straight," she reminded him.

His smile faded. "It's best not to offer too many details.
We met in Atlanta, and now we have Ben."

She turned to face him, adjusting the lap belt as she
shifted. "Your family's not going to question you showing
up with a six-month-old baby? Like maybe you would
have mentioned it to them prior to now?"

One bulky shoulder lifted and lowered. "I told you we
aren't close."

"Your mom not knowing she has a grandchild is a bit
more than 'not close,'" Cory felt compelled to point out.
"Will she be upset we aren't married?"

"I'm not sure."

Her stomach tightened at his response. "Will she want to have a relationship with Ben after this weekend?"

"Good question."

"I have a million of them where that came from," she said. "I don't even know how your father died."

"Heart attack."

"Sudden." She worried her lower lip between her teeth. There were so many potential potholes for her to tumble into this weekend, and based on the tight set of his jaw, Jordan was in no shape to help navigate her through it. In fact, she had the feeling she'd be the one supporting him and he'd need solace well beyond a distraction.

"Can you answer a question with more than two words?" She was careful to make her voice light and was rewarded when his posture gentled somewhat.

"I suppose so."

"A bonus word. Nice. I'm sorry about your father's death," she said, giving in to the urge to reach out and place her hand on his arm.

*Don't miss*
His Secret Starlight Baby *by Michelle Major,*
*available March 2021 wherever*
*Harlequin Special Edition books and ebooks are sold.*

Harlequin.com

# *Love Harlequin romance?*

## DISCOVER.

Be the first to find out about promotions,
news and exclusive content!

Facebook.com/HarlequinBooks

Twitter.com/HarlequinBooks

Instagram.com/HarlequinBooks

Pinterest.com/HarlequinBooks

YouTube.com/HarlequinBooks

ReaderService.com

## EXPLORE.

Sign up for the Harlequin e-newsletter and
download a free book from any series at
**TryHarlequin.com**

## CONNECT.

Join our Harlequin community to
share your thoughts and connect
with other romance readers!
**Facebook.com/groups/HarlequinConnection**